Praise for the novels of Susan Mallery

"Mallery's authentic characters and their refreshing summer escapades are sure to resonate. The emphasis on the power of friendship and the joy of new romance make this sparkling novel a sure hit with women's fiction fans."
—*Publishers Weekly* on *The Friendship List*

"Mallery brings her signature humor and style to this moving story of strong women who help each other deal with realistic challenges, a tale as appealing as the fiction of Debbie Macomber and Anne Tyler." —*Booklist* on *California Girls*

"Susan Mallery never disappoints and with *Daughters of the Bride* she is at her storytelling best."
—Debbie Macomber, #1 *New York Times* bestselling author

"Mallery's latest novel is a breath of fresh air for romantics, a sweet reminder that falling in love is never how you plan it and always a pleasant surprise."
—*Library Journal* on *The Summer of Sunshine & Margot*,
starred review

"The characters will have you crying, laughing, and falling in love…. Another brilliantly well-written story."
—*San Francisco Book Review* on *The Friends We Keep*, 5 stars

"Heartfelt, funny, and utterly charming all the way through!"
—Susan Elizabeth Phillips,
New York Times bestselling author, on *Daughters of the Bride*

"Heartwarming… This book is sweet and will appeal to readers who enjoy the intricacies of family drama."
—*Publishers Weekly* on *When We Found Home*

SUSAN MALLERY

the friendship list

HQN

HQN

Recycling programs
for this product may
not exist in your area.

ISBN-13: 978-1-335-45272-6

The Friendship List

First published in 2020. This edition published in 2022.

Copyright © 2020 by Susan Mallery, Inc.

For questions and comments about the quality of this book, please contact us at CustomerService@Harlequin.com.

HQN
22 Adelaide St. West, 41st Floor
Toronto, Ontario M5H 4E3, Canada
www.Harlequin.com

Printed in U.S.A.

I had the best time writing this book—seriously, it was just plain fun from start to finish. I love the relationship between Ellen and Unity. They made me laugh and cry and I was so excited to learn what happened next. It seemed there was a surprise around every corner.

In the spirit of surprises…I'm dedicating this book to six lovely readers.

Brenda R., Cindy G., Courtney T., Nicole W., Teresa B., Zina O.

As many of you know, I'm a huge supporter of animal welfare, and my favorite organization is Seattle Humane. In the summer of 2019, Seattle Humane asked me to help them with an upcoming project—using "Bad Poetry Month" to drive awareness of pets looking for a home. I asked my Facebook friends to pitch in and we all wrote some very fun poetry in support of those pets.

From all the submissions, Brenda, Cindy, Courtney, Nicole, Teresa and Zina had their poems chosen to be featured. And to give them an extra thank-you (and a surprise!) I'm dedicating this book to them.

So, my friends, this one is for you.

the friendship list

one

"I SHOULD HAVE married money," Ellen Fox said glumly. "That would have solved all my problems."

Unity Leandre, her best friend, practically since birth, raised her eyebrows. "Because that was an option so many times and you kept saying no?"

"It could have been. Maybe. If I'd ever, you know, met a rich guy I liked and wanted to marry."

"Wouldn't having him want to marry you be an equally important part of the equation?"

Ellen groaned. "This is not a good time for logic. This is a good time for sympathy. Or giving me a winning lottery ticket. We've been friends for years and you've never once given me a winning lottery ticket."

Unity picked up her coffee and smiled. "True, but I did give you my pony rides when we celebrated our eighth birthdays."

A point she would have to concede, Ellen thought.

With their birthdays so close together, they'd often had shared parties. The summer they'd turned eight, Unity's mom had arranged for pony rides at a nearby farm. Unity had enjoyed herself, but Ellen had fallen in love with scruffy Mr. Peepers, the crabby old pony who carried them around the paddock. At Ellen's declaration of affection for the pony, Unity had handed over the rest of her ride tickets, content to watch Ellen on Mr. Peepers's wide back.

"You were wonderful about the pony rides," Ellen said earnestly. "And I love that you were so generous. But right now I really need a small fortune. Nothing overwhelming. Just a tasteful million or so. In return, I'll give back the rides on Mr. Peepers."

Unity reached across the kitchen table and touched Ellen's arm. "He really wants to go to UCLA?"

Ellen nodded, afraid if she spoke, she would whimper. After sucking in a breath, she managed to say, "He does. Even with a partial scholarship, the price is going to kill me." She braced herself for the ugly reality. "Out-of-state costs, including room and board, are about sixty-four thousand dollars." Ellen felt her heart skip a beat and not out of excitement. "A year. A year! I don't even bring home that much after taxes. Who has that kind of money? It might as well be a million dollars."

Unity nodded. "Okay, now marrying money makes sense."

"I don't have a lot of options." Ellen pressed her hand to her chest and told herself she wasn't having a heart attack. "You know I'd do anything for Coop and I'll figure this out, but those numbers are terrifying. I have to start buying lottery scratchers and get a second job." She looked at Unity. "How much do you think they make at Starbucks? I could work nights."

Unity, five inches taller, with long, straight blond hair, grabbed her hands. "Last month it was University of Oklahoma and the month before that, he wanted to go to Notre Dame. Cooper has changed his mind a dozen times. Wait until you go look at colleges this summer and he figures out what he really wants, then see who offers the best financial aid before you panic." Her mouth curved up in a smile. "No offense, Ellen, but I've tasted your coffee. You shouldn't be working anywhere near a Starbucks."

"Very funny." Ellen squeezed her hands. "You're right. He's barely seventeen. He won't be a senior until September. I have time. And I'm saving money every month."

It was how she'd been raised, she thought. To be practical, to take responsibility. If only her parents had thought to mention marrying for money.

"After our road trip, he may decide he wants to go to the University of Washington after all, and that would solve all my problems."

Not just the money ones, but the loneliness ones, she thought wistfully. Because after eighteen years of them being a team, her nearly grown-up baby boy was going to leave her.

"Stop," Unity said. "You're getting sad. I can see it."

"I hate that you know me so well."

"No, you don't."

Ellen sighed. "No, I don't, but you're annoying."

"You're more annoying."

They smiled at each other.

Unity stood, all five feet ten of her, and stretched.

"I have to get going. You have young minds to mold and I have a backed-up kitchen sink to deal with, followed by a gate repair and something with a vacuum. The message wasn't clear." She looked at Ellen. "You going to be okay?"

Ellen nodded. "I'm fine. You're right. Coop will change his mind fifteen more times. I'll wait until it's a sure thing, then have my breakdown."

"See. You always have a plan."

They walked to the front door. Ellen's mind slid back to the ridiculous cost of college.

"Any of those old people you help have money?" she asked. "For the right price, I could be a trophy wife."

Unity shook her head. "You're thirty-four. The average resident of Silver Pines is in his seventies."

"Marrying money would still solve all my problems."

Unity hugged her, hanging on tight for an extra second. "You're a freak."

"I'm a momma bear with a cub."

"Your cub is six foot three. It's time to stop worrying."

"That will never happen."

"Which is why I love you. Talk later."

Ellen smiled. "Have a good one. Avoid spiders."

"Always."

When Unity had driven away, Ellen returned to the kitchen where she quickly loaded the dishwasher, then packed her lunch. Cooper had left before six. He was doing some end-of-school-year fitness challenge. Something about running and Ellen wasn't sure what. To be honest, when he went on about his workouts, it was really hard not to tune him out. Especially when she had things like tuition to worry about.

"Not anymore today," she said out loud. She would worry again in the morning. Unity was right—Cooper was going to keep changing his mind. Their road trip to look at colleges was only a few weeks away. After that they would narrow the list and he would start to apply. Only then would she know the final number and have to figure out how to pay for it.

Until then she had plenty to keep her busy. She was giving pop quizzes in both fourth and sixth periods and she wanted to update her year-end tests for her two algebra classes. She needed to buy groceries and put gas in the car and go by the library to get all her summer reading on the reserve list.

As she finished her morning routine and drove to the high school where she taught, Ellen thought about Cooper and the college issue. While she was afraid she couldn't afford the tuition, she had to admit it was a great problem to have. Seventeen years ago, she'd been a terrified teenager, about to be a single mom, with nothing between her and living on the streets except incredibly disappointed and angry parents who had been determined to make her see the error of her ways.

Through hard work and determination, she'd managed to pull herself together—raise Cooper, go to college, get a good job, buy a duplex and save money for her kid's education. Yay her.

But it sure would have been a lot easier if she'd simply married someone with money.

"How is it possible to get a C-in Spanish?" Coach Keith Kinne asked, not bothering to keep his voice down. "Half the population in town speaks Spanish. Hell, your sister's husband is Hispanic." He glared at the strapping football player standing in front of him. "Luka, you're an idiot."

Luka hung his head. "Yes, Coach."

"Don't 'yes, Coach' me. You knew this was happening—you've known for weeks. And did you ask for help? Did you tell me?"

"No, Coach."

Keith thought about strangling the kid but he wasn't sure he could physically wrap his hands around the teen's thick neck. He swore silently, knowing they were where they were and now he had to fix things—like he always did with his students.

"You know the rules," he pointed out. "To play on any varsity team you have to get a C+ or better in every class. Did you think the rules didn't apply to you?"

Luka, nearly six-five and two hundred and fifty pounds, slumped even more. "I thought I was doing okay."

"Really? So you'd been getting better grades on your tests?"

"Not exactly." He raised his head, his expression miserable. "I thought I could pull up my grade at the last minute."

"How did that plan work out?"

"*No bueno.*"

Keith glared at him. "You think this is funny?"

"No, Coach."

Keith shook his head. "You know there's not a Spanish summer school class. That means we're going to have to find an alternative."

Despite his dark skin, Luka went pale. "Coach, don't send me away."

"No one gets sent away." Sometimes athletes went to

other districts that had a different summer curriculum. They stayed with families and focused on their studies.

"I need to stay with my family. My mom understands me."

"It would be better for all of us if she understood Spanish." Keith glared at the kid. "I'll arrange for an online class. You'll get a tutor. You will report to me twice a week, bringing me updates until you pass the class." He sharpened his gaze. "With an A."

Luka took a step back. "Coach, no! An A? I can't."

"Not with that attitude."

"But, Coach."

"You knew the rules and you broke them. You could have come to me for help early on. You know I'm always here for any of my students, but did you think about that or did you decide you were fine on your own?"

"I decided I was fine on my own," Luka mumbled.

"Exactly. And deciding on your own is not how teams work. You go it alone and you fail."

Tears filled Luka's eyes. "Yes, Coach."

Keith pointed to the door. Luka shuffled out. Keith sank into his chair. He'd been hard on the kid, but he needed to get the message across. Grades mattered. He was willing to help whenever he could, but he had to be told what was going on. He had a feeling Luka thought because he was a star athlete he was going to get special treatment. Maybe somewhere else, but not here. Forcing Luka to get an A sent a message to everyone who wanted to play varsity sports.

He'd barely turned to his computer when one of the freshman boys stuck his head in the office. "Coach Kinne! Coach Kinne! There's a girl crying in the weight room."

Keith silently groaned as he got up and jogged to the weight room, hoping he was about to deal with something simple like a broken arm or a concussion. He knew what to do for those kinds of things. Anything that was more emotional, honest to God, terrified him.

He walked into the weight room and found a group of guys huddled together. A petite, dark-haired girl he didn't know sat on a bench at the far end, her hands covering her face, her sobs audible in the uneasy silence.

He looked at the guys. "She hurt?"

They shifted their weight and shook their heads. Damn. So it wasn't physical. Why didn't things ever go his way?

"Any of you responsible for whatever it is?" he asked.

More shaken heads with a couple of guys ducking out.

Keith pointed to the door so the rest of them left, then returned his attention to the crying girl. She was small and looked young. Maybe fifteen. Not one of his daughter's friends or a school athlete—he knew all of them.

He approached the teen, trying to look friendly rather than menacing, then sat on a nearby bench.

"Hey," he said softly. "I'm Coach Kinne."

She sniffed. Her eyes were red, her skin pale. "I know who you are."

"What's going on?" *Don't be pregnant, don't be pregnant*, he chanted silently.

More tears spilled over. "I'm pregnant. The father is Dylan, only he says he's not, and I can't tell my m-mom because she'll be so mad and he said he l-loved me."

And just like that Keith watched his Monday fall directly into the crapper.

KEITH LEFT WORK exactly at three fifteen. He would be returning to his office to finish up paperwork, supervise a couple of workouts and review final grades for athletes hovering on the edge of academic problems. But first, he had pressing personal business.

He drove the two short miles to his house, walked inside and headed directly for his seventeen-year-old daughter's room.

Lissa looked up from her laptop when he entered, her smile fading as she figured out he was in a mood. Despite the attitude, she was a beauty. Long dark hair, big brown eyes. Dammit all to hell—why couldn't he have an ugly daughter who no guy would look at twice?

"Hi, Dad," she said, sounding wary. "What's up?"

"Spot check."

She rolled her eyes. "Seriously? There is something wrong with you. I heard what happened at school today. I'm not dumb enough to date a guy like Dylan who would tell a tree stump he loved it if it would have sex with him. I'm not sleeping with anyone and I'm not pregnant. I told you—I'm not ready to have sex, as in I'm still a virgin. You're obsessed. Would you feel better if I wore a chastity belt?"

"Yes, but you won't. I've asked."

"Da-ad. Why are you like this? Pregnancy isn't the worst thing that could happen. I could be sick and dying. Wouldn't that be terrible?"

"You can't win this argument with logic. I'm irrational. I accept that. But I'm also the parent, so you have to deal with me being irrational."

He pointed to her bathroom. She sighed the long-suffering sigh of those cursed with impossible fathers and got up. He followed her to the doorway and watched as she pulled the small plastic container out of the bathroom drawer and opened it.

Relief eased the tension in his body. Pills were missing. The right number of pills.

"You are a nightmare father," his daughter said, shoving the pills back in the drawer. "I can't wait until I'm eighteen and I can get the shot instead of having to take birth control pills. Then you'll only bug me every few months."

"I can't wait, either."

"It's not like I even have a boyfriend."

"You could be talking to someone online."

Her annoyance faded as she smiled at him. "Dad, only one of us in this house does the online dating thing and it's not me."

"I don't online date."

"Fine. You pick up women online, then go off and have sex with them for the weekend. It's gross. You should fall in love with someone you're not embarrassed to bring home to meet me."

"I'm not embarrassed. I just don't want complications."

"But you do want to have sex. It's yucky."

"Then why are we talking about it?" He pulled her close and hugged her, then kissed the top of her head. "Sorry, Lissa. I can't help worrying about you."

She looked up at him. "Dad, I'm taking my pills every day, not that it matters because I'm not having sex. *I'm not.* I've barely kissed a guy. Having you as my father makes it really difficult to date. Guys don't want to mess with you and risk being beat up."

"Good."

She smiled even as she hit him in the arm. "You're repressing my emotional growth."

"Just don't get pregnant."

"You need to find a more positive message. How about 'be your best self'?"

"That, too. Gotta go."

"I'm having dinner with Jessie tonight. Remember?"

"No problem. Be home by ten."

He got back in his truck but before starting the engine, he quickly texted Ellen. I need a couple of beers and a friendly ear. You around tonight?

The response came quickly. *Only if you bring fried chicken. I have beer and ice cream.*

You're on. See you at six.

ELLEN COULDN'T FIGURE out why a six-foot-five-inch, seventeen-year-old guy crying bothered her more than pretty much any teenage girl crying. Was it reverse sexual discrimination? Because boys cried less often, their tears had more value? Was it the sheer size of Luka juxtaposed with the implied vulnerability of tears? As she was unlikely to figure out an answer, she decided to ignore the question.

"Luka, you're going to be fine," she said, reaching up to pat the teen on his shoulder as Cooper hovered nearby. "You'll take the online Spanish class and you'll do great. You're plenty smart. You just got complacent."

"He thought because he's such a hotshot on the field, his shit didn't stink," Coop said, then groaned. "Sorry, Mom. Um, I meant to say, ah, poop."

She turned to her son and raised her eyebrows. She

was pleased that, despite his age and size, he took a step back and swallowed.

"I'm really sorry," he added.

"As you should be. Luka, Coach isn't throwing you off the bus."

"You didn't see him. He was really mad. He said I was an idiot."

Not exactly the word she would have chosen, but then she didn't spend much time in the jock/jockette world.

"You're a leader, so he expects better of you."

More tears filled Luka's eyes. Next to him, Coop winced.

"What if I can't get an A?"

"You won't with that attitude."

Luka sniffed. "That's what Coach said."

Cooper leaned close. "It's a teacher thing. They think alike. Welcome to my world."

She did her best not to smile. Her boys, she thought fondly. Cooper and his friends had been running in and out of her life since he'd been old enough to invite kids back to play. Luka had been a staple in her life for nearly a decade. He and his family had moved here from Yap (a tiny island in Micronesia—she'd had to look it up). Luka and Coop had met the first day of second grade and been best friends ever since.

"Luka, I forbid you to think about this anymore today. Your mom is waiting for you. Go have a nice dinner and relax this evening. Tomorrow, get your butt in gear and get going on the Spanish studies." She hesitated. "I'll talk to Coach and make sure you're still on the college trip."

His dark eyes brightened. "You will? Thanks, Ms. F. That would be great."

Before she could step back, Luka grabbed her and lifted her up in the air. It was not a comfortable feeling, but all of Coop's friends seemed to do it. He swung her around twice before setting her down. Both teens headed for the door.

"I'll be back by ten," Coop yelled over his shoulder. "Have fun."

Ellen gave herself a little shake to make sure nothing had been crushed, then stepped out on her small deck to check out the heat level. The front of the house faced south, leaving the backyard in shade in the early evening. The temperature was close to eighty, but bearable.

The deck overlooked a small patch of lawn edged by fencing. Nothing fancy, but it was hers and she loved it. She quickly wiped off the metal table and dusted the chairs before putting out placemats, plenty of paper napkins and a cut-up lime. She'd already made a green salad to counteract the calories from the fried chicken. Shortly after six, she heard a knock on the front door, followed by a familiar voice calling, "It's me."

"In the kitchen," she yelled as she opened the refrigerator and pulled out two bottles of beer. Dos Equis for him and a Corona for herself. She glared when she saw the extra to-go container in his hand.

"What?" she demanded. "We agreed on chicken."

He held up the KFC bucket. "I brought chicken. Original, because you like it."

"Don't distract me. Are those potatoes? I can't eat those."

"Actually you can. I've seen you. You have no trouble using a fork."

She set his beer on the table. "Do you know how

many calories are in those mashed potatoes? I'm not some macho athletic guy."

Keith gave her an unapologetic smile. "I'd still be friends with you if you were." He set down the food. "Stop worrying about it. You look fine." He glanced at her. "As far as anyone can tell."

She ignored that and refused to look down at her oversize tunic and baggy pants. "I like to be comfortable. Loose clothing allows me to move freely on the job." She ducked back into the house to get the salad, then joined him at the table.

He'd already taken his usual seat and opened both to-go containers. The smell of fried chicken reminded her she hadn't eaten since lunch, which felt like two days ago. Her stomach growled and her mouth watered.

Keith put a chicken breast on her plate, then handed her the mashed potatoes. She put slices of lime in both their beers. Their movements were familiar. Comfortable.

Coach Keith Kinne and his daughter had moved to Willowbrook five years ago. He'd joined the faculty of Birchly High as the football coach and athletic director. Washington State might not have the religious fever of Texas when it came to high school football, but there was still a lot of enthusiasm and the six-foot-two-inch, good-looking, dark-haired former NFL player had caught a lot of ladies' attention.

Not hers, though. Mostly because she didn't date—there wasn't time and no one she met was ever that interesting. So when she'd found him cornered by a slightly aggressive novice teacher from the English department, Ellen had stepped in to save him and their friendship had been born. They hung out together because it was easy and they complemented each other. He'd helped her when she'd bought a new-to-her car a couple of years ago and she went Christmas shopping with him for his daughter.

"Why are you smiling?" he asked, picking up his beer.

"Just thinking that it's nice we're friends. Imagine how awkward things would have been if I'd gone after you when you first moved here."

He frowned. "Don't say that. If you had, we might not be friends now. I was fresh off a divorce and I wasn't looking for trouble."

"I'm not trouble."

"You would have been if we'd dated."

What on earth did he mean? "Trouble how?"

"You know. Boy-girl trouble." He put down his beer. "Speaking of dating, Lissa got on me about my internet relationships."

"You don't have internet relationships. You find women to have sex with."

He winced. "That's what she said. Have you two been talking about me behind my back?"

"Oh, please. We have so many more interesting things to talk about." She'd never understood the appeal of casual sex. It seemed so impersonal. Shouldn't that level of intimacy be part of a relationship? Otherwise sex was just as romantic as passing gas.

"She told me to find someone I wasn't embarrassed by so she could meet her."

"That's nice."

"It freaked me out."

Ellen grinned. "That's because there are emotions attached to relationships and you don't like emotions."

"I like some of them. I like winning."

"Winning isn't an emotion."

"Fine. I like how winning makes me feel." His expression turned smug. "I get emotions."

"You're faking it." She let her smile fade. "Cooper wants to go to UCLA."

"Are you sure? He told me Stanford."

She heard a ringing in her ears as her whole world tilted. "W-what? Stanford? No. He can't."

"Why not? They have a better wrestling program. I've spoken to the coach there and he's really interested. I'm working on getting Coop a one-on-one meeting when we visit the school. With his skills and grades, he's got a good shot at getting in."

"I'm going to faint."

"Why? You should be happy."

She glared at him. "Happy? Are you insane? I can't afford UCLA and it's a state school. How on earth would I pay for Stanford? Plus, why isn't Cooper telling me about things like meeting a coach? I should know that."

"Breathe," Keith told her. "If he goes to Stanford, you'll be fine. With what you make, his tuition will be covered. If he gets a partial scholarship, it could go toward room and board. Stanford would be a lot cheaper for you than UCLA."

Her panic faded. "Are you sure?"

He looked at her. "You have to ask me that?"

"Sorry. Of course you're sure. You do this all the time." She picked up her chicken. "Yay, Stanford. Go team."

"You don't have any contact with his dad, do you? Because his income would count."

"No contact," she said cheerfully. "Jeremy disappeared before Coop was born. I hear from him every five or six years for five seconds and then he's gone again. He signed his rights away and he's never given me a penny." She smiled. "I say that without bitterness because I'm loving the Stanford dream."

Keith grinned. "You're saying you can be bought for the price of tuition?"

She smiled back at him. "I can be bought for a whole lot less than that. So why didn't he tell me about wanting to go to Stanford? Why is he keeping secrets?"

"He's becoming a man. He needs his own dreams and plans."

"But I'm his mom and he's my baby boy. Make him stop growing up."

"Sorry. Not my superpower."

She remembered what it had been like when Coop had been younger. It had been the two of them against the world. "I miss being the most important person in his life, but you're right. He needs to make his own way. What are the Stanford colors? Will they look good on me?"

two

KEITH REACHED FOR his beer, not bothering to hide his amusement. "Is that going to be part of the decision-making process? How you look in the college colors? Because you care so much about how you look?"

"Hey!" Ellen balled up her napkin and tossed it at him. "I care. Sort of."

Keith had been around women enough to know this was not a winning line of conversation. When it came to pretty much everything, women had rules men couldn't possibly understand. He'd often thought that if Ellen put even five minutes into her appearance, she would be chasing men off with a stick. Yet if he mentioned that, he was the bad guy.

Like her clothes. They were always at least two sizes too big. Even when she wasn't teaching, she wore baggy jeans and oversize T-shirts or sweatshirts. She never put on makeup. Despite having long, wavy dark hair, she never wore it other than in a ponytail or a braid.

Not his rock, he reminded himself. Ellen was his friend and whatever made her happy made him happy, too.

"I'm sure the Stanford colors will be glorious on you," he told her.

She rolled her eyes. "Glorious? Is that the best you could come up with?"

"It is."

"Fine. Tell me about your day."

He reached for a chicken leg and put it on his plate, then added two more. "I had to deal with another pregnant girl. Why does this keep happening and why do they come to me?"

"In reverse order, they come to you because you're capable and the odds of the guy involved being an athlete are high. As for why they get pregnant, that's easy. Men don't control their sperm."

He stared at her. "What?"

"Sperm. It's not the sex that's the problem." She waved her beer bottle. "Think about it. Women can have sex all day long and not get pregnant. They can have orgasm after orgasm and nada. It's all about ejaculation. If the male half of the species made sure that didn't happen inside women, there would be no unplanned pregnancies. Everyone looks to the girl, but she's not the one who made it happen. He did."

Despite the hell that had been his day, Keith chuckled. "You always have a unique perspective."

"I know. What was it you said? I'm glorious."

"You are. So if you're right, then the system is rigged

against women, but that doesn't change the pregnancy outcome."

Her expression turned sympathetic. "You worry about Lissa too much."

"Do I? As you just pointed out, she's one wayward ejaculation away from getting pregnant."

"She's on the pill."

"If she takes them."

Ellen put her hand on his forearm. "Your daughter doesn't want to get pregnant, Keith. She's a smart girl and she's on birth control. Plus, from what I can tell, she's not seeing anyone. You know how she gets—once she likes a guy, that's all she ever talks about. On the boy-girl front, things have been quiet."

"I hope you're right. The whole situation makes me crazy." Lissa was his daughter, his world. He wanted to do everything in his power to make her life perfect.

Ellen reached for the mashed potatoes. "When we're back from the college bus trip, Lissa and I will be working at the fruit stand for the rest of the summer. I'll find out what's going on. Between now and then, she's busy with school, then she'll be with you on the bus. She should be perfectly safe. And speaking of the bus trip, I think we're pretty much done with the details. What do you think?"

"I agree. I'm buying the Disneyland tickets this week," he said. "The hotel reservations are all made."

"You're a good man for doing this."

He raised one shoulder. "I don't mind it."

Since moving to Willowbrook, he'd started taking a group of his athletes on a tour of West Coast colleges. The students spent the school year raising money to pay for gas, hotels rooms and food. Keith made appoint-

ments with the various colleges the students were interested in. The trips were about two weeks long, with
a few fun stops along the way. This year's students had
decided they wanted to spend an afternoon on the beach
in Santa Monica, a day in Disneyland and a day at the
Monterey Bay Aquarium. They'd raised enough money
and Keith always let them plan the agenda. They would
visit a half dozen colleges, see the West Coast and, for
many of his students, leave the state for the first time.

"You excited about the trip?" he asked.

Ellen smiled at him. "Excited is strong, but I'm happy
to be the bus mom."

It would be her first time joining him, but with Coop
going, she'd volunteered. He was bringing Lissa.

"Too bad it's only guys," he said. "I think Lissa
would have liked a couple of girls along."

He always had more students apply than he could
manage. In November, he held a drawing with twelve
students chosen at random. This year both of the female
students who had won a slot had dropped out.

"She'll have me," Ellen said. "Plus Coop's like her
brother. And all the guys are scared of you, so no one
will bother her."

"Damn straight they're scared of me," he grumbled.
"If I catch any of them with my daughter, I will let my
fists do the talking."

She tsked. "Violence? Is that the best you can come
up with?"

"When it comes to Lissa, yes."

They finished dinner and talked for another hour before he helped her clean up. Close to eight, she walked
him to the front door.

"Thanks for listening," he said, hugging her.

"Thanks for the info on Stanford. I'll sleep easier tonight knowing I just might be able to pay for college."

She looked up at him as she spoke. As always, her bangs were too long, almost touching her big eyes. She looked impossibly young—as if there was no way she could have a seventeen-year-old son. Only she'd been Lissa's age when she'd gotten pregnant.

"You did a great job with your kid," he told her.

"Thank you. Back at you."

"Yeah, but I wasn't still in high school when she was born. And I had a wife."

"I had my parents."

"Hey, I'm trying to pay you a compliment here."

"Sorry." She smiled. "Thank you, Coach Kinne."

"You're welcome, Ms. Fox."

She laughed. "See you tomorrow."

"Always."

He walked toward his extended cab truck. Despite the hour, the sun still hadn't set. This time of year, there was a ridiculous amount of daylight in the Pacific Northwest.

As he got behind the wheel, he glanced at the duplex where Ellen lived. She'd told him how when her parents had sold their house and moved to Palm Desert to retire, they'd given her enough money for a down payment on a house. She'd impressed them by buying a duplex instead, so she would have steady income to help her pay down the mortgage.

She'd confessed that she would have preferred a single-family home, but she'd known the duplex was the smarter decision. That was Ellen—always sensible and doing the right thing. She was a good friend, one he could depend on. In some ways, not counting Lissa, Ellen was the best relationship he'd ever had.

"PETER, MY YOUNGEST, called last night," Howard said, as he checked his toolbox. "His divorce is final. Maybe you'd like to meet him."

Unity Leandre stared at the big dry-erase board mounted on the wall of her garage. It was divided into five columns, one for each day of the week. The jobs were listed on the day they would be done, with an arrival time next to them. Every morning she went over the jobs with her team and decided who would do what and how long it should take.

"She doesn't want to go out with Peter," Jerry said. "He's what? In his forties?"

"Forty-five."

"That's too old for her. How old are you, Unity?"

"Thirty-four."

"See?" Jerry sounded triumphant. "That's too big an age difference. Plus Peter lives in Bellingham. The drive would be at least three hours, maybe four."

"He's a good guy," Howard insisted. "An entrepreneur."

"He owns a yard mowing service."

"It's a landscaping company. They'd have a lot in common."

Jerry snorted. "Leave the girl alone. She'll find the right guy on her own. She doesn't need us butting into her business."

"I'm not butting, I'm offering to help. Unity, am I butting in?"

Unity put Howard's initials next to the backed-up drain and Jerry's by the new shower fixture.

Only then did she turn toward the two seventysomething men who worked for her—part-time, of course. Because being retired didn't mean a person wasn't busy. Something she'd learned in the past three years. She had a team of five men working for her—all well over the age of sixty-five, all good at their jobs. Sure, there were times when they couldn't move as fast as someone younger, but they were skilled, careful and thorough. She would rather the job took a little longer, but was done right. Besides, most of her clients were at the Silver Pines retirement community, so they appreciated having handymen of a certain age around. As for Howard's youngest and his recent divorce, just no.

She smiled. "You're not butting, Howard, but I'm also not interested."

"You haven't met him yet. What if he's everything you've been looking for?"

Unity shook her head. Three-plus years after Stuart's death, she wasn't the least bit interested in finding a replacement.

"I'm sure he's wonderful," she said kindly. "Just not for me."

"It's because he's too old, right?" Jerry asked hopefully. He turned to Howard. "I told you to stop butting in."

The two men were fast friends. They both had gray hair, wrinkled faces and slight beer bellies. Howard was a little taller, but still shorter than Unity. She was five-ten and, as more than one of the old ladies at the retirement community had remarked, a strapping girl. Broad-shouldered and sturdy. In high school she'd been on the swim team and had almost made it to the state championships. These days her exercise program came with her job. There was plenty of bending, lifting, dragging and reaching. Maybe she wasn't the media's idea of a beauty, but she didn't care. Stuart had thought she was pretty and that was enough for her.

She wrote down the addresses of the jobs on two pieces of paper and handed them to the guys. "Keep track of your hours and parts, please," she told them. "I'm heading over to help Dagmar this morning. You can reach me on my phone if you need me."

Jerry shook the note. "If you got a real phone, you could text us the address. And you could get one of those apps to keep track of our hours and the parts we use. Paper is so last century."

Howard rolled his eyes. "He has an e-reader, so he thinks he's all that."

"I love my flip phone." Unity patted her jeans pocket. "It's dependable and the battery charge lasts forever."

"That's because your phone doesn't do anything," Jerry grumbled. "Embrace technology. By the time we die, you'll be replacing us with robots."

"Not likely." Unity smiled at them. "And please don't die."

"It's gonna happen eventually," Howard said cheerfully. "See you later, Unity."

The guys left, speaking for a minute on the sidewalk before heading for their cars. Unity confirmed that she'd listened to all the messages left on the answering machine, then scanned her date book to make sure the current week's work had been transferred to the dry-erase board. Old-school, she thought. But simple and dependable. She wasn't really a technology kind of person.

After closing the garage door, she walked through the house to double-check the back door. She paused in the hall, by the wedding picture taken the week after she'd graduated from high school. She and Stuart had been so young, she thought wistfully, touching the glass protecting the photograph. But they'd been in love and so sure they would be together forever.

The familiar sadness was pushed aside for a moment when she caught sight of the tiny glass beads on her wedding dress. There were hundreds of them, all sewn by hand. She should know—she and Ellen had spent dozens of hours carefully adding the beads to the inexpensive dress that had been all Unity could afford. She'd wanted the beautifully beaded dress, but it had been double her budget. She'd placed the order for the cheaper one, but had left the store in tears.

The next day Ellen had dropped a small, heavy box on Unity's bed. Inside had been little plastic bags filled with beautiful, iridescent glass beads.

"It'll take us right up until the wedding," Ellen had told her. "But you're going to have the perfect dress when you marry Stuart."

It was an Ellen kind of thing to do, Unity thought. She believed in showing her love rather than just talking about it. From April until the end of June that year, Ellen had demonstrated her affection with hours of beading, and in the end, Unity had married Stuart…all the while wearing the dress of her dreams.

Her gaze shifted to her late husband's face, remembering everything about that day. They'd been so thrilled to get married. It had been a magical day, but not the best day. With him, there hadn't been a best day—there couldn't be. They were all too good.

And thoughts like that were not helpful, she reminded herself, as the ache of missing him returned.

Dagmar was waiting and Dagmar wasn't the type to take lateness in stride.

Unity drove the three miles to The Village at Silver Pines, otherwise known as just plain Silver Pines, and was waved in by the guard at the gate.

Silver Pines was the largest retirement community in the Pacific Northwest. There were single-family homes, condos, a golf course, several clubhouses, three restaurants, a workout facility, two pools, tennis and pickleball courts, and a grocery store. Deeper into the multi-acre complex were the independent living apartments, assisted living apartments, memory care and rehab facilities, a skilled nursing home and an out-patient surgery center.

The community hosted weekly garage sales, movie nights and all kinds of clubs. The senior center—housed in the largest of the clubhouses—was open to the public.

Unity had discovered it and Silver Pines when she'd first moved back, three years ago. She'd decided to take up knitting, and the senior center had offered a class. She'd enjoyed the company so much, she'd joined the local pickleball league and was a regular at various events. Now, with the exception of Ellen, all her friends were over the age of sixty-five.

She drove through quiet, well-maintained streets. The association took care of all front lawns—freeing the residents from worry. Unity smiled. Maybe Howard should tell his son about the work his lawn business could have here. Not that she was interested. Too many of her friends were trying to fix her up. They liked Unity and wanted to see her "happy." When she tried to tell them it had been only three years and she was nowhere near over Stuart, they told her she shouldn't wallow. As if she had a choice about the amount of grief in her life. She also tried explaining that she'd had one great marriage and didn't need another one, but that didn't work either. Only Ellen let her be.

Unity turned onto a side street, then another, before pulling in front of a small rambler. The house was two bedrooms and two baths—about twelve hundred square feet. Sadly, Betty had fallen the previous week and broken her hip and would be moving into an independent living apartment.

Betty's soon-to-be former house, like all the other houses, was on a single level with no stairs. The path from the street to the dark blue front door had a gentle incline. There were no steps anywhere in the house. The doorways were wide enough to accommodate a wheelchair. Inside the finishes were upscale. There were several floor plans and this was one of Unity's favorites.

Dagmar met her at the front door. "You're here. Good. We can get started right away. I went and saw Betty yesterday and got a list of all the things she wants us to pack for her. The movers come in the morning and take care of the rest of it."

Dagmar, a seventysomething former librarian, had the energy level of a brewing volcano. She wore her straight hair in a chin-length bob. The color varied, sometimes significantly. Currently her swinging, shiny hair was a deep auburn with a single purple stripe on her left side. Her clothes matched her personality—vibrant hues battled prints for attention. She was as likely to show up in a Hawaiian-print caftan as riding pants and a bullfighter's bolero jacket.

Today she had on a calf-length wrap skirt done in a balloon animal print. Her twinset picked up the lime green of one of the balloons and seemed conservative enough until she turned around and Unity saw a sequined version of the Rolling Stones open mouth logo. As always, reading glasses perched on Dagmar's head.

"Let's start in the bedroom. All she wants us to pack up there are her unmentionables." Dagmar grinned over her shoulder as she led the way through the cheerful living room to the short hallway. "She used those exact words. Unmentionables. What is this? The set of *Little Women*? I told her unless she had some fur lined G-strings, the movers weren't going to care, but you know how Betty is."

Unity was used to Dagmar's whirlwind, take-charge attitude. The first time Unity had come to Silver Pines to take her knitting classes, Dagmar had spotted her immediately. Within ten minutes, she pretty much knew Unity's life story. By the end of the fifty-minute lesson, she'd introduced Unity to everyone in the class and had invited Unity to a potluck and a pickleball game. They'd been friends ever since.

"I packed up her medications yesterday," Dagmar told her, pointing to the bathroom. "I'm hiding them at my place until she's out of rehab. You know that doctor of hers is going to mess with everything and it will take her weeks to get back on track. This way I have a stash so we can figure it out as we go."

"Because self-medication is always the answer?" Unity asked wryly.

"At our age, it can be." Dagmar pointed to the roll of packing paper on the bed. "You get going on her Swarovski collection while I pack up the girl stuff. That's mostly what she's worried about. Her glass animals and the pictures, of course." Dagmar's smile faded.

"She won't have room to hang them at her new apartment. I've been thinking that I should put them all in a photo album for her."

Before Unity could say anything, Dagmar pointed to the paper. "Chop-chop. I have bridge this afternoon and I'm sure you have work you should be doing."

"Yes, ma'am."

Unity didn't take offense at the instruction—it was simply Dagmar's way. She unrolled the paper, then she walked around the small house, collecting the crystal animals in a sturdy box.

Betty had them in her hutch, of course, but also on floating shelves in the living room and den. As Unity gathered crystal swans and frogs, dogs and birds, she looked around at various rooms. The kitchen was recently remodeled, with quartz countertops and stainless steel appliances. There was plenty of storage and a back deck with room for a table and chairs, along with a barbecue.

The neighborhood was quiet. Safe, too, she thought, carefully wrapping the crystal pieces and placing them in the box.

Dagmar appeared a few minutes later with an empty box and an armful of framed photographs. Betty had been a background dancer in Hollywood musicals back in the late 1940s and early 1950s.

"She was a beautiful girl," Dagmar said. She held up a photograph of a very young Betty in a scanty costume with a spray of feathers on her head.

"She was. What an exciting life."

"She was brave." Dagmar sighed. "I never was. I studied dance all through high school. I wanted to run off to New York and be a Rockette." She smiled. "Back then you didn't have to be so tall and I just made the height requirement. But my parents were very opposed and I was too scared to do it on my own. So I went to college and got my degree in library science."

"You've led a pretty interesting life," Unity told her.

"No, dear. But I have married interesting men, so there's that."

"This is a really nice house," Unity said as she continued to pack. "The rooms are all a good size."

Dagmar's brown eyes narrowed. "Oh my God! Don't tell me you're checking it out."

"What? No. Of course not. I've never been in Betty's house before."

Dagmar put her hands on her hips. "You're what? Thirty-two?"

"Thirty-four."

"Whatever. You're a baby. You should not be eyeing houses in an age-restricted community. You already spend too much time here as it is. Not that I don't love your company but you should be with people your own age."

"I am. All the time."

Dagmar's eyebrows rose. "Really? Is this before or after you come here for whatever classes you've signed up for this time?"

Unity tried not to sound defensive. "The classes are open to the entire county."

"Yes, but you're one of the few not collecting social security who bother to take advantage of that."

"So I'm smart."

"You're troubling me, Unity. It's been three years. Don't you think it's time to want more than you have?"

"No."

Dagmar sighed. "Maybe you want to think for a second before you answer."

"Why? I like my life. I have my friends and my business."

"Yes, you have all that, but what about a man?"

"I had my man. Dagmar, let it go."

"I can't. You had a wonderful marriage and Stuart died and it's all very sad, but at some point you need to move on. Start dating. Have you thought about dating at all?"

"Since the last time you asked? Not really."

Unity did her best to keep her tone friendly. She didn't like this line of questioning. No, she hadn't thought of dating. She'd been married to Stuart and that had been enough. One month after their wedding, he'd left for basic training. She'd joined him when he'd been assigned to a base in Colorado.

That had been their life. She'd made a home at whatever base he'd been assigned to. When he'd had leave, they'd traveled everywhere together. When his work had taken him overseas, she'd waited for him to come back to her. Being married to Stuart was all she knew. Three years after his death, she still only knew how to be his wife. Even her handyman business had grown out of her life with Stuart. Now it supported her and gave her something to do with her day.

There were supposed to have been children, but they'd wanted to wait until they were thirty and then his mom had died, so they'd waited another year and then Stuart had been gone.

"I'm sorry," Dagmar said unexpectedly, pulling Unity close. "I'm pushing you and that never goes well. It's just I hate to see you wasting your life, hanging out with a bunch of old farts with cataracts and spider veins. You should be with some young people, going out and having fun."

"I have fun with you."

Dagmar released her and smiled. "I am a good time, aren't I? And while I appreciate the compliment, I was thinking more in the lines of sex. Darling, you desperately need a man."

"I was thinking more of getting my bangs trimmed."

"How very sad. All right, young lady. One more house check for silly crystal figurines. Although I'm in no position to cast stones. After all, my house is a shrine to all things Thomas Kincaid. I can't help it. His work moves me. Plus, I can get new things dirt cheap at the estate sales around here."

Unity did one more pass through the house. For now she was happy to live in what had been Stuart's house, surrounded by his life as a boy. The familiar was comforting. But in another twenty-one or so years, she would qualify to move to Silver Pines and wasn't that something to look forward to?

three

THE SHRIEKS, laughs and yells were louder than usual, as the last day of school wound down. Ellen sat at her desk, thinking her students would be shocked to know Ms. Fox was just as excited as they were at the thought of having the summer off. But while they were done for the semester, she still had final exams to finish grading.

Ah, to have a subject that lent itself to Scantron testing, she thought wistfully, eyeing the tall stack of papers she would be wading through. But on her tests, partial credit was always available for the work done correctly, so every pencil mark had to be studied for its potential value to the final answer. She pulled the top test off the stack and uncapped her red extra-fine-point Sharpie and went to work.

Two hours and thirty-three minutes later, she had a mild headache and a slightly sore hand, but she had finished. She entered the grades into the computer, then happily hit the send button.

"I am done," she said aloud, tapping her feet on the floor as she threw her arms in the air.

She'd already cleaned out her desk, so only had to gather a few personal things before walking around her classroom one last time to make sure nothing had been forgotten.

It was nearly five and the school was quiet. She locked her classroom as she left before making her way to her car. She would dump her things, then check on Coop before heading home. She wanted to work on her to-do list for the upcoming bus trip, but first she would get some takeout to celebrate. What it would be depended on whether or not Coop was, or Coop and Luka were, joining her for dinner.

She put everything in her trunk, then headed for the gym. Cooper and Luka were, as always, working out. They were obsessed with their muscles, and their earnestness about the whole thing made her giggle. Not that she let them know—they would be horrified to think they were anything but manly men.

She rounded the corner and caught a reflection out of the corner of her eye. As she glanced toward it, she saw the mirrored wall in the trophy case.

It was one of those moments when she wasn't expecting to see herself and therefore had a microsecond of wondering "Who is that?" only to realize it was her. In that second of time she had a brief impression of a nondescript person swallowed up by clothes that were far too large.

Ellen came to a stop and stared at herself. She wore a loose tunic shirt that came to midthigh. Her pull-on pants billowed as she walked. The dark colors weren't flattering.

Heat burned at her cheeks, although why she was embarrassed, she couldn't say. So she wasn't a fashionista—she was still a good person.

She remembered Keith's comment when they'd had dinner the previous week—that no one could tell if she gained weight because her clothes were so baggy. It was just her thing, she told herself. She'd always dressed this way, hadn't she?

Ellen continued to stare at herself as she remembered the summer before she began her first teaching job. Money had, as always, been so tight and she'd needed clothes to wear to work. She'd gone to a nice thrift store just outside Seattle where she'd found some wonderful, high-quality outfits at swoon-worthy prices. The only problem had been that they were two sizes too big.

Given her need and her budget, she'd bought them and worn them. Funny how all these years later, she'd never thought to start wearing things that actually fit.

She shook off the thought and started for the weight room. As she approached, she heard voices. Cooper was there, along with Luka. Ellen hovered just to the side of the door, figuring she didn't get all that much opportunity to eavesdrop and that she wouldn't be much of a mother if she didn't take advantage of a situation that presented itself.

"There's no reason to go," Coop said, sounding dejected. "I should stay home and get a job."

Go? Go where?

"You have to take the bus trip, man," Luka told him. "Don't you want to see Stanford?"

"Why? I can't go away to college. Not that far away."

Ellen pressed a hand to her mouth to keep from making any noise. Not go away to college? Where had that come from? They'd always talked about him going away. It was what he wanted.

"Coop, come on. Don't say that."

"You know I can't leave her. She needs me."

No, no, no, no! Ellen battled panic. Who needed him? She didn't even know Coop was seeing someone. What bitch had trapped him?

She went cold all over and the unthinkable pushed its way into her brain. What if some girl was pregnant? There was a lot of that going around.

She closed her eyes. That couldn't be it. They'd talked and talked about safe sex. She bought him condoms. She reminded him of how hard it was for just the two of them and how using a condom protected him from unplanned pregnancies and STDs. Hadn't he been listening?

"You know her," Coop continued. "You know what our relationship is like. She depends on me. She won't make it without me."

Who was it? Ellen wanted to scream the question. She ran through the list of girls she knew her son hung out with and tried to figure out which one might be holding him back. Did Keith know? No, he would have said something. Maybe she should talk to Lissa. Maybe—

"That's no reason to stay here," Luka told him. "You want to go away to college."

"I can't. Luka, I can't. She's my mom and she needs me."

Ellen sagged against the wall as all the air rushed out of her body. Heat replaced the cold as she battled with the impossible. Her? The person he was talking about was *her*?

"We've always been a team," Coop said. "I'm her life. She doesn't date. I'm seventeen years old and my mom hasn't been on a single date my whole life."

"Not even one?"

"Nope. She's never gone in the evening, unless it's to hang out with Unity or Coach Kinne. She doesn't do anything but work and take care of me. How can I leave her? Who will take care of her?"

The horror returned, but this time it was laced with confusion and shame. How could her son think like this? She was perfectly capable. She'd raised him, she'd graduated from college, she had a good job. She didn't need her kid to take care of her. Why would he assume he was her everything? She had a life.

Without thinking, she began backing away from the door. She retreated to the main corridor and stood there, trying to clear her mind.

This was nothing but a misunderstanding, she told herself. Coop was reading the situation wrong. Of course she had a life and she would be fine when he was gone. Why wouldn't she be? She was more than capable of being on her own. He had to know that. He was free to go live his life—be his own person. She wanted that for him, of course, but just as important, she never wanted him to resent her the way she'd always resented her parents.

She would take a second and gather her thoughts, then return to the weight room. She would find out about his plans for the evening, then go home and... And... Well, she didn't know what she was going to do, but it would be something fun and exciting. Because of course she had things to do. Not dating didn't mean anything. Lots of people didn't date. She was absolutely and totally fine and happy and living the dream. That was her. For sure.

UNITY FINISHED TIGHTENING the new faucet in place. She ran water, then checked under the sink to make sure there were no leaks. When she was confident everything was perfect, she collected her tools, put the old faucet in the box the new one had arrived in and wiped down the counter. Only then did she go get Mr. Sweetman who was in his recliner, watching TV.

"I'm all done," she said loudly, so the eightysomething gentleman could hear her over *Judge Judy.*

Mr. Sweetman, as adorable as his name, looked up and smiled. "All done?"

"I am."

He nodded and got to his feet, a slow process that was painful to watch. When Unity couldn't bear the struggle anymore, she grabbed him by both forearms and pulled until he was standing.

She matched his slow pace to the kitchen, then showed him the new faucet.

"If you press this button, the water goes from a steady stream to a nice spray," she told him. "You don't have to make it go back to a steady stream. The next time you turn it on, it's on the steady stream automatically."

"Oh, that's very nice."

She demonstrated the hose feature, showing him how he could easily rinse out his sink. He watched carefully, then practiced using the faucet before turning to her.

"Technology's a marvel. When I was growing up,

we had to pump water out of a well and carry it into the house. We've come a long way."

"We have. I'll send you a bill in a day or so."

He patted her arm. "You're a good girl, Unity. Thanks for my new faucet."

She gave him a wave and let herself out.

After stowing her tools, she slid onto her seat and called her answering machine back home to pick up messages, then started her truck and drove through Silver Pines. Phyllis, the head of the local pickleball league, had asked her to stop by after work.

She was lucky that way, she thought, driving through the tidy community, waving at people she knew. Being her own boss meant she could come and go as she wanted. Although there were days when she had more work than she could handle, even with her part-time helpers.

She knew the solution was to hire a full-time employee—something she'd thought about and talked about and whined about. Ellen had threatened to place an ad online herself, just to force Unity to make a decision. It was probably the right thing to do, but Unity just couldn't seem to make herself take the step. Hiring someone seemed like a big responsibility.

A real employee would be different than her part-time team. She would have to pay him or her every week, and do payroll.

She parked in front of Phyllis's duplex. The seventy-something woman lived alone, with her two cats. Phyllis was a stern kind of person who intimidated Unity—not that she ever let herself show it. Until moving to Silver Pines, Phyllis had been a member of a tennis club and had played several times a week. Now she put the same devotion and energy into the local pickleball league. She was president of the club and in charge of all the tournaments. Phyllis had a forceful personality and got things done.

Unity had discovered the world of pickleball after she'd moved home and joined the league nearly two years ago. She liked the exercise, the comradery and the company.

"Good, you're here," Phyllis said, showing her into her living room.

They sat on opposite sofas. The room was just like Phyllis—no-nonsense and practical. Unity noticed the lack of refreshments, which surprised her. Most meetings, social or otherwise, came with at least an offer of iced tea and a cookie.

"I'll get right to the point," Phyllis said, her tone curt. "Several league members have been complaining about you, Unity."

"What?" The unexpected statement shocked her. "I don't understand. I'm on time, I support my team members. I always bring refreshments when it's my turn." She pressed her lips together to make herself stop talking.

Phyllis, a tall woman with close-cropped gray hair and small brown eyes, frowned. "It's ridiculous you were ever allowed to join the league. Look at you. You're a big, strapping girl. It's not a fair fight. None of the other pairs can defeat you. No one wants to play against you."

Unity felt herself flush. She suddenly felt all arms and legs, not to mention completely rejected. "I don't win every game."

"Nearly. I've gone through the statistics for the last

three tournaments. You and your partner won all of them. You're just too young and fit. The league was always meant to be for the people living here. You're a ringer and we don't want you around. I'm sorry, Unity, but you're being given the boot."

"You're kicking me out?"

"We are."

She said *we* but Unity had a feeling it was more a *her* decision. The whole situation was desperately unfair. "But the league is open to everyone in town. There are a lot of other people under sixty-five playing pickleball."

"They're all older than you and mostly fat. They're terrible players. We've changed the rules. You have to be fifty or over to join the league. We took a vote."

"Without me?"

Phyllis's expression wasn't the least bit sympathetic. "Yes. Without you."

Unexpected tears burned in her eyes. Unity felt exposed and foolish and ashamed. This was so much worse than being picked last for a team in school— mostly because she never had been. She loved pickleball. What was she supposed to do now?

"I'm sorry," she whispered, standing. "I didn't know."

"Now you do. Find a league with people your own age. You'll do fine."

Phyllis hustled her to the front door, showed her out, then closed it firmly in Unity's face. Unity tried to summon a little righteous anger, but she couldn't get past the giant slap of rejection.

She got in her truck, silently called Phyllis a bitch, then drove the short distance to Dagmar's house. When she was parked out front, she called her.

"You busy?" she asked, when Dagmar answered.

"Darling, I beg you, get a phone that texts. Even my friends text rather than call."

Dagmar's tone was light and Unity knew the comment was teasing, only it felt like one more judgment.

"Are you busy?" she asked again, trying to keep her voice from shaking.

"Oh, no. What happened?"

"Phyllis threw me off the pickleball league. She said I was a big, strapping girl and didn't belong."

"She's a wizened old cow who hasn't had sex in over a decade. I'm sure her girl parts are about as interesting as day-old bread."

Despite everything, Unity smiled. "That's a very weird analogy."

"I know. I was struggling to make one work." The curtain at the front of the house moved. "Oh, good, you're here. Come on inside and we'll talk about it."

As always, just being in Dagmar's house made Unity feel better. While most of the residents surrounded themselves with items from their past—pictures, mementos, ornate pieces of furniture not suited to the smaller space—Dagmar had decorated her house with an elegant, beachy vibe. Pale gray grounded all the shades of blue. The sofas were comfortable, the accessories minimal. A white shag rug defined the living area. The blue-and-gray backsplash colors were repeated in the throw pillows.

The cool elegance was a contrast to Dagmar's Bohemian style. Today she had on black-and-red striped wide-leg trousers and a red T-shirt dominated by a picture of Marilyn Monroe. A dozen or so bangles rattled on her wrist.

Unity unlaced her work boots at the door and walked

into the kitchen. Dagmar set a bottle of red wine on the counter and got out two glasses, then opened her refrigerator. She pulled out a fresh veggie plate, two containers of dip, a bowl of hummus and some pita chips. By the time Unity had removed the cork and poured them each a glass, the snacks were set out on the island. They each took a stool, then Dagmar held up her glass.

"Tell me what happened."

Unity briefly recounted her conversation with Phyllis. "It feels really arbitrary and, at the same time, incredibly personal. She never liked me."

"That's because she needs to be the queen bee and with you kicking her bony ass, that was never going to happen." Dagmar sipped her wine. "You could take her advice and join a league with people your own age. Take Ellen with you. She can be your partner."

Unity smiled. "Ellen doesn't believe in organized sports. Or exercise."

"What about your other friends?" There was something in Dagmar's tone as she asked the question. Something Unity couldn't put her finger on.

"You mean outside Silver Pines?"

Dagmar's brown eyes turned sympathetic. "Yes, dear. Your friends not getting social security."

Unity let her gaze slide to the window. "I have Ellen. Everyone else is pretty much, you know, here." She turned back to Dagmar. "I like the activities here. I like being busy." Her full calendar made her feel less alone. "Besides, I enjoy the people here. I think they're interesting and fun and well traveled. I have an old soul."

"What you have is an inability to move on with your life. Darling, I love you as much as if you were my own daughter, but come on. What are you doing? Pickleball with old people? The knitting club? Do you do anything with people your own age, ever?" She held up a hand. "Excluding Ellen and Cooper?"

Unity grabbed a slice of red pepper and took a bite.

"I'll take that as a no." Dagmar sighed. "It's been three years, Unity. You're thirty-four. You've been in mourning nearly 10 percent of your life."

Ten percent of her life? Unity had never thought about it that way. Not that it changed anything—time wasn't the issue.

"I've buried four husbands," Dagmar told her. "I loved each of them and the end was always painful, but you have to keep moving forward or you stagnate and die."

Unity shook her head. "You don't understand. It's different for me."

"Because you loved Stuart more? You had a greater love? I'm a terrible person for finding someone else?"

"No, of course not. It's just—" She looked at her friend. "I only want to love Stuart."

"He's not coming back. Would you rather mourn him and be alone than risk the chance of finding happiness again?"

Yes. Unity didn't say it, but she thought it and knew it to be true.

"I would accept you not wanting another relationship if that was all it was," Dagmar told her. "But it isn't. You're stuck, my love. What I don't understand is how you can be that way with all you see around here."

"What do you mean?"

Dagmar waved to take in the room. "We come here to die. Oh, it's a lovely place with lots to do, but we are in the final years of our lives. Look at Betty. She has plans—a river cruise, Christmas in New York. Will she still get to do that? Who knows? How long until she's gone? What about me?"

Unity's eyes widened. "What about you? Are you sick?"

"Not that I know of. But at my age, we're all one bad diagnosis away from a terrible turn in our lives. Yes, it can happen to anyone, but for those of us living here, it feels more inevitable."

She squeezed Unity's hand. "Darling, you're so young and vibrant. I hate to see you hiding from your own life. I wish you'd make friends your own age and go do exciting things. I wish you'd find a handsome man and use him for sex. I'm not saying you have to find another one true love, but you do have a responsibility to be alive, and right now, you're not."

Unity knew the words were said with love, but they still hurt. She thought of Dagmar as a second mother and the scolding, however gently delivered, made her feel uncomfortable and embarrassed.

"Are you cutting me off?" she asked, her voice trembling.

"Never. And if you stop coming to see, I'll hunt you down and drag you back here." Dagmar smiled gently. "Just think about it. Life is wonderful. I want you to remember there's so much out there you can experience. If not with men, then at least new horizons, new experiences. Although some of the old ones are quite wonderful." Her smile turned sly. "The feel of a man's tongue on your—"

Unity jumped to her feet. "Oh, my God! Don't say whatever you were going to say."

"I can't believe your Stuart never did that to you."

Heat flared on her cheeks and it was all Unity could do not the cover her ears and hum. "Of course he did, but I'm not discussing sex with you."

"Yes, you made that clear the time I started to tell you about my threesome. It wasn't the smartest decision I've ever made but it was a night."

"I'm leaving," Unity said, hurrying toward the door. "You're impossible."

"I'm alive. It's something you should consider."

Unity shoved her feet into her boots. "I'm alive, too. Just in a different way."

Dagmar followed her to the door. Her expression was serious. "Before you know it, you're going to be my age. It's true what they say—regrets are the very worst."

Unity hesitated, then nodded, as if she believed what she was being told. She hugged her friend, let herself out and hurried to her van.

What had started out as a good day had turned into something else very quickly, she thought as she headed for home. She felt battered and picked on and all she wanted to do was climb into bed and wish it all away. And if that didn't work, she would think about Stuart because no matter what, he was always with her. And that was never going to change.

four

"BY THE WAY, you're fired," Thaddeus Roake said as he used the bottle opener on his beer and tossed the cap into the trash.

Lela pulled a cookie sheet of mini quiches out of the oven. After setting it on the hot pads on the counter, she turned and grinned at him. "You can't fire me. I don't work for you."

"You're still fired. You're a terrible matchmaker."

The petite brunette sighed heavily. "Yes, well, I want to apologize for that last setup. I totally misread the situation."

Thaddeus thought about the lunch Lela had arranged for him with Kristie—an attractive thirtysomething woman who seemed to check all the boxes on his wish list. She was smart, funny, caring and single.

He'd met her at Ruth's Chris Steak House. She'd been upbeat, attentive and charming. Forty-five minutes in, he'd allowed himself to hope his dating situation might be looking up. Then she'd mentioned wanting two hundred thousand dollars for her charity.

"It was an ask, not a date," he said.

Freddy, Lela's husband and Thaddeus's best friend from the age of six, wandered into the kitchen. He looked between them.

"What?"

"Thaddeus is firing me as his matchmaker."

Freddy kissed his wife on the cheek. "A good idea. You're not very good at it."

"Hey. I know lots of great single women. I just haven't quite figured out how to sort through them yet."

Freddy leaned against the counter. "What about that one with the weird name. Katie-Jane, Katie-Marie—"

"Katie-Lynn," Thaddeus and Lela said together.

"She's very successful," Lela said defensively.

"You're right." Thaddeus reached for a quiche. "She never got off the phone our entire lunch and when we were done, she called me Theodore."

"It's close," Lela murmured.

"And that other one," Freddy said, grabbing a beer from the refrigerator. "The one who was—"

"Married?" Thaddeus asked dryly.

"I was going to say too old, but you're right. One of them was married." Freddy shook his head. "Honey, I love you to the moon and back but you gotta leave Thaddeus alone. He's such a loser. You're going to make things worse."

Thaddeus eyed his friend. "I'm not a loser."

Freddy waved away the comment. "Look at you. You're what? Thirty-seven? So old with nothing to show for it."

"I have a very successful business that employs you, along with a couple dozen other people."

"That's nothing. I got Lela and three kids."

"Smug bastard."

They clinked bottles.

"You know it," Freddy said. "Come on. The Mariners are ahead."

A huge sectional sofa sat in front of the TV mounted on the wall in the family room. The kids were off playing with friends. In a couple of hours, they would come racing into the house with demands for food and attention. The house, a sprawling two-story place with a big backyard, was often loud and chaotic.

Thaddeus looked around, admitting that after years of chasing his business and financial dreams, he was finally ready to make a shift in priorities. This was what he was looking for—home, family. He was finally ready to settle down and because life was a mean bitch with a sense of humor, he couldn't find anyone he wanted to settle down with. In the past six months he'd been on more first dates than he could count. A few had led to second dates, but none to third dates. He could find a failing business, turn it around and then sell it for five times what he paid, no problem. He could chat up a gorgeous woman at any trendy bar in the area and get laid. But finding someone special, someone he wanted to have kids with and spend the rest of his life adoring, someone he wanted to introduce to his great-aunt Dagmar, was not in his skill set.

Was wanting to find someone special so impossible? He knew part of the problem was separating himself from his success. He wanted a woman who cared about him, not his bank account.

"I can hear you thinking from here," Freddy said, never taking his gaze from the TV.

"Sorting things through."

"Should have married young, man. You could have had it all by now."

"Not my style."

"Your style has you screwed." Freddy grinned. "Tell you what. If you end up old and alone, I'll build you an apartment over the garage."

Thaddeus sighed. "Sadly, that's the best offer I've had this month."

Freddy's humor faded. "Seriously, bro, you've got to keep looking. There has to be someone out there hard up enough to want a guy who looks like you."

"You're right. You managed to convince Lela to marry you and I'm way better-looking than you."

"Yeah, maybe, but I have a bigger dick."

"Your mama."

Lela carried in the quiche, along with egg rolls and dipping sauce. "Really? Is that what we're reduced to? Bragging about your penis and talking trash about your mothers?"

Freddy waited until she'd put down the food, then pulled her onto his lap. "You picked me. You could have had any man you wanted and you picked me. Now you have to live with it."

She wrapped her arms around his neck and snuggled close. "I know. Sometimes you get lucky."

Thaddeus turned his attention to the game, ignoring the disquiet inside. Because saying disquiet was easier than saying loneliness, which was really what it was.

He swallowed the last of his beer, then stood. "I'm gonna go."

Lela slid to her feet. "What? Don't. Come on, Thaddeus. Stay to dinner."

He kissed her cheek, then nodded at Freddy. "I'll see you at work tomorrow."

His friend narrowed his gaze. "You're going to the office, aren't you?"

"Just for a couple of hours."

Freddy rose and walked him out. "You okay, man? You need me to come with you?"

"To watch me work? I'm fine. I just have to figure it out."

Freddy nodded. "Maybe plastic surgery would help."

Thaddeus laughed and got in his car. As he drove the short distance to his condo's parking garage, he told himself maybe it was time to accept the fact that he wasn't meant to find "the one." He'd already been married once and that had been a disaster. Maybe he was meant to be the fun uncle, the charming party guy who had a string of interchangeable women. There were worse fates. Think of the time he would save if he stopped looking. Given the choice between alone and disappointment—maybe alone didn't look so bad.

At 2:57 a.m. Ellen woke from a restless sleep and sat straight up in bed. She didn't know what she'd been dreaming but whatever it was, it had left her sweaty, with her heart racing. As she stared into the darkness, she was overwhelmed by a sense of dread. Not only did she have to worry about her son resenting her the way she'd resented her parents, but Cooper had been right. She didn't have a life.

She did the same thing every day. She lived a routine that revolved around her work and her friends and her son. She didn't date. She, in fact, hadn't been on a date since she'd found out she was pregnant. Worse, she hadn't had sex with a man since she'd gotten pregnant.

She flung off the covers and jumped to her feet where she tried to catch her breath.

How had it happened? How had she forgotten to do things like have a life? No wonder her kid was worried about her. She was pathetic, which she could live with, but she was also holding Cooper back, which was unforgiveable. And the worst part? Now that she knew the truth, she was going to have to do something about it.

ELLEN NEVER GOT back to sleep. Sometime around four thirty, she stopped faking it and got up and showered. She tried to distract herself by playing computer games, but her mind was too busy racing for her to focus.

Shortly before six, she wrote a note for Coop, in case he got up before she was back. As it was the first day of summer vacation, she was pretty sure she wouldn't see him until noon, but if the unexpected happened, she didn't want him to worry. She swung by Starbucks, got two venti lattes and a couple of breakfast sandwiches, then headed for Unity's house, three blocks away.

She used her key to let herself in and tiptoed down the hall. When she saw a light on in her friend's bathroom, she breathed a sigh of relief.

"It's me," she called. "Don't freak."

There was a scream from the bathroom, then Unity stuck her head out, a toothbrush in one hand.

"You gave me a heart attack. What are you doing here?"

Ellen held up the Starbucks tray. "Sorry. I have a crisis. I figured you'd be up already."

Unity, annoyingly pretty with bedhead and no makeup, stared at her. "It's barely six. What time did you get up?"

"I don't know. Fourish."

"Then it must be bad. Give me thirty seconds."

Ellen retreated to the kitchen. It was already well past sunrise, so she didn't bother with lights, instead collapsing on one of the kitchen chairs and reaching for a coffee. A couple of minutes later, Unity joined her.

Her friend had pulled a T-shirt over jeans. Her feet were bare, as was her face. Unity wasn't one to bother with things like makeup. Not that Ellen did much, either. It was such a pain in the ass, and time-consuming. Not only did you have to put it all on, later, when you were dog tired and just wanted to go to bed, you had to take it all off. She had better things to do with her life. Like panic.

Unity took the remaining coffee. "Why didn't you call me last night?"

"I didn't think it was bad. Or I was mulling." Maybe she had been a little embarrassed to share. Yes, Unity was her best friend and they talked about nearly everything, but there was something about what Cooper had said that had made her want to go hide rather than spill her guts.

Unity passed out the sandwiches. She unwrapped hers and took a bite. "Tell me."

Ellen sucked in a breath, then explained about the overheard conversation. As she spoke all the embarrassment rushed back, along with a good dose of despair, some fear and a bit of chagrin.

"I can't believe he thinks I'm not capable of being on my own. I'm very capable. I've raised him. Yes, my parents helped and I'm grateful but it was mostly me taking care of him. I'm his mom. I handle things. Sure, we talk about being a team, but that's a family thing, not an 'I need him to survive' thing."

She finished in a rush, then sucked in a breath, only to realize that instead of looking sympathetic, Unity was smiling.

"You think this is funny?" Ellen asked, outraged. "It's not funny at all. It's awful. I love Coop with all I have and it turns out I'm holding him back." She felt her eyes burning. "I'm making his life smaller. That's terrible."

Unity stunned her by giving a little wave of dismissal. "It's not all that. Come on. Last week you were upset he wanted to go away to California to college. Now he doesn't. Your problem is solved."

Ellen genuinely couldn't understand why her friend said that. She might as well have mentioned the price of grapefruit.

"This is serious," she snapped, feeling tightness in her chest as different emotions struggled for dominance. "I know what it's like to be trapped by a parent. My folks were great to me, but in order to live with them, after I had Cooper, I had to follow their rules. There was school and homework and taking care of him and going to my part-time job and nothing else. I never had a life and while I know they were trying to teach me a lesson, a lot of the time their actions felt vindictive and cruel. Every second of every day was spent making sure I remembered how I'd screwed up."

She felt her temper rising. "After we graduated, you were gone. You don't know what I went through. I'm not saying I shouldn't have taken responsibility for my

kid, but there was never a break. While I appreciate the
support, I resented the hell out of them. When I finally
got my teaching credential, it took me six months to
save enough to move out into my own apartment. Coop
and I were dirt-poor, but I didn't care. I was finally free
of them. I never want him to feel that way about me."

Restless, she sprang to her feet and began pacing
the length of the room. "I love my folks. I do, but there
were times when I hated them." She glared at Unity. "I
don't want Cooper to hate me."

"He doesn't." Unity still looked amused. "You're
blowing this out of proportion."

"No, I'm not. Don't you get it? My parents aren't bad
people, but for them, the rules were more important
than their only child. Since they've moved away, I talk
to them every few months and that's it. How much of
that is because of their stupid rules? They were wrong
in how they treated me and I never wanted to be that
person with Cooper."

"Ellen, you're not," Unity told her. "Cooper's fine.
You know he is. He adores you and he's a really good
guy. Just sit down and talk to him about all this."

"And say what? That I have life? I don't. I figured
that out in the middle of the night." Ellen looked at her.
"I have school and you and Cooper and that's it. I don't
have any hobbies. I don't date. God knows I haven't had
sex since I was a teenager. I resented how my parents
made me live and yet here I am, seventeen years later,
still following their rules. Living the life they told me
to live, even though I hated it."

Unity reached for her sandwich and took a bite. "So
change."

The casual words felt like a slap across the face.

"That's it?" Ellen asked bitterly. "That's your advice? Change? How is that helpful? How does that show any understanding of the problem? How would you have liked it if when you called me to tell me Stuart was gone that I had told you to get over it?"

Unity's eyes widened. "That's not fair."

"Isn't it? This is a crisis and you're sitting there smiling, telling me it will be fine. It's not fine. It's my son and I want him to be happy." Her voice was rising and she honestly didn't care. Maybe shouting would get her point across. "I want him to have a wonderful college experience and not worry about me for even one second. Why can't you see that? Why aren't you helping?"

Unity stood and faced her. "I'm sorry you think I'm not being supportive. That isn't how I feel. Of course I want to help you. I just think you're making this way bigger than it is. You've lost perspective."

"What perspective do you have about anything? You're living in your late husband's house, sleeping in his high school bed, wearing his old clothes, wishing your life away. It's been three years and you're still in the same place you were when I dropped everything and flew to South Carolina to bring you home. I handled everything, Unity. Everything. You needed me and I was happy to be there when you needed me. It would be nice, if just once, you could stop thinking about yourself and realize sometimes I need you, too."

They stared at each other. Ellen's chest hurt. She didn't want to be fighting. She wanted understanding and support and maybe a hug. But Unity only stared at her, wide-eyed before saying, "You really hurt my feelings."

"You hurt mine. You're dismissing me and what's going on."

"Maybe because it isn't a big deal. Certainly nothing like losing my husband. You still have your child. You're not in pain every single day. You've never lost anyone and you don't know what it's like. Maybe when you understand that, I'll decide to understand you."

The words were like a physical blow. Ellen felt sick to her stomach. Was she wrong about every relationship in her life?

"I didn't realize that caring and concern came at a price in our friendship," Ellen told her, hoping her heart wasn't really breaking. "It would be helpful if you'd send me some kind of accounting so I could see what you think I've paid for and what I haven't. That way I won't make the mistake of coming to you for help when there's not enough credit in my account."

She turned then and ran out of the house. She got in her car and drove home, then locked herself in her bedroom where she curled up, pulling her knees to her chest, and started to cry.

five

RIGHTEOUS INDIGNATION GOT Unity through most of the morning. She couldn't believe how horrible Ellen had been and the awful things she'd said. They were family—you'd think Ellen would remember that. But by noon, Unity started to question what had happened and was thinking maybe she could have been a little more supportive.

Ellen had been her best friend her whole life. Before Unity's parents had been killed in a car crash, she and Ellen had split their time between their two houses, understanding that when they were at Ellen's place, there were lots of rules and when they were at Unity's, they could do whatever they wanted.

After working in the garden for a while, she went inside for lunch, only to find she wasn't really hungry. In fact, she felt more than a little sick to her stomach. Instead of seeing the contents of her refrigerator, she saw the tall, solemn-eyed policeman telling her that her parents weren't going to be coming home.

She'd been thirteen—old enough to understand but too young to truly process the information. She shut the refrigerator and sank down on the floor as she remembered Ellen and her parents holding her tight as she sobbed out her pain. She'd gone to live with Ellen and her folks—there'd never been a question of that. Although she had her own room, for the first year, she'd slept with Ellen, her friend hugging her when Unity woke screaming from the nightmares.

Years later, Ellen had helped her plan every part of her small, inexpensive wedding to Stuart. They'd made the centerpieces themselves, after they'd finished the beading on Unity's dress. Ellen had been her maid of honor and Ellen had emailed her every single day that Stuart was deployed. And yes, when Unity had once again opened her front door to find stern-faced men waiting to tell her Stuart was gone, Ellen had dropped everything to fly out to South Carolina and bring her home. Because Ellen showed her love by doing. She always had.

Unity leaned against the cabinets and closed her eyes as the uncomfortable truth wormed its way into her soul. Ellen had needed her and she hadn't been there. Worse, Ellen had asked for help and Unity had practically laughed in her face as she told her to get over herself. So what if she didn't think what Coop had said was a big deal? Ellen did and wasn't that what mattered? Only the things Ellen had said—they had been awful.

Unity forced herself to her feet, made her way out to her work van and drove to Silver Pines.

She'd joined the Saturday afternoon Moving on

After Loss grief group shortly after coming home. The group met in one of the community center rooms. A licensed therapist acted as facilitator, but there was no set agenda. People were allowed to talk or not talk, sharing as they liked. Just being with other people who had gone through what she had made her feel less alone.

About a year ago they'd gotten a new facilitator—Carmen. She was a fortysomething woman with dark hair and eyes, and a calming way about her.

Unity walked into the community center room and saw there were about fifteen people attending today. She greeted everyone as she made her way to the coffee machine in the back. Every few weeks someone new joined, but today all the faces were familiar.

When Carmen announced it was time, they took their seats in the loose circle formed by their chairs. Carmen welcomed them and asked who wanted to share. Unity tried to listen but kept finding her attention slipping back to her fight with Ellen. The more she thought about it, the more she wondered if she'd been wrong.

Just considering the possibility made her sick to her stomach again.

"Unity?"

Unity realized everyone was looking at her. She glanced at Carmen. "Sorry. I was lost in thought."

"I could tell. Want to talk about it?"

"She's thinking about Stuart," Veronica, a short, plump woman in her seventies said with an eye roll. "It's what she's always thinking about."

"I wasn't thinking about him," Unity said, surprised by the harsh statement. "Although this is a grief group. Isn't dealing with the loss of my husband the point?"

The pain of missing him joined her regret and guilt

about Ellen. None of this was supposed to have happened, she thought bitterly. She was supposed to be happily married and the mother of two or three kids by now. But she was left with nothing but memories and the flag that had draped his coffin.

Veronica sighed heavily. "No, it's not. Because you're not dead yet, despite how you act. Yes, you lost your husband, and it's tragic, but come on. You're not the only one. We've all lost someone. You're acting like this is some unique event only you have experienced. It's not like your pain is any bigger than ours, no matter how much you love reveling in it."

"All right," Carmen said. "That was a little bit more of a response than I was hoping for."

"I'm not wrong, am I?" Veronica asked, motioning to the group.

To Unity's surprise and discomfort, several people murmured words of agreement.

Unity folded her arms across her chest as if she could protect herself from the biting assessments. "But Stuart was my husband."

"Like Veronica said, we've all lost someone," Edward reminded her. "That's why we're here."

"It's called moving on after loss," Veronica said. "Be grateful for what you were given. Not living your life is a dumb ass way to spend your day."

Carmen sighed. "Veronica, we've talked about this."

"What? I can't say dumb ass? Really? Is anyone here genuinely offended?"

Unity wanted to say she was, but she was too focused on surviving the unexpected attack.

"I'm not stuck," she whispered.

Carmen gave her a sympathetic look. "Are you sure?"

Unity wanted to say she was happy loving Stuart, even if he wasn't with her anymore, but knew that would open her to another round of blunt statements she couldn't stand to hear. She felt raw and exposed and she wished she'd stayed home.

"Your points are good ones," she lied, just wanting them to focus on someone else. Their words made her feel raw and unwelcome and way too close to losing control.

Carmen seemed to sense that and changed the subject. Unity got through the rest of the meeting. When it was over, she hurried to her van and drove home. Her stomach ached, her head pounded and she felt like she could throw up, but worst of all she wanted to call Ellen and tell her what had happened and she couldn't because they were fighting.

The enormity of that slammed into her, making her eyes fill with tears even as her body seemed to contract in on itself. She felt like a squashed bug—all flat and bleeding. Her chest got so tight, she couldn't breathe.

Ellen was her family. Unity couldn't remember a time when she and Ellen hadn't been friends. She also couldn't remember them ever fighting—certainly not as adults.

She sat at the kitchen table and replayed the early morning conversation in her head. Ellen had been upset about Cooper and had wanted help. Ellen had needed her and she hadn't been there.

No wonder Ellen had felt dismissed and ignored. Unity of all people should have seen that.

She sat up straight. What if the fight had ruined everything? What if their relationship could never be made right? What if it was broken beyond repair?

Panic seized her, forcing her to her feet. But when she was standing, she didn't know what to do. How could she show Ellen she understood and was sorry? Because she was sorry and she was scared. More scared than she'd ever been because whenever she'd faced something bad, she'd known Ellen would be there for her, no matter what, and she didn't have that certainty anymore.

An apology was required, but that didn't help Ellen. Not really. There had to be another solution—one that made Ellen feel heard and maybe fixed the problem.

Unity walked into her small office. She pulled out a pad of paper and reached for a pen. Ellen needed to convince Cooper she had a life, even though she didn't. Which meant she had to start doing things to show him she had things she looked forward to, like going out and dressing in clothes that fit and—

Unity started making a list of ways Ellen could change her life. When she'd nearly filled a page with items—some helpful, some ridiculous—she studied it. There were a few good ideas here. She should tell Ellen how she could fix the problem.

"Because people love to be told what to do?" she murmured aloud, thinking about how she'd been attacked at her grief group.

She thought about what people had said. She hadn't enjoyed everyone piling on her, as if she were the only one with a problem. It wasn't as if they had their acts together either.

Unity started a second list—this one about herself. She took some items from Ellen's list and added a few others for herself.

She knew she had zero interest in changing. She didn't want to heal and move on, but that wasn't the point. She needed her friend back more than she needed to breathe. She'd hurt Ellen and now they were fighting. Unity would do anything to make that right. She didn't have to believe—she just had to convince Ellen she believed. And maybe this was a start.

BY LATE AFTERNOON Ellen had lost her mad and she just missed Unity. The fight had been stupid. She and Unity had been friends forever. Shouldn't they do better than they had that morning?

She was just about to call and say that when Cooper walked into the living room, a basketball under one arm, his dark hair falling in his eyes.

"I'm meeting Luka at the park," he said, looking more like a kid than a young man in his baggy shorts and oversize T-shirt. "Then we're going back to his place for a barbecue. I'll be home by eleven."

She smiled at him. "Have fun."

"I will." He hesitated, his blue eyes darkened with concern. "What are you going to do, Mom?"

As in it was a Saturday night and she was a carefree single woman who should have plans. Plans that made her sound like she didn't need her teenage son worrying about her.

She waved her cell phone. "I'm about to call Unity. We're, ah, going to hang out with some friends." She tried to look amused. "Sort of an old people party."

Coop looked doubtful. "Really?"

"Uh-huh."

"Okay. Have fun."

"You, too."

He left. Seconds later, she heard his car start up. When he'd pulled out of the driveway, she told herself at least half of the statement had been true—she was going to call Unity.

But before she could dial, her phone rang. She glanced at the unfamiliar number.

"Hello?"

"Ellen, it's Jeremy."

Who? She didn't know any...

Crap, crap, crap. Actually she did know a Jeremy, or she had back in high school. They'd dated for a month, he'd gotten her pregnant and then he'd disappeared. Since then she'd heard from him every five or so years. He asked about Coop but never wanted to see him. She supposed every now and then the guilt got to him.

"This is unexpected," she said.

"I know. How are you?"

"Good and you?"

"Good."

There was a moment of silence. She heard him clear his throat.

"I, ah, I've been thinking about what happened all those years ago. About Cooper and how he's doing. I'm in a different place now and thought maybe, if you wouldn't mind, I could meet him."

If Ellen had been standing, she would have fallen. Or fainted.

"He's seventeen. He's practically an adult and you just now want to meet him?" She knew she sounded shrill, but was the man on crack? "You signed your rights away before he was born. You walked out on me and him. You've shown absolutely no interest in him."

Something she'd had to explain to her son over the years, when he'd asked about his father. She'd always had to go out of her way to make sure Jeremy wasn't the bad guy. She'd always had to take the high ground and say things like he hadn't been ready to be a father and no, she hadn't been disappointed to be physically and emotionally abandoned as she'd gone through her senior year of high school pregnant.

"People change, Ellen."

"Oh, do they?"

"I can see you're still upset. I suppose you have reason to be. You're right—I have no legal rights, but he is my son and I was hoping I could get to know him."

She wanted to tell him not a chance. That he didn't deserve to know Cooper or have anything to do with him. That neither of them was interested. Only she knew that last one wasn't true. Cooper might not show it, but she knew he was curious about his father, and in her gut, she was pretty sure he would like a chance to meet him.

"Are you still there?" Jeremy asked.

"Yes."

Why did she always have to be the adult in the room?

"I need to think about this," she said.

"Of course. Let me give you my contact information."

She got up and walked into the kitchen where she grabbed a pen and a piece of paper, then scribbled down his number and email address.

"I'd really like a second chance with him," Jeremy told her.

She thought about how alone she'd felt as she'd struggled as a single parent, how much he'd missed and how bitterly unfair his request was, and then she remembered Coop.

"I'll get back to you," she told him. "Give me a few days."

"Thank you, Ellen."

She hung up and swore. Now? Did this have to be happening now?

Her phone rang again. She answered without looking at the screen.

"Yes?"

"It's me," Unity said. "I'm sorry. Please forgive me."

Relief eased the tightness in her chest. "Only if you promise to come over and get drunk with me."

"I'll be there in five minutes."

"The front door is open."

ELLEN DUG OUT a frozen pizza and turned on the oven, then opened a bottle of red wine. When she heard the door open, she ran out of her kitchen and met Unity in the living room where they hugged each other tight.

"I'm sorry," Unity said, tears filling her eyes. "I'm sorry. I should have understood. I should have listened."

"No, it was me. I was so upset that I lashed out. I'm sorry. I was insensitive about Stuart. I hurt you."

"No, I hurt you."

They looked at each other, then hugged again. Ellen hung on, feeling her world right itself.

"I've had a horrible day," she admitted.

"Me, too. I missed you. I can't believe we had a fight."

"I can't, either. Let's promise to never do it again."

They smiled at each other.

"Deal," Unity said.

They linked arms and walked into the kitchen. After

taking a seat at the table, Ellen poured them each a glass of wine. Unity sat across from her, her expression sad.

"I really am sorry."

"Me, too. I'm okay if you're okay."

Unity hesitated, then nodded.

"You sure?" Ellen asked.

"Yes. I'm fine, or I will be." She bit her bottom lip. "I was thinking about what you said about Coop and how you're worried about him. Plus what you said about me."

Ellen winced. "Do we have to talk about that?"

"I'm not complaining. I have an idea." Unity pulled a pad of paper out of her large handbag and slid it across to the table.

Ellen glanced down. "The Friendship List?" She looked at her friend. "What is that?"

"So you need to convince Coop that you're totally fine on your own and I maybe need to get out of my rut."

Ellen wanted to tease that *maybe* wasn't the right word, but knew it was too soon. "Okay. And?"

"And we do it together. We make a pact to challenge each other to use the summer to make some changes. Cooper won't apply to colleges until the fall, so there's time for you to show him you have a life. Let's take advantage of that. We would each have a list of things to do and whoever does the most wins."

"Like a game show?"

"Kind of. The winner treats the loser to a weekend at the Salish Lodge."

That caught Ellen's attention. She and Unity had been talking about a girlfriends' weekend at the Lodge forever. The Salish Lodge was an upscale resort on the Seattle side of the mountains. There was a spa, a couple of great restaurants and amazing views of Snoqualmie Falls. But the glorious accommodations came with a price tag her schoolteacher's salary couldn't afford very easily.

"I could really get into a spa weekend," she said slowly.

"Me, too. And regardless of who wins, going away will help convince Cooper that you're really okay without him."

It was an interesting idea. Ellen knew Unity wasn't the only one in a rut. As she'd been unable to come up with a single idea to fix things with Coop, she was willing to give this a try.

"What about you?" Ellen asked. "Do you want to change? I'm not trying to start anything, but you haven't even hinted that you're looking for more than you have."

"I know, but what I'm doing isn't working." She reached for her wine. "I got thrown out of the pickleball league."

"What? How could that happen? You're a star player."

Unity's mouth twisted. "That was part of the problem. I was told that I'm too young and fit and that I should go find a league with people my own age."

"I hadn't thought about it that way, but they're right."

"According to Phyllis, I'm a big, strapping girl."

Ellen couldn't hide her smile. "Strapping? She said strapping?"

"She did."

"I hate her."

"Thank you."

The oven dinged. Ellen got up and slid in the frozen pizza, then resumed her seat.

"Have you thought about joining another pickleball league?"

"Not really, but I should think about it. Maybe put it on the challenge list."

Ellen tore off a couple of sheets of blank paper, while Unity dug pens out of her bag.

"Let's do this," Ellen said. "Let's come up with a list of challenges. Things that are scary and fun and help us grow as people."

"Ugh." Unity wrinkled her nose. "Sorry. I'm not a fan of change."

"Me, either, but circumstances being what they are, I don't think we have a choice." She pointed to Unity's paper. "Pickleball. Write it down."

"I'd rather do something else."

"Like what?"

"I don't know." Unity thought for a second. "Sky-diving."

"What?" Ellen lowered her voice. "Are you insane? Skydiving?"

Unity grinned. "Yes, and you should get a tattoo."

"You first."

Unity picked up her pen and wrote the word *tattoo*, followed by *skydiving*. Her expression turned smug. "Match that."

"Fine." Ellen wrote down *tattoo* on her list. Then she thought about her recent realization that not only hadn't she been on a date in the past seventeen years, she also hadn't had sex. Well, at least not with some-one other than herself.

Her pen hovered right above the paper.

"You can do it," Unity whispered.

"What I'd really like is sex with a handsome man. Unlikely, but whatever." She scribbled the words. "I have no idea how I'm going to make that happen." She looked at Unity. "I challenge you to think about doing the same."

"Sex with a man?"

"Or a woman."

Unity rolled her eyes. "As if."

"Oh, and in your case, he has to be age appropriate."

She thought Unity might get upset at that, but her friend only started to laugh.

"I'm definitely not ready for that," Unity admitted.

"I know, but isn't that the point? Oh, I have one for you. Get a phone you can text with."

"Fine. Get some clothes that fit you."

Ellen winced. "I really should do that."

"Yes, you should."

The timer dinged. Ellen sliced up the pizza and set it in the center of the table. Over wine and dinner, they continued to brainstorm their lists. Nearly an hour later, they looked at each other.

"I'm excited and uncomfortable," Ellen admitted. "Which I think is the point. What about you?"

Unity shrugged. "The same."

"I'm not sure you're ready to move on."

"I'm not, but do I have a choice?" Unity split the last of the wine between them. "I got yelled at in my grief group."

"Grief group is giving you grief?" Ellen slapped her hand over her mouth. "Sorry. That's the wine talking."

"Yes, it is and you're right. It's kind of funny."

"No, it's not. What happened?"

"They told me I'm stuck. That I'm not moving on." She set her elbows on the table and leaned forward. "They said I think my pain and loss are more special than anyone else's and that's why I can't move on."

"I'm sorry. That must have been awful."

"It was. They ganged up on me." Unity looked at her list then back at Ellen. "Are they right? Am I making what happened more than it is?"

"No. You suffered a horrible loss. You're not wrong to miss Stuart. You loved him."

Unity's gaze was steady. "But?"

"But maybe it's time to stop assuming that your life has to be over, too. Stuart is gone, but you're still here. You could find someone, have kids."

"I don't want kids if I can't have them with Stuart."

Words Ellen had heard before. "Maybe it's the wine talking," she said slowly, "but I think it's more you won't *let* yourself have kids with anyone but Stuart."

Unity stared at her. "That's not true."

"Are you sure? Like I said this morning, I had to deal with a lot of arbitrary rules in my time. I'm good at recognizing them. You've made a lot of decisions based on grief. Maybe they were right at first, but I don't think they're right now."

"I can't think about that now."

Ellen nodded rather than push. "Just think about them later, okay?"

"I will because you're my family and I love you." Unity sighed. "Okay, we're doing this?"

"We are. We need to." Ellen picked up her list. After half a bottle of wine, the words swam a little, but she could still read them. "Learn how to do a smoky eye. Get a tattoo. Sing karaoke. Wear clothes that fit for a least a month, which I have to say is really dumb because if I'm buying new clothes, I'm going to wear them for more than a month."

Unity motioned for her to keep going.

"Have sex with a hunky guy. Get drunk, and not by myself. Hey, does tonight count?"

"No."

"You're kind of a pain in my ass." She returned her attention to the list. "Go out dancing. Wear a bathing suit at the beach." She grimaced. "I'm so pale, I'll blind people."

"Not the point."

"Be that way. Is that all? Oh, rent an impractical car for the weekend and go wild." She put down the list. "I'm not getting a ticket."

"That is entirely up to you." Unity reached for her own list. "Get a tattoo. Go skydiving. Learn to rock climb. Wear a dress and three-inch heels."

Ellen waved her hand. "Without a bra."

"What?"

"You heard me. Just wearing a dress and heels is no big deal. No bra, missy. You have great boobs. You'll be fine."

Unity shook her head, then dutifully noted the change. "Look at three houses or condos, even though I don't want to move."

"Not at Silver Pines," Ellen added. "No wistful shopping with the old people."

"I wasn't going to look at Silver Pines. I can't move there until I'm fifty-five."

"It pains me that you know that."

Unity smiled. "Get a phone that texts."

"Hallelujah."

"Bite me. What else? Join a pickleball team with people my own age. Hire a full-time employee who isn't past the age of retirement and, last but not least, move my business into an office."

They looked at each other.

"Some of these are good," Ellen said. "Like you getting a real office. Even if you never move out of Stuart's house, it would be nice to get all that inventory out of your garage. You'd have more separation from work."

"I do like the idea of that one," Unity admitted. "I'm nervous about hiring someone full-time, though. It's a lot of responsibility."

"You're a responsible person. Besides, you always have more work than you can do." Ellen looked at her list. "There's very little on here I can do on my own or even with you."

"The point is to get out so Cooper realizes you have a life beyond him. He's afraid he's all you have."

Ellen covered her face with her hands. "I didn't tell you. Jeremy called today."

Unity's blue eyes widened. "Jeremy as in Cooper's father? He called? It's been seventeen years. What, did he lose your number until today?"

Ellen smiled. "Thank you for the righteous indignation. He's called a couple of times before. Just to, I don't know, get an update, I guess."

"Is that what he wanted today?"

Ellen thought about the call. "No. He wants to see Coop. He wants to get to know his son."

"Oh, no. Are you all right with that?"

"No. The thought of it terrifies me. Jeremy is some Hollywood movie producer in LA. He's new and interesting and I'm just the mom."

"You're afraid you're going to lose him?"

Ellen nodded.

"But you know you have to tell him."

Ellen nodded again. She didn't want to, but it was

the right thing to do. She reached for her pen and added one more thing to her list.

Let Cooper meet his dad.

six

THE DISTANCE BETWEEN Thaddeus's downtown Bellevue condo and his great-aunt Dagmar's house was one hundred and seven miles. In the winter, the mountain pass between them could be difficult but in late June, the interstate was an easy two-hour drive.

As he paused to check in with the security guard at the entrance to The Village at Silver Pines, he found himself once again wishing she would consider moving to his side of the mountain. There were plenty of very nice retirement communities in the Seattle area and he'd told her price was no object. But no matter how he cajoled, Dagmar refused to move. She'd lived in Willowbrook her entire life. She claimed not to be a big city kind of person.

When he'd relocated from Las Vegas seven years ago, he'd looked around Willowbrook, but the small community with its early twentieth-century storefronts hadn't been the least bit appealing. Even though he could run his business from anywhere, he'd been unable to imagine himself living in a town with a grange, where the bowling alley was still a hot spot and the main road off the interstate road was dotted with gas stations and fast-food places to service the travelers going somewhere else.

Yes, just a mile or two north of the highway, there were charming residential streets and plenty of parks and even a handful of cows, but nothing about the place was him. He liked urban views and being close to a decent airport.

Now he drove into his aunt's retirement community, turning on the narrow streets before stopping in front of her house. The front door opened before he'd even gotten out of his car.

Despite her age, Dagmar looked as she always had—vital and eccentric, with her auburn hair swinging around her face. She was dressed in camo-patterned cropped pants and an olive green wrap blouse covered with applique black flowers.

"Darling!" She held out her arms as he approached. "You made it. I'm delighted."

"You asked and I answered."

He was gentle as he held her, mindful of the fact that she was more frail this year than last. She was as sharp as she had ever been, but he worried about her as she got older.

"Come inside. You're staying to dinner, aren't you? I'm planning something wonderful."

"You always do."

Two days ago, Dagmar had texted, inviting him over. She'd told him to come early and to plan on having a good time. With Dagmar that could mean anything from an evening going over old photos or playing bridge with her cronies. Regardless, he was in. Dagmar was the last of his family and he loved her.

His mother was Dagmar's niece. He'd known her all his life. When he was little, he and his mom would fly up to Washington and spend the holidays with her. Unlike Seattle, the eastern part of the state usually had snow in December. Everything about staying with Dagmar had seemed magical—especially the hill out back and the sled she kept for him.

As she'd approached her retirement, she'd wanted to sell her place and move to Silver Pines. When she refused to relocate to Seattle, Thaddeus had insisted on buying the house she had now, telling her to keep the proceeds from her house sale for whatever she needed. Not that she would ever go wanting—he would make sure of that. But he knew she enjoyed being independent.

He wrapped his arm around her as they walked into the house. "What have you planned for us tonight?"

"Dinner with a friend."

They went into her living room. He saw she'd set out appetizers on the coffee table and the ingredients for cocktails on her kitchen island.

"Who's the friend?" he asked, moving into the kitchen and studying what she'd left out for him. There was his usual bottle of Scotch, along with a bottle of bourbon. Beside that were a bowl of sugar cubes, sliced oranges and Angostura bitters. Next to that were several highball glasses, an ice bucket and a bottle of club soda.

He added a sugar cube to the highball glass, then sprinkled it with the bitters. After adding a splash of soda, he muddled the mixture until it coated the bottom of the glass. He added ice and bourbon before gently mixing the drink and garnishing it with an orange slice. When that was done, he poured himself a Scotch and joined her on the sofa.

They clinked glasses.

"How are you feeling?" he asked.

She waved away the question. "I'm in perfect health, my love. At least as much as one can be at my age." She laughed. "Now I want to talk to you about doing me a favor."

"Of course."

"I need you to seduce one of my friends."

Thaddeus was pleased that he managed to stay seated and not react in any way beyond taking a very healthy slug of his drink.

"No."

Dagmar pursed her lips. "But you haven't heard me out."

He reached for one of the chilled shrimp on a plate. "I would throw myself in front of a bullet for you or give you a kidney, but there is nothing you can say or do to convince me to have sex with one of your octogenarian friends."

"What if she's in amazing shape?"

Something he didn't want to think about. "No."

His great-aunt's smile turned sly. "What if she's not eighty?"

"I'm not sure her being in her sixties makes a difference. Why are you setting me up?"

"Technically I'm setting her up. Not that you don't need a woman in your life. You do. The divorce was ages ago and while I'm sure the mindless sex you engage in is exciting in the moment, it has to leave you feeling empty afterward. Or am I assuming an emotional depth you don't have?"

Better to have her think he was shallow than to tell her the truth, he thought humorously. There was no way he wanted Dagmar to know he was actively seeking a relationship. She was nothing if not determined and if she started looking for his future wife, then God help him.

"Why are you setting up your friend?"

She looked at him over her glass. "Don't for a moment think that I didn't notice your slick change of subject. But fine. We'll talk about Unity." She smiled. "She's thirty-four and very sweet. She's a handyman." Dagmar held up a hand. "An unusual occupation, but I thought you'd find that intriguing. She's tall and very athletic."

"Please don't tell me she has a great sense of humor."

"As a matter of fact, she does, but she's also very pretty. But you worrying about that isn't fair. Not everyone can be beautiful."

"How would you know? You've always been a looker."

"And this is why I love you. Now about Unity. She's been a widow for three years and she's having trouble getting back in the game."

He shook his head. "There's no game."

"Of course there's a game and I miss it desperately. But that's neither here nor there. You'll like her and you should have sex with her."

"When I first meet her or did you want me to wait?"

Dagmar rolled her eyes. "You're so difficult. Whenever it's appropriate. Just show her a good time. She needs to remember what it's like to be young and single and still have firm breasts."

"You've never set me up before." Something he was grateful for.

"As I explained, I'm setting up Unity."

"So I'm being used."

"Yes, but for a good cause. Besides, you like a challenge and I have a feeling she's going to be that. Are you interested?"

To go out with Dagmar's sad friend? "No. I can find my own women."

"And yet you remain single."

"I'm not married. There's a difference."

"Not one I can see. Darling, don't you want more?"

He had a feeling she didn't mean his drink.

The doorbell rang, saving him from answering. Dagmar smiled and rose to let in her guest. It was only as she opened the door it occurred to him that "dinner with a friend" was going to be dinner with the widow his great-aunt wanted him to seduce.

He thought briefly of bolting out the back door before reluctantly standing. Dagmar returned, a tall blonde at her side.

"Thaddeus, this is Unity. Unity, my great-nephew, Thaddeus."

"Hello," he said with a neutral smile.

She had long blond hair and big blue eyes. She was about five-ten, with broad shoulders and long legs. Not a beauty, but pretty enough, he supposed. Unlike his great-aunt's, Unity's clothing choices were designed to blend in. She wore a white T-shirt over khakis and absolutely no makeup.

His first impression was she wasn't anything close

to his type. His second was to be surprised at her obvious shock at the sight of him.

"I'm not sure I knew you had a great-nephew," she said, looking between them.

"I am pretty special," he murmured.

Dagmar shot him her "Really? Do we have to?" look before smiling at Unity. "I'm sure I've mentioned him before. However, I know you've never met until now."

No doubt by design, he thought. "She's been keeping you a secret, as well," he said, holding out his hand. "Nice to meet you, Unity."

She still looked confused as they shook hands. Dagmar guided them to the sofa, careful to take a club chair for herself.

"Be a dear and get Unity a drink." Dagmar waved her glass. "Thaddeus makes a wonderful old-fashioned. Of course Thaddeus has other skills, don't you, darling?"

He ignored her and went into the kitchen to make Unity her drink. When he delivered it, he took Dagmar's empty glass from her, leaning close to murmur, "You're laying it on a little thick."

She smiled. "It's a style thing."

He made another old-fashioned. When they were all seated again, Dagmar beamed at them both. "Isn't this lovely? I've been waiting for the right moment to introduce you two."

Unity looked more baffled than intrigued. She shifted uncomfortably before glancing at him. "So, um, what do you do?"

"He's a farmer," Dagmar said.

"I'm not a farmer."

"You farm," his great-aunt reminded him. "You've told me." She looked at Unity. "It's all very confusing.

The man lives in Bellevue, so I genuinely don't understand how it all works, but he's very successful."

He thought about explaining he hadn't farmed in
the way most people thought then decided it wasn't
worth the trouble. Instead he smiled and said, "I sold
the farm."

"What do you do now?" Unity asked.

"Some real estate development. Property manage-
ment. Business turnarounds."

"He's very successful," Dagmar added helpfully.

"That's a lot," Unity said, looking more uncomfortable by the second. She'd yet to take a sip of her drink
and her fingers clutched the glass so tightly, he was
afraid the crystal would shatter.

Unable to help himself, he took the drink from her
and put it on the coffee table. She stared at her empty
hand, then at him and flushed.

Thaddeus had been in dozens of relationships—some
lasting all of two nights and one ending in marriage.
None of them had been especially successful. Regardless, he considered himself fairly experienced when it
came to women. Unity showed all the signs of someone
completely out of her element. She was scared and uneasy and, if her darting glances toward the door were
any indication, wishing she could run for freedom.

Which meant she'd had no idea he was going to be
here, meaning the setup had been on both sides. What
was up with that? Dagmar rarely got into his business.
So why was this time different and why was Unity so
apprehensive? If Dagmar had never talked about him,
then all she knew was what she saw.

He was clear on how the outside world viewed him.
He was tall, fit and good-looking enough to be appeal-

ing, but not so pretty that it got in the way. He commanded attention and understood his place in the world. But he wasn't anyone to fear.

"What do you do, Unity?" he asked, deliberately keeping his voice quiet.

"I, ah, own a handyman business. My customers are local. We do home repairs."

"She's wonderful," Dagmar added. "Everyone adores her. She has several employees, all retired men who know exactly what to do in any given situation."

Unity managed a smile. "They work part-time for me."

"Did you grow up in the area?"

She brightened. "I did. I went to school here. I married when I graduated and Stuart joined the army. I went with him after he finished basic training." She paused. "He, um, died three years ago. I moved back here then."

The widow part. He'd forgotten about that. "I'm sorry for your loss."

"Thank you."

"Unity is very involved with the Silver Pines community," Dagmar said.

Unity winced. Thaddeus had no idea why.

"A lot of the activities are open to the public," she said. "I've taken a few classes. Until recently I was on the pickleball league." She met his gaze. "Do you play?"

"Pickleball? It's not my sport." He and Freddy had a couple of pickup basketball games they liked to join. Pickleball? Was that like badminton with a tennis ball? Ah, no.

Unity reached for her glass. Her hand shook so much, she couldn't pick it up. She quickly pulled back her arm and tucked it behind her.

Thaddeus had impressed his share of women but he'd never petrified one before. He stood and looked at his great-aunt.

"Could I speak to you for a moment, please?"

Dagmar put down her drink and allowed him to pull her to her feet.

"We'll be right back," he told Unity, then led Dagmar down the hall to her bedroom. When he'd shut the door behind them, he exhaled. "This has got to stop. The poor woman is actually trembling with fear."

"I know. I'm sorry. I had no idea she would be so—" Dagmar waved her hand. "I can't even describe it."

"I'm going to go." He shook his head before she could speak. "Whatever your plans were for this evening, they're not going to happen. You have a nice dinner with Unity and I'll see you later."

"But I wanted to spend time with you."

"I wanted the same, but it's not as if you can ask her to leave. I'll come back soon. I promise." He kissed her cheek. "I love you."

"I love you, too."

They returned to the living room. Unity looked at him.

"Is everything all right?" she asked.

Thaddeus smiled at her. "It is, however I need to start my drive back to Seattle. It was very nice to meet you, Unity."

She stood. "I hope I didn't chase you off."

"Of course not."

Her mouth twisted. "It's just I was surprised and I'm not very good at small talk and you're a little imposing."

Her honesty surprised him. "I'm far from imposing."

"Have you seen yourself?" She flashed him a smile.

"But it was nice to meet you. Next time I'll do better. Oh, wait. I should go so you two can—"

Without thinking, he took her hand in his. As his fingers curled around hers, he felt an unexpected jolt of heat and interest. Because it made all the sense in the world that he would be attracted to a woman who literally quaked in fear around him.

"You stay. I insist," he said, releasing her and stepping back.

He kissed Dagmar's cheek again, then let himself out. As he walked to his car, he told himself that when he got back to Bellevue he would work out for an hour, get to bed early and start fresh in the morning. There were several billion people in the world and at least half of them were women. Surely he could find one, just one, who was the right one for him. Or at least semi-right or half-right. At this point, he wasn't looking for a miracle, he just wanted a good woman to love and a couple of kids. Even if lately, that had felt like wishing for the moon.

KEITH WALKED IN his house and threw his keys into the basket on the table by the back door. The bus he was taking on the college road trip had been serviced and declared ready for the twenty-four-hundred-mile journey. He didn't want to jinx anything, but he had a feeling he was just about ready.

He walked into the family room and saw Lissa curled up on the sofa, reading. In the second before she looked up and acknowledged him, he took a moment to deal with the reality that his baby girl was growing up.

She'd turned seventeen two months ago and she was about to be a senior in high school. Gone were the gap-toothed smile and the pigtails. In their place were short-shorts and a young woman who looked closer to thirty than ten. It wasn't anything he was happy about, but he'd yet to figure out a way to stop time.

He crossed to where she was on the sofa and took a seat on the coffee table in front of her. Reluctantly, she put down her book and stared at him.

"Hi," he said pointedly.

"Hi, Dad."

"Whatcha reading?"

She held up a paperback with a kissing couple on the cover. "Want it when I'm done?"

He recoiled. "No, thanks."

She smiled. "You sure? Maybe you could learn a few moves."

He ignored that. "The bus is ready for the trip. You have everything you need?"

She sighed heavily. "It's a road trip, Dad. I don't need anything special."

"But you'll be visiting the colleges we're stopping at. Walking around campus, getting a feel for them."

"Dad, you're making this more than it is. I'm fine."

"Which of the colleges are you most interested in? UCLA? University of Oregon?"

Her brown eyes, the same color as his, glazed over. "I have no idea."

"But there must be one you want to see."

"Not really."

She'd been like this for a while, he thought, frustrated by her lack of interest in college. "Lissa, you're going to be a senior. College applications go out in the fall. So far you haven't mentioned one school that you like, you won't talk about your major, nothing. What's going on?"

She shifted so her feet were flat on the floor. "Why are you pushing me? What's the big deal? It's just college, Dad. I'll get there, but not with you in my face, every second of every day."

"I'm not in your face."

"You're sitting less than two feet from me. What would you call it?"

"I'm curious and supportive. Lissa, what's going on? You know you're going to have to make some decisions about your future. You're not going to be in high school forever. At some point you have to grow up and take responsibility for yourself."

"And you can't wait for that, can you?" she snapped, coming to her feet. "You're just like those birds that push their babies out of the nest. You know what, Dad? Sometimes the babies can't fly. Sometimes they crash to the ground and they die."

With that horrific image, she stalked out of the room, down the hall and slammed her bedroom door behind her.

Keith held in a groan. Lately it seemed all his conversations with her were going off the rails and he had no idea why. Was it him? Was it her? Was it a generic teenage thing?

He rubbed his face wishing he were doing a better job at raising a teenage daughter. Maybe if Becky lived closer. But his ex-wife was still in Missoula and had very little contact with Lissa.

Keith shifted to the sofa and leaned his head back. It wasn't supposed to be like this, he thought. He'd married Becky with the best of intentions. Okay, sure, she'd been pregnant, but he'd been happy about that. Maybe that had forced them to rush things, but he'd been in love with her.

Keith had been drafted by the NFL out of the University of Oklahoma. His five-year career had been spent with him mostly on the bench, as a backup quarterback. He'd had a couple of great games, but not the career he'd hoped for. When his contract hadn't been renewed, he'd transitioned to coaching at a small college in Montana.

He and Becky had divorced almost immediately. They'd coparented Lissa until Becky had remarried, once again pregnant before the wedding. After the first of two kids had been born, he'd taken on more and more responsibility for their daughter.

Five years ago, he'd been looking for a different kind of challenge when he'd been offered the athletic director position at Birchly High School. He'd thought Becky would fight him on the move, but she'd immediately agreed to give him sole custody of Lissa. At the time he'd worried his daughter would feel rejected by her mother, but she'd seemed happy with the relocation and had settled in nicely.

Now, he thought maybe he was dealing with some serious payback for not suffering before.

He forced himself to his feet. He might not know what to say to his daughter but that didn't mean they shouldn't be talking. He headed down the hall and stopped in front of her bedroom door.

"Lissa," he said as he knocked. "Open up. I want to talk."

There was no response.

"Lissa?" He waited. Again, nothing. "Lissa, either you open the door or I'm opening it for you."

He waited thirty seconds, then tried the knob. It was locked. His irritation grew. Did she think she could frustrate him so easily? He went into his bedroom, opened a drawer and pulled out the long, skinny pick that would pop the lock.

Only when he opened her bedroom door, she wasn't lying on her bed, glaring at him. She wasn't anywhere. The window was open, the screen on the ground and his daughter was gone.

seven

"YOU'RE DISTRACTED," Freddy said conversationally. "We're talking about buying a business. You always like that. What's up?"

A question Thaddeus couldn't answer. No, scratch that. A question he didn't *want* to answer.

They were in his office on the twentieth floor, with a north-facing view. He could see much of Bellevue and Kirkland beyond. To the west was North Seattle and to the northeast, on a clear day, Mount Baker.

Several files lay open on the large conference table. There were reports, sales projections and all the details that usually captured his interest, but today he couldn't get excited about buying an underfunded software company with potential.

He got up to pour himself more coffee, but instead crossed to the window where he stared out at the horizon.

"I met someone."

Freddy got up and joined him at the floor-to-ceiling window. "You sound more cautious than excited. Who is she? Where'd you meet?" His friend eyed him. "Not in a bar. You have terrible luck with women in bars."

Thaddeus raised his eyebrows. "I always have good luck with women in bars."

"No. You always get laid, but it never goes anywhere. There's a difference."

Freddy had a point. "I didn't meet her in a bar. She's a friend of Dagmar's." At Freddy's expression of surprise, he added, "She's thirty-four."

"Thank God. Because if you start dating some woman in her seventies, I'm going to take you to the doctor. So, who is she?"

"I don't know. She's a widow. Her husband was in the military. I assume he was killed in the line of duty."

He could ask his aunt for details, but that would be giving Dagmar way more power than he wanted her to have.

He shoved his hands into his front pockets. "We were at Dagmar's. We were supposed to have dinner."

"It was a setup?"

He nodded. "She didn't tell me until I got there. I ended up not staying long. Our meeting didn't go well."

Freddy shook his head. "So why are we talking about her?"

"Because there was something about her." At least he believed there had been. He'd thought about her the whole drive home and for the next couple of days. He was still thinking about her. There'd been chemistry and Dagmar liked her, which was about the best reference possible.

"She was nervous," he said. "More than nervous. She was scared."

"Of you?"

"Some. Or maybe it was the situation."

"She sounds like a real catch," Freddy muttered sarcastically. "Don't you want someone who likes you?"

"Everyone likes me."

"Not this girl. Man, what is it with you? Why do you always go looking for trouble?"

"I have no idea."

"Are you going to call her?"

"Haven't got a clue."

"You want to buy this business?"

"Not today."

Freddy walked back to the conference table, muttering in both English and Spanish that he didn't know why he'd ever come to work for Thaddeus in the first place and that he needed to find somewhere else to work where the people weren't so crazy.

As he opened the conference room door to leave, he glanced over his shoulder. "Is she the one?"

"There is no *one*."

"You don't believe that. You want there to be a one. Maybe the problem is you're looking for something that doesn't exist. Whatever it is, you gotta get this girl out of your head. She's not doing you any good in there."

Thaddeus smiled. "Tell me something I don't know."

KEITH CALLED LISSA'S PHONE, but she didn't pick up. Nor did she answer his texts telling her to get home now. When she finally walked into the house, three hours later, her gait was unsteady and her eyes were glazed. He stared at her in disbelief.

"Are you drunk?" he demanded. "You're seventeen. You know better than to drink. Where have you been? Did you drive? Tell me you didn't drive."

She waved toward the front of the house. "No car, Dad. I didn't drive."

At least she'd had that much sense, he thought grimly. "What has gotten into you?"

"Me?" she asked, her voice overly loud. "What about you? Pushing, pushing, pushing. Don't you have anything better to do?" Her voice rose with each word until she was shouting.

This was not the girl he knew, he thought in confusion. What was happening to them?

"Come on, Dad." She took a step toward him. "Punish me. You know you want to. What are you going to do? Hit me?"

He instinctively took a step back. "Lissa, what is going on?" He'd never hit her. He didn't believe in spanking or hitting. Punishments were a matter of finding a point of leverage that fit the crime.

She glared at him. "There has to be something. There's always something."

He moved toward her. She tried to sidestep him, but she was too uncoordinated. Before she could react, he'd pulled her phone out of her shorts back pocket. He held it tightly, then pointed to the hallway.

"Go to your room and sleep it off. We'll talk when you're sober."

"Whatever."

She stalked away. The door slammed. Seconds later came the sound of a loud alarm. Her door flew open and she surged toward him.

"What did you do?" she asked, screaming to be heard over the earsplitting alarm.

He pushed a button on his phone, silencing the shrill sound.

"You booby-trapped my window?"

"You snuck out, Lissa. You've never done that before. If you're trying to show me you can't be trusted, then that's how I'll treat you. Every time you open your window, the alarm's going off."

"How did you do that? I was gone like three hours."

"Ever hear of a hardware store?"

She glared at him. "I hate you."

"You're not my favorite right now, either. If you're going to act like a kid, I'm going to treat you like a kid. You snuck out. That's unacceptable behavior. Now go to your room. We'll talk in the morning."

She held out her hand "I want my phone."

"I want a daughter who acts her age. We're both going to have to live with the pain of disappointment."

She literally stomped her foot, screamed out loud, then disappeared into her bedroom. The door slam was hard enough to rattle a couple of pictures on the wall.

Keith sucked in a breath and wondered where his baby girl had gone and how he was going to get her back.

ELLEN SAT IN her Subaru in the parking lot of the North Bend outlet mall and tried to gather her courage. There was not a bone in her body that wanted to be shopping today. She had plenty of clothes in perfectly good condition. Yes, they were baggy, but they were comfortable and practical and, perhaps most important of all, *paid for*. She'd been raised to be frugal and while she might rail against her parents and their weird rules, she couldn't escape them. Not wasting money was a biggie. Plus there was the whole "saving for college" thing.

But a deal was a deal. She would get a few things for the bus trip and the summer. Shorts and T-shirts for home, some crop pants and maybe a blouse or two for the college visits. She had a budget, she had a free morning. All she was lacking was the will.

"I'm already here," she muttered, getting out of the SUV.

As she stepped up onto the sidewalk, her thighs reminded her that day two of her yoga video had been just as painful as day one. Not that she wanted to do yoga—it was stupid—but in an attempt to prove to her son she had a life, she'd dutifully dug it out and had gone through the whole, tedious thirty minutes of stretching and reaching and breathing.

It all felt like a stupid waste of time. She wasn't a bendy person. She liked to think that her flexibility was more mental. Still, it had been worth it when Coop had asked her what she was doing and she'd been able to tell him she was practicing yoga so she felt comfortable going to a class. He'd been surprised, she'd been only mildly uncomfortable lying. All in all, a moment.

Ignoring the general why-did-you-do-this-to-us ache in her body, she walked into the store and looked around.

There were plenty of sale racks, which she appreciated. She whipped through crop pants and shorts, only to remember she wasn't going to buy her usual size fourteen clothes. She tried to figure out her actual size. A twelve? A ten?

One of the few advantages of having a baby at seventeen was there were virtually no lingering effects. She didn't have stretch marks or a poufy stomach. She wasn't skinny but she was the same weight she'd been since she was twenty, and she honest to God had no idea what size she should wear.

Deciding jeans were the best way to find out, she picked three sizes of the same style and took them into a dressing room. The twelves looked nice, but a little loose and the eights didn't make it over her butt. She put on the size ten jeans and looked at herself in the mirror.

They fit. Sort of. They were much tighter than anything she ever wore but they weren't uncomfortable. She turned sideways to look at herself. She had to admit, she looked fairly decent. Not, you know, like a model or anything, but she wasn't hideous. She'd never liked her thighs, but her butt was okay and she had something of a waist.

"Size ten it is," she murmured.

Thirty minutes later she had an impressive pile of yeses. The at-home clothes were easy. She went for cheap and washable. For the road trip, she found several cute crop pants that would be comfortable, appropriate and weren't denim. She also chose a sleeveless wrap-front cotton blouse in several colors. They would be easy wearing on the long bus trip and would go with the two above-the-knee skirts she'd bought. For reasons not clear to her, she fell in love with a red floral-print dress with black lace at the hem. It was ridiculously cute and she found she really wanted it. Hopefully there would be a dinner or two where she could wear it. And at twenty-two dollars, it wasn't going to blow her budget.

Once she was home, she carried her purchases into her room and sorted through them. On the whole, she was happy with what she'd bought. She had a new wardrobe, she hadn't broken the bank and she'd checked off an important item on her list. Or at least she would once she started actually wearing the clothes. And speaking of the list...

She pulled it out of her underwear drawer and studied it. So many of the items seemed impossible. While sex with a handsome man was the most unlikely, the one that scared her the most was letting Cooper spend time with his dad. She knew she had to do it and having it happen while they were in LA made the most sense. But thinking that and following through were two very different things.

But what if he liked his dad better? What if he wanted to move to LA and never spoke to her again? What if everything about Jeremy's Hollywood life was more exciting and somehow he blamed her for his dad not being interested in acting like a father?

She returned the list to the drawer and drew in a breath. She would tell Coop about the phone call and potential visit, she vowed. Once they were on the bus, she would let him know and set up some kind of meeting. That would give her time to brace herself and a distraction once he heard the news. Cowardly, perhaps, but it was pretty much the best she could do.

UNITY HAD BATTLED low-grade nausea for days and this morning was no different. She'd dealt with customers, sent out her guys, installed floating shelves and a multifunction Toto toilet that was genuinely more fancy than any car she'd ever owned, ate her meals and lived her life, all with a stomach that wouldn't settle.

She had acted like an idiot. No, that was unfair to

all the idiots in the world. She'd been incoherent. She'd been shaking. She'd acted like she'd been trapped in a cage of lions or snakes or, worst of all, spiders.

After Thaddeus had left, Dagmar had asked if she wanted to talk about what had happened. When Unity had said no, they'd had a nice dinner together, never mentioning the bigger-than-an-elephant in the room.

So her friend had tried to set her up. It happened all the time. Not to her, but in other people's lives, it happened. Yes, she'd been caught off guard. She had the excuse of shock and not being used to having drinks with a man, but still. She'd been so awkward and dumb about the whole thing that just thinking about it made her insides writhe. She might never want to date again, but shouldn't she be able to sit in close proximity to a man without having some kind of social seizure?

As she drove to Ellen's, she thought about everything that had happened in the past few weeks. The pickleball rejection, the fight with Ellen, the grief group rebellion, her reaction to meeting Thaddeus. Maybe the Universe was trying to send her a message. And if it was, maybe she should listen.

She knocked once on Ellen's front door, then let herself in.

"It's me," she called.

Ellen walked into the living room and paused, her hands on her hips. At the sight of her, Unity momentarily forgot her own discomfort. Her friend had on denim shorts and a pale pink T-shirt, neither of which was surprising given the promise of a high around eighty-two. No, the shocker was how the clothes actually fit, showing off Ellen's body. Just as startling were the eye shadow and mascara enhancing her big blue eyes.

Unity stared at her. "You look great."

"I feel stupid."

"You look amazing. Are you wearing eyeliner?"

"Yes. And it's not easy to put on. I tried a smoky eye yesterday, but I just looked like I got in a fight. How do those YouTube girls do it? Plus, I got mascara in my eye and let me tell you, that's painful." She tugged at her T-shirt. "I feel exposed. It's so tight."

"It's not tight. It fits."

They went into the kitchen. Ellen poured them each a cup of coffee and joined Unity at the table.

"I have all new clothes for the trip."

"You leave Monday, right?"

"Uh-huh."

"Excited?"

Ellen groaned. "No. I mean I'm glad I'm going but all that time with a bunch of teenagers on a bus? Keith is dealing with some unexpected attitude from Lissa. I'm hoping to have some time with her to try to figure out what's going on. And I do want to work through a few items on my list."

"And Disneyland," Unity teased.

"I'll confess the aquarium in Monterey is probably more my thing, but the kids will love it." She paused. "You okay?"

Unity clutched her cup of coffee and shook her head. "No. Something happened."

Ellen leaned toward her. "What? Tell me."

Unity recounted how Dagmar had invited her to dinner without warning her there would be a man there.

"He's her great-nephew or something. It was so surreal. I was shocked and confused and then I just got scared. I'm not kidding. I almost couldn't speak and I was shaking. I can't imagine what he was thinking. I feel stupid and inept."

Ellen held up her hand. "Wait a minute. Dagmar set you up without warning you? Has she met you? You still sleep in Stuart's room, in the bed he had in high school. You're still going to a grief group and she set you up without telling you?"

Unity nodded. "It was awful. Not the guy. He was nice enough, I guess. I don't really remember very much about him."

"Were you interested?"

"What? No. How could I be? I'm not kidding. I don't even remember what he looks like." She thought about that evening. "He's got dark hair, maybe. I don't know." She looked at Ellen. "I'm so embarrassed by my behavior. It's one thing to not want to let go of Stuart but I should be able to survive in a normal social situation. I completely overreacted. I don't want to date or anything, but I hate feeling like this. I'll accept being stuck, but I don't want to be broken."

"This isn't your fault. You can't be expected to just meet some guy. That's too much, too fast. Dagmar shouldn't have done that to you. I'm not dealing with the Stuart stuff and I'd have trouble meeting some random guy without knowing what was happening."

Unity managed a slow smile. "Yes, but you're socially awkward, too."

Ellen laughed. "Gee, thanks. So you're saying we're both a mess?"

"Apparently. Although look at you, wearing the fancy clothes."

Ellen tugged on the short sleeve of her T-shirt. "Twelve dollars, baby. I'm living in style." Her smile faded. "Maybe it's time to get out of your life rut. Just a little."

"I know. Someone's sending me a message." She pressed a hand to her stomach. "I need to listen."

One corner of Ellen's mouth turned up. "You could get the guy's number and ask for a do-over."

Unity shuddered. "Not happening." But she knew she had to do something. She'd never felt the need to change before now, but being uncomfortable with herself and her actions wasn't good, either.

"So you didn't like him at all?"

"I didn't register him. I was so freaked out, I couldn't focus on anything. It was really bad."

"So he could be gorgeous."

"Yes, or he could have been wearing a superhero costume."

"I doubt that. If he'd been dressed up like a superhero, you would have remembered that. A cape is hard to forget."

Cooper wandered into the kitchen. He waved at them both before heading to the refrigerator and pulling open the door.

"Morning," Ellen said.

Coop nodded.

Ellen smiled at Unity. "It's nine thirty, so a predawn morning for him."

Cooper sighed. "Mom, it's summer vacation. This is my only week off. After the bus trip, I'm going to be working until school starts. I need my sleep."

Despite being a couple of inches taller than her, with his mussed hair and T-shirt and pajama bottoms, he looked more like the little boy he'd been a few years ago than the man he was becoming.

"Excited about the college trip?" Unity asked.

Cooper set a frozen breakfast burrito on the counter next to the gallon of milk. He yawned and stretched before answering Unity.

"I guess. I'm glad I get to see some things, but I'm not thinking about going away to college. UW is a good choice for me."

Unity met Ellen's worried gaze.

"What about UCLA?" Unity asked. "Or Stanford? They're both great schools. I thought you were interested in them."

"Maybe. I don't know. It's a long way to go. I won't be able to get home very much."

"True, but I'm here and I'm way better at fixing things than you. Let us all remember the great flood last year when you tried to fix a leaky faucet."

Coop's expression turned sheepish. "Okay, yeah. That didn't go well."

Unity waved her hand. "Fly, be free, little grasshopper. I'll hold down the fort while you're off dealing with higher learning."

Coop glanced from her to his mom and back. "I'm still thinking UW."

With that, he put the breakfast burrito in the microwave and poured himself a giant glass of milk.

Ellen rose. Unity followed her into the living room.

"See?" Ellen sounded worried. "I have to do something."

"You are. Look, you're going to show him you're fine on your own. By the time you're back from your trip, he'll be convinced."

"I hope so. He can't stay here because of me."

"He won't." Unity hugged her. "We'll make sure of it."

An easy promise, mostly because Unity would do whatever she had to in order to make her friend's life right. As for herself, she was just beginning to think there might be the tiniest of problems. Now she just had to figure out what to do next.

eight

TRADITIONAL SCHOOL BUSES used to transport schoolchildren on bus routes were required, by law, to be yellow. Activity buses, used for purposes other than transporting children on bus routes, didn't have the same restrictions. As Keith stared at the white bus he would be driving for the next two-plus weeks, he tried to find some comfort in that fact.

When he'd moved to Birchly High School, he quickly realized that coordinating a bus driver for different games and meets could be a challenge so he'd required all coaches, including himself, to have a valid school bus driver's licenses. Every August the coaching staff took a refresher course. The district, grateful not to have to find drivers and pay them, had given the department two new-to-them activity buses. The larger one could handle the bigger events like track meets and football games. The smaller bus—with ten rows and lots of storage—was the one Keith would be taking on the college road trip.

As he pulled the bus into the high school parking lot where he would pick up his passengers, he glanced in the rearview mirror. Lissa sat in the last row, looking out the side window, her arms crossed, her expression sullen. They still weren't speaking. Keith couldn't remember the last time they'd gone this long before making up and he didn't like it. In the last few months, Lissa had changed and he had no idea why.

He knew part of her sulk was his fault. She'd caught him going through her luggage. He'd wanted to make sure she was bringing her birth control pills, a fact she hadn't found amusing.

"What do you think I'm going to do?" she'd screamed. "Have sex right there on the bus with everyone watching?"

She'd grabbed her tote bag from him and had stomped out of the room, muttering to herself about becoming an emancipated minor.

He vowed to do better, then got off the bus to wait for the rest of the students to arrive for their early morning departure.

Right on time cars pulled into the parking lot. He greeted the parents and their kids, confirmed paperwork and contact numbers, promised he would do his best to make sure no one got into trouble.

Best friends Aidan and Andy complained (again) about the aquarium. "It's so dumb, Coach. Why do we have to go there?" Aidan asked, his too long hair falling in his eyes.

Andy agreed.

They were both tall, rangy boys who played basketball. Aidan also ran track. He was a decent athlete, but Andy was the real star. He had a good shot at a basketball scholarship. UCLA was unlikely, but maybe UC San Diego. Keith was going to try to work some magic there.

"Everyone voted," he reminded them. "Your side lost. It's one day, guys. You'll survive."

They grumbled as they got on the bus.

A familiar Subaru pulled up. Unity waved from the driver's side. Ellen and Cooper got out. Coop unloaded the luggage while Ellen walked toward Keith, a folder in her hands.

"I have paperwork," she said with a smile. "Lots of paperwork. You really should figure out a way to go digital with this."

"I like having hard copies," he said automatically, as he stared at her in confusion. Something was different with Ellen, he thought, trying to figure out what it was.

He cataloged her appearance. Her long hair was pulled back in a ponytail, just like always. She had on makeup maybe, which was a surprise, but made her eyes looked bluer than usual. As for what she was wearing, it was just some shirt thing and pants that stopped just below her knee. Nothing out of the ordinary except—

He swore silently. The clothes fit. For once they weren't swirling around her, the extra fabric concealing every part of her body. He could see the shape of her waist and her hips, the outline of her thighs. And breasts. Ellen had breasts!

He realized he was staring and forced his gaze away. Of course she had breasts. Women had breasts. Ellen's were no big deal. Only he'd never noticed them before and he didn't want to see them now.

Okay, that was too strong. It's not that he didn't want to see them, it was that he didn't want to *notice* them. It wasn't like that for them. They were friends. They supported each other. There wasn't any awareness or tension or…

For the second time he jerked his attention away from her body. What was wrong with him? Obviously he was more stressed about the trip than he'd realized. Or the fight with Lissa was affecting him.

He took the folder from her and put it in his backpack with the others. Cooper loaded their luggage in the bus, then went up the steps. Ellen returned to her car and hugged Unity. They had a whispered conversation, laughed, then Unity drove away. Ellen returned to his side.

"I can't believe we're really doing this," she said. "I can't believe you've done this before and are willing to do it again."

"It's not so bad. The time goes fast and the kids have fun." He nodded toward the back of the bus and lowered his voice. "Lissa still isn't speaking to me."

"But it's been nearly a week. I'm sorry. Maybe I'll get a chance to talk to her on the road."

He grimaced. "She caught me going through her bag, looking for her birth control pills."

Ellen stared at him. "You know you're an idiot, right?"

"Pretty much."

Another car pulled up and Luka got out.

"Coach, Coach, I got an A on my first Spanish test!"

"Good for you."

Luka beamed.

Keith knew reminding him that if he'd applied himself in the first place, he wouldn't have to take summer school wouldn't be helpful, so he only thought it.

He collected paperwork from the kid's tearful mother, who gave him three bags of homecooked food.

"For the trip," she explained. "The boys get so hungry. There are forks and plates for everyone." She smiled at Ellen. "Luka has never been away from me for this long. I worry about him."

Ellen patted her shoulder. "I'll be sure to look out for him. And Coop's along. Try not to worry, Kiki."

"I can't help it. He's my baby."

A baby who could flatten any offensive player in the league, Keith thought.

Luka hugged his mother, then got on the bus. Keith saw he went all the way to the back and sat next to Lissa. Maybe the two of them could talk about how horrible he was. Although with an A under his belt, Keith would guess Luka was feeling pretty good about things today.

When Luka's mother had driven away, Keith tucked her paperwork in the backpack. "That's all of them. You ready for this?"

Ellen stared at the bus. "It's an adventure. I need an adventure in my life, so let's do it." She smiled at him, before turning and climbing up the stairs.

As she did so, her pants tightened around her butt. Keith found himself staring at the curves, something he would swear he'd never done before. Not with Ellen. Worse, he imagined himself putting his hands on her—

He took a step back and shook his head. Back the truck up. He had to stay focused, he told himself. Whatever was going on with Ellen wasn't his business, nor was her ass. They worked together and were friends.

Nothing more. But as he climbed in behind her, he had the sudden thought this was going to be a very, very long journey.

UNITY GOT HOME about three thirty after her last job was canceled. She restocked the van, confirmed her jobs for the next day and went through all the messages on the answering machine. Not sure what else to do with herself, she wandered through the house.

Stuart's parents had bought the place when they'd first been married. The three bedroom, two bath house had originally been about fourteen hundred square feet. They'd added on a family room when Stuart had still been a kid, taking the house to eighteen hundred square feet.

Stuart's dad had passed away when Stuart had still been in elementary school, leaving him and his mom devastated. Unity hadn't met him until high school. She remembered he'd been quiet, responsible and goal-oriented. He knew what he wanted to do with his life.

When they'd started dating, Stuart's mom had been excited to have Unity hang out. There had been countless dinners at the round table and lots of evenings with the three of them watching TV.

There were so many memories in the house, Unity thought, walking into the master bedroom his mother had used until she died four years before. The furniture was gone—sold after her death. The closet was empty. Unity had packed away the few treasures Stuart had wanted to keep and those boxes were stacked neatly in the corner of the large, bright room.

Family pictures lined the hallway. There were his parents' wedding pictures, along with several photos from her wedding to Stuart. On the opposite wall were dozens of pictures of Stuart, marking his passage from adorable baby to handsome man, with blond hair and green eyes.

She touched his framed senior picture, wishing she could touch him instead. But he was gone and she was alone and no matter how she fought against that truth, she couldn't change it.

She went into the garage and stared at the shelves she'd hung on the walls. She kept her tools there, along with basic supplies she needed for her business. There was an old washer and dryer in the back, a freezer she never used and a door to the backyard. All in all a good house, she thought. Too big for her, but she had no reason to move. This was her home. Even more important, it had been Stuart's home and living here allowed her to still be close to him.

Only… Only… Maybe that wasn't enough. Unity returned to the living room where she stared out the front window and wondered what she was supposed to do with herself. Ellen was gone, there was no pickleball league. She felt weird about her grief group and hadn't gone on Saturday. She was sure there were other activities at Silver Pines, but she was beginning to wonder if she was really welcome there. She supposed she could call Dagmar and ask if she wanted to have dinner or something, only she hadn't spoken to her friend since that disastrous dinner. Honestly, she was a little embarrassed to get in touch with her.

Which left her restless and more than a little lost. Maybe she should—

Her phone rang. She answered it, grateful for the interruption.

"Hello?"

"Unity? It's Thaddeus."

Her mind went totally blank for at least three seconds. Thaddeus, as in Thaddeus? He'd called? Her mouth opened and closed as she sank onto the living room sofa. "Oh. Um, hi."

"Am I catching you at a bad time?"

"No. Of course not."

"Despite the wrinkle in our first meeting, I was wondering if you wanted to get together and do something. Maybe go to dinner or a movie."

Wrinkle? Was that how he thought of her subpar ability to exist in a fairly normal social situation? While his word choice was polite, she knew that disaster was much closer to the truth.

Then the rest of what he'd said sank in and she found herself standing, then sitting again. Dinner? A movie?

"Are you asking me out?"

She heard a soft, low chuckle over the phone. "Yes."

"Why? I wasn't interesting or even coherent." *I don't even remember what you look like.* Although probably best not to say that.

"And yet here I am, calling and asking."

She was too surprised to be freaked out, which was probably a good thing. Was it a date? No, he couldn't want to date her. That was too strange to consider.

"I appreciate the offer," she said, prepared to tell him no, only to remember the list. The list she'd created to help her friend, after which she'd realized that maybe getting out of her head and her rut wouldn't be such a bad thing. "Can you hold on a second?"

"Of course."

She put down the phone and raced into the small bedroom that had always been used as a study. She found the list on the desk, then ran back to the living room, only to stare at her cell phone and realize she could have brought it with her. Wow—she really was out of her element with pretty much everything.

"I *would* like to do something," she said, scanning the list. House hunting was too strange and sex was completely out of the question. She hadn't made up her mind about the tattoo.

"I don't suppose we could go skydiving."

Thaddeus laughed. "Unity, I have to tell you, I wasn't expecting that. Do you like to skydive?"

"I've never been, but I've been thinking about doing it." Or at least she'd written it down, which was nearly the same thing.

"All right. Would you accept indoor skydiving or does it have to be the real thing?"

"Indoor skydiving?"

"Yes. There's a place by the airport. I've driven by it several times. Let me go online and see what's involved, then text you the information."

"I don't have a phone that texts. It's a long story." She looked back at the list. "But I might be getting one, soon."

"Good to know. Then I'll call you with the information. If it works out, I'll pick you up at nine Saturday morning."

Skydiving. She was going to do it. "That sounds good. Oh, wait. That means you have to leave Bellevue really early. It's a couple of hours' drive."

"I'll come over the night before and stay with Dagmar."

"Okay. Then I'll wait to hear from you and I'll see you Saturday. For skydiving."

"I'll be in touch."

They hung up. Unity returned to the study and did a search for indoor skydiving. There really was a place, just like Thaddeus had said. She was going to do this.

She smiled to herself, thinking progress was good and she was making some. She was glad Thaddeus had called. They would go skydiving, she would check an item off her list and then he would bring her home. As for spending time with the man himself, well, she just wasn't going to think about that.

THE BUS WASN'T the most comfortable ride, but it was for a good cause, Ellen told herself. The students all sat in the back half of the vehicle, giving the two adults plenty of buffer between them and their noise. Ellen made a place for herself in the front seat across from Keith, loosening the seat belt so she could sit with her back to the window and her legs stretched out on the bench.

The plan was to drive all the way down to San Diego in two and a half days, turn around and start the college visits on the way back.

Their first stop was UC San Diego. Ellen was looking forward to seeing the campus and the nearby town. She'd been to Southern California, but not San Diego, and had always heard it was a wonderful coastal town. She was also thinking she might get at least one item on her challenge list checked off there. Assuming she had the courage. But before they got there, she had to have a conversation with her son.

Around twelve thirty, Keith pulled into a McDonald's just outside Portland. After he opened the door, he stood and faced the group.

"Thirty minutes, people. Use your gift cards. Remember, you are responsible for maintaining possession of your gift cards. If you lose them, you will go hungry."

Ellen was facing him, with the kids well behind them. She grinned as he spoke, knowing there was no way he would let anyone on the bus miss a meal.

Rather than give the students cash, she and Keith had bought lots of gift cards. They would be handed out before each meal, then collected when they were done. Everyone had worked hard to raise plenty of money to fund the trip. One of the parents had even donated Marriott points, allowing them to stay for free at several hotels up and down the route.

"Use the bathroom," he continued, his voice stern. "I want to drive straight through to Medford. It's four hours. I need you to go now so you can hold it for four hours."

"You're just so tough," she said quietly, so she wouldn't be overheard. Keith winked.

Andy groaned. "Coach, we got it. We can manage lunch and the bathroom."

"We'll see about that."

With that, he went down the stairs. Ellen followed. She helped him pass out the gift cards, then fell into step with Cooper.

"Can we have lunch together?" she asked with a fake smile, knowing she couldn't put off her confession any longer.

He looked at her. "Really, Mom?"

"Just this once. I promise not to make a habit of it."

She hesitated, feeling her smile fade. "I need to talk to you about something."

His face tightened with concern. She knew he would take her request as yet more proof that she couldn't be left on her own, but that would quickly change when she told him about his dad. She'd already put it off long enough. They were only a few days away from arriving in Los Angeles. If Cooper was going to set something up with Jeremy, it had to happen now.

They placed their order then she claimed a relatively quiet table in the back. Cooper waited for the food and carried the tray toward her.

As he approached, she looked for traces of his father. She hadn't seen Jeremy in over seventeen years and his image wasn't as clear as it had been, but she knew there were parts of him in her son's square jaw and broad shoulders.

He passed her the kid's burger and salad she'd ordered, then opened the first of his two Quarter Pounders with cheese.

She waited until he'd finished half of the first burger before saying, "I heard from your dad."

Cooper looked at her, then raised and lowered one shoulder. Not an unexpected response.

The first time Jeremy had contacted her, she'd debated for days before telling her son. He'd been so excited and had waited for nearly a month to find out if his dad would call back and want to see him. But Jeremy hadn't and Coop had slowly gotten over his disappointment. Over time they'd both learned that Jeremy checked in every few years, but never made any attempt to take things further. Until now.

"He lives in LA," she said, poking at her salad. Suddenly she wasn't hungry. "He's married, again, with a couple of little kids."

Cooper finished the first burger. "Big deal. This is his what? Third marriage? Mom, why are you telling me this?"

She met his dark gaze. "He said he wants to get to know you. He regrets what he's missed and would like to have some kind of relationship with you."

Cooper's eyes widened. "He said that?"

"Uh-huh."

"But he never wanted to before. Why now?"

"I don't know. Maybe he's grown up enough to realize what he missed. Maybe having more kids has shown him being a dad is a great gig." She made herself smile. "He's your dad, Coop. You should think about getting to know him."

"Are you okay with that?"

"Of course," she lied. "I'll admit that I've loved having you all to myself, but I always knew you wanted to have a relationship with him. Why don't you get in touch and see if you can set up a meeting? There would be time for lunch after the UCLA tour. You could meet him and then join the rest of us on the beach."

Cooper looked both hopeful and worried. "You're sure?"

"I am." She picked up her burger, as if she were comfortable enough to eat. "He's a movie producer. That could be fun to talk about."

"He's in the movie business?" Coop sounded excited.

"He is." She pulled Jeremy's phone number out of her back pocket. "Text him and see what he says. We're going to be hanging out by the pier in Santa Monica.

Have him pick a place and we'll drop you off there, then you can meet up with us."

He gave her a wide grin. "This is the best, Mom. Thanks."

"You're welcome." She pointed at his lunch. "Finish eating before you text him. If you don't, you'll be starving later, and I'm pretty sure Coach Kinne meant what he said about not stopping."

Coop nodded eagerly and grabbed a handful of fries. Ellen put down her burger and told herself she'd done the right thing and eventually she would feel good about it. But right now her stomach hurt and she wanted to crawl into a corner and make the whole Jeremy thing go away.

nine

DINNER AT A local Medford restaurant was a raucous affair. They had a long table for all thirteen of them. Ellen and Keith sat at one end. Ellen noticed Lissa was still keeping her distance from her father and had planted herself as far away from him as possible. At some point Ellen would have to talk to the teen about what was going on, but not today. Ellen didn't feel she was in a position to give anyone advice about anything. She was feeling too emotionally frail.

As she'd suggested, Coop had texted his father. The two had gone back and forth for nearly half an hour and now her son had plans to meet Jeremy for lunch at a restaurant in Santa Monica. Ellen told herself she should be happy and excited, but she was having trouble summoning any enthusiasm for the event.

She supposed she should look at the bright side—having them meet would check off one more item on her list. She should think about that, and how Unity was going to treat her to a great spa weekend at the end of summer. Because there was no way Unity was going to do anything to get out of her rut.

She pushed away her half-eaten dinner. Thinking about Coop and his dad wasn't doing much for her appetite. She looked around for a distraction, but Keith was talking to Aidan. Realizing no one was paying attention to her, she pulled the list out of her handbag and studied it.

"We should go out and sing karaoke," she said loudly.

The table went silent as everyone stared at her with identical expressions of shock and horror. Even Keith.

"Don't you have to be twenty-one?" Luka asked tentatively.

"To go into a bar," she said, hearing her defensive tone. "But what about a bowling alley or something? Don't they have karaoke? It would be fun."

"Mo-om," Coop said, his teeth clenched. "No one wants to do that."

"Why not? It's an experience."

Lissa shot Coop a sympathetic look. He sank down in his seat. The other teens avoided making eye contact.

"You ready for the check?" their perky server asked Keith.

"We are." He pulled out his wallet and handed her a credit card. "Thanks."

"No problem."

"We done here?" Aidan asked, already stepping away from the table.

Keith nodded.

"Then we'll, ah, head back to our rooms." He glanced at Ellen, then away. "Night, Ms. F."

She couldn't believe it. They were going to run out on her?

When they were alone, Keith looked at her. "Karaoke?"

"Why is that so surprising?"

"Because in all the years I've known you, you've never once mentioned karaoke as a hobby." He flashed her a grin. "Having said that, I'm impressed by your ability to clear the room."

"I didn't want to clear the room. I wanted them to go sing with me."

He frowned. "For real?"

"Yes." Unexpectedly annoyed, she picked up her purse and glared at him. "You don't know everything about me. I have a whole life that doesn't include you. A social life, in fact."

Which wasn't exactly true, but why worry about details?

He stared at her. "You okay?"

"I'm fine." She got up.

"Are you going to try to find a karaoke bar?" he asked, sounding worried.

In a strange town when they had an early start in the morning?

"Probably not. But I could if I—"

"Wanted. Yes, I know. Are you all right?"

"Fine. Perfectly fine."

She flounced out of the restaurant and headed back for the hotel. She was hurt and mad and confused and a lot of other emotions that made no sense.

Stupid list, she thought as she went up in the elevator. Stupid everything.

She stood in the center of her room, not sure what to

do now. It was barely seven. No doubt the teens had all retreated to the safety of their rooms, hoping to avoid other adult encounters. The boys were doubled up while Keith, Lissa and she each had their own space.

After pacing for a few minutes, she walked over to the closet and stared at the clothes hanging there. It took only a few seconds to pull off what she was wearing and put on a blue sleeveless wrap dress. She tugged off the band holding her ponytail in place, slipped on the wedge heels, slung her purse over her shoulder and marched out of her room.

There was a bar downstairs. She was going to sit there and get drunk. Okay, maybe not drunk, but she was going to have a glass of wine, just like regular people did all the time. And if she got a little drunk, then yay her. So there!

KEITH WAS USED to the road trips being stressful but he'd never thought any of his worries would be about Ellen. She was dependable, unflappable and a good friend. Or at least she had been before tonight. What had gotten into her?

Thirty minutes after she'd walked out of the restaurant, he couldn't stand it anymore and went up to her room. Only she didn't answer when he knocked. He tried texting, but she didn't answer that either.

Not sure what to do, he went back to the lobby. On a hunch, he made his way to the bar where he found her at a small table, staring at what looked like an untouched glass of white wine.

He crossed to the table and took the seat opposite.

"Go away," she said without looking at him.

"Why do you have a glass of white wine? You hate white wine."

"It's what women order in bars." She glared at him. "Did I tell you to go away?"

"You did. I'm ignoring you. Why do you think women order white wine in bars?"

She waved her hand. "It's what they always do in books and movies. They have a glass of white wine. It's classy."

"Not if you don't like it." He rested his forearms on the table and leaned toward her. "Ellen, why are you here?"

Her gaze met his. "Are you asking in the existential sense?"

He ignored the need to laugh. "No. Why are you sitting in a bar?"

"I want to get drunk. I rarely do that, you know, except with Unity. I'm very responsible. It's boring. I'm boring." She glared at him. "There's your answer. I'm sitting in a bar because I'm tired of being a boring person."

She usually wore her long hair up in a ponytail, but now her hair was loose and tumbling over her shoulders. The new style suited her, making her look sexy and appealing. Not that he would notice. There was no sexy Ellen for him. No way. She was firmly in the friend column in his life. That was how he liked his relationship with her. Friendly and uncomplicated.

There was a reason he avoided getting involved with a woman close to home—he didn't want the messiness. He had a good life that he enjoyed—his present difficulties with Lissa aside. Ellen was a part of that. He depended on her and he wasn't comfortable with all the changes.

But leaving wasn't an option. He and Ellen had each other's backs. Something had obviously happened to her and he was going to figure out what it was and then fix it. After that, things would go back to what they'd been.

He waved over the server. When she pulled out her pad, he pointed to the white wine. "She's not a fan. Why don't you bring her a cosmo and I'll have a vodka tonic."

"Sure thing."

Ellen's eyes widened. "A cosmo. That's perfect. I love *Sex and the City*. I should have thought of that." She sighed. "You know, I've never had one, probably because I don't live a cosmo kind of life." She shook her head. "Is it wrong to blame my parents for that?"

He leaned toward her again. "Ellen, what's going on?"

She hung her head. "It's too embarrassing."

"I doubt that."

She put her hands on the table, then tucked them under the table. After shifting in her seat, she opened her mouth, closed it, then groaned.

"I hate this."

He waited.

She glared at him. "You're so annoying. All right. If you have to stick your nose in everyone's business. Why is that?"

He still didn't speak. No way he was getting pulled into a distraction.

She muttered something he couldn't hear, then sighed loudly. "I overheard Cooper talking to Luka. He said he was giving up his dream of going to college out of state because he was worried about leaving me. He said I depended on him too much." She looked away. "He told Luka I never date and while he didn't say it, I'm sure he was thinking about the fact that I haven't had sex since before he was born."

Her mouth twisted. "My son thinks I'm a loser, which is awful, but I can live with that. What I can't stand is him ruining his life because of me. I want him to go away to school. Okay, I don't *want it*, want it, but it's important. He should have the chance to follow his dreams without worrying that I'm dragging him down."

There were a lot of words and a lot of information. Keith planned to deal with it all, but right now he couldn't get past one incredible statement.

"You haven't had sex since you were seventeen?" he asked, unable to keep the incredulity out of his voice.

"Oh, my God! *That's* what you got from all that? I have a problem with my son."

"Yes, and we need to talk about that, but you haven't had sex in seventeen years?"

She glared at him. "We can't all be famous football players who have hundreds of women throwing themselves at us."

"You don't like women that way."

She made a strangled sound in her throat. "It was an example." She leaned toward him and lowered her voice. "I lived with my parents until I graduated from college. They had very strict rules. Doing something fun like dating was not allowed. By the time Coop and I got our own place, I'd kind of forgotten how to date. It just happened." Her gaze narrowed. "It's not like I haven't had an orgasm, you idiot."

Whoa. He had not planned for the topic to take that turn. He tried to push away the automatically generated images, but they were stubborn. How did she do that? By hand? With toys? Both?

Heat flared unexpectedly. Thankfully their server arrived with the drinks, offering a distraction.

Ellen thanked the woman, then took a sip of her cosmo. Her happy smile hit him square in the gut.

"That's nice," she said. "I feel so sophisticated. Anyway, like I said, my parents were strict. They were disappointed in me when I turned up pregnant. Not that I blame them. But they did overreact. I wasn't allowed to have anything like a social life. I raised Coop, went to college, did homework and had a part-time job. There were no boys." Her expression turned wistful. "No time for anything fun, except what I did with him. They firmly believed love came at a price."

She took another drink. "I moved out into an apartment as soon as I could after I finished college. A year later, my folks sold their house and gave me enough for a down payment on the duplex. Then they moved away." She sighed. "We never see them. It's weird, like they were waiting for me to prove myself so they could be done with me."

"I'm sorry."

"I'm used to it. Coop and I have been fine, at least I thought we were. But now I find out that he thinks I don't have a life, which I don't. I could live with that problem, but if he's afraid to go away to school because he thinks he can't leave, then I have to do something."

There was too much information coming at him too quickly. Plus the whole orgasm comment made it difficult to concentrate.

"So talk to him. He'll understand."

She gave him the "why are you so stupid" look. "He won't. Words are empty. I have to show him I'm okay."

She reached for her purse and pulled out a sheet of

paper. "Unity and I have a bet going. She needs to get out of her rut nearly as much as I need to get out of mine. We're trying to help each other." She waved the paper. "One of the things on my list is karaoke."

He took the paper from her, not sure what to expect. The first item was a smoky eye and he had no idea what that was. Sure enough there was karaoke, along with wearing clothes that fit, which explained the new wardrobe.

Sex with a handsome guy? He swore under his breath. Who had put that on the list?

He handed the paper back to her. "You're making too much of this."

"I'm not and if you thought about it for even a second, you'd see that I was right. Do you know what's going to happen in LA?"

"You're getting a tattoo?"

"No, not there." She picked up her drink and waved it toward him. "Cooper is meeting his father. Jeremy has finally come to realize he would like to get to know his son, which should make me happy but it doesn't. Jeremy is going to be cool and special and I'm just the old mom he's had for years."

Finally a topic he could embrace. "You're not going to lose him. Sure, Jeremy's new right now, but Coop knows his biological father has had zero interest for seventeen years. He's not going to forget that. He'll enjoy the experience and get on with his life."

"I wish. I feel so lost." She waved at their server and held up her empty glass.

Keith glanced at his. Yup, still three-quarters full.

"You're just in a bad place," he told her, wondering how the drink would hit her in the next few minutes, not to mention in the morning. "You need to give yourself credit for all you've accomplished." He stiffened as an uncomfortable thought occurred to him. "You were Lissa's age when you got pregnant and had Cooper."

"I was. Seventeen. Did you know there was some song in the 1970s about being seventeen? I heard it a few times. It was sad."

"You're starting to not make sense." He eyed her drink. "How much did you eat at dinner?"

"Not much. I can't eat when I'm upset." Tears filled her eyes. "I love Cooper so much."

He stared at the tears. Ellen was crying? She never cried. He'd seen her angry, frustrated, sad and bone weary but she'd never once cried. He didn't like seeing it now. He had to make it stop.

He searched frantically for a distraction. Could he offer to buy her something? Take her somewhere?

A single tear rolled down her cheek, nearly sending him to his knees.

"I'll help," he blurted.

She reached for her glass only to put it down when she saw it was empty. "Help with what?"

The server appeared with a second cosmo. Ellen exchanged glasses with her and took a big sip before looking at him expectantly.

"The list. I'll help. Give advice, go with you when you sing karaoke, whatever."

Not with the sex, though, he told himself. Ellen was his friend. Friends didn't do that with each other. Sex had a way of changing things and he liked what he had with Ellen just as it was.

"You can't help me with a smoky eye," she murmured.

"I don't know what that is."

"It's a makeup thing and it's hard. I've tried like three times and I look ridiculous. Maybe my eyes are the wrong shape. Does that make a difference? It's all so wrong. Guys just have to put on a suit and they look great. Of course Unity has to wear a dress without a bra, which, frankly, I don't see happening."

She wasn't making any sense. He eyed the half-finished drink. She couldn't be feeling hers yet, could she?

"Maybe we should get you back to your room," he told her.

She nodded and gulped the rest of her drink. "Okay." When she stood, she wobbled a bit. "I feel funny."

"I'll bet. Can you wait a sec? I have to pay for the drinks."

She plopped back in her chair and reached for his half-finished drink. Before he could stop her, she'd downed that as well.

"You're going to have a hangover in the morning."

She smiled. "I've never had a hangover. I've never done a lot of things."

Like sex.

The thought came out of nowhere and he didn't like that one bit. No sex, he told himself as he walked over to their server and quickly paid the bill. Zero sex, at least with Ellen. He wasn't going there. Nope. Not him. No way.

He got her to her feet and guided her toward the elevators. As they went up to their floor, he said, "Promise me you'll stay in your room tonight."

She frowned. "Where else would I go?"

"I'm not sure, but you're acting wild."

Instead of looking chagrined, she beamed at him. "Wild? I like that. Wild!"

When the doors opened, he grabbed her by her elbow and eased her toward her room. When they were there, she looked at him expectantly. He dug in her purse for the key and opened the door. She stepped inside before turning back to him.

For one insane second, he had the impossible idea of simply following her inside, taking her in his arms and demonstrating what she'd been missing. He found himself wanting to kiss her and touch her and show her that an orgasm with someone else could be even better than one she had by herself.

The visuals shocked the hell out of him, but not nearly as much as the rush of need and hunger. Not just *I want to get laid* hunger, but a specific burn for the woman in front of him. What was up with that?

Before he could bolt, or figure out a way to go back in time forty minutes and not go into the bar, Ellen smiled, raised herself up on tiptoe, kissed him on the mouth, grabbed the key, then turned away.

"Night."

As he tried to gather his senses and maybe pick his jaw up off the floor, she walked toward the bed, stepping out of her sandals.

She reached a hand behind her and began pulling down the zipper of her dress. Keith held in a yelp as he quickly stepped into the hallway and shut the door. As he made his way to his room, he wondered how everything had gone so incredibly wrong, so incredibly fast and what he was supposed to do now.

ten

UNITY HAD NOT thought through her day with Thaddeus. Not the skydiving part—she'd gone onto the website and it looked fun and interesting. No, that would be easy— it was the being with a man thing that had her rattled.

She couldn't figure out why Thaddeus had called her in the first place. Or what he was thinking. Or, honestly, remember what he looked like, which was why she was pacing and nervous before he'd even arrived.

She'd nearly canceled every hour since they set up the date, um, appointment. Each time she stopped her- self. She knew that even though she was never going to get over Stuart, she needed to learn how to behave more normally. She needed to stop hiding and have something close to a life. This was the very first step.

Her doorbell rang right on time. Unity rubbed her hands up and down her jeans before pulling open the front door and staring at the man standing there.

He was tall, with dark hair and eyes, muscled, but lean and shockingly good-looking. Like better-looking than most humans. How could she not have remembered that? How had she not noticed in the first place?

He smiled. "Good morning."

Okay, so it *was* him and not just some random stranger. "Thanks for the invitation."

They looked at each other. Unity had no idea what to say. Thaddeus motioned to his car in the driveway.

"Ready to go?"

"Sure."

She collected her purse, then made sure the front door was locked behind her.

He held open the passenger door, which freaked her out a little. Fortunately, the interior of his car was so nice, she could think about that rather than the fact that she was in a car with a man she barely knew, about to take a two-hour drive to go indoor skydiving.

Not that she was worried about him being a serial killer or anything. He was Dagmar's great-nephew. Still, it was very strange.

"I brought my camera," she said, as they headed for the freeway. "I'm hoping I can take a picture and then email it to my friend Ellen."

He glanced at her. "Because if your phone doesn't text, it probably doesn't take pictures, either."

"Not everyone needs the latest technology."

"It might be nice to have something from this century."

She grinned. "My phone's not that old." She thought of her list of challenges. "I might be getting a new one."

"Let me know when you decide."

They merged onto I90, heading west. Thaddeus's car

was quiet, with comfortable seats. It felt expensive and powerful. Nothing like her van, that was practical for work but not exactly a fun machine to drive.

She was aware of the man next to her. His T-shirt left his arms bare and they were sitting close together. Everything was just so strange, she thought, torn between wishing she'd refused his invitation and the knowledge that she really had to do this.

The rolling hills and hay and alfalfa fields quickly gave way to forest. The mountain range stretched north and south, heading up to Canada and down to California. The highest peaks still had snow while the lower elevations were thick with vegetation.

"I'm sorry about before," she said, deciding to address the issue head-on. "When we met. You were unexpected."

"I get that a lot." His voice was teasing.

She smiled, then glanced at him. "I don't do this."

"Drive in cars?"

"Go out with people." She waved toward him. "Male people."

"Men?" he confirmed.

"Men."

"Because you're not over your late husband?"

A blunt statement that got right to the heart of the issue, she thought, trying not to writhe in her seat. "Yes, that."

"Why did you say yes to me?"

"I had to." She closed her eyes, then opened them. "I might be trapped. I don't feel trapped—I like my life—but circumstances are conspiring to show me that maybe I'm more stuck than is healthy."

"I'm part of your rehab?"

"Maybe. Is that bad?"

"I don't know. I've never been anyone's rehab before." He glanced at her. "Just to confirm, your late husband has been gone for three years?"

"Yes. His name is Stuart." *Was* Stuart, but she didn't correct herself.

"And you haven't been on a date since then."

"No."

"Okay, then. Thanks for the information. I'm going out on a limb here and saying we're probably not having sex then."

He spoke so casually, she almost didn't get what he was saying. When the meaning sank in, she was so shocked, she nearly threw herself out of the moving car. Then the ridiculousness of his statement struck her and she started to laugh.

Thaddeus smiled at her. "A man likes to know these things in advance."

"I guess."

"And that was a no?"

She laughed again. "It was," she said as she leaned back in the seat, more relaxed than she had been. "Are you really a farmer?"

"No. I was never a farmer. I was an investor in a Bitcoin farm, but I sold my interest a couple of years ago."

"I don't know what Bitcoin is," she admitted. "Something with computers, right?"

"It's a cryptocurrency."

"And you farm it?"

"That's what people call it. The system is totally open to anyone who wants to see what's going on. Transactions with Bitcoin have to be verified before they can become part of the blockchain and unless you're having problems falling asleep, you really don't want me to explain it all to you."

"I doubt I'd fall asleep, but I don't think I would understand it. How did you start investing in the farm?"

"Someone asked me to. I did my research and when it seemed like a good idea, I bought in."

"Did you make a lot of money doing it?"

He smiled at her. "I did."

She shifted so she was angled toward him. "Dagmar has told me you own property and you also help companies that are in trouble. Is that right?"

He nodded. "I have real estate holdings and I own a company that does turnarounds. I don't go in and fix the companies. I have people who do that."

He was so different from anyone she'd ever met. "When did you move here?"

"About seven years ago. I went from San Diego to Las Vegas to Seattle."

"Las Vegas?" She wrinkled her nose. "I've never been. I'm not a gambler."

"I'm not either." He glanced at her, then back at the road. "I was working construction in San Diego and I met this girl. She wanted to be a dancer in a Vegas show. I followed her."

Unity smiled. "How old were you?"

"Twenty. Young and foolish."

"What happened with the girl?"

"We broke up but I stayed in Las Vegas. I managed to put myself through school. I have a degree in finance. I started investing and here I am."

"That's quite a journey."

"What about you?"

She resumed sitting straight in her seat. "I married

Stuart out of high school. He joined the army and went off to basic training. When he was done with that, I joined him. I've lived in a bunch of places around the US, in military housing."

"No kids?"

She shook her head. "Stuart planned on staying in for his twenty years. We were going to start our family when we were thirty so the kids wouldn't have to move around a bunch with his various assignments. Once he retired, we were going to move back to Willowbrook. But his mom passed away unexpectedly about the time we were going to start trying and that put it off. Then Stuart was killed."

She got through the telling without getting too much into the emotion of it. If she didn't think about the details, about how much everything had changed once she'd lost him, she would be fine.

While the biggest regret was losing Stuart, of course, she also mourned the children she would never have. Without Stuart, she wasn't going to be a mother.

"I'm sorry," Thaddeus murmured.

"Thank you." She faked a smile. "You don't have kids either?"

"No. I want them, but so far it's not happening." He slowed as they passed a doe and a fawn standing beside the road. "You doing okay with the talking thing?"

It occurred to her then that even though Thaddeus was like no one she'd ever met, he was also a kind man.

"I am. Thank you."

"You're welcome."

Unity drew in a breath. This wasn't so bad. Maybe change was possible. Maybe she was going to be just fine.

ELLEN'S PRIDE IN her hangover nearly made up for the headache that took two ibuprofen and three hours to go away. When they stopped for their midmorning gas and potty break, she followed Lissa into the convenience store.

"I need advice," she told the teen as they picked out sodas for the next leg of the journey. "I want to get a couple of fashion magazines and I don't know which ones are good."

Lissa grinned. "Let's go look."

They walked over to the magazine racks. Lissa pointed out *Vogue* and *InStyle*.

"Both of those would be good for you."

"*Vogue* scares me," Ellen admitted. She picked up *InStyle* and flipped through it. "This is more my speed." Maybe she would get some ideas for cute clothes. If nothing else, it would be good for Coop to see her reading a fashion magazine.

They chose a few snacks, then headed for the checkout line. When they were back on the bus, Ellen flipped through the magazine. She paused at an ad that showed a sexy couple embracing. She studied how the man's hands were on the woman's impossibly narrow waist. They were staring into each other's eyes and doing a good job of convincing Ellen she'd stumbled on a personal moment.

She'd never had that, she thought. Not the sexy guy or the embrace or any of it. To be honest, until recently, she'd never much thought about having a man in her life. She'd been too busy, scrambling to get through every day. And maybe she'd been a bit unwilling to take a risk. Dating, at her age, seemed fraught with potential disasters. Plus, in her town, the dating pool was small.

But suddenly she was thinking it would be nice to have someone who cared about her. The sex thing was different. She'd never really thought about pursuing it. How would that even happen? Was it a natural progression of dating? She had no one to ask. Unity hadn't dated since high school and Keith found women online. That was hardly traditional.

Everyone else trooped back on the bus. Keith pulled out onto the street that paralleled the freeway, then merged into the southbound traffic. In the rear of the bus, Luka opened the Spanish language app on his phone. In a matter of minutes, all the kids were speaking along with him, teasing each other about mispronunciations.

Ellen shifted from her seat to the one behind Keith.

"How are you feeling?" he asked, meeting her gaze in the mirror. "You were quiet this morning."

She grinned. "I had a hangover."

"You sound proud."

"I am. I'm better now."

"Drink lots of fluids. You need to hydrate."

"If I do that, I'll need to stop more often and you know how cranky you get when we stop to let someone pee."

He smiled. "I'll make an exception in your case."

"Thank you." She thought about their conversation the previous night. "Thanks for listening. And buying me drinks."

"Anytime."

"I'm starting to get together a plan. For the list."

His gaze met hers again, before returning to the road. "What does that mean?"

"I'm getting a tattoo. In San Diego. I've done my research and I think that's the best place. There are a lot of tattoo parlors in the area because of the navy base." She popped a can of soda and took a sip. "Although it's not just military guys anymore. Everyone has tattoos. I want to say it's a strange thing to do, but I guess we've been marking our bodies for thousands of years."

"You don't need me here for this conversation, do you?" he asked.

"Not really, but it's nice to have you here all the same." She took another drink. "I found the place I want to go to. It gets very good reviews."

"You picked a tattoo parlor based on Yelp?"

"Not just Yelp. Other review sites. I don't want to be disappointed."

He shook his head. "What's the tattoo?"

She smiled. "You'll have to wait and see."

More laughter erupted from the rear of the bus. Ellen glanced at the students, then back at the windshield. She thought about the magazine and the couple in the ad.

"Maybe I'm not a sexual being," she said with sigh.

The bus swerved slightly. Keith glared at her. "Don't say stuff like that while I'm driving."

"What does your driving have to do with anything?"

"It's distracting."

"Well, I've said it now. Can we talk about it?"

"No."

She ignored him. "It's just why haven't I found a guy to sleep with? Why hasn't a guy found me? Why have I been okay with just masturbating all these years?"

He made a strangled sound.

She waved the can at him. "Oh, please. Like you don't. Everyone does it."

"Nobody talks about it."

"Whatever. But shouldn't I have been looking? It was really awful with Jeremy, but that was a long time ago. Maybe I give off a nonsexual vibe. Tell me about the women you meet online."

"No."

She sighed. "Come on. I'm serious. You must have a favorite site you like where the women are nice. I don't know if I could do that. Meet someone online and have sex with them." She considered the thousands of ways the situation would be both awkward and disappointing.

"I don't do it that much."

She held in a smile. "Online dating or masturbating?"

He shook his head. "You're impossible. Online dating. I tried it a few times and it's convenient, but it's not perfect. The temporary nature of it gets old."

"So why not just date someone you can be with long-term? Oh, wait. I know. We live in a small town. It could be messy and you don't like messy in your personal life."

He gaze narrowed. "How do you know that?"

"I know things about you. Plus, I think the same thing. The Willowbrook dating pool is pretty small. Obviously self-pleasure is the answer, but it's lonely. I need to think about dating." She leaned forward and grinned. "Do you know any guys I might like?"

"We're not having this conversation."

"I had no idea you were such a stick-in-the-mud."

"Live with the pain."

THADDEUS WASN'T ONE to think about how much a date cost, but in this case he had to admit he'd gotten a lot of bang for the buck. Unity had been enthralled with the indoor skydiving from the second they'd walked into the tall building.

She'd listened attentively to the instructions, had happily put on the gear and when it was her turn in the wind tunnel, she'd enjoyed every second.

"That was incredible," she said as she unzipped her jumpsuit and handed her helmet to the guy at iFly. "It was the most indescribable experience I've ever had."

She was grinning as she spoke, her eyes bright and happy. Completely different from the terrified woman he'd met a few days ago.

"I'm glad you enjoyed it."

"I did, so much! I was doing all kinds of somersaults and stuff, right in the air! It felt great. Like flying in a dream, but better, because it was real. I want to do this again. I wish my friend Ellen would go with me, but there is no way. I could bring Cooper. That's her son," she added. "He's seventeen. He would think it's a blast."

They walked out toward his car, Unity nearly bouncing with each step.

"Thank you," she said earnestly, turning to him. "Really. Thank you."

"You're welcome. Want to get some lunch before we head back?"

"Yes, please. I was too nervous to eat this morning and now I'm starving."

She got in the car without waiting for him to hold the door. As he walked around to the driver's side, he thought about where they were and how they were dressed. Not fast food, he thought. Somewhere nicer, but casual.

They drove a few miles north to the Hyatt on Lake Washington. Thaddeus valet parked the car, then led the way to a restaurant right on the water. They were shown to a table with a view.

She glanced around at the quiet restaurant, then back out at the water. He had no idea what she was thinking, but she looked delighted with the world. He supposed, if nothing else, he should be pleased that he'd given her that.

She was still a puzzle. Beautiful, in a girl-next-door, I-don't-care-about-my-looks kind of way. Unselfconscious, yet incredibly closed off. He should have walked away after that first meeting, yet he hadn't and now he found himself wanting to know more about her.

"You're glowing."

She laughed. "I'm emotionally floating as much as I was physically. Now I'm wondering if I want to try the real thing."

"Whole different ball game."

"Have you been?"

He didn't have a problem with heights, but actual skydiving was a push. "No, and while I would be happy to drive you, jumping out of a plane isn't my idea of fun."

"What is?"

Had any other woman asked that question, he would have assumed she was flirting. But not Unity. He doubted she knew how.

"I find my work fun, which makes me a lucky man. We're in boating season, so I enjoy that. Snowboarding in the winter. Basketball with my friends when we all have time."

"You have a boat?"

He nodded.

"A big one?" Her tone was teasing.

"One big, one small. The larger one is for weekend trips, the small one is for playing around on the lake."

Her eyes widened. "Two boats? I guess I shouldn't be surprised but I am. You're really successful, huh?"

He held in a smile. "Yes."

Their server appeared. "Good afternoon. Welcome to Water's Table. What can I get you to drink?"

Thaddeus opened the wine list and scanned a page. "It's early for a bottle, but I see you have Veuve by the glass. We'll start with one of those."

The twentysomething woman smiled. "Of course."

Unity waited until she left before leaning forward. "What did you order?"

"A glass of Veuve." He paused. "Veuve Clicquot. Champagne, to celebrate your uplifting experience."

"But it's lunch," she said, sounding shocked.

"Should I cancel the order?"

"No. Sorry. It's just not how I spend my day." She looked down, then back at him. "I don't think I've had champagne before. It just wasn't our thing. I know people often have it at weddings, but we were only eighteen, as were all our friends. We didn't have much money. Ellen's parents gave me some, but I didn't want to take advantage of them."

She was in her thirties and she'd never had champagne? He filed the information away and returned to what she'd just told him.

"Why Ellen's parents and not your own?"

"Mine died when I was thirteen." Her mouth twisted. "It was a shock, of course. They were traveling. We had a small farm and they were creative and spent the winters making beautiful candles they sold at craft fairs. I usually went with them, but that summer Ellen and I were taking a class together at the park and so I stayed with her and her folks while my parents were gone."

The happiness faded from her eyes. "They were killed in a car accident. There wasn't any other family. Ellen's parents took me in so I didn't have to go into foster care."

"I'm sorry."

"Thanks. Anyway, that's why they helped pay for the wedding."

"How old were you when you met Stuart?"

"Fifteen."

"So just two years after losing your parents." The first boyfriend becomes the husband, becomes the only family. Was that why Unity wasn't comfortable dating? She'd never had to and didn't know how?

Their server brought over the glasses of champagne. Thaddeus raised his glass.

"To your adventure."

She smiled and touched her glass to his, then took a sip. She paused for a second, took a second sip, then smiled.

"It's wonderful. I like the bubbles. It's not sweet at all. I thought it would be."

"I'm glad you like it."

They placed their order and handed over menus. Unity fiddled with her napkin for several seconds, then looked at him.

"Why did you call me? Our first meeting didn't go very well."

With anyone else, he would have had a glib nonanswer ready. He rarely gave away too much this early on. But Unity was different. She obviously didn't date and had little or no experience with men beyond her late husband. There was a guilelessness about her that made him want to protect her—something that rarely happened.

"I couldn't stop thinking about you."

Her eyes widened as she stared at him. "What does that mean?"

He smiled. "I would think the sentence was self-explanatory."

"You're right. I mean why? I'm nobody. I'm not interesting. I might even be lost." She seemed to shrink as she spoke, hunching in the chair.

"I'll accept confused or in transition," he told her. "Not lost. Being lost implies a lack of strength. You have strength."

His words obviously startled her. "Maybe you're seeing more than there is."

"I have good instincts about women." An inability to find one he wanted to marry, but that was different. "You have potential."

"Potential without action is wasted."

"Then act."

One corner of her mouth turned up. "You're very free with advice."

"Most people are. Tell me about your business. It's unusual for a woman to be a handyman."

She reached for her champagne. "It is, but where I live, I think it gives me an advantage. I'm instantly trustworthy." She smiled. "Let's see. I grew up knowing when something broke, new wasn't an option. We repaired, reused, made do. When I was little, I helped my dad a lot. He showed me how to do things."

"Sounds like a good dad."

"He was. When I married Stuart, we lived in base

housing. It's not luxurious, as you can imagine. My sink had a leaky faucet that was driving me crazy. I reported it, but they said it would be a couple of weeks for someone to get there. So I went to the hardware store and bought a couple of washers and fixed it myself."

He liked that she'd taken action. He also enjoyed listening to her talk. When she forgot to be sad, her whole face relaxed. She was animated and genuine.

"I started helping out a few friends with small projects. Word got out and people I didn't know called me to do things. I made a price list and it became a part-time job. When we moved to the next base, I started up again."

"So when you had to move back to Willowbrook, opening your own business was a natural transition."

She nodded. "I like what I do. Having Silver Pines nearby means there is always work. I have a good reputation in the community and I'm one of their go-to people."

She drank more champagne. "My friend Ellen thinks I need to hire a real full-time person to work for me."

"Who works for you now?"

"A group of retired guys. I have help, they get to travel when they want. It works." She leaned toward him, her elbows on the table. "I'll admit I don't take my business as seriously as I probably should. I turn down work constantly. Having someone full-time would mean getting more jobs, especially the bigger ones that pay more."

"But?" he asked.

"I work out of my garage. If I got a full-time person, I'd probably need to move into a real business location. That scares me. I've never had a rent payment."

"Have you run the numbers?"

She ducked her head. "I don't even know what that means."

"You figure out what your expenses would be, then look at how much you think you would earn."

Their food arrived. He'd ordered fish and chips, while Unity had chosen a burger.

"Math isn't my thing," she said before taking a big bite. "I don't do computers and spreadsheets. My guys are always after me to get a smartphone so we can use one of the business apps to schedule jobs and stuff."

"And yet you resist."

"I don't like change."

"You're afraid of change, there's a difference."

She put down her burger and wiped her hands. "How did you know that?"

"It's pretty obvious, Unity. You're bright, you're capable, but you don't want to challenge yourself." He smiled. "Excluding today's adventure."

"I don't think I like being that transparent."

"Too late now."

"What else can you see?"

A smart man would change the subject. "You're in a lot of pain and you don't know how to process it. I'm not sure if you want to move forward, or if you simply think you should. As you said, you're afraid of change."

"Actually you said that." She picked up a french fry and ate it. "You're not wrong."

"Thank you."

She smiled. "You're welcome. All this talk of what you can see makes me uncomfortable, but I don't think you're being mean about it."

"I'm not."

She studied him. "You'd be a good dad."

"My ex and I broke up before that could happen. I want children."

"Me, too," she said, then frowned. "I mean I did."

"But not anymore?"

She looked surprised by the question. "I can't. Stuart's gone."

More information he should pay attention to. "You won't have children without him?"

She paused, a french fry halfway to her mouth. "You're saying I could have a child with someone else." She sounded scandalized by the concept.

"It's not unheard of."

She set down the fry. "I never really thought about it—having children now." She shook her head as if trying to dislodge the concept.

"Let's change the subject," he said gently. "Great weather we're having."

She glanced at him, then away. After returning her attention to him, she said, "You're different than I thought you'd be. Although to be honest, I had no idea what to expect."

"Is reality better or worse?"

She smiled. "Better. But I am confused about one thing. You're this rich, good-looking, successful guy. Why are you here?"

An excellent question he'd asked himself several times. "I told you. I can't stop thinking about you."

"In a boy-girl way?"

"Some. Why did you say yes?"

"I wanted to go skydiving."

Ouch. "Honest, but painful."

"Why? Oh, because I wasn't thinking about you."

She ducked her head, then straightened. "But I'll think of you now. After today."

"Yay, me."

"This is very confusing."

"For both of us."

She finished her glass of champagne. "What happens now?"

He flagged the server and ordered Unity a second glass. When they were alone, he said, "That's up to you. My suggestion is we try this again and see what happens."

"You mean go out?"

"Yes."

She considered the question. He watched her, looking for clues as to what she was thinking. There weren't any.

His head told him they were doomed—that he was a fool and he should get out while he could. His gut was less sure. Unity intrigued him. Maybe it was just the appeal of the unfamiliar. Maybe it was something else. Freddy would tell him he had a death wish.

She pulled a sheet of paper out of her handbag. "So I have this list I made with my friend Ellen. We're both in a rut and we're going to spend the summer helping each other get out of it. We've set it up as a contest. Whoever does the most stuff on the list wins."

"Is there a prize?"

"A spa weekend." She smiled. "I want to win."

"You have a competitive side?"

"Sometimes. Would you mind if we did some stuff on my list? You know, for the challenge with Ellen?"

She passed over the piece of paper. He read it cautiously, not sure what to expect. Item five caught his attention. *Sex with a handsome (and age-appropriate) man.* He was up for that. The other one he liked had her wearing a dress without a bra. But he had a feeling she wasn't going to want to go for any of those.

"How about we try rock climbing?" he asked, picking one of the items least likely to scare her off.

"That would be a good one. Or something else, if you'd prefer," she added primly, as if aware she was being demanding while offering little in return.

"Unity, do you *want* to go out with me again?"

She fidgeted in her seat, glanced away, then back at him. "Yes."

The answer he'd been hoping for, the answer that should have relieved him. Yet he knew that nothing about what they were doing was simple for either of them.

"Then we'll go out," he told her. "We'll figure out the rest of it from there."

"I like that," she said with a smile that kicked him in the gut and warned him he was playing a very dangerous game.

eleven

ELLEN COULDN'T BELIEVE how much getting a tattoo hurt. The needle just kept going and going, making her want to scream that she had changed her mind. Only she couldn't. Last night Unity had told her she'd gone skydiving. *Skydiving!* At an indoor place, but still. Ellen still couldn't figure out the stupid smoky eye and Unity was flinging herself into some air tunnel.

Even more startling, she'd gone with a man! And they'd agreed to go out again. Had anyone but Unity told her that, Ellen would have assumed the person was lying. But Unity had always been totally honest, which meant in less than a week, she'd gone on a date and been skydiving.

Game on, Ellen thought, gritting her teeth against the jabbing, piercing pain. She was getting a tattoo for sure. How much longer could it take?

After what felt like three days of torture, she was finally done. Ellen listened carefully to the instructions, took the offered salve and soap she was supposed to use while it healed and walked gingerly to the waiting area.

Lissa came to her feet. "Did you do it? How was it?"

"Yes and painful."

The teen grinned. "Can I see it?"

"Not for a couple of hours. I have to keep on the bandage." Ellen pressed her hand against the throbbing on her left, rear hip. "Then I wash it and apply this stuff." She waved the salve. "Then I live my life."

There were other instructions. No soaking in water for three weeks, no scrubbing. She had a list.

Lissa hugged her. "I'm so proud of you. That's impressive."

"Believe me, I was tempted to stop about fifty times."

Ellen opened her Uber app and requested a car, then the two of them went outside. The afternoon was a balmy seventy-two degrees, the sky a perfect blue.

They'd arrived in San Diego the previous afternoon. Two of the students had appointments at the college. The rest would simply tour the campus and get a feel for what attending UC San Diego would be like. Ellen had decided to use the tour time to get her tattoo. She'd been surprised when Lissa had offered to go with her.

Now as they waited for their car, Ellen looked at her. "You know, we don't have to go directly back to the hotel. We could make a quick trip to the campus if you want."

Lissa wrinkled her nose. "No, thanks. It's not the school for me. It's tough to get in and I'd have out-of-state tuition. Why would I want my dad to pay all that when I haven't figured out my major yet? Community college makes more sense."

"All the schools we're looking at are out of state."

"I know." Lissa's voice was heavy as she spoke. "I tried explaining that to my dad, but he…" She turned away. "Is that our car?" She waved to the Prius pulling up to the curb.

On the drive back to the hotel, Ellen tried to make sense of what Lissa had told her. Was it really a money thing? She had trouble believing that. Keith had played in the NFL. He'd had a couple of endorsement deals. Although he'd never been a big star, he was articulate and good-looking. Sponsors had loved him.

She wouldn't say he was wealthy, but she knew there was some money—enough that a pricey college wouldn't be financially debilitating. Surely Lissa understood that as well.

They arrived back at the hotel. Lissa went up to her room to change into a bathing suit so she could hang out by the pool. Ellen collected her e-reader and joined her, careful to stay in the shade.

Getting comfortable in the lawn chair was nearly impossible, she thought, shifting on the chair.

"You okay?" Lissa asked.

"It's a dumb place to get a tattoo," Ellen complained, reaching for a towel to shove behind her back. "How am I supposed to sit?"

Lissa tried not to smile. "At least you can sleep on your other side."

"I know. I shouldn't whine. I did this to myself. It'll be better tomorrow. It's just, it looks so much easier on TV."

She tried to read and watch the clock at the same time. At exactly two hours, she went upstairs to her room and took off the bandage before washing the area with the special liquid soap she'd been given. After that, she applied the salve, then pulled out the granny panties she'd brought along just for this moment. She pulled them on over her bikini ones to keep the cream off her crop pants.

"So sexy," she murmured, laughing at herself as she left the room.

She went into the lobby and saw all the guys were back. Aidan was high-fiving everyone. When he saw her, he rushed over, grabbed her and spun her in a circle.

"Hey, Ms. F. You should have come with us. The campus is close to the beach and the girls are beautiful." He released her and grinned. "Man, I so need to go here. I know it's a UC school, but my academics are good and they have my major and maybe I can run track or something."

His enthusiasm made her laugh. "Good for you, Aidan. Now let's see if you still feel that way after you see the next campus."

The rangy teen shook his head. "I'm a Triton all the way."

"They'd be lucky to have you," she told him, secretly suspecting Aidan was going to be just as interested in every college they visited. He just seemed like the type.

She made her way to Cooper. "How was it?"

Her son shrugged. "Good. It's a nice campus, but not for me." He glanced at his friend and grinned. "Aidan's stoked."

"I heard. So you're still waiting for Stanford and UCLA?"

"Uh-huh."

They would head out midmorning to arrive in Westwood in time for lunch. Cooper and Luka had afternoon meetings with the athletic department. The following morning, everyone would go on a tour of the UCLA campus, then Coop was meeting his dad for lunch while the rest of the group hung out on the beach.

When she'd first told him about his dad, he'd been super excited, but in the last day or so, he hadn't mentioned the lunch. She wasn't sure if he was trying to spare her feelings, or if he was nervous.

"Are you excited to see UCLA?" she asked, searching for some level of enthusiasm. Something that would show the plan was working.

"I guess."

She held in a sigh. Not exactly what she'd been hoping for. "From what I've heard, it's huge. Nearly a hundred thousand people go through it each day. That's three times as many people as live in Willowbrook."

He smiled at her. "You've been doing research."

"I like to stay up on things. Don't forget, after the morning tour, you're meeting your dad."

Emotions she couldn't read raced through his eyes. He glanced away. "It's no big deal."

She wished she knew what he was thinking. "Coop, it is. Are you nervous?"

He shrugged. "Some. Maybe. He's just a guy."

She pulled him over to one of the sofas in the large, open lobby. When they were seated, she said, "Coop, this *is* a big deal. You need to be prepared for a lot of emotions that don't make sense. You have ideas in your head about who your father is and they may not be close to the truth."

"You're saying I won't like him?"

"What? No. Of course not. I'm saying that you have to understand that whatever expectations you have are about you and what you need. Jeremy won't be able to read your mind. So if it doesn't go how you imagine, that's okay. It doesn't mean your dad doesn't care about you."

"If he cared, he would have shown up a long time ago."

An excellent point. One she wanted to linger on, but knew she had to stay neutral with a slightly positive chaser. In her heart of hearts, she wouldn't be the least bit sad if Coop and his dad didn't get along—but if that were to happen, she wanted it to occur organically and not because of anything she'd done.

"I'm sure he regrets his decision. How could he not? But he's here now, so have a good time, then come join us on the beach."

Her son met her gaze. "You all right with this, Mom? If you don't want me to go, I won't go."

Ack! "Go," she said with as much enthusiasm as she could muster. "Go and have a good time. I'm happy you're doing this. I'm a little jealous of your lunch because I think we're getting hot dogs on the pier and that's hardly the same as some fancy restaurant in Santa Monica. Maybe you'll see a movie star."

"Oh, Mom. It doesn't work like that."

"Why not? They have to eat eventually."

He didn't smile. "I want you to be okay."

"I am okay." She squeezed his hand and smiled. "I'm having a lot of fun already. I got a tattoo today."

He stared at her, as if he hadn't heard her. "What did you say?"

"I got a tattoo." She pointed to her left rear hip. "It was very painful, let me tell you. I nearly told the guy to stop, but then what? I would have had half a tattoo."

Cooper came to his feet, towering over her. "A tattoo?" he roared loud enough for the entire lobby to turn in their direction. "Are you serious?"

She held in a smile. "What are you so upset about? I'm an adult. I can do what I want."

"You're not the tattoo type. You're a mom."

She stood and patted his arm. "I'm not *just* a mom, kid, and I get to have a life if I want to." She turned and reached for the front button of her pants. "Want to see?"

Coop looked horrified. "Not here. Mom!" He muttered something she couldn't hear. "I can't believe you did that."

"It's nice that I can still surprise you."

He groaned. "I'm going up to my room."

"Chicken." She made a clucking sound.

"I don't know you," he called over his shoulder as he walked away.

She was still chuckling when she let herself into her room. She liked that Coop was shocked about the tattoo, but she wished he was more enthused about the various campuses they would be seeing.

As for him hanging out with his dad, that was a different kind of problem. Nerves were natural, but with her luck, Jeremy would be nothing but charming and by the end of the meal, her son would want to relocate to LA and leave her behind. Although that would solve the "I can't leave my mom" problem, that wasn't how she wanted it to happen.

"Don't start worrying about things that haven't happened yet," she told herself as she reached for her phone.

Want to see my tattoo?

Keith responded instantly. *I can't believe you really did that.*

I said I would.

There wasn't a response, but seconds later, she heard a knock on her door. She opened it and found Keith standing in the hallway.

"What were you thinking?" he asked.

"It was on my list. I told you I was going to do it. All you guys act so tough and worldly, but you're not at all. Coop was practically hysterical."

"That his mother got a tattoo? Hmm, I wonder why that is."

She grinned. "Want to see it?"

Keith hesitated. "Where is it?"

She rolled her eyes. "Nowhere bad. Just on my hip." She turned her back and unfastened her pants, then pushed them and the granny panties down. "It's a shooting star."

"Uh-huh."

He sounded farther away as he spoke. She glanced over her shoulder and saw he was at the far end of the room.

"It's not a disease," she told him, pulling up her pants. "What are you afraid of?"

"I'm being cautious. I didn't know how many clothes you were going to take off."

The unexpected statement hurt her feelings. "Because it would be so awful to see me naked? Gee, thanks for the compliment."

He groaned. "It wouldn't be awful. It would be—" He took a step toward her, stopped. His whole body tensed. "Could we please not talk about you being naked?"

"Because it's too gross?" She squared her shoulders, determined to be strong in the face of what seemed to be mean comments. "I'll have you know I look good naked."

His jaw clenched. "I'm sure you do. I just don't need that in my head right now. Thinking about you naked isn't comfortable." He held up a hand. "It's a guy thing, okay? Can you trust me on that? It's not that I wouldn't like to see your body. This is not me dissing you."

Some of her hurt faded. "So you *would* like to see me naked?"

He swore. "Ellen, please. Change the subject."

She looked at him. He was a big strong guy. Very masculine and comfortable in his own skin. Which was weird to think about because they'd always only been friends. But now, studying his body and thinking how much they enjoyed each other's company, she wondered what it would be like to be more than friends.

Not, you know, in love or anything, but intimate. She smiled. Sex. She was talking sex.

She would guess he knew what he was doing, which was good. One of them should. She'd seen him shirtless, when Coop had been at camp and Keith had mowed her lawn. If the rest of him was, ah, proportional, that would be interesting. Not that she actually cared about penis size. After all this time, she would pretty much be accepting of whatever she could get.

"Do you want me to see you naked?" she asked, still caught up in her thoughts.

Keith dropped into the chair by the small desk against the wall and covered his face with his hands.

"I can't do this," he said, his voice muffled. "I can't. I'm begging you, show a little mercy."

"I have no idea what has your panties in a bunch, but whatever. Sure. We should talk about Lissa."

Keith's head snapped up. "Do not tell me my daughter got a tattoo."

Ellen waved away the question. "She didn't even ask about it, so no."

She crossed to the bed and gingerly sat down. The mattress was relatively soft, so her hip didn't hurt.

"I offered to take her to UCSD for a quick look around and she wasn't interested. She said the out-of-state tuition would be expensive and she didn't see the point because she didn't know what she wanted to study. She mentioned going to community college instead."

His head snapped up. "She said that to you? She's never mentioned community college to me. If she wants to, that's fine, but why not go away and have the college experience? She's bright, she's social, she gets good grades." He expression turned pleading. "Tell me what's going on."

"I have no idea. I'm sorry. That was all she said. She's a good kid, Keith. Give her some time. Seeing all the different colleges may spark her interest."

"I want her to be happy."

"I know. Maybe talk to her after the UCLA tour. Not in a pushy way. Just ask her what she thought. Oh, at dinner tonight, talk about what it was like for you when you went away to school. The boys will love hearing about that and maybe she'll catch their enthusiasm."

"Good idea. Thanks."

He stood. She rose, as well.

"We have an hour before we all meet for dinner," she said. "Want to go get a drink?"

"What?" His voice was more high-pitched than usual. He cleared his throat. "No. I have stuff I need to do. No drink. Not a good idea."

Before she could ask what was wrong with him, he'd bolted from her room, moving so fast, he didn't bother shutting the door behind him.

Ellen stared after him. Men were weird. Why had no one told her that before?

THADDEUS DID HIS best to get Unity off his mind. He began negotiations to sell one of the companies he'd turned around, looked into a hiking trip in Patagonia and nearly signed up for yet another matchmaking service. In the end he continued with the negotiations, but trashed everything else. Until he got Unity out of his head, he wasn't going hiking anywhere south of the equator and there was no point in dating someone else.

He had no idea what combination of qualities allowed her to get to him. Did he want to rescue her? Was it the blend of honesty and raw vulnerability? Yes, she was pretty, but so were a lot of women. She wasn't unusually funny or smart. So why couldn't he just walk away?

He tried talking to his great-aunt about the problem but she'd insisted that wasn't a phone conversation. If he wanted to talk about Unity, he was going to have to come to Silver Pines.

He ignored her ultimatum for two days before finally making the drive. When he arrived at her house, there was a note on her front door that said she was at the east community room and he should join her there. As if she knew he would be arriving this afternoon.

"I hate being predictable," he muttered, following the signs to the building in question and going inside.

Inside, double doors were propped open and music with a classic Cuban beat spilled out. He moved toward the sound, knowing he would find Dagmar in the middle of whatever party was going on. He was so caught up in his own thoughts that he didn't recognize the danger until it was too late.

He was all the way inside the room when he realized it wasn't a party—it was a dance lesson. Before he could bolt for safety, the music stopped and he heard a familiar voice calling, "Darling, you made it. And your timing is perfect. You know how I love to rumba."

His great-aunt sailed toward him. She'd replaced the purple streak in her hair with a green one. Today she had on a dress with a full skirt that came to midcalf, and dance heels. The music began again and he instinctively took her in his arms and began to dance.

The movements were familiar. Slow, quick, quick. He moved her around the room, keeping pace with the other ten or so pairs of dancers. He guided her through a crossover break, then spun her expertly before returning to the basic step. As they continued around the room, he noticed about five or six women standing in a group. They were all staring at him expectantly.

Dagmar waved at them. "You know you're going to have to dance with my friends who don't have partners."

"I could tell you no."

She smiled. "I doubt that."

She was right, so he surrendered to the inevitable and danced with all the single women for the better part of two hours. At least he wouldn't have to worry about getting in his workout today.

When everyone was finally sated, he drove Dagmar home. She fixed a plate of appetizers while he made cocktails. After everything was prepared, they made their way to her living room.

"Thank you for dancing with my friends," she told him, toasting him with her drink. "That was very sweet of you. We'll be talking about it for weeks."

"Just don't give any of them my number."

Her expression turned impish. "How disappointing. Hearts will be broken." She picked up a shrimp and dipped it into the sauce she'd put out. "Now, tell me what's going on with Unity."

He leaned back in the sofa. "We went out."

"Yes. Skydiving. She had a wonderful time and thought it was all very exciting. Are you going to ask her out again?"

He leaned forward and rested his forearms on his knees. "I don't want to. I want to walk away and never see her again."

"I thought you liked her."

"I do and I don't know why. She's made it clear she's not that interested in me. She's obsessed with her late husband. She's only going out with me because of some bet with her friend Ellen. They've challenged each other to do different things and the winner gets a spa weekend." He looked at Dagmar. "I'm a means to an end."

His great-aunt didn't seem the least bit offended on his behalf. "She's using you. How delicious."

"You're supposed to take my side."

"I will when you need me to." She patted his shoulder. "Let me get this straight. You know Unity isn't looking to have a man in her life and yet you can't seem to forget her. Is that right?"

"Yes, and I don't like it. Why her? What about her gets to me?"

"Sometimes there's just a knowing between two people. No one can explain it."

"But this isn't between two people. This is me interested and her not."

"I can see how that would be more awkward."

He grimaced. "You're not very sympathetic."

"I know and I'm almost sorry about that. What are you going to do?"

"I'm not sure. Keep seeing her until I can get her out of my system, I guess." He reached for his drink. "Do you think she's ever going to let go of Stuart?"

"In time. She's healing, but it's slow going. Sometimes I think Unity hangs on because she doesn't have anything to let go for. Maybe you can give her that." She brightened. "Oh, maybe that's the appeal. You've never fought against a ghost before. You're challenged by the unknown outcome."

"I'd like to think I'm not that shallow."

"I would like that for you, as well, but we can't be sure, can we?"

Despite everything, he chuckled. "You're impossible."

"And yet you love me anyway."

"That I do."

twelve

UNITY WAITED FOR the picture to download on her computer, then stared at it in disbelief. There, in full color, was a picture of a slightly red, puffy tattoo.

Ellen had done it. She'd gotten a tattoo!

Unity grabbed her phone and quickly called. Ellen picked up on the first ring.

"Ha!" she said with a laugh. "Take that, skydiving girl."

"I can't believe you did it."

"Me, either, but we both have proof. Even better, tomorrow not only is Cooper having lunch with his dad, but I'm wearing a bathing suit at the beach. A total score. Two more items checked off my list." Ellen sighed happily. "I think I'm going to get a massage and a facial when you take me to Salish Lodge."

Unity stood up, then sat down. "I'm so impressed," she admitted. "Ellen, you're doing it."

"I am. It's really not that hard. I'll admit your sky-diving totally inspired me. I can't believe you did *that*."

"It was fun. I didn't know what to expect, but I loved it. I'm thinking of trying the real thing one day."

"You know that makes me question your sanity."

Unity laughed. "Go ahead. You won't be the first person." She shifted the phone to the other ear. "Is Coop noticing?"

"I think so. He was incredibly shocked about the tattoo, so that was kind of fun. He's also having second thoughts about spending time with his dad. I know it makes me small, but I'm glad about that. Still, I told him to go, even though I know Jeremy's going to be totally cool and chances are good my feelings will be crushed by the whole thing."

"But you're doing what's right."

"Yes, and it sucks. So what about you? There's a guy? How did that happen?"

"Not a guy, exactly."

"A hermaphrodite?"

Unity laughed. "No. He's the one I met when it went so badly. He asked me out and I suggested skydiving."

"That must have made him think twice about calling."

"Maybe, but he was up for it."

"Did you like him?"

"I don't know what that means. I was more comfortable around him this time. We talked and I managed full sentences." Unity swiveled on the chair in her home office. "He said he wants to go out again. Like a date."

"And?"

"And I don't want to date. Why would I want a man in my life?"

"For the sex? And don't tell me you don't want to have sex. You and Stuart were like rabbits. I was always jealous of that."

"But that was with Stuart. I don't know how to be with anyone else."

"I don't know how to be with anyone at all. Sell it somewhere else, sister."

Unity smiled. "You'll figure it out."

"So will you. Unity, the guy sounds nice. He comes with references and he's interested. Maybe you should just go with it for a little while. Deal with emotions as they come up, because at some point you really do have to move on. Believe me, I'm living the lesson right now. Ever since you moved back we've been enabling each other to stick with what was safe. I like that we're pushing each other to stretch a little."

"That sounds really mature," Unity said, hoping her voice sounded teasing instead of scared.

"Good. I was going for mature. Try the dating thing. It will be good for you."

"To what end?" Unity asked. "I love Stuart. I don't want to love anyone else."

"You love me."

"That's different. I don't want to love another man."

"That makes me sad. You're giving up so much of your life. You could still have kids, Unity. Don't you want that?"

"That's what Thaddeus said. Not those exact words, but he talked about me having children without Stuart."

"What did you say?"

"That I'd never considered the possibility."

"Not even once?"

"How could I? Ellen, he was my everything."

"So without him you're nothing?"

"Sometimes."

"Don't you want more?"

The softly asked question should have elicited an automatic "No, of course not." But for once Unity wasn't sure what to say. Was she really going to live the rest of her life in mourning? Was she really going to give up every dream she'd ever had? And what about a family? She'd always wanted babies to hold and love and nurture.

"Maybe I could get artificial insemination," she offered.

"You're just so romantic, I don't know how I stand you. Yes, you could do that. You'll be a great mom, with or without a partner. But speaking from experience, being a single parent isn't easy. And you know what? Not a decision you have to make today. I'm just saying maybe you can think about letting a guy in for a little while. If you don't like it, you can stop seeing him, but right now you're making decisions without a lot of information."

Unity knew Ellen was right. "You're right. That's good advice."

"Thank you. I gotta run, but know that I'm going to revel in my ass kicking on the challenge. Winning!"

Unity laughed. "Yes, you are, but I'm going to catch up. Love you."

"Love you, too."

They hung up. Unity looked back at the tattoo picture. Getting one was on her list, too.

She'd just done an internet search of local places when her phone rang again.

"Hello?"

"It's Thaddeus."

"Oh, hi."

She turned away from the computer, aware of a slight sense of anticipation. He'd called. It had been a couple of days, so she'd started to wonder if he would. Not that she wanted him to. Not exactly. Of course she hadn't wanted him *not* to call, so there was that. Sometimes it was hard to be her.

"I know it's last-minute, but I've been visiting Dagmar and wondered if you wanted to grab dinner or something."

He was here? In Willowbrook?

She looked back at the screen. "I'd like that, but could we make a stop first?"

"Sure. Where do you want to go?"

"I'd like to get a tattoo."

Thaddeus pulled up in front of her house ten minutes later. She met him at the front door, wondering why he seemed taller than she remembered. And possibly better-looking.

His eyes were dark, his hair layered. He had a three-day beard. The slightly scruffy look suited him, as did the polo shirt and jeans. The man had a body, she thought, wondering what he did to stay in shape.

"Tattoo?" he asked, stepping onto the porch. "For the challenge?"

"Yes. It's the only reason. I'm not really the tattoo type."

"You're going to be the type now." He smiled teasingly. "Once you get one, you can't stop doing it."

"I doubt that."

"Do you know what you're going to get?"

She smiled "A peace symbol. For my parents."

"Okay, let's do it."

He waited while she locked the front door, then put his hand on the small of her back as they walked to the car. She was aware of the light pressure and the heat from his skin. There was only her thin T-shirt between flesh-on-flesh contact.

It wasn't awful, she thought, but it wasn't comfortable. Not in a don't-touch-me way, but more because no one ever did that. And that entire chain of thought was exactly the reason she needed the challenge, she admitted to herself.

"I forgot to ask Ellen if it's going to hurt," she said as he pulled away from the curb.

"It's going to hurt."

She glanced at him. "You don't have to sound so cheerful about it."

He smiled. "I don't think the news comes as a shock to you."

"No, but you could have pretended it would be fine. Do you have any tattoos?"

"No."

"But everybody's doing it."

He glanced at her. "Everybody isn't and I was never interested. Still, I will be your tattoo wingman for the evening."

They arrived far more quickly than Unity would have liked. After going inside, she explained what she wanted. The young man at the counter showed her several different peace symbols.

"I didn't think there would be a choice," she said, flipping through the pages before picking a simple design. "That one."

"Where do you want it?" the guy asked.

"By my shoulder blade."

That question she'd planned for. While waiting for Thaddeus, she'd put on a plain, modest sports bra with a T back, giving the artist plenty of room to work.

She filled out the forms, handed over her credit card, then signed the receipt.

"Give me about ten minutes," the guy said. "You can have a seat over there, or wait outside. We have a table and chairs right in front."

"Thank you." Unity turned to Thaddeus. "Can we wait outside? I'm a little nervous and I'd like to pace."

He held open the door.

She stepped into the warm afternoon and sucked in a breath. "I feel sick." She pressed a hand to her stomach. "It's going to be okay, isn't it?"

He smiled. "You'll be fine."

"You don't actually know that."

"You didn't like it when I said it was going to hurt and now you don't like me saying you'll do great. I don't see a win here for me."

"Sorry. I don't mean to be difficult. Maybe we should change the subject." She sank into one of the chairs at the small metal table, then sprang to her feet. "So, you went to see Dagmar. How is she?"

"Her usual self." His expression turned rueful. "She had me meet her at the community center, where there was a rumba class going on. I got roped into being a partner."

"You know how to rumba?"

Something flashed in his eyes. "I do."

"How can you possibly know that? It's so random." She thought about what she knew about him. "Oh, the girlfriend. The one you followed to Vegas. She was a dancer. You must know a lot of fancy steps."

"It makes me popular with Dagmar's friends."

He was saying all the right things, but Unity couldn't help thinking there was something he wasn't telling her. She couldn't say exactly why she thought that—maybe it was the way he was standing or how he wouldn't quite meet her gaze.

Or she was just on edge because she had no dance secrets in her past.

"You were very sweet to indulge her," she said.

"She's my family. It's what I do."

"I know what you mean. Ellen and Cooper are my family. I would be lost without them." She smiled. "I guess we have that in common."

"Ellen and Cooper? I don't think so."

She laughed. "That we would do anything for the people we love."

"Like the challenge?"

She groaned. "Yes, like the challenge. Although I'm starting to think it's good for me to stretch myself."

The door opened and the guy from behind the counter stuck out his head. "I'm ready for you."

Unity's stomach lurched. She grabbed Thaddeus's hand. "Stay with me?"

"Promise."

They went into the back room. Unity was directed to sit backward on a straight chair, her arms folded and resting along the back.

"Once we start, I need you not to move," the guy told her.

She nodded and pulled a clip from her bag. She pinned up her hair, then hesitated only a second before pulling off her T-shirt. As she felt herself flushing, she told herself she was perfectly covered and no one cared about her boobs anyway.

Thaddeus politely looked away until she was seated, then pulled a chair close to her and met her gaze.

"You can do this," he told her.

"I hope so."

"I'll distract you with stories about my misspent youth."

She had the brief thought that he was a really nice man and that she had no idea why he was taking so much time with her, then she felt something cold and wet on her back.

"Disinfectant," the guy said. "As this is your first time, I'm going to do a test run so you'll know what to expect. There's no ink in the needle. Try not to jump."

She nodded before sucking in a breath. Thaddeus put both his hands on her forearms and leaned close.

"The gang I joined had an initiation," he told her. "You had to kill someone and you couldn't use a gun."

"What?" she asked, wide-eyed. "You've killed some-one?"

Before he could answer, she felt a sharp, intense jab right above her shoulder blade. Nerve endings screamed, then so did she.

"Stop! Just stop!" She half rose, turning to face the guy. "Is that really what you're going to do?"

He nodded. "That's what it feels like."

"How many pokes would you have to do?"

"I don't know. It's gonna take a while."

"No," she said firmly, stepping away from the chair and pulling on her T-shirt. "I'm not doing this."

"I can't give you a refund."

"You keep the money. It's fine." Her shoulder still throbbed from the needle punches.

As she pulled out her hair clip, she heard a snuffling sound. She spun toward Thaddeus who was obviously trying not to laugh.

"Don't," she snapped. "It hurts."

"Obviously."

"You think you're so tough, let's see you endure that."

He held up both hands. "I wouldn't think of it."

"My pain is not funny."

"Of course not."

She grabbed her bag. "We're leaving now."

She stalked out, Thaddeus trailing behind her. When they reached his car, she glared at him across the hood. "We're never going to talk about this again."

"Whatever you say."

She reached for her door handle. "Did you really kill someone?"

The grin returned. "No."

"You weren't in a gang?"

He shook his head.

"So you lied?"

"It got your attention."

"Not enough." She got into the car and leaned back against the seat, only to wince when her shoulder came in contact with the leather. "I'm going to have a bruise."

He took her hand in his. "You were very brave."

"Oh, stop it," she said, trying not to smile.

He was still laughing when they left the parking lot.

THERE WERE DAYS and there were days. Keith sat on the beach in Santa Monica, questioning nearly everything about his life. Why had he thought agreeing to bring a bunch of teenagers to the beach was a good idea? The ocean was big and dangerous. He'd had to use his stern voice to get everyone to use sunscreen and now the guys were out in the surf, like they knew what they were doing.

The morning tour of UCLA had gone well, so that was something. Coop had been a little distracted, no doubt thinking about his upcoming lunch with his father, but he'd done a good job on his interview yesterday. Lissa, on the other hand, could not have been less interested. He'd tried to talk to her about how great it all was, but she'd given him the *why did I think having parents was a good idea* look and had avoided him for the rest of the tour.

Keith adjusted his baseball cap, trying to keep tabs on everyone. Ellen should be arriving shortly. She was dropping Coop off at the restaurant where he was meeting his father, then joining the group on the beach. Tomorrow was the Disneyland visit and the day after, they would head up to Santa Barbara.

He tried to clear his mind and enjoy the moment. The temperature was in the high seventies, the sun was out, the sand was warm. He had to focus on the little things.

Keith did a quick head count and realized Lissa was missing. He stood up and looked around frantically, only to catch sight of her talking with a lifeguard. Of course she was, he thought grimly as he started toward them. When the guy put his arm on his daughter's shoulder, Keith began swearing.

Lissa stood with her back to him, so didn't see him approach. He hated her tiny bikini and wished she'd put on the T-shirt he'd asked her to wear. Instead of agreeing, she'd rolled her eyes and walked away. She was doing that a lot lately.

"Can I help you?" the lifeguard asked.

Lissa turned and saw him. "Dad!"

Keith ignored her and stared into the reflective sunglasses of the lifeguard.

"She's seventeen," he said bluntly. "I'll press charges."

The lifeguard took a step back. "You said you were twenty."

Keith grabbed her arm. "She lied. You should know better, in your line of work."

"Da-ad!" She shook off his hold and starting walking toward their pile of belongings. "You're so annoying."

"Back at you." He pointed to the towels. "Go destroy your skin by tanning. Or hang out with the guys in the water."

"Oh, you'll trust me with them?"

"Sure." He smiled. "They're all afraid of me. I like that in a young man."

"You think you know everything but you don't."

"I know a lot."

Lissa darted toward the water. He watched her go, relaxing when she joined Andy and Luka in the surf. The guys would take care of her.

Just then his phone buzzed. He pulled it out and saw he had a text from Ellen.

Where are you?

Lifeguard station 20, he texted back. *Can you see it?*

There was a pause. Yes. I'm at 18. Be right there.

He headed north, looking for her. He spotted her, a large tote bag in one hand, her sandals in the other. Her long dark hair blew in the breeze and she had on sunglasses. When she saw him, she smiled and instantly the world righted itself.

Damn, she looked good, he thought absently. All female and sexy. The skirt of her wrap sundress was blowing open in the breeze. He found himself wanting to pull her close and kiss her until they...

He came to a stop. Kiss her? Kiss Ellen? No. Not going there. No kissing. No anything. They were friends. He liked being friends with her. She was a constant in his life and he liked that, too.

She walked up to him and leaned her head against his chest. "I'm trying to be brave, but it's hard. Jeremy was there. I'll admit I was half hoping he wouldn't show, but he did and Coop was so excited."

Keith put his hands on her upper arms. "It's going to be fine."

"I don't think so, but I don't have a choice. I know I'm doing the right thing. I just wish he'd never called." She straightened. "Okay, I'm done whining. Show me where we are so I can text Coop the location. Jeremy's going to walk him to the beach after lunch and point him in the right direction."

"Too bad he's not walking him the whole way. I'd like to meet him." And crush him like a bug, he thought, unexpectedly feeling territorial. "How did you feel, seeing him after all these years?"

"Strange. He looks different. I guess we all do. He's like a grown person. There was no chemistry, if that's what you're asking." She shuddered. "Thank you, no."

She stopped and looked out at the ocean. "That's beautiful. I'm going to pay attention to the view and forget everything else."

She pulled a large towel out of her tote bag and spread it on the sand, then looked around. "Why is everyone so perfect?"

He followed her gaze. All he saw was a bunch of people lying in the sun. There were teens, young families and a few people pushing retirement age.

"Who's perfect?"

She pointed to a couple of women in maybe their early twenties. "They are. My boobs were never that perky. Do you think they're real? I've always wondered what implants must feel like. Is it different to have them or different for the guy when he touches them? I wish I knew someone who had implants so I could ask."

Boobs? They were talking about boobs? A couple of days ago it had been whether or not he wanted to see her naked. What was going on with Ellen?

She unfastened the tie at her waist, then looked at him. "Don't laugh, okay? I just couldn't do a two-piece bathing suit. I felt too exposed. So I went with the old lady version. Whatever you're thinking, don't say it."

Before he could figure out what she was talking about, she shrugged out of her dress, folded it and tucked it into her tote bag. She fished a straw hat out of her tote, plopped it on her head, then stood there, staring at the ocean.

"This is nice," she murmured.

This is nice? This is *nice*!

He took a step back. Ellen was in a one-piece bathing suit. And nothing else. He could see everything. The outline of her breasts, her hips, her butt, her long legs. Yes, she was pale, especially compared to the average LA beachgoer, but her skin was soft-looking and smooth.

He'd always known Ellen had a body, but she'd kept it hidden for all the time he'd known her so he'd never thought about it, or her, *that way*. Worse, now when he thought about her slightly scornful "Of course I've had orgasms" comment, he could picture things a lot more clearly. At this moment he knew exactly how her legs looked and could imagine them spread wide, her body arched as her fingers rubbed faster and faster and—

He dropped to his towel, bending his knees, hoping to hide his rapidly growing erection. WTF! This had to stop. Ellen was a safe zone. She couldn't become dangerous—he needed her.

She sat on her towel, which she'd happened to put next to his. After pulling out a bottle of sunscreen, she handed it to him and presented her back.

"Put it on heavy, please. I don't want to burn."

As she spoke, she pulled her long hair out of the way. Holy crap, he was going to have to touch her.

He looked around frantically, hoping Lissa had come back so he could pass the task to her, but his daughter was still playing in the water. He sucked in a breath, then poured the thick lotion into one palm. After rubbing his hands together, he quickly spread the protection all over Ellen's back and shoulders.

Her skin was just as warm and soft as he'd imagined it would be. Wanting ignited. He thought about leaning close and kissing the side of her neck. No, first he would shift close so he could do that while reaching around to cup her breasts. Then they would—

He slammed on the mental brakes and quickly searched for a distraction. What about that game against New England when he'd been intercepted and the entire stadium had erupted in boos? It had been his own fault—Rogers had been open, but he'd thrown to Jefferson, and after that, his team couldn't do anything right. He should have thrown to Rogers. Everybody knew that.

The familiar litany of self-recrimination did the trick. The desire eased, as did his dick, and by the time he was done with her shoulders, equilibrium had been restored.

UNITY HAD TO make an executive decision. Did she want the full Apple Store experience and a ninety-mile drive, or was she willing to buy her new iPhone from an authorized retailer a mere thirty-five miles away? As much as she wanted to see the T-shirt of the day and have the total immersion moment, practicality won out.

"I'm impressed," Dagmar said as they drove south on highway 82, heading to Yakima. "You're finally getting a phone manufactured in this century."

Unity smiled. "Don't mock my little flip phone. It's been very faithful to me."

"Then you should give it a ceremonial burial when you get home. Something tasteful, with a choir and lots of flowers."

They were in Dagmar's car, with Unity driving. The BMW was a nice size, small, but not too small, with all-wheel drive. It handled a whole lot better than Unity's work van. Dagmar had mentioned the car was a gift from Thaddeus—yet another example of the man's generosity.

They'd had a good time the other night, she admitted to herself. After the tattoo fiasco, they'd gone out to dinner at a local restaurant. Conversation had flowed easily between them and the evening had zipped by. Being around Thaddeus was getting easier and she appreciated that.

"So what prompted this great change?" Dagmar asked. "I would have sworn you would never voluntarily give up your beloved flip phone."

"I have a bet with Ellen." She shrugged. "It's more of a challenge." She explained about Cooper and his belief that his mother couldn't get along without him. She left out the fight, instead talking about how she'd come up with the idea as a way to help her friend.

"Only now I'm thinking it's probably good for me, too. So I can get out of the rut everyone thinks I'm in."

She did her best not to sound defensive as she spoke, but wasn't sure how successful she was.

Dagmar only smiled. "That sounds like an excellent plan and explains the skydiving."

They drove to the Yakima Verizon store. Once inside, she listened to an explanation about the different iPhones. Unity chose the simplest model they had, then agonized over the different cases.

"You'll want something sturdy," Dagmar told her. "With the work you do, you need your phone protected. But you can still get a pretty color."

More quickly than she would have thought, her credit card was charged and the new phone was hers.

When the transaction was complete, she and Dagmar took a seat in the back of the store and waited for the phone to finish activating. Given that she was starting with no apps and no contacts, it didn't take long.

Dagmar showed her how to work the basic functions. Unity quickly input Ellen's number, then Thaddeus's.

"I want to text Ellen," she said.

"You should. Let me show you the emojis."

Dagmar pushed a couple of buttons, then showed her the smiley face. "They're all there. Hundreds of them. Once you start using a few, they'll stay up front, where they're easy to keep using. Oh, and beware of the eggplant." She waggled her eyebrows. "That's the symbol for a penis."

"An eggplant? Poor vegetable. Why does it have to be a penis?"

"I don't know, dear, but it does."

Unity typed in a text to Ellen.

I have a new phone—one that texts. Take that, tattoo girl.

Seconds later, three dots appeared on the screen.

"That means she's answering you," Dagmar told her. "This is so exciting."

Welcome to a brave new world. I'm so proud of you. How's it going?

Great. I'm excited about the phone. How did it go with Jeremy and Coop?

He got back about an hour ago and didn't say much. Only that he had a really good time and his dad is cool.

You worried?

Yes, but I'll deal. Gotta go. Love you.

Love you, too.

Unity clutched the phone to her chest. "I think I love it. Is that wrong?"

"Of course not. Apple love is pure."

They drove back to Willowbrook. When Unity was about to turn into Silver Pines, Dagmar shook her head.

"Go around the back way," she said, patting Unity's arm. "I want to show you something."

"Sounds mysterious."

She circled around Silver Pines, heading north. Just beyond the retirement community was a big, fancy golf course. There were two in the area. The public one out by the interstate and this one, which was private. Unity had never played golf and she didn't run in private club circles, so she'd never been on the grounds.

As they approached, Dagmar pointed to an entrance to a residential community.

"In there," she said.

Unity glanced at her. "Are you moving? Why would you leave Silver Pines? It has everything."

"I'm not going anywhere. This is for you."

Unity immediately pulled to the side of the road. Tension formed a knot in her stomach, making her want to get out of the car and run so far, no one could ever find her.

She drew in several slow breaths, then looked at her friend. "What are you doing?"

"Showing you a townhome. It's just an open house. I happened to see an ad for it and thought of you."

"Did Thaddeus tell you?"

Dagmar looked confused. "Tell me what?"

"Looking at houses is on my challenge list."

"He never mentioned that, darling. The first I heard of your competition was when you told me a couple of hours ago." She smiled. "But it is interesting that all your friends have the same notion."

"It's suspicious."

"How can you say that? Ellen and I love you. It's just an open house," Dagmar added gently. "Come look. If nothing else, you can brag about it to Ellen."

Unity didn't want to think about moving. She loved living in Stuart's house, sleeping in his bed, having her clothes hang in the same closet as his still did. She often pretended he wasn't dead—that he was just gone, like on a deployment, and soon he would be back. She wanted the pictures on the hallway walls, the memories in every corner. If she moved, she would lose all that. If she moved, she would lose him.

But she couldn't say that to Dagmar, or anyone. No one understood what she was going through.

"For me?" Dagmar asked.

Unity nodded because it was easier to agree. In one respect, her friend was right. It was just an open house.

She followed the signs to an unexpectedly large complex. They parked in the visitor's lot and made their way to the unit for sale. On the way they passed a community pool, several barbecues and a nicely kept garden.

The unit for sale had a two-car garage. She and Dagmar took off their shoes before walking into a surprisingly open foyer that led to a big living room with floor-to-ceiling windows overlooking a beautiful garden.

A well-dressed real estate agent greeted them.

"Hello. I'm Miranda. Thank you for coming." She handed them each a brochure on the property. "It's a wonderful end unit, so there are extra windows. The HOA dues cover all the outside maintenance, including the pool, along with a social membership at the club."

"That sounds wonderful," Dagmar said. "There are three bedrooms?"

Miranda nodded. "And two and a half bathrooms. I'll let you look around."

The living room led into a formal dining room. Beyond that was the oversize kitchen.

Unity did her best to ignore the growing sense of unease and instead pretend she was watching her favorite episode of *House Hunters*.

The kitchen looked brand-new. The cabinets were dark cherry and the countertops were a gorgeous quartz pattern. She opened a drawer and saw it was high quality. There was a five-burner stove, a farm sink and a walk-in pantry.

From the eating area, they opened sliding glass doors that led to a deck overlooking the golf course.

Miranda joined them. "Isn't it wonderful? So peaceful. You're near the water feature. We get a lot of geese passing through and there are resident ducks." She smiled. "Because everyone always asks, there is a window replacement policy. If a wayward golf ball takes out a window, the club will have it replaced within forty-eight hours."

"That is important," Dagmar said, taking Unity's arm. "Let's go upstairs."

They saw two secondary bedrooms with a connecting bath. Across the hall was the laundry room. At the end of the hall was the master. The room was huge, with vaulted ceilings and a balcony overlooking the golf course. The master bath was as modern and lovely as the kitchen.

They went downstairs, thanked Miranda, then left.

When they were standing by the car, Dagmar asked, "What do you think?"

Unity glanced back at the townhouse. "It's nice."

"There was so much light. And the appliances were fantastic. Did you see the jetted tub? Plus, there's a pool. Didn't you tell me you used to swim?"

"Back in high school," Unity whispered, feeling herself start to shake.

She braced herself against the car as her eyes filled with tears. Seconds later, sobs clawed at her throat.

"I can't," she gasped, hunching over as the pain washed through her. "I can't. I can't."

Dagmar held on to her. "Keep breathing, my love. You'll be fine."

She pulled away. "I'm not fine. Stop pushing me. Everyone's pushing me. I don't want a condo. I want to stay where I am."

Dagmar only smiled. "Don't be frightened, Unity. Healing isn't easy and sometimes it hurts, but you will be better for it."

"I don't want to be better. I want Stuart back." The sobs returned as she covered her face with her hands. "I want him back."

"That isn't going to happen. He's dead. If you can't do anything else, maybe it's time to accept that. Your husband is gone forever."

Unity gasped. "How can you say that?"

"I'm stating the obvious. Yes, you miss him. Yes, he was wonderful, but he's not here, is he? He's never going to be here, and the sooner you accept that, the sooner you can—"

"Let go," Unity said bitterly. "You've told me a thousand times."

"Then maybe you should start listening." Dagmar's usually friendly gaze had turned steely. "Do you have any doubt that I love you?"

"No."

"Then perhaps it's time to accept that I'm doing this for your own good. We all are. I'm worried about you. This is more than mourning, Unity. This is a kind of mental torture I can't understand. Your love for Stuart wasn't any greater than any other love, but your determination to stay trapped in the pain of your loss certainly is."

The harsh words shocked her enough that she stopped crying. "There's nothing wrong with me."

"All evidence to the contrary." Dagmar waved at the building. "It was an open house and yet here you are, acting like I've just sold you into sexual slavery. You need to get over yourself."

"Are you mad at me?"

Dagmar sighed. "No. Disappointed."

Unity stiffened. "Then I should probably take you home."

"Yes, you probably should."

AFTER A MORNING of rides and more rides, Ellen and Lissa decided to escape from the guys and get in a little shopping time. Main Street in Disneyland had dozens of stores filled with fun items they discovered they could not live without.

Ellen fingered an Elsa dress. "Why don't they make these in adult sizes?" she asked. "I could so rock an Elsa dress."

Lissa's eyes widened. "Where? You know you couldn't wear that at school."

Ellen thought about the looks on her students' faces if she waltzed into class wearing an Elsa dress. Impossible, but so fun to think about.

"It would change the classroom dynamic," she said with a laugh.

"You'd hear from the parents for sure."

Ellen picked up a tiara. "I can't help it. I love all things *Frozen*."

Lissa showed her a stuffed Sven. "How about this instead?"

The friendly reindeer doll was smiling. And pricey, but she'd yet to buy anything for herself. "I'm tempted," she admitted, as her phone buzzed.

She pulled it out of her pocket and saw she had a text from Jeremy. Ugh, she thought, opening it. But maybe he would give her a little insight into his lunch with Coop yesterday. All her son had told her was he'd had a good time and that his dad was a really cool guy.

Thanks again for letting me have lunch with Cooper yesterday. He's such a great kid. You must be so proud of him. You did a wonderful job, Ellen. I want to tell you I have regrets, but I gave up that right a long time ago.

Yes, you did, she thought, watching the three dots that indicated he was typing again.

I appreciate you being willing to let him come stay with me later this summer. He and I talked about a week, but maybe we can make it two. I told Lucy and the girls about him last night and they're all excited. Let's firm up the details when you two get back to Willowbrook.

Ellen stared at the words, reading them a second, then a third time. What was he talking about? There was no visit planned. She hadn't agreed to any visit and Coop hadn't said a word.

But Jeremy and Coop had talked about it, she thought, fighting the hurt growing inside of her. Coop obviously wanted to spend more time with his father— something she might not like but could understand. What she didn't get was the fact that he hadn't said anything to her.

"You okay?" Lissa asked, studying her.

Ellen shoved her phone into her pocket. "I'm fine. Everything is great." She hoped she was lying convincingly. She didn't want to get into any of this with Lissa. "Aren't we supposed to meet the guys by Star Tours? We should get going."

Lissa hesitated before nodding slowly. Ellen returned stuffed Sven to the shelf, then hurried out of the store.

They made quick time to the meeting place. The guys were all there, looking tired and happy. Keith spotted her and waved.

"Ready for round two?" he asked.

Her throat was tight and her chest ached. She glanced at her son, but Coop was talking to his friends and didn't even look at her.

Why hadn't he told her about the invitation? What else had he and Jeremy talked about that he was keeping from her?

"Ellen?"

She looked at Keith and faked a smile. "You go ahead. I'll wait here."

His dark gaze searched her face, then he turned to the group. "Everyone go on the ride, then meet back here.

We'll discuss the rest of the afternoon and evening. We need to be on the road by eight tomorrow morning to get to Santa Barbara before eleven."

"Sure, Coach," Luka said. "Come on, Lissa. You can sit with me this time."

They all rushed to get in line for the ride. Ellen motioned toward them. "You should go with them."

"You should tell me what happened."

She shook her head and looked away. "I can't. I'm going to cry and you don't want to be a part of that." She held up a hand. "I'm fine. Everything's fine."

"It's not fine if you're about to cry. Come on, Ellen. You can tell me anything."

She thought maybe that might be true. Keith was her friend and he'd always been there for her. He'd rescued her when she'd had a flat tire, even though it had been seven on a Saturday morning and he'd been asleep when she'd called. He'd finished the job in what felt like minutes, all the while teasing her about her lack of car knowledge, then he'd bought her breakfast.

He'd been the one she'd texted with a frantic plea because her period had started early and with gusto, leaving her unable to get up from her seat in her classroom. He'd taken her class to the gym, giving her the chance to duck out and head home to change clothes.

No matter the problem, he was her rock, she thought, swallowing against the thickness in her throat before stepping into his open arms and letting the tears flow.

"Coop had lunch with his dad yesterday," she said between sobs.

Strong arms held her close. He moved his hands up and down her back. "We knew this."

"He hasn't talked about it. I've asked a couple of times, but he won't say anything."

"He probably doesn't know what's okay to say. He doesn't want to hurt you."

She sniffed and nodded, liking how strong Keith was and how being held felt so nice. "Jeremy texted me a bit ago and said he and Coop had talked about Coop visiting over the summer. Jeremy wanted to know if it was okay to have him stay for two weeks instead of one. As if I even knew about the invitation. He didn't tell me. He didn't say a word."

"He's a kid," Keith said gently. "He doesn't know how to handle this."

She sniffed again, then raised her head. "Because he's excited about his dad and he doesn't want me to feel bad about that?"

He nodded.

"I get the logic of it, but it hurts. I don't want him to go. I don't want him to have a relationship with Jeremy. I'm just not that big a person."

Keith smoothed the hair off her face. "You going to tell him no?"

"I can't. Of course he has to go. I won't like it, but I won't stand in his way. I just want him to tell me."

"Give him some time."

"I hate Jeremy."

He smiled at her. "No, you don't."

"Maybe I do."

"You don't know him well enough to hate him. You can hate the idea of him, but not the man himself."

"This is not a time for logic. This is a time for listening and offering to beat up Cooper's father."

One corner of his mouth lifted. "I'm happy to do that, if you'd like."

She sighed. "No. He'd probably press charges and I think he has a lot of money, so there's no way we could afford a better lawyer."

Keith shifted, putting his arm around her. "You're going to get through this."

"Maybe."

"That's my little ray of sunshine. Come on, I'll buy you a churro."

She wiped her face, then managed a smile. "I love a churro."

"Sugar is always the answer."

"Not always, but most of the time."

thirteen

For the first time since moving back to Willowbrook, Unity wasn't comfortable in her own house. Despite the familiar rooms, the sofa she'd sat on for years, the dishes in the cupboard, the place didn't feel like home.

She hadn't slept, she couldn't think and even working all day hadn't cleared her head.

She'd never fought with Dagmar before. They'd been friends for over two years and there hadn't once been a harsh word between them. The same could be said about Ellen, and they'd been friends their whole lives. But they'd disagreed just a few weeks ago.

Unity wanted to say it was everyone else—that she was the victim here and the whole world should get off her back. But she couldn't help thinking, she was the one person both situations had in common, and if she accepted that premise, then wasn't it possible that she was the problem, not her friends?

She retraced her steps, coming to a stop in what had been the master bedroom. After Stuart's mother had died, he and Unity had flown back to Willowbrook to take care of the funeral arrangements. Stuart had gone through her things, donating her clothes and cleaning out the bedroom.

At the time Unity had told him all that could wait. They could handle it when they moved back after his twenty years in the army were up. He'd said it was easier to do it then. It helped him accept she was gone. Plus, when they came back permanently, they would have kids and dealing with the move and cleaning out the master would be too much for them to take on. He'd mentioned taking a week or so of his leave later in the year to clean out the other two bedrooms.

They'd ended up going to Australia instead, promising each other they would be back the following year. Only then Stuart had been killed and when Unity had retreated to the house where he'd grown up, the last thing she'd wanted to do was make any changes.

She turned in a slow circle, taking in the bare walls, the worn carpet. The whole house needed painting, she thought absently. She ducked into the master bath and looked at the old-fashioned sink and the bright green tiles in the small shower.

A gut job was the only solution, she admitted, looking at the patterned linoleum flooring. A neutral tile would make the space look bigger. Using the same tile in the shower and on the floor would help, too. She could do a lot of the work herself. The guys would help her with the demo and she could handle the plumbing. She was less sure of her tile skills, so could hire out that part.

The remodel might be a good project for her. She could fix up the bathroom and the bedroom, then maybe move in here, instead of staying in Stuart's room. That would be a step forward. Progress that could get her friends off her back.

Feeling better than she had in a while, she left the master, went into the small study and sat at her desk. She got an empty folder out of a drawer and labeled it "Master bath" and made a few notes. When she'd put the folder in her current jobs tray, she got out her phone.

Are we still speaking?

She sent the text to Dagmar. Seconds later, she had an answer.

Funny you should ask that.

Her doorbell rang.

Unity walked through the living room and opened the front door to find Dagmar standing on the porch. She had her phone in one hand and a pink box from a local bakery in the other.

Unity's restlessness faded and her stomach unknotted.

"Eclairs," Dagmar told her. "An offering of peace."

Unity drew her friend into the house, took the box and put it on the coffee table by the sofa, then hugged the older woman. Dagmar hugged her back.

"I shouldn't have pushed," Dagmar said when they released each other. "I'm sorry for that, and for upsetting you."

"But not for what you said?" Unity asked, amused by the distinction.

"I'm not wrong, although I might not have handled the situation the best way I could have. But I never meant to make you cry."

"I know. I've been thinking a lot about what you said. It's hard for me to imagine moving on."

"Because you don't want to?"

"Mostly."

"They say admitting the problem is half the battle, but I've always thought that was a crock. It's more like an eighth of the battle. But at least progress has been made, yes?"

Unity smiled. "It has."

"Excellent. Come on. I'll buy you dinner and we can celebrate your eighth."

"What about the eclairs?"

"Put them in the refrigerator, darling. They're for breakfast."

THADDEUS ARRIVED AT the upscale downtown Seattle restaurant a few minutes before the hour. He told the hostess he was there for the senator's luncheon and was shown to a private room in the back.

Political fund-raising went in and out of season, depending on whether or not the legislature was in session. For weeks at a time, his email was silent, but then it all ramped up again with pleas for money.

Thaddeus gave generously to the candidates he supported. Today he was attending a lunch hosted by one of Washington State's two senators. He didn't have an agenda, but he liked to know if there was ever a problem, he had contact information for senior staff in the senator's office.

The group of twenty or twenty-five attendees was eclectic, as always. A few businesspeople, some retirees, a handful of what he would guess were activists representing different causes. The lunch would follow a familiar pattern—once the senator arrived and everyone was seated, they would go around the room and introduce themselves. The senator would make a few remarks, then open up the room to questions. Some ninety minutes later, it would all be over.

The room was set up with a long table in the center. The senator's seat was identified with a sweater thrown across the back. A few eager souls had already claimed the seats on either side. Thaddeus wondered what it said about a person that they were so determined to be close to power. He preferred to get the lay of the land, so to speak, then sit where he could observe what was going on. If he had something he wanted to discuss with the senator, he would make an appointment, not sidle up at a luncheon.

"Hello."

He turned and saw an attractive woman approaching. She wore a well-tailored suit and high heels. Her dark red hair hung down her back and her stride was confident. He would guess she was about his age. Her name tag identified her as Perri.

"A fan of the senator?" she asked, stopping in front of him.

"I am."

"Me, too." She smiled, then tilted her head. "You own a business. Hmm, let me guess. Not aerospace or retail." She took one of his hands in hers and rubbed her fingers across his palm. "Not construction. So finance?"

"Real estate."

"I own several day spas."

"Are the ladies of Seattle into that sort of thing?"

The smile returned. "They are. Lucky me."

She wore large diamond studs and an expensive watch. Not a surprise considering the lunch tickets were a thousand dollars a seat.

She released his hand. "Too bad your wife couldn't make it."

Hardly subtle, but then he preferred women who got right to the point. "I'm not married."

"Me, either."

They looked at each other.

Thaddeus knew what came next. They would sit together at the lunch and exchange a few words. At the end of the meal, she would offer her card and suggest they get together.

On the surface, she seemed to have much of what he was looking for. She was bright, successful, attractive and confident. He should be intrigued.

"Can you excuse me for a moment?" he asked.

"Of course."

He walked toward the front of the restaurant. When he was outside, he scrolled through his contacts and placed a call.

Unity picked up on the first ring. "Hi. It's the middle of the day. Shouldn't you be working?"

"I could say the same thing about you."

"I am working. I'm just finishing up hanging a replacement blind in the bedroom."

"And then what?"

"I go back home and work on tomorrow's schedule."

"Want to go rock climbing instead? There's a place right there in town."

She laughed. "Don't you have an empire to run?"

"I have good staff. So yes or no on the rock climbing?"

"I'd love to."

"Great. I'll see you in about three hours."

He walked to the parking garage across the street and collected his car, then headed across Lake Washington, back to Bellevue. He would stop at his condo and get changed, then drive out to Willowbrook. Anticipation made it difficult not to speed. He had no idea what it was about Unity that got to him, but he'd already made the decision to simply see this thing through. When she was out of his system, he would be able to move on. Until then, he had a date with a beautiful woman.

It was only when he was driving across Snoqualmie Pass that he realized he'd never gone back to the luncheon. Oh, well, he thought. Apparently he and Perri were not meant to be.

He made good time and pulled up in front of Unity's house about fifteen minutes earlier than he'd expected. She must have been watching for him because she came out before he'd turned off the car engine.

She had on leggings and a T-shirt, with her hair pulled back in a ponytail. She looked long, lean and sexy as hell, which meant he was in all kinds of trouble.

"Hi," she said as she got in next to him. "I've never been rock climbing before. This is going to be fun."

He pulled away from the curb. "How coordinated are you, anyway?"

She slapped his arm. "Hey, you. I'll have you know

I'm very athletic. I was a swimmer back in high school. I almost made it to the state championships."

"What were your events?"

"Backstroke, freestyle and the individual and team medley."

He glanced at her. "Swimming isn't rock climbing."

"Oh, like you rock climb all the time."

"I've done it a time or two."

"Don't get all smug," she told him. "For all you know, I'm a natural."

They arrived at the athletic center and were directed to the rock climbing wall. Once Unity had put her bag in a locker, they walked into the tall, open room that held four different heights of rock climbing walls.

She stared up, then glanced around. "They really are walls."

"What did you expect?"

"I don't know. I thought maybe it was a metaphor."

He grinned. "It's a wall."

"I can see that."

He led her around the area. "There are different types of climbs. Easy to challenging. We'll start with easy. You're going to wear a harness and you'll have a spotter. Don't worry if you fall. He'll catch you and lower you to the ground."

She scoffed. "I'm not going to fall."

"You're very confident."

"There is butt kicking in your future." She turned and walked back to the beginner's wall, her ponytail swaying with each step.

He waited while she stepped into her harness, then helped her adjust the leg and waist loops. He ignored the feel of her body as his fingers brushed against her.

When she was secure, he handed her a helmet then stepped back to watch.

"You're not climbing with me?" she asked.

"I want to see how you do first."

"Prepare to be amazed."

Her belayer—the spotter—gave her a few basic safety instructions, then took hold of her rope. Unity reached for the first holds and started to climb.

She went slowly, carefully choosing her handholds, then moving her feet. She got about eight feet off the ground before stopping.

"The green one on your left," Thaddeus called out helpfully.

"I don't like that one."

"Why not?"

"I don't want to let go to grab it."

"You'll still be holding on with your other hand and your feet are secure."

She eyed the green hold but didn't reach for it.

"Is it the height or letting go?" he asked.

"Do not make this into a metaphor about my life," she told him, her voice sounding determined.

He saw her tense, then she stretched out toward the green hold. And promptly slipped. She reached again, lost her footing and fell toward the mat-covered floor. Her belayer held the rope, then slowly lowered her down until she was standing.

Thaddeus moved next to her. "You okay?"

She was pale, but she straightened and squared her shoulders. "I can do this."

"I know you can."

Thirty minutes later, Thaddeus had to admit that while Unity had grit and a strong will, she had zero rock climbing skills. She didn't want to let go of the holds she had and she couldn't seem to keep her feet from slipping.

"But I'm athletic," she said on her fifth tumble. "I'm strong. Some old lady told me I was a big, strapping girl."

"Maybe you'd do better at golf," he teased.

"I need to be better at something."

"Do you still swim?"

"No."

"Then how about that?"

She looked at the wall and sighed before taking off her helmet. "I can wait while you scamper up to the top."

"I don't scamper."

"But you can get to the top."

He glanced up at the wall. "Not a problem. Do you need to see it to believe me?"

"No." She sounded glum. "I thought I'd be good at this."

"It takes practice."

"I didn't get above eight feet. That's pathetic."

"How about I buy you a burger to make up for it?"

"I could eat a burger."

He helped her out of the harness, then waited while she collected her bag. Unity paused to study the bulletin board where they offered classes.

"Maybe I should try a beginner session," she said. "A lesson might help."

"I'm thinking the swimming is a better option. Is there a club in town?"

"Uh-huh. I've never joined but I should look into it for sure. At least there I know what I'm doing." She paused by his car. "First the tattoo incident and now this. What if I'm a loser?"

He stared into her blue eyes and fought the need to kiss her. Just one over-the-top, on-the-mouth kiss. But it would only be good if she kissed him back and he had no idea if she would.

"You're not a loser. You're challenged."

She glared at him, then got in the car.

"We are so not speaking," she grumbled when he settled in beside her.

"Is this where I remind you of the burger I offered?"

"I can't be bought."

"Want to bet?"

She laughed. "Okay, I can be but I don't want to talk about it."

He drove them to the local burger place. They went inside and claimed a table. Unity flipped through the menu before glancing at him.

"May I order a chocolate shake?" she asked.

"Yes. You have to keep up your big, strapping girl strength."

She put her arms on the table and dropped her head to them. "I'm a disaster," she groaned.

"In many ways, yes."

Not able to stop himself, he reached out and lightly stroked her head. Her hair was soft against his fingers. He suspected the rest of her would be, as well.

If wishes were horses, he thought to himself, reaching for his own menu.

Unity straightened. "I'm done whining," she announced. "I want to talk about you."

Their server came and they ordered. As promised, Unity asked for a chocolate shake with extra whipped cream, along with a bacon burger and fries. Thaddeus went with iced tea and a regular cheeseburger.

When they were alone again, Unity looked at him expectantly.

"What?" he asked. "I'm not going to start sharing random facts about myself. What do you want to know?"

"You said before you followed a girl to Las Vegas. And that you put yourself through school. Was this when you were doing construction? That must have been hard. And how did you get from that to investing?"

He'd wondered if the question would come up, although he hadn't decided how he would answer it. Generally, he avoided the truth. People—women—frequently got the wrong impression.

No, he mentally amended. There was nothing wrong with their impression. It was their reaction he had trouble with.

Her eyes widened. "You're not sure what to say. That means there's a secret."

"You sound happy about the possibility."

"Sure. I don't have any secrets. I never have. My life is pretty much what you see." She leaned forward, her expression eager. "Tell me. Please? Tell me, tell me, tell me."

Their server brought them their drinks. Unity ignored the massive chocolate shake in front of her, instead staring at him with both delight and intrigue—an irresistible combination that made him unable to deny her anything.

"I told you the girl I followed to Las Vegas was a dancer."

She nodded eagerly.

"When we met, I didn't know how to dance. Not beyond what you do in high school and at clubs. I really liked her and wanted to impress her, so I took lessons."

"That's so romantic. She must have been excited when you first took her out dancing."

"She was, but the real surprise was that I had some ability. Dancing came easily to me."

Unity dipped her spoon into her milkshake and tasted it. "No wonder Dagmar wants you to come and dance with her. Oh!" She stared at him. "Dagmar wanted to be a dancer when she was younger but her parents would have disapproved, so she became a librarian. You probably get your ability from her."

"She told you about that?"

"Uh-huh." Unity licked her spoon again, distracting him with the sight of her tongue. "Go on."

It took him a second to remember where he'd been in the story. "When Amari and I moved to Las Vegas, she had a job in a big production show, but I couldn't get work in construction. There weren't any jobs and without a job, I couldn't get into the union—"

Unity interrupted him with a sigh. "Amari? Is that her name? It's beautiful. She was really pretty, huh?"

"Yes, she was."

"That's nice."

It had been but right now he was more concerned about her lack of jealousy. If nothing else, Unity was doing an excellent job of keeping him humble.

"I was doing odd jobs when someone we knew mentioned open auditions for a show I could be in."

Unity smiled encouragingly. "Did you try out?"

"I did."

"And you got in?"

He nodded.

She smiled happily. "That's so great. What was the show?"

He had no idea what she was going to say or do, but knew that she was likely to surprise him.

"I was a stripper."

UNITY WAITED FOR the rest of the sentence. Some addition that would change the meaning. Like "I'm kidding. I worked as a clown." But Thaddeus only watched her watch him, as if gauging her reaction.

"A stripper?" she asked.

He nodded.

"You took off your clothes."

"Down to a G-string."

"I don't know what that means," she admitted. "I understand all the words and I know what a stripper does, but you can't have been one."

"Why not?"

"Because I know you and it's just too unexpected."

Their server returned with their food. Unity immediately reached for a french fry. A stripper. She tried to picture it, wasn't sure if she wanted to, then realized even if she did, she couldn't.

"I have no experience with strippers," she admitted. "I've never seen anything like that."

"Why does that not surprise me?" He picked up his burger. "I did it for about seven years. The money was good, especially after I became a headliner. I put myself through college, bought a house, moved my mom in with me."

"If you made that much money, you must have a really great body," she blurted before she could stop herself. "I'm not sure I could earn enough to buy a coffee if I took my clothes off."

He'd just swallowed and started to choke. Unity watched him anxiously until he motioned that he was fine.

"It's not about perfection," he told her. "It's about making the audience happy."

"Yeah, I couldn't do that, either. How did you get into investing?"

"Someone I knew was starting a business and needed cash. I helped him out. The business took off. I invested in a few apartment buildings and they did well. I got a divorce and my mom passed away the same year. That's when I packed it up and moved to Seattle."

"To be close to Dagmar?"

"She's my only family. I tried to get her to move over to Bellevue with me, but she's a stubborn lady."

"She loves Silver Pines. She would never leave it."

"That's why I make the drive."

Stripping. She couldn't imagine. "Was it difficult to do? At the audition?"

"Not really. They tell you to come in with a bathing suit on, so it's not that big a deal. The guy who told me about the auditions gave me some pointers. I took a few classes." He watched her as he spoke. "You don't seem upset."

"Why would I be upset? You mean morally?" She shook her head. "No. I have no problem with that. It's more the strangeness of it. Like I just found out you have a llama herd or something."

"A llama herd?"

"I've never known anyone with llamas. It must have been hard working nights. I know people do, but it's not our bodies' natural rhythm. I would guess entertainers have a whole different sleep cycle. I get up early—I'm not sure I could adjust."

Thaddeus's expression was unreadable, but if she had to guess, she would say he was wondering when she'd grown her second head.

"What?" she demanded.

"That's your big concern? My sleep cycle?"

"What did you expect? How do most women act?" She ate another fry, then wrinkled her nose. "Oh, no. Do they ask you to strip for them? That could be awkward. I mean if it was organic to the moment, but to have someone you care about expect that sort of thing... It could be demeaning. Or maybe dehumanizing. One of the *D* words. I absolutely could not handle that."

She looked at him and grinned. "No offense. I couldn't handle anyone stripping. Seeing another man naked? I would totally freak out."

The two-headed look returned. "Why? Guys pretty much all look the same."

"Yes, but I've only ever seen Stuart naked."

"Now you're the llama farmer."

She waved her burger. "Why is that shocking?"

"You've only been with one guy?"

"That's not unusual. I was a virgin when we married." She smiled. "Well, maybe not technically. But it was really close."

"How was it close?"

"I felt guilty that we'd had sex."

Thaddeus laughed. "Guilt counts?"

"Yes. Everybody knows that. Anyway, we started dating young. He was the only guy I dated or kissed or anything." She took a bite and chewed. "I think it was because I lost my family. I was looking to belong somewhere and Stuart made that possible. We could belong to each other."

"That's very insightful."

And unanticipated, she thought, in surprise. She hadn't married Stuart to belong—she'd married him because she loved him. There was no other reason.

"So what's your thing with llamas?" Thaddeus asked.

"I've never known what you used them for," she admitted, grateful for the change in subject. "Alpacas have those fibers, but what do llamas do? Aside from spit?"

"You have a fancy smartphone. You could look it up."

"Later," she told him. "Then I'll report back."

fourteen

AFTER DINNER, Unity and Thaddeus decided to catch a movie. When it was over, he drove her home. Despite the fact that it was close to nine, it was still light outside. The sun had set, but the last rays had yet to fade.

Unity found herself getting more and more nervous as they approached her house and she had no idea why. They'd had a great time with each other. Being around him was always so easy. Yes, she'd sucked at rock climbing, but at least she'd tried. She'd learned more about him and she had a homework assignment to study up on llamas. So why was there a knot forming in her stomach and a sense of impending doom?

When they reached the house, Thaddeus turned off the engine and got out of the car. She did, as well, oddly reluctant to walk to the front door. She told herself not to be ridiculous, that she was fine. This was her neighborhood, it wasn't even totally dark. What was she afraid of?

"This was fun," she said as they reached the front porch and she faced him. "Thank you."

"You're welcome."

His dark gaze locked with hers. The tension inside of her doubled in size and she wanted to throw herself inside the house. But first there was the pesky matter of getting out her key, then opening the door, and right now both tasks seemed impossible.

He took a step closer. She was torn between backing away and staying where she was. The indecision gave him just enough time to reach up and cup her face in his hands.

The feel of warm skin against her own immobilized her. She could only watch as he moved closer, then lightly brushed his mouth against hers.

The kiss was soft and brief, barely any contact. She wasn't sure she even felt it. She was too caught up in the fact that, for the first time in her life, a man other than Stuart had kissed her.

Oh, there had been kisses on the cheek from friends, but nothing like this. Nothing that was romantic. No, she told herself. Not romantic. Sexual.

He drew back enough to meet her gaze. "You okay?"

Her nod was automatic and possibly a lie, but she wasn't going to admit she was uncomfortable with something that innocuous.

He leaned in again, pressing his mouth to hers. This time he lingered and she felt the heat of his body, the sensation of his lips against hers. Everything was unfamiliar. She was used to kissing Stuart and this wasn't that. But it wasn't awful, either. Thaddeus smelled nice.

When he dropped his hands to her waist, he didn't grab her and pull her close. He held her loosely, as if he wanted her to know she could pull away at any second.

He slowly moved back and forth, just enough to create a little friction. Her lips seemed to become more sensitized and she nearly dropped her bag so she could wrap her arms around him. Deep down inside, she felt a familiar spiraling need as the most female part of her struggled to come back to life.

Without thinking or planning, she put her free hand on his shoulder and parted her lips in a silent invitation. He lightly touched the tip of his tongue to hers, then withdrew.

He stepped back and gave her a rueful smile. "I don't think we should push it," he told her. "Good night, Unity."

He walked to his car and waited until she let herself inside, then he drove away. She stood in the living room, her body painfully awakening, making her uncomfortable, and her lips still tingling from Thaddeus's kiss.

THE BUS PULLED into Santa Barbara late in the morning. The drive had been quiet, with most of the teens dozing on the way. Ellen appreciated the chance to relax in her seat, enjoying the scenery on the way up from Los Angeles.

As they drove into the city, she moved to sit behind Keith.

"We're going to be too early to check in to the hotel," she said. "But I'd like to swing by anyway and make sure the rooms are all blocked to be close together."

"Sounds like a plan. We can have lunch there, then head down to the beach. There's a place to buy kites. I thought the guys would enjoy flying them before they have to get dressed up for tonight."

UC Santa Barbara was hosting an evening for potential freshmen. Over a hundred had been invited, including their eleven. The program began at four and went until eleven. There was a dinner, speakers who would talk about life on campus and a chaperoned party where the students could get to know each other.

Lissa joined Ellen. "Are you talking about this afternoon?"

"We are," her dad told her. "Want to go fly kites?"

Lissa sighed heavily then turned to Ellen. "Want to go shopping? There are some cute boutiques downtown. I remember them from last year."

Ellen met Keith's gaze in the mirror. He gave her a slight nod.

"Sure," she said easily. "Let's do that. I can't remember the last time I shopped in a boutique. I'm sure the prices will make me faint and then you can use your first aid certificate knowledge to revive me."

Lissa grinned. "We'll find you some cute clothes. That will make you feel better. Are you two going out to dinner or something while we're on campus?"

"We haven't talked about it," Ellen said. She'd forgotten they had a night off. "We should do something."

Keith grinned at her. "I promise not to make you starve."

Two hours later Ellen and Lissa walked along State Street. The sidewalks were busy for a weekday afternoon. The temperature was in the midseventies, the sky was a perfect California blue.

"This is the life," Ellen said with a sigh.

"Being on a bus with ten teenage guys?"

"I was thinking more of the not having to go to work and visiting new places."

Lissa grinned. "Not the bus part."

"No. How are you holding up? Are they starting to get on your nerves?"

Lissa shook her head. "I'm used to it. I was little when Dad was still in the NFL, so I don't remember that. Just his coaching. Guys have always hung out at the house and stuff." Her smile faded. "My mom didn't like that students would show up without warning."

"She's still in Missoula, right?"

"Uh-huh. She remarried and has a couple of kids."

"Do you see her much?"

Lissa stopped walking and stared at a window display. "Not really. I've visited a few times, but it never goes well. She's busy with the family she has now."

Ellen knew there was a lot of information in those three sentences. "Do you want to see her more?"

Lissa touched the glass. "No. She's not interested in me." She glanced at Ellen. "She rarely calls or texts. She used to but it got less. I think she picked my dad because she wanted to be married to a guy in the NFL. The fame and stuff. She had me to keep him."

Ellen tried to hide her shock. "Sweetie, you can't know that."

"I can guess. I was really little, but I remember them fighting. She would tell him he had to try harder to become a star. He got mad because of course he was trying. When he started coaching, she wasn't happy. It wasn't what she wanted. I don't think she wanted me, either."

Ellen put her arm around Lissa, not sure what to say.

I'm sure she loves you came to mind, but there was no way to know if that was true.

"She sounds like a really dumb person," she said instead. "I think you're amazing and I would love to have you as my daughter."

"Thanks."

"Your dad thinks the world of you. You know that, right? He loves you and is so proud of you."

Lissa stepped away. "I know, but everything is different now."

"In what way?

"With me growing up and all. It won't be the way it was."

"No, but you can still be close. Your dad isn't going to turn his back on you, Lissa. Do you believe that?"

Lissa nodded, but didn't look convinced. Ellen knew there was friction between father and daughter. While she wondered if the answer was buried in their conversation, she couldn't figure out what it was.

Lissa pointed to the boutique. "Let's go in there. We'll both find cute dresses."

"I have higher hopes for you than me. They don't look like an old lady place."

Lissa grinned. "You're not that old. There will be something you'll like."

They went inside and looked around. Ellen saw cuteness everywhere. The dresses, the tops, the little flirty skirts. Then she glanced at the price tags and worried that she really would faint. These were not outlet store prices.

Lissa joined her. "You look funny."

"Everything is so expensive."

"Sometimes you have to pay retail."

"That violates my upbringing."

"Maybe it's time to be a rebel."

"Maybe I'd rather have a savings account."

Still, the clothes were tempting. She wandered over to the sale rack and found several dresses that called to her. She picked three and went back to the dressing room. Lissa went into the one next door and they took turns modeling their outfits.

Lissa came out in a plain white sheath dress. The color contrasted with her tanned skin and dark hair, and showed off her perfect body without revealing anything.

"Wow," Ellen said. "Just wow. You look incredible. I'm torn. The girl side of me says to go for it. The parent side of me says your dad will lock you in your room."

Lissa laughed. "I know. It's a total win." She pointed to Ellen's dress. "You look amazing, too. That's the best one of the three."

The dress was lined black lace and sleeveless. The deep V dipped lower than she was comfortable with, but still worked with her bra. The fit and flare style flattered, although she was a little nervous about the skirt ending several inches above her knee.

"I don't know," she said, glancing at herself in the mirror. "There's a lot of cleavage."

"Duh. That's the point." Lissa's expression turned impish. "Make sure you wear a thong so if you twirl, everyone gets a show."

"Lissa!"

The teen giggled.

"A thong. As if." She didn't own any thongs. Just her regular bikini panties.

A saleswoman stopped by and smiled. "You both

look fabulous." She held out a black push-up bra. "I took a chance and guessed you're a thirty-four C."

Ellen took the undergarments. "I am."

"Then see what the right foundations can do." The woman left.

Ellen looked at Lissa. "I can't wear a push-up bra."

Lissa pointed to the dressing room. "You have to try it on. Just to see."

Ellen retreated to her dressing room where she took off the dress and put on the bra. She looked at herself in the mirror and felt her jaw drop. Holy crap—where had those come from? Her breasts were high and full and even she was impressed. She slid the dress over her head and zipped it, then returned her attention to the mirror.

"I don't think I can go outside like this," she admitted.

Lissa opened the door and started to laugh. "You have to buy that, Ellen. You really do."

"No one needs to see this much breast."

"You're not showing anything you shouldn't. Be brave. Go for it."

Modesty battled with the reality of how sexy she looked. In the end, she took the bra and the dress and even a black thong. Then, because she didn't have any shoes to wear with the dress, they had to go find a pair of strappy sandals and a little evening clutch.

They met Keith as they returned to the hotel. He glanced at the shopping bags they both carried.

"Should I be worried?" he asked, hugging his daughter. "Is my credit card crying?"

"Just two dresses and some shoes," Lissa told him.

"Just, huh." He looked at Ellen. "What about you?"

Be brave, she told herself before saying out loud, "I

have a new dress, too. We need to go somewhere nice for dinner."

He grinned. "We're going fancy, huh? I'll make reservations."

"I need to run," Lissa said, heading for the elevator. "The bus will be here soon and I have to curl my hair."

Keith watched her go. "Are the dresses okay? Should I be worried?"

Ellen thought of the white sheath. "All the scary bits are covered."

"That's a relief." He glanced at her shopping bags. "What did you buy?"

She smiled. "You'll have to wait and see."

UNITY WALKED INTO the bedroom she used as an office and stared at her computer, not sure what to do. Curiosity battled with a sense of propriety. It would be wrong to invade Thaddeus's privacy, she told herself, only to have a voice in her head whisper that if the man was so very concerned about privacy he probably shouldn't have worked as a stripper.

She inched toward her chair, finally settling in place and going online. Once there, she hesitated. Maybe there weren't any videos of him, um, dancing. Maybe nothing was posted. Maybe she was worried for no reason.

Cautiously, she typed his name in the search bar, then pushed Enter. The page filled with information about his company, articles in *The Seattle Times* about various acquisitions and a link to his LinkedIn profile.

She moved the cursor to the search bar and added the word *stripper* after his name. The page loaded again, this time giving her links on YouTube and several Facebook pages, along with articles with headlines like "The Most Fantasized About Man in Las Vegas." She clicked on the first video, then drew back in her chair and braced herself.

The video quality was grainy and the sound was hard to hear, but there was no mistaking the stage and the pounding beat of the music. A man stood in the center, smiling at the crowd. He was barefoot and wearing only pants and a shirt, and yes, it absolutely was Thaddeus.

Unity held in a shriek, closed her eyes, then opened them again. After a couple of seconds he started to move, his body keeping time. He turned and strutted and slid across the stage, his perfect body on display. He was all muscle, but lean rather than bulky.

As she watched, he began to unbutton the shirt. The crowd screamed for him to take it off. Women threw themselves on the stage and had to be dragged away. Thaddeus took his time, going slowly, one button then another until the shirt was open.

He left it that way, dancing more, letting his movements open the shirt more and more until he finally pulled it off and tossed it to the crowd.

The women jumped for it, tearing the fabric into pieces and holding up their trophy of scraps. Onstage he continued to move, showing off his chiseled chest. A woman jumped onstage and ripped off her shirt. She had large breasts that bounced as she ran toward him.

Rather than retreat, he danced toward her, staying at arm's length, but moving around her. Seconds later, security pulled her off stage.

Thaddeus watched her go for a second, gave a little shrug, then turned his attention back to his audience.

Unity heard cries of "I need you, Thaddeus" and "Take me, please. I'll do anything you want."

The beat of the song increased, as did the screaming. Without warning, Thaddeus grabbed the sides of his pants and gave a sharp tug. The garment split along the side seam and he pulled them away. Dressed only in a G-string, he paused to let them enjoy the show. Seconds later, the video ended.

Unity closed the window and tried to make sense of what she'd seen. Despite the visual proof, she couldn't reconcile the man she knew with the man in the video. Thaddeus was nothing like that. He was funny and kind and he loved his aunt. She couldn't imagine him dancing like that in front of her. She would die of embarrassment.

She wasn't offended by what he'd done—if she had to pick an emotion, she would say she was confused. Obviously he'd done well and used the money and time to prepare for the next stage of his life, which spoke well of his character. She supposed part of the problem was the sexuality of it all. In her world, that stuff was private.

She clicked on one of the articles about him and scanned the text. Thaddeus had been voted the man women would most like to make love with three years in a row.

"Oh, honey, I've been married ten years," one fan told me for this article. "When I've had a bad day with the kids and my husband gives me the look, I know I just have to picture Thaddeus and I'm good to go. That body, those hands, the way he fills his G-string. It's all so yummy. I hear the music in my head and it's about five seconds to launch."

Unity felt her eyes widen. "Maybe people are different in Las Vegas," she murmured aloud.

She couldn't imagine thinking about someone else while making love with her husband. She'd only ever thought of Stuart. And if she were with a different man, she would be thinking of him. Not that she was going to have sex with someone else. She was—

She stood as unexpected tears burned in her eyes. Was that true? Was she never going to make love ever again in her entire life? Was she done with that?

Stuart was gone and she didn't plan on being with anyone else, so not having a sexual partner was a natural outcome. She would be fine. She didn't really need that kind of closeness or touching.

"But I don't want to give any of that up."

The words were forced out of her, against her will. She took a step back, as if moving away from whatever had caused her to speak. But there was no escaping the truth. She wasn't just lonely—she wanted to have sex. She wanted the touching, the tasting, the heat. She wanted need and release and the closeness after.

Worse, when she closed her eyes, the man she pictured wasn't faceless. He wasn't a stranger. He was Thaddeus. It was his hands on her body, his smile that made her giddy, his body pleasing hers. She could accept generic wanting, that was human. But this need wasn't generic at all.

As the thoughts formed, her body responded. Her breasts became more sensitive and a heaviness grew, low in her belly. The sensation fanned out, making her uncomfortable.

"No," she said, hurrying out of the room, as if she could outrun the need. "I don't want him. I don't."

In the kitchen she leaned against the counter and closed her eyes. But instead of remembering what it was like with Stuart, she felt Thaddeus's mouth on hers. She wanted more of that. She wanted his lips, his tongue and then she wanted his hands on her—

"I can't."

But instead of a scream, her voice was a whimper. She sank onto the floor and curled up on the hard linoleum, telling herself there wasn't any need. No desire gripped her. The memories were enough because she loved Stuart. She would always love Stuart. She'd married him because they were meant to be together.

I think it was because I lost my family. I was looking to belong somewhere and Stuart made that possible. We could belong to each other.

She sat up. "That wasn't why," she said loudly. "Stuart and I fell in love. We did!"

Even as she battled the past and what might be the truth, in the back of her mind, she could see Thaddeus moving around the stage. She saw him take off his shirt, then his pants, and she hated herself for the steady wanting that pulsed between her legs.

fifteen

"HOLY SHIT."

Keith knew it was too late to call back the words, but that was the least of his problems.

Why was this happening to him? He worked hard at his job, he went out of his way to be there for the kids he coached and spent many an hour lying awake, worrying about his daughter. So why, exactly, was his life falling into the toilet?

"What?" Ellen asked, staring at him from the doorway of her hotel room. She flushed and looked down at herself. "Too much?" Her shoulders slumped. "Sorry. I'll go get changed."

He managed to drag his gaze from incredibly impressive cleavage and pull his mind out of the gutter in time to quickly clear his throat and say, "No. Sorry. You look amazing." He gave her a rueful smile. "You knocked me on my ass. I wasn't braced. I'm braced now."

She worried her bottom lip, which made him want to kiss it. And her. All over. Yup, that would do it. He would start at the bottom and work his way up. No, he would spend about an hour on her breasts and *then* he would start at the bottom and work his way up. He would part her legs and take her places she'd never—

"I need a drink," he said, reaching for her hand and pulling her into the hallway. "You're spectacular. Own it and ignore me being a guy with his head up his butt."

She pressed a hand to her chest. "You sure it's not too much?"

"Oh, it's too much and that's why it works." He tugged on her hand. "Come on, wild girl. We have dinner reservations."

The restaurant the hotel had recommended was only a block away. Keith found himself enjoying the feeling of Ellen's hand in his. Technically this wasn't a date, so he should probably let go, but if she didn't object, he was going to enjoy the sense of connection their linked fingers gave him.

They were quickly shown to their table. It was only when they were seated across from each other that he realized he was going to have to keep reminding himself he was having a conversation with Ellen and not her breasts.

Ellen ordered a cosmopolitan and he got a vodka tonic. When their server left, he said, "Has Cooper mentioned anything about his dad yet?"

"No." She picked up her fork and put it back down. "I'm determined to let him tell me himself. At some point he has to. He can't just disappear for a week or two." She managed a smile. "Besides, someone has to drive him to the airport."

"Are you still upset?"

"Less than I was. You're right. I'm not going to lose him, even though that's what it feels like. He'll tell me. I just wish he already had."

He reached across the table and squeezed her hand. "Want me to slap him around for you?"

She laughed. "Thank you but I'm good." Her smile faded. "Lissa and I talked when we went shopping today."

His good mood vanished. He pulled back his hand and told himself whatever it was, he could handle it.

"Is she pregnant?"

"What?" Her voice was a shriek. She looked around, then lowered it. "No. Why do you always go there?"

"It's the worst-case scenario."

"No, it's not. There are plenty things much worse than an unexpected pregnancy."

He remembered she'd had to deal with one and winced. "Sorry. You're right."

Their server brought the drinks. When he'd left, Ellen said, "Lissa talked about her mom. She thinks Becky only had her to keep you around."

He sagged back in his chair. "She said that?"

"Kind of." She sighed. "Yes, but it was more the point of the conversation that concerned me." Her tone gentled. "I know they don't see each other much."

"Or at all. Once Lissa and I moved here, Becky lost interest. I've been worried about that. I love Lissa, but I'm not always enough." He looked at her. "What with being a guy and all."

"You do have your flaws, but you're a great dad. I'm sorry Becky is such an indifferent mother. That must hurt both of you. Was she like that when you were still married?"

"Some. I was way more excited about the pregnancy than she was." He grimaced. "Becky was always on me about my football career. She seemed to think if I tried harder, I could become a starter and a star. That was her goal. It wasn't like I didn't want that, too."

He'd worked as hard as he knew how. He'd taken his body to the limits of his endurance, then had pushed past them. There was skill and there was experience and then there was a God-given gift. He had the first two but the last one had eluded him.

Oh, he'd been good. No one got as far as he did without talent, but that extra ability needed to cross the line to greatness had eluded him.

"When I finally retired from the NFL, our marriage really suffered," he said. "Becky hated everything about my coaching job at the community college. In a twist of fate I can't explain, she loved the town. Just not me."

"What about Lissa?"

He tried to remember. "I guess she lost interest in her, too." He thought about all that had happened, all he never talked about. "She cheated. That's why we finally split up."

Ellen stared at him. "No way. She had an affair?"

"More than one." He tried to smile. "Ironic, huh? Not that I was ever unfaithful, but what with playing football and all, I'd be the one who was expected to do that."

"I'm sorry."

He shrugged. "I was at the time, but now I see it was her way of ending things. She wasn't subtle about it and when I gave her an ultimatum, she chose to stay with the other guy. So I moved out."

"Did you take Lissa with you?"

"We shared custody until I got the job here. When I told Becky I wanted to move, she said I should take Lissa with me. I know it was the right decision, but I hope I didn't mess her up."

Ellen smiled at him. "You did the right thing. She's great and she knows you love her."

"Then why is she acting out?"

"That, I don't know."

Their server returned with menus and told them about the specials.

"I'll give you a few minutes to decide," he said with a smile. "And don't forget tonight we have live music and dancing, starting at eight."

Ellen looked at Keith, her eyes bright. "Live music and dancing? People do that?"

"The band plays the music, but yes, people dance. You've never been—"

He stopped himself, remembering what she'd told him. Of course she hadn't been out dancing—she hadn't been on a date since she got pregnant with Coop. She hadn't done anything.

Not even make love with a man.

That unhelpful comment, compliments of some twisted part of his brain, caused him to look at her breasts, which basically emptied his mind of rational thought.

She looked around, as if trying to figure out where it all happened. "Can we… Would you…"

She wanted to stay and dance. He couldn't remember for sure, but he thought maybe it was on her list of things to do to be wild. Although dancing in a restaurant wasn't anyone's definition of wild, unless you'd never done it.

He supposed the good news was if she was that close to him, he wouldn't have to worry about being distracted by looking at her breasts.

"We'll take our time over dinner," he told her. "And then we'll dance."

"You know how, because I'm not an expert."

"We'll wait for the slow songs."

She smiled happily and reached for her cocktail. "You're the best date ever."

"I hear that all *the* time."

ELLEN SPENT DINNER in a state of anticipation. The last dance she'd been to had been her junior prom. Jeremy had taken her and later that evening, in a brief, unsatisfying encounter, he'd gotten her pregnant. She'd spent the night of her senior prom caring for a colicky newborn.

But now she was going dancing with Keith. She knew that even if she didn't know what she was doing, he would take care of her. He was good that way.

When he'd paid the bill, they made their way to the bar and sat at a small table in the back. The band was already set up and, exactly at eight, started to play.

The music was quiet, old-fashioned and slow. Perfect for dancing. Two couples got up and moved to the open floor. The women stepped into the men's arms and they began to move. She watched intently, telling herself it didn't look difficult.

"What are you thinking?" Keith asked.

"That I would do better if I wasn't wearing high heels."

He chuckled, then stood and held out his hand. "Shall we?"

Nerves clutched at her, making her want to stay where she was. But curiosity and a desire to be more than she had been had her placing her hand in his and standing.

He led her to the small area and drew her close, still holding her one hand. He put her other on his shoulder, then rested his fingers on her waist. Before she could wrap her mind around what was happening, they were moving to the soft strains of "Stormy Weather."

After a few minutes, she was able to relax. Keith used his hand at her waist to kind of direct her where he wanted to go. They moved well together and she liked being able to look up into his eyes.

"This is nice," she said. "We should have done this ages ago."

He smiled at her and pulled her closer until they were pressed against each other. She rested her head on his shoulder and put her hand on his back. Her eyes drifted closed.

Better, she thought, inhaling the scent of him and liking how secure she felt. Secure and maybe a little tingly. Her breasts were pressed against his chest and his leg brushed against hers every few steps.

The man had powerful thighs and she knew he was strong. She'd seen him working out, all sweaty with the muscles. And his hands were big.

Aware that she'd had wine after her cocktail, she thought maybe she was flirting with being a little drunk and should probably watch herself. Only...

"I'd rather watch you."

Keith shifted so he could look at her. "What did you say?"

She tried not to panic. Had she spoken that out loud? "What? Me? Nothing."

She put her head back on his shoulder, only this time she didn't close her eyes. How could she when his neck was right there, just above the collar of his shirt?

She wondered what he would taste like. Salty maybe. Had she ever tasted a man's skin before? Did it taste different than a woman's skin? The question made her giggle because she had no idea what a woman's skin tasted like. She didn't go around licking people.

"What's so funny?" he asked.

"Just thinking stuff."

He felt really good, she thought as they continued to dance. The room heated, or maybe it was just her. Every time their legs brushed she had the oddest idea that she should rub herself against his hard thigh. That would feel really good. She could rub and rub and rub.

Need began slowly, trickling down to her center. Without thinking, she let her hand drift from the center of his back to his waist. At the same time, she moved her head those few inches so that she could press her mouth against his neck and—

He swore quietly and jumped back. "What are you doing?"

The question shocked her into awareness. They were on the edge of the dance floor. No one seemed to be paying attention to them, but that didn't stop the wave of humiliation from crashing through her.

What *had* she been doing? She couldn't go around touching and kissing people. She and Keith weren't together. She had no right, and based on the way he'd reacted, he also had no interest.

Horrified at her behavior and embarrassed beyond words, she bolted for their table, grabbed her small evening clutch, then hurried out of the restaurant. Once she was on the sidewalk, she frantically tried to figure out where the hotel was so she could hide in her room until the mortification killed her.

She'd barely taken a step when a strong hand clamped down on her arm, holding her in place.

"Ellen, what's going on?"

Her cheeks were on fire. She desperately wanted to be anywhere but here, only she had no superpowers and she probably deserved to suffer for what she'd done.

"I'm sorry," she whispered staring at the sidewalk. "I'm so sorry. That was inappropriate and I never meant to try to—" She couldn't even say what had been happening. She forced herself to look at him. "I'm sorry."

She did her best not to cry. She didn't want him thinking she was playing the tears card. It was just so awful.

Keith studied her, as if trying to figure her out. "What were you doing?"

She hung her head again. "Don't make me say it. I can see you're upset and mad and you have every right to be."

"I'm not mad. I'm confused. You kissed me."

Could someone please kill her now? She nodded.

"On the neck."

Another nod.

"You touched my butt."

Her head snapped up. "I didn't. I got close, but I never actually... You know."

"Were you coming on to me?"

Oh God, oh God, oh God. "I don't know. Maybe. I'm not sure what that means. I was thinking about how nice it was in your arms and, you know, how it felt and then it all got out of hand."

He turned away and said something she couldn't hear before looking at her again.

"I wasn't mad," he told her. "I was surprised. And uncomfortable."

She'd made him uncomfortable? Had she just sexually harassed one of her closest friends?

"Oh, no. I'm so sorry. Please forgive me. It will never happen again, I promise."

"Stop," he told her. "I said that wrong. I wasn't uncomfortable because of the kiss. I liked the kiss. I was—" He swore again and pushed a hand through his hair.

"I didn't want to stand there with a giant erection, okay?" He glared at her. "You're making my life difficult, Ellen. I thought the worst thing I'd have to deal with on the bus trip was arguing teenagers, but then you bounced on board with your tight clothes and your breasts and then you get a damned tattoo on your ass."

"It's my hip," she said primly. "Hip, not ass."

"Whatever. You get it somewhere I'm not used to seeing then show it to me like I'm your hundred-and-eighty-year-old uncle. You strip down to a bathing suit and ask me to rub on lotion and talk about masturbating and toys and then kiss me. I can't take it anymore. I'm only human, Ellen. At some point, I'm going to snap."

She might not be an expert on the boy-girl thing, but he didn't sound like he minded that she'd kissed him.

If she had to guess, he was saying he was admitting he was attracted to her. As in wanting to do it with her.

"Are we talking sex?" she asked, keeping her voice low.

He glared at her. "Yes, Ellen, we're talking sex. I want to make love with you. Are you happy? I think about it all the time. It's driving me crazy. I can't stop thinking about it and just when I get myself under control, you wear a dress like that. I know I should have more control, but I don't."

The bubbles of joy nearly made her float. Keith wanted to have sex with her!

She reached for his hand. "Which way is the hotel?"

He hesitated. "Ellen, you have to be sure."

"I'm very sure. I'm seventeen years of not doing it sure. I want to feel someone else give me an orgasm."

He surprised her by smiling. "That, I can do."

They practically ran back to the hotel.

"My room," he said when they got off the elevator. "I have condoms."

"You travel with condoms?"

He flashed her a smile. "They weren't for me. I keep them around for emergencies."

"And now you have one."

sixteen

ELLEN WAS TOO excited to be nervous. It was going to happen. Finally. She was tingly and wet and excited. She wanted to do everything she'd ever read about or seen in the movies. She wanted to feel him inside of her because she really couldn't remember much about her brief encounter with Jeremy.

They went into his room. He locked the door behind them and looked at her.

"Are you sure?"

"Yes. We've talked about this. The surest of the sure." She stepped out of her shoes. "Come on. Let's do this."

He smiled. "Give me one second."

He walked over to the king-size bed and drew back the covers, then turned on a floor lamp in the corner. She danced impatiently from foot to foot as he pulled a box of condoms out of his duffel and put them on the nightstand.

When he turned to her, she launched herself across the room. He caught her in his arms and pulled her close. She rose on tiptoes, he lowered his head and they met in a kiss full of heat and hunger and need.

Ellen liked how his lips claimed hers. There was no delicate dance, just complete going for it. His tongue swept inside, tangling with hers. Excitement shot through her as she realized this was actually going to happen. All of it. Finally!

She kissed him back, stroking his tongue, then clamping her lips around it and sucking. He hauled her against him and dropped his hands to her butt, holding her still, then rubbing himself against her. It took her a second to realize he was already aroused.

She pulled back. "I want to see. I want to see!"

He stared at her. "See what?"

She pointed to his crotch. "That. I never got to see one before. Not in real life. Please? I'll show you mine."

He smiled. "That is an offer I can't refuse."

He made quick work of his shirt, then stepped out of his shoes and socks. At the same time, she unfastened her dress and stepped out of it.

His gaze locked on her body. She smiled and half turned.

"Look. I'm wearing a thong. I never have before. It's not very comfortable, but—"

He lunged for her, grabbed her around the waist, then turned her and gently bit her on the curve of her rear. When he straightened, he kissed her on the mouth.

As she moved her tongue against his, she reached behind herself, unfastened her bra and tossed it away.

His hands settled on her breasts, cupping the curves even as he moved his thumbs against her hard nipples.

Fire shot through her. She had to stop kissing him to take it all in. Every stroke was like magic, teasing her into a higher state of arousal as the feelings in her breasts traveled directly to her clit.

"Oh, wow," she breathed, meeting his dark gaze. "Keep doing that."

He smiled. "I can make it better."

"Not possible."

He nudged her toward the bed. "Go lie down."

She did as he requested. He stepped out of his jeans but left his briefs in place, which was very disappointing. But before she could complain, he joined her. After lightly kissing her lips, he shifted so he could take one of her nipples in his mouth.

The warm heat and gentle friction was incredible, she thought, letting her eyes sink closed. Better than that, even. He moved his tongue across her nipple, then sucked deeply. Pleasure shot through her, causing her to arch up toward him. He repeated the action on her other breast, sucking harder and deeper, making her whimper and beg.

She felt his hand on her thong and realized he wanted to take it off. She helped him, even though it meant not doing the breast thing anymore. But before she could complain, he moved between her legs.

"Hold yourself open," he told her, guiding her hands to the edges of her labia and parting the flesh.

She did as he requested, then watched as he lowered himself to the bed and gave her an intimate, open-mouthed kiss right on her clit.

Nothing had prepared her for the sensation of his

tongue on her. Not her fingers or the vibrators or the books or anything. It was indescribable pleasure—all hot promise and teasing touch.

She dug her heels in the mattress and spread her legs as wide as she could, wanting to feel it all. He moved at a steady rhythm designed to send her over the edge and even though she wanted that, too, what he was doing felt too good for him to ever stop.

"Keith," she breathed. "I can't believe it. What are you doing to me?"

She felt him chuckle, then gasped as he slid a finger inside of her. He pushed all the way in, then curved up and touched something she couldn't explain and then, suddenly, she was coming and coming, crying out as the wonder of it filled her. She shook and gasped and still she came, more and more and more until she was finally nothing but a panting, glorious puddle of afterglow, which would have been fine if only she hadn't started to cry.

The sobs were as unexpected as her orgasm had been. She couldn't stop and couldn't catch her breath. Strong arms pulled her close. Soft murmurs told her she would be fine. He held her and rocked her gently until she could breathe.

When she had a bit of control, she grabbed a couple of tissues from the box on the nightstand.

"Sorry. I don't know what that was."

"Emotional release."

"I guess." She drew back enough to see him. "That was amazing."

He gave her a smug smile. "Yeah?"

"You know it was."

"You didn't take long to get there."

"I never do."

One eyebrow rose. "You don't say."

They were in a bed, she was naked, she'd just had the best orgasm of her life and then she'd cried. She supposed she should feel awkward or something, but she didn't. It was all too glorious.

She tossed the tissues on the nightstand, then looked pointedly at his very large erection hiding in his briefs. "Come on. I still want to see."

The smile returned. "As you wish."

He rose and stood beside the bed before unselfconsciously taking off his briefs.

And there it was. Her first penis. Okay, not her first, but the first one she'd seen in the flesh, so to speak. He was hard and while it looked painful, she doubted it was. She reached out and put her hand around him, moving back and forth.

He groaned and took her hand away. "That's dangerous."

"Oh, right. Because if you come now, we can't have intercourse for a while." She picked up the box of condoms and shook it. "Let's do it."

"You're such a romantic."

"Hey, I've been waiting a long time for this, mister. We can do the romance thing later."

He took out a condom and put it on. She watched his practiced movements, then slid over so there was room for him on the bed. He knelt between her thighs, his gaze locking with hers.

"You're sure about this?" he asked.

"Yes." She waved her hand. "I want this. Please. Just impale me."

"Impale?"

"I thought humor would make you feel better."

"You're weird."

"Fine. Yes. Do it."

"So impatient." He braced his arms on either side of her. "It helps if you guide me inside."

She reached between them and did as he suggested. He eased inside of her, entering her slowly, as if giving her time to get used to him. She focused all her attention on how he seemed to fill her, stretching her a little, but not in a bad way.

"You okay?" he asked, staying perfectly still.

She wiggled her hips, getting used to the feel of him inside of her, then clamped down her muscles. He inhaled sharply.

"Yeah, don't do that."

She instantly relaxed. "Sorry. Did it hurt?"

He smiled. "No. It felt great, but it's been a while and I don't want this to end before it should."

"You should masturbate more. It takes the edge off."

He laughed, then stared into her eyes. "Why didn't I know about this side of you before?"

"We never talked about sex. We were an asexual couple."

"You had a secret life I never knew about." He withdrew, then pushed in her again. "Still okay?"

"Uh-huh."

What he was doing felt nice. She shifted so she could wrap her legs around his hips, which caused him to go in deeper. The steady in and out felt really good. Different than when he'd gone down on her, but still arousing. She liked how he felt inside of her. There was a completeness to it she couldn't explain—a sense of rightness.

"I'm going to go faster," he told her. "Let me know if it gets uncomfortable and I'll stop."

"You're worried about me. Is it the almost virgin thing?"

"Yes."

"That's so nice."

Later she would think about how he'd been so considerate. Later she would do a lot of things, but the second Keith increased the rhythm, she found herself unable to do anything but feel him.

The sensation of fullness expanded. She felt a pressure way down low and it spread through her in a way she couldn't explain. She tilted her hips more and pulsed so she met him stroke for stroke. Her chest tightened as her breathing quickened and her gaze locked with his.

Something was happening, she thought frantically. Something incredible.

She grabbed his hips and pulled him in deeper, straining toward what could only be another release. He went faster still, pushing in so deeply she had no choice but to surrender to the moment.

She cried out as she came, her body shuddering. She felt her muscles contracting around him and couldn't help squeezing even harder because it felt so good. He filled her twice more before groaning loudly as he found his own orgasm.

They looked at each other. One of his eyebrows rose. She smiled.

"Not bad."

He laughed. "You're a screamer."

"What? No. I didn't scream."

"It was pretty loud." He winked. "I like that."

They got up and shared the bathroom as they cleaned

up. Ellen tried to stay centered in the moment. Here she was, naked, in a hotel bathroom, with Keith, and they'd just made love. Her mind simply couldn't take it in.

But the proof was right there in front of her. And in the mirror, if she wanted to look there, which she did. The man had a great body. Every inch of him looked good.

He met her gaze in the mirror. "You're checking me out."

"I can't help it."

"Look as much as you'd like. You can touch, too. I need a little time before there will be any action, but it shouldn't be long."

She put her hand on his rear—his naked rear—and he just stood there. Emboldened, she traced the muscles in his back before circling around to the front where she ran her hands across his chest. He felt good. Warm and strong and masculine.

Without warning, he pulled her in front of him and turned her so they were both facing the large bathroom mirror. Her hair was a mess, her makeup was smudged, but what really got her attention was the satisfaction in her eyes. She looked like what she was—a woman who had been completely pleasured.

"Nice," he murmured, moving her hair so he could nibble on her neck. "Very nice."

"It is. Are we going to do it again?"

He met her gaze in the mirror. "Are you saying that it's better with me than by yourself?"

She smiled. "Yes, I am."

"I'm glad." He straightened and took her hand. "Come on. While I recover my strength, let's see how many more times I can make you scream."

"A man with a mission. I like that."

THADDEUS PUSHED THE button to dial Unity. He wanted to see her with an intensity that made him feel like a kid again. Anticipation quickened his breathing, which made him feel ridiculous, but there was no getting around the truth.

She got to him. The kiss they'd shared had kept him up nights and he wanted to repeat it. He wanted to do more, but knew that wasn't likely. Not for a while. Unity was still feeling her way.

But he wasn't. The more he spent time with her, the more he liked her. He liked how genuine she was, how she wore her heart—and her pain—on her sleeve. He liked looking at her and being with her and thinking about her. He'd been with a lot of women in his life, but she was different. She got to him in a way no one had before.

"Hello?"

He smiled at the sound of her voice. "It's Thaddeus."

"I saw your name on the screen. Hi."

"I thought maybe we could do something on Saturday. Hang out for the day. I doubt you want to give rock climbing another try but maybe we could go for a day hike. Or we could come back over here."

He told himself to stop talking. He sounded too eager and hopeful. He was the man—he should be cool.

"I can't," she said, her voice soft.

"I'm free Sunday, if that works better."

"It's not the day."

She hesitated and in that pause, he knew. It wasn't about availability. It wasn't the day—it was him.

"I don't want to see you anymore," she told him, then winced. "I'm sorry. That came out more harshly than I meant it to. I like you, it's not that. We've had fun and it's been great, but I just can't go out with you. I'm not ready to date anyone."

The surge of anger was unexpected in its intensity. He had a feeling that behind it was a truckload of hurt, but this was not the time for self-examination.

"It's been three years, Unity. What's the timeline? Five years? Ten? Never? You're thirty-four. Shouldn't you get on with your life? Isn't there something you want beyond waiting for something that's never going to happen? Are you giving up on everything? No husband, no kids, just you waiting to die?"

When he finally got himself to stop talking, he realized he'd gone too far, but what did it matter? He wasn't getting through to her.

"You know what? Forget it." He shifted the phone to his other ear. "You don't want to go out, that's fine with me. I get the message. I won't bother you again."

With that, he hung up. After tossing his phone on his desk, he picked up the report he'd been looking at it and threw it against the wall.

"This is bullshit," he growled, standing up, thinking this would be a good time to go find a fight. Only he wasn't a kid anymore and there wasn't anyone to fight. There was just anger and disappointment and the realization that he'd lost Unity. Even sadder, he'd lost something he hadn't thought he would ever find—*the one*. Stupid, but there it was.

No, he told himself bitterly. Nothing was lost. There had been nothing to lose. She wasn't gone—she'd never been available in the first place and he'd been the moron who'd refused to see that.

KEITH DROVE THE bus north toward Monterey. Despite his lack of sleep, he was feeling pretty good. The last two nights with Ellen had been incredible. She was the perfect lover—enthusiastic, easy to please and up for anything. She wanted to make up for lost time and he was happy to let that happen.

As per usual, the teens were in the back of the bus and Ellen was up front. She slid from her seat to the one behind him and smiled at him in the mirror. He smiled back.

She leaned forward, resting her arms on the bar behind the driver's seat. "So I've been thinking," she said, her voice low. "Could we do it from behind? I've always wondered about that—there are logistics—but I think we could make it work."

The image was clear enough to give him an instant hard-on. "Not while I'm driving," he told her, trying to sound stern.

"So many rules." Her smile was impish. "But fine. We'll talk about it later."

He had no doubt about that. When it came to sex, she would talk about anything. "Speaking of rules, we need to come up with a few."

"Why?"

He glanced up in the mirror, making sure his other passengers weren't in earshot.

"You can't keep running in and out of my hotel room. We'll get caught."

"You're such a worrier. So you want to put this on hold until we're back in Willowbrook?"

Go without Ellen for the next week?

"I'm not saying that."

Her smile returned. "We'll be extra careful and be sure that we set the alarm."

Last night they'd forgotten and they'd both fallen asleep, not waking until almost six. Ellen had dressed in a hurry, then bolted for her room before everyone else was up. He'd sweated one of the guys getting up early for a workout before they hit the road. Fortunately for them, everyone had slept in.

She lightly touched his shoulder. "I don't want to give this up."

"Me, either."

"Then we'll figure it out," she told him, before returning to her seat.

He hoped she was right but knew there was more than logistics while they were on the road. What happened when they got home? He and Ellen had always been friends—he liked them being friends. What were they going to do when they weren't on the bus? Date? Just have sex? Did he want them to be dating?

He liked Ellen. He liked them together—both in and out of bed. Dating could be interesting. Assuming she wanted that, too. Which they should have talked about before anything happened. Only she'd worn that dress and then she'd kissed him and he'd wanted her and now he couldn't resist her.

If it was just the best sex of his life, he knew he would be okay. But it was more than that—it was the best sex of his life with Ellen, which honestly scared the crap out of him. Not that he would change a thing, which circled back to where he'd started. Tired, happy and more than a little confused.

seventeen

"WHY DIDN'T YOU tell me sex was so great?" Ellen asked with a laugh. "I'm seriously mad at you."

Unity grinned as she sank down on the tarp-covered floor in the apartment she was painting. "When was I supposed to bring up the topic?"

"I don't know. We talk nearly every day of our lives. It would have been nice for you to mention it casually in conversation."

Unity put her cell phone on speaker, set the phone on the tarp, then stretched out next to it. "Sorry. It never crossed my mind."

"Are you kidding? It's all I can think about. I'm glowing so much, I'm practically radioactive. I know that's the hormones talking, but who cares!" Ellen sighed dramatically. "I'm having the best time."

"Make sure you pee after."

"What are you talking about?"

Unity laughed. "After sex. Make sure you pee. You don't want to get a urinary tract infection. All that action down there can cause one."

"Thanks for the tip. There is a world of things I don't know. It's embarrassing. So how are you?"

"Good." Unity knew that was a lie, but she wasn't going to talk about her ongoing funk and spoil her best friend's mood. "I'm busy with work. There were a couple of unplanned move-outs and the in-house maintenance team can't keep up with the workload, so I've stepped in. They're doing the major refurbishing, but I'm taking care of the painting."

"I'm glad you have lots of work, but please tell me you're not working twenty-seven hours a day."

"I'm not working twenty-seven hours a day," Unity told her, knowing it was true. She was working closer to eighteen. Painting was quiet, so the other people in the building didn't mind if she stayed late and started early.

Work was safe, she thought, knowing that was something else she wouldn't share with Ellen. Work kept her from feeling unsettled and confused and lonely. She didn't like where she was in her life, but she also didn't know how to change. And even though she knew she'd done the right thing, she missed Thaddeus. A realization that made her feel sick to her stomach—as if she'd somehow betrayed Stuart—something she knew wasn't true, but couldn't make herself believe, and once she went down that rabbit hole, she just wanted to curl up in a ball and sob her heart out.

"You doing anything fun?" Ellen asked. "Have you found a new pickleball league?"

"I haven't been looking but I probably should. After

the rock climbing fiasco, I know I should stick to sports I'm good at."

"You could start swimming again. You were good at that."

"I'm thinking about it."

"Do more than think. Go join the club or whatever it is. I'd tell you to have sex, because it's the best, but I don't think you're ready."

There was a muffled noise in the background. Ellen sighed.

"I have to run. Keith is calling for everyone to get on the bus."

"Where are you?"

"Close to Monterey. We'll be there in a couple of hours, then we go to the aquarium tomorrow. After that, Stanford. Yikes, he's honking the horn. That man. Love you. I'll call tomorrow."

"Love you, too."

They both hung up.

Unity scrambled to her feet. She missed Ellen and Cooper. She needed some hugging and Cooper had always been a great hugger. She wanted to hang with Ellen, talking and laughing until everything felt right again. As that wasn't likely to happen until her friend was back from her road trip, lunch was next on her list.

Unity wrapped her paint roller and tray in plastic, put the lid on the can, then turned out the lights. After making sure she didn't have any paint on her shoes, she stepped out into the hallway, then made her way to her van.

Fast food called, but she knew it would make more sense to go home. She could make a sandwich and then bring food back for dinner, so she could work straight through until nine or ten o'clock that night. If all went well, she would be too exhausted to think when she finally fell into bed.

At the stop sign at the end of the street, she saw a notice for an open house. Hesitating only a second, she made a quick left turn and followed the arrows until she parked in front of a small duplex. The yard was full of flowers, there was a big bay window and an open front door.

Unity walked up the path and stepped into the home. She wasn't familiar with the floor plan but, based on the size of the living room, assumed this was a one-bedroom with a den. Maybe twelve hundred square feet.

A man in his forties walked into the living room and smiled at her. "Good afternoon. I'm John. Are you looking for a place for your parents?"

A perfectly reasonable question, she thought, fighting both laughter and tears. Because Silver Pines was an age-restricted community and she had no business looking at houses here.

"I am," she lied, knowing she was a fool and probably needed mental professional help.

"Excellent. Do you know much about the area? The Village at Silver Pines is a wonderful community full of activities and friendly residences."

He did a quick three-minute sales pitch on the area, then took her on a quick tour of the house. She saw a nice patio off the back, the safety bar in the large walk-in shower and took the brochure he offered before thanking him and leaving. She stepped out front to find Dagmar's car blocking her van and the woman herself waiting on the sidewalk.

Unity battled guilt and a need to defend herself. She

clutched the folder to her chest as she approached her friend, knowing she was going to get yelled at, or worse.

But instead of complaining that Unity had no right to be looking at houses in Silver Pines or pointing out that instead of moving forward, she was moving backward, Dagmar only smiled at her.

"Come on back to my place. I'll make you lunch."

Unity nodded and got in her van. Ten minutes later, she was seated at the island in Dagmar's kitchen, watching the older woman set out a beautiful cheese plate along with three kinds of crackers.

"Start on that," Dagmar told her. "I'll cut up some fruit, then make you an omelet."

"I'm not that hungry."

"You should be. From the looks of things, you haven't been eating." Dagmar raised her eyebrows. "Don't try to tell me otherwise. Women lose weight in their faces first. Yours is gaunt."

Unity dutifully cut off a piece of cheese and put it on a cracker. "I've been busy."

Dagmar put out grapes, then sliced up two peaches, along with a nectarine. She slid the plate close to Unity before joining her at one of the stools.

"Busy doesn't make you sad," the older woman said bluntly. "You look sad. What happened?"

"He didn't tell you?"

"There's only one he we have in common, so no. Thaddeus hasn't said anything. I repeat my question. What happened?"

Unity desperately wished she hadn't said anything, but it was too late now. "He asked me out and I told him we shouldn't see each other anymore."

Dagmar tapped the cheese plate. "Eat. You're not eating."

"Aren't you mad at me?"

"I have no reason to be."

Dagmar tucked her hair behind her ears, revealing a bright red streak in the strands. She had on a ruffled blouse over what could only be called harem pants. Her makeup was perfect, her jewelry jangled. Just looking at her made Unity feel better.

"What happens between you and Thaddeus is your business," Dagmar told her. "I will admit to being curious about what went wrong. I thought the two of you were doing well together."

"We were. I like him. He's nice and funny and—"

Dagmar rolled her eyes. "Darling, Thaddeus simply can't be described as nice. I won't allow it. Tell me you think he's sexy and exciting and a little bit dangerous."

Unity ate more cheese on a cracker. "Sexy, yes. Dangerous? I don't think so."

"So if he's sexy and you like him, why don't you want to see him?"

Unity sighed. "I'm not ready."

She braced herself for the lecture, the angry words that made logical sense but didn't affect her heart.

Dagmar surprised her by shaking her head. "No, that's not the reason. If you really weren't ready, there wouldn't be a problem. You'd be relieved to not be going out with him. It's something else. Let me think."

Unity continued to nibble on cheese and fruit, hoping her friend would let the topic go so they could discuss something safer or easier or, hey, funny.

"Children or sex," Dagmar announced.

Unity felt her eyes widen. "Excuse me?"

"It's either children or sex. Unless it's both." She smiled. "Oh, sweet girl, have you thought about having children with Thaddeus? I would love great-great-nieces and nephews. I am wonderful with children."

"I'm not having children with Thaddeus."

"As long as you have them with someone. Regardless of the father, I want to be involved."

"I can't do that."

Dagmar's smile faded. "I know. Having children would break the rules, wouldn't it? Having a life, being happy. That's what's not allowed."

Unity fought tears and the bone-crushing pain she lived with every day. "There aren't rules," she whispered, even though she knew she was lying.

"Of course there are," Dagmar told her. "The rules keep you safe. The rules tell you what to do when you're so lost, you know you'll never be found. The rules keep you normal enough on the outside so no one notices you're dying on the inside."

Unity stared at her. "You can't know that."

"And yet, it appears I do." Dagmar patted her arm. "I told you I buried four husbands, and I loved all of them. You may think what you feel, what you're experiencing, is unique, but it's not. I'm not trying to take away from the actual pain—that is yours alone. But the experience of loss and the fear of moving on, I'm sorry to say, is fairly common."

Dagmar picked up a grape. "Do you think that one day you'll wake up and simply know it's time be yourself again? Are you waiting for an epiphany? It doesn't work like that. You have to have faith that it's going to be okay and start challenging yourself to take a little step forward."

"I've taken steps."

"And now you're retreating. Hiding from all you accomplished. Is it because you're thinking you'd like to have sex with Thaddeus?"

Unity nearly came off her stool. "Why would you say that?"

"Because you're breathing. You should hear my friends go on about him. It's not my favorite topic, let me tell you. The man is family. There are things I don't want to know." She patted Unity's arm. "I'm making an exception for you, dear. Talk away."

"I don't think about that." Unity spoke the lie proudly, then felt herself crumble. "I have thought about it. I want to."

"Have sex or have sex with him? There is a difference."

"Have sex with him."

"Interesting. And you're telling yourself you can't, and it's wrong to feel those things. It's your friend Ellen's parents, isn't it? Didn't you tell me they had all kinds of rules for their daughter and you lived with them for a while after you lost your own parents, so I suppose it makes sense that their provincial attitudes rubbed off on you."

The words came so fast, Unity didn't have time to move out of the way, so they slammed against her, right in the head and the heart.

"You think I'm doing what they would want me to do?"

"I think they're a strong influence. And as I said before, the rules do keep you safe."

"I don't feel safe. I feel scared and lost and empty."

I want a baby. The thought formed before she could

stop it and once it breathed life, she couldn't wish it away. She didn't even have to close her eyes to imagine the precious weight in her arms or inhale the sweet scent. Even as the image took form, she felt Thaddeus's warm hands on her shoulders as he stared down at the child they'd created.

Unity scrambled to her feet. Her chest felt tight and her body started shaking.

"I don't want to love anyone else," she said, the statement more hope than reality. "I don't. I *don't*."

"I'm sorry," Dagmar whispered.

"For what?"

"For you. That is so sad. Loving people is the best of who we are as a species. Our ability to love and be loved defines us. Without that, we have no purpose, no reason to live. Be careful, darling. You're in a very dangerous place. If you get much more lost, you might never find your way back."

ELLEN HAD NEVER considered herself a fish person. She'd been a math major in college, so chemistry had been pretty easy, but the biological sciences had all seemed too squishy for her. Standing in the middle of the Monterey Bay Aquarium, she wondered if it was too late to change her major.

She *loved* fish and sea creatures. The otters were adorable and the Kelp Forest was so beautiful. She was trying to identify different kinds of fish when Cooper joined her.

"Hey," she said, surprised to see him, but trying not to show it. He'd mostly been keeping his distance since Los Angeles. No doubt guilt about the plans he'd made with his father.

"This place is cool," he told her. "I didn't think it would be, but I like it."

"Me, too." She pointed to several fish swimming past them. "I think that's a rockfish. I've eaten rockfish and now I feel guilty."

Coop grinned. "You didn't eat that one."

"No, but I could have scarfed down a cousin or sibling. I'm a horrible person."

"You're not."

She glanced up at her very tall son. "Are you having a good time?"

"Yeah. Seeing the different colleges is interesting."

"Stanford's tomorrow. Are you nervous?"

He shifted his weight. "A little. I want to make a good impression."

"You will. You know what to do. You're smart and, thanks to me, you're articulate."

He raised his eyebrows. "Thanks to you?"

"Excellent genes and years of training. I know what I'm doing when it comes to the kid thing. I have mad skills."

He surprised her by hugging her. "You do, Mom."

She held on as long as he did, then released him when he stepped back.

"Let's go look at the otters," she said, pointing in the direction of their habitat. "I won't feel so guilty watching them play. I've never eaten an otter."

"Mom. No one eats otters. They're like dogs or something."

"Someone has. You know they tried."

"That's gross."

"Yes, it is."

They stood together, watching the otters swim

around. Ellen sensed there was more conversation to be had, so she kept her body language relaxed, as if she had plenty of time to wait and listen.

"I've heard from my dad," Coop told her, keeping his gaze on the playful mammals.

"I'm glad he's staying in touch. You didn't say much about your lunch with him. Did it go well?"

"We talked a lot. He's got a couple of kids. Girls. Seven and maybe five. I can't remember. I guess they're my half sisters."

Ellen did her best not to react to that bit of information. She'd known Jeremy had more children but hadn't put together that they were Cooper's half siblings. She was not happy about the connection but knew there was nothing to be done about it.

"You're good with children," she pointed out, proud of herself for sounding so reasonable. "You've been a mentor at the elementary school for three years."

"But this is different." He turned to her. "How come you never said anything bad about him? He got you pregnant, then left. He was my age. I'd never do that."

"Everyone's different. I don't think his parents were happy about what had happened. For all I know, it was their idea."

"You wouldn't want me to walk away from the girl or the baby."

She debated how to answer, then went for humor. She poked him in the chest and said, "Then wear a condom, young man. Your penis should never be naked around a girl, even if you are."

"Mo-om." He looked around, then lowered his voice. "Don't say penis. We're in public."

"Are you wearing a condom?"

He flushed. "I'm not doing that with anyone."

"You were last year."

"I had a girlfriend. And I wore a condom. Can we please stop talking about it?"

"Yes." She sighed. "Don't be mad at your dad on my behalf, Coop. You should get to know him. If you don't like who he is, then be mad at him."

"Why are you so nice about him?"

"Because he's your father. While I don't like that he disappeared on me, I like how you and I turned out. I can't miss having Jeremy around because he never was. I'm sorry for what you went through, wanting to know him, but other than that, I don't think about him."

"He should have paid child support."

"That would have been nice, but the deal we signed absolved him of that." Jeremy had given up his rights and she'd given up the promise of child support.

"You wouldn't be mad if I spent time with him?"

Finally, she thought, grateful he'd gotten around to talking about the situation. "No. I'd miss you, but then I'd have a party every night."

He didn't laugh at that. When she glanced at him, she found him studying her. "You're different, Mom. Not just the clothes, but something else."

She felt herself flushing and quickly turned back to the otters. "You're just saying that because I got a tattoo," she said, hoping to change the subject. Because she had a feeling the difference wasn't the tattoo but was instead the delicious nights with Keith.

"I can't believe you did that," he admitted.

"Me, either, but it's pretty cool." She drew her eyebrows together. "Not that I want you getting one."

He grinned. "Too late. I'm already thinking about

it." His smile faded. "I want to spend some time with Dad this summer. Fly down to see him and stay with him. You okay with that?"

No, she wasn't. She hated the thought of him with his father. She was still terrified Jeremy would be more interesting and exciting and tempt him with a fancy car and the promise of meeting movie stars. What if he went away and never came back?

But she couldn't say any of that. Whatever she was feeling, she had to think of the greater good. It was the sucky part of parenting, but no less important than all the others.

"I'll miss you," she admitted, "But if you want to get to know him, this is a really good time."

"Thanks, Mom. We've been talking about dates. We'll pick them when we get home, okay?"

She nodded rather than saying anything. She didn't want him to hear the sadness in her voice or figure out how scared she was. Her baby boy was all grown up. She'd done the best she could to raise him. Now she had to hope she didn't end up losing him forever.

"Unity, could you stay after a few minutes?" Carmen asked.

Unity had already started out of the community center meeting room, wanting to get back to work. She'd almost skipped grief group but had decided to attend at the last second. She was even more sad than she had been. No, not sad. Uneasy. She couldn't get comfortable in her own skin.

She'd been unable to forget what she and Dagmar had talked about and she'd been unable to stop thinking about what it would be like to have a baby. She and

Stuart had always talked about having a family, but somehow that had seemed more in theory than real. But the child she'd seen in her arms, the child she'd *felt*, seemed to already be alive.

She nodded at Carmen, then sat. Nothing the group facilitator had to say would be good news, she thought grimly.

As if to prove her point, Carmen began with a rueful smile followed by, "This is so difficult."

Carmen held out a piece of paper with three names and phone numbers on it. "I've been thinking a lot about your situation, Unity, and I believe the grief group isn't helping you. The average stay for our members is eight months. You've been coming here nearly three years."

She continued to hold out the paper until Unity took it.

"Any one of these counselors would be able to give you the one-on-one support you need to figure out how to heal. Regardless of who you pick, you'll be in good hands."

Unity stared at the neat printing, then looked at Carmen. "Are you throwing me out of grief group?"

"I think it's time you tried something else."

Unity nodded because there was nothing to say. She could beg to be kept around only Carmen wasn't wrong. Still, there was no denying the rejection hurt.

"I like everyone," she whispered. "I like coming here."

"I know and we like you, too. All of us. Please promise you'll contact the people on the list."

Unity nodded, mostly to get away rather than because she intended to follow through.

Carmen sighed. "You're allowed to be happy, Unity,

even after you lose someone. I wish you could believe that."

Unity rose. Carmen walked over and held her tight. "You're a wonderful person. Please stay in touch with me."

"Thank you."

Unity walked out of the room. Part of her wanted to go back and ask about the ethics of tossing out a member who was obviously in pain. Weren't there rules against that? But to what end?

She drove back to her house. Once she was inside, she sat on the living room sofa. The blows just kept coming, she thought. She wasn't welcome anywhere.

She looked at the names and the numbers Carmen had given her. A therapist would tell her she had to get busy living. That for now, going through the motions was plenty—that wanting to get better would follow action, but first she had to force herself to do something constructive. She'd been through it before—when she'd first moved back to Willowbrook.

She'd faked her way into a few activities. The grief group, pickleball. She'd hung out with Ellen and Cooper. She'd started her business. And now she was back where she'd begun, feeling awful all the time. If she was completely honest with herself, she was tired of it. Tired of feeling bad, of being lonely and sad. She wanted to be different, but didn't know how.

Her phone buzzed. Unity opened the text from Ellen to find a half dozen pictures from the Monterey Bay Aquarium—otters and fish, and one with Ellen standing between Coop and Luka, both teens dwarfing her.

Miss you. Xoxo

Unity texted back the same, then scrolled through the pictures again. Ellen looked happy.

Before she could put down her phone, Howard sent a text saying they were done with the window replacement and were heading out for tacos and did she want him to bring some back for her.

At least she had tacos to look forward to, she thought, trying to find humor in the situation. And seeing Ellen again. And hanging out with Dagmar and talking to Coop about which college had been his favorite. She had her business. She had friends who made her happy, and she had the promise of tacos. None of them were big, Stuart-size things, but it was more than a lot of people had.

Carmen was right—grief group wasn't helping. Unity didn't want to try therapy again, but she was willing to admit that she'd been miserable, she'd been stuck and neither of them had felt very good. Maybe it was time to try something else.

I'll meet you guys at the taco place, she texted Howard, then got up and walked out to her van. She was tired of being tired, she told herself. Moving backward meant more suffering, and staying stuck was just as bad. That left moving forward. There had to be an answer somewhere. All she had to do was find it.

eighteen

KEITH FELT HIS heart thundering in his chest as his body tried to recover from yet another extraordinary love-making session with Ellen. She straddled him, her long, wavy hair tumbling down her back, her whole body arched as she claimed the last ounce of pleasure from what he would guess was her third orgasm of the night. With her, it was difficult to keep track.

Not that he was complaining. Ellen was the perfect sexual partner. She was game for anything, had zero inhibitions, was always in the mood and came easily. There was no bad here.

She drew in a deep breath and gave him a satisfied smile. "You're really good at this."

"So are you."

She slid off him and stood, then stretched before turning to head to the bathroom. He watched her go, his gaze settling on her still-healing tattoo. He had to admit, the shooting star looked good on her.

She glanced over her shoulder. "Don't judge me."

He got up and followed her. "Why would I judge?"

"Because I'm ordinary and you've been with perfect." She waved her hand. "You know, back when you were a football god. You could have had anyone."

They went into the bathroom to clean up. He met her gaze in the mirror.

"Have I or my dick ever given you a reason to think you're not perfect?" he asked.

She laughed as she passed him a washcloth. "You're not separate entities."

"The question still stands."

"No. You have both been gratifyingly eager."

He pulled her close and kissed her. "Then accept your level of perfection."

"If I must."

They returned to bed and pulled up the sheets. Ellen snuggled close, her head on his chest, her legs tangled with his.

He liked this part, too, he thought. The touching, the talking. The connection.

"The Stanford visit went well," she said. "Coop loved everything about the campus."

"The coach was excited about him. He said he would be a good member of the team. I think he's got a shot."

"Me, too. It would be a good fit." She raised herself up so she could meet his gaze. "The best part was him talking about going there. I think he's starting to realize that I'll be perfectly fine on my own." She flopped back down. "I'll miss him like crazy but I want him to be free to follow his dreams without worrying about me."

"You're a good mom."

"I hope so. I still hate Jeremy, which makes me less of a good mom."

He smiled. "I think you're allowed to hate him. Just remember that a lot of his appeal is that he's new."

"And the Hollywood thing. But you're right. Once Jeremy isn't new, he won't be so exciting."

"Just like me."

Keith meant the words to be a joke, but as he spoke them, he realized they were true. Even more uncomfortable, he didn't like what that meant.

Ellen rose up on her elbow again. "Why would you say that?"

He tried to look casual. "This is new and you find everything about it interesting."

"Keith, I'm pretty sure I'm always going to find the whole sex thing with you interesting. Besides, I've known you for years. We're friends. We're important to each other. That isn't going to change."

He groaned silently as he realized he'd inadvertently stumbled into a conversation they should have had days ago—before the sex had started.

He pushed himself into a sitting position. Ellen did the same. Being Ellen she didn't bother to cover up, which meant she was naked. Sitting cross-legged and naked, her hair just long enough to half cover her breasts, and her pussy all out there for him to admire.

He told himself to act his age and look her in the eye, which was harder than it should have been, but he managed.

"It's different now," he told her. "Things have changed."

"Because we're lovers? You're saying the sex is the problem?"

"Not a problem, but something we should talk about."

She looked confused. "Why? It's great. I'd like to do it more."

They were already doing it three times a night. "I don't know that I can."

She flashed him a grin. "Men are so weak."

"Back on topic. Our relationship has changed. Are you okay with that?"

"Definitely." Her eyes widened. "Wait. Aren't you?"

"Yes, but I want to make sure you understand." He paused, not sure what to say. Ellen waited, her expression expectant.

Why had he started this? "You haven't had a lot of man-woman experience. I want to make sure we have the same understanding about what we're doing."

"You mean you're worried I'm going to fall in love with you?"

"No, just…" Damn. He had no idea what he was supposed to be saying, but he knew it was something.

She smiled at him, looking more amused than concerned. "Keith, you're so sweet. Really, I'm fine. I love this." She motioned to the bed. "What we're doing and how fun it is. You're an incredible lover and easy to talk to and I've always liked you. Don't worry about me. I'm doing great. Better than great. As for what this is, I think we should wait until we get home to decide that. Right now we're on the road and it's all new. This is vacation. We're in Eugene day after tomorrow for our University of Oregon visit, so it's only a couple more nights until we're back. Let's talk then and see what we both want."

The words all sounded reasonable, but he couldn't help thinking she made it all sound so simple and easy.

In his experience, changing direction in a relationship was a lot of things, but simple and easy weren't any of them.

"You're sure?" he asked.

"Absolutely." She stretched out on the bed and patted the space next to her. "I've set my phone for five. Lie down and get some sleep. I promise not to attack you even once tonight."

He slid down on the mattress and pulled her close. "I like it when you attack me."

"Even in the shower?"

"Especially in the shower."

He turned out the light and closed his eyes. Maybe he was worrying about nothing. Maybe everything was going to be just fine. They were both adults who had been friends for a long time. They could handle the change in their relationship. He fell asleep with the faint whisper of a voice in his head telling him that there was no way his luck was that good.

THADDEUS STARED AT the paperwork in front of him. The apartment complex was in east Kirkland, close enough to the main Microsoft campus to command high rents. The roof was new, and Thaddeus's preliminary walk-through hadn't revealed any big problems. The current owner had a gambling problem and needed an influx of cash fast. In the morning, a team of building inspectors would cover every inch of the property and report back. Once he knew there weren't any big repair costs in his future, Thaddeus would make a decision. He wanted to buy the property—he had the cash on hand and the guy was willing to make a deal. But if the numbers didn't work, Thaddeus would walk away.

His office phone buzzed. He pushed the button. "Yes."

"There's someone to see you. Her name is Unity Leandre. Should I tell her you're busy?"

Unity was here? His first reaction was a rush of anticipation, followed by the more rational question of why. It had been over a week since she'd told him to get lost.

No matter how much he might be interested, she obviously wasn't. Only a fool would see her again, and he was never foolish. There were dozens of warning signs he needed to pay attention to. He would tell her—

"Send her in," he said, then mentally slapped himself. Really? Send her in? Because that was such a good idea?

His door opened. He rose as she walked into his office.

She looked different and it took him a second to figure out what had changed. Her clothes, he thought. He'd only ever seen her in jeans or cargo pants, with a bare face and straight hair either hanging loose or pulled back in a braid. Today she had on a sleeveless dress that buttoned up the front. Her hair hung in soft curls and he was pretty sure she was wearing makeup.

"Hi," she said, looking both scared and resolved. "I appreciate you letting me see you. I wasn't sure you would."

Looking at her made him weak, and hearing her voice nearly brought him to his knees. Why her? Why not that woman from the political luncheon or any of the other women he'd tried dating recently? Why did it have to be her? Chemistry? Was his mother trying to teach him a lesson from the great beyond? Was he just unlucky in love?

She shifted her small handbag from one hand to the other. "Your office is really nice. I got a bit confused when I got to downtown Bellevue. There are so many high-rises." She managed a quick smile. "It's nothing like Willowbrook."

"That's true. Where did you park?"

"In the garage." Her smile turned more genuine. "I'm not totally sure I'll be able to find my car again."

"You mean your van?"

She looked away, then back at him. "I have Ellen's Subaru."

"Give me the parking ticket. I can validate it for you."

He swore silently. This was the most inane conversation he'd ever had. Validate her parking? What was that? He should be asking why she was here, or telling her to get out.

Unity opened her mouth, closed it, then half turned away. When she looked back at him, her eyes were filled with tears.

"Do you want to go out with me?"

He literally took a step back. No way he'd seen that question coming. Before he could figure out how to answer, she continued.

"I know I'm a mess," she said quickly, her fingers clutching her purse so tightly, her knuckles were white. "I've been thinking a lot about my life and what I'm doing and not doing. I got thrown out of grief group." Her mouth twisted. "There has been one hit after the other, lately. People telling me I'm stuck and that I need to move on and I've fought them so hard. I'm exhausted by the fight. It's all of them against just me and for so long, I believed I was right. But what if I'm not?"

She drew in a breath. "I want to change. I don't know how, exactly, or what is okay and what isn't, but I want to find out. So I wondered if you still wanted to go out with me because I'd like that very much. You're easy to be with and I feel safe around you. Plus, I keep thinking about you, so there's that." She gave him a faint smile. "And, you know, the skydiving."

The smile faded and she cleared her throat. "Which is all about me, right? And dating should be about both people. You asked me out before, which makes me think maybe you like me enough to want to try again, because I know I can do better. If you would be willing to give me another chance…"

No. It was the right answer, and an easy word for him to say. He said no all the time. Get involved with Unity? He didn't need the drama or the pain in his ass. She was trouble and a mistake and the fact that he wanted her in his bed was meaningless because what were the odds of that ever happening?

He looked at her, at her fear-filled eyes and the faint quiver in her lower lip. Coming here had taken a lot of courage, he had to give her that. She'd put herself out there, risking rejection. She probably thought she was braced for it.

If only, he thought grimly. For reasons he couldn't explain, he didn't have the power to resist her. If she hadn't said she couldn't stop thinking about him, he might have had a chance, but she had and now he was well and truly stuck with his feelings and his wanting and being a damned idiot when it came to this one woman.

"We can go out," he said, giving in to the inevitable. One day he would be over her, but he wasn't there yet.

Her eyes brightened, her mouth curved up and her entire body relaxed. "You're sure?"

He nodded.

"Oh, good. Thank you. That's so great. Is there something you'd like to do? Set up a date or—" She paused. "I don't know what you want."

"How about the next time I kiss you, you kiss me back?"

She flushed, but kept her gaze on him. "I agree. That would be good." She took a tentative step toward him. "Did you want to kiss me now?"

The offer surprised him. "I think the moment should be a little more spontaneous."

"Okay." She looked at her watch. "It's four o'clock. I should let you get back to work. Did you want to have dinner later?"

He had to give her credit—she'd gone all in. "Unity, did you have a plan for today?"

"What do you mean?"

"Are you driving back tonight? Are you staying? Did you just get in the car and drive over to see me?"

"I didn't really think much of that through," she admitted. "I told the guys I was going to be gone, packed a bag and came. I probably should have called, but this seemed more like an in-person conversation. Are you busy tonight?"

She sounded so earnest, he thought, being sucked in by the second. And vulnerable.

"I'm having dinner with friends," he said. "You'll come with me."

"Are they expecting you to bring a date?"

"They're not expecting me at all, but I'll call them. I think something low-key will be good for both of us." He wanted Freddy and Lela to meet Unity. Partly because he liked her but mostly to get their opinion.

The smile returned. "That sounds nice. What time would you like to meet?"

"So you can what? Drive around the city until it's time to go?"

"I thought I'd find somewhere to stay."

He was being tested—he got that now. And he knew in his gut that somehow his mother was involved. This was payback for all the trouble he'd gotten into as a kid.

"I have a guest room," he told her. "The bedroom door has a lock, so you'll be safe there."

She moved toward him, stopping when she was inches away. "I don't have to lock the door, Thaddeus. You'd never do anything to make me feel uncomfortable."

He was sure she meant the words as a compliment but as she spoke he felt like she'd just cut off his balls.

He was about to suggest they should get her settled when she raised herself on tiptoe and pressed her mouth to his. Her lips were soft and warm, with a slight hint of determination.

He stayed perfectly still, not wanting to assume anything. She rested one hand on his shoulder and pulled a bit, as if urging him to bend. He leaned toward her and put his hands on her waist. She tilted her head and moved her mouth against his, parting slightly in an age-old invitation.

Desire slammed into him, making him want to haul her against him and do a whole lot more than kiss. Instead he straightened and eased back enough to break contact. He braced himself for her to cry or bolt, but she only smiled.

"I believe you promised me a validation," she said, pulling her parking ticket out of her bag. "I like that in a man."

As easy as that? "You're okay?"

"Yes." She sighed. "I'm sorry I've made it so hard for you to trust me. I'm okay."

He either believed her or they were done. He wanted to tell himself he needed a minute, only he knew he didn't. For whatever reason, she got to him and he couldn't resist her. Until that changed, he was going to have to see how it all played out.

nineteen

UNITY FELT GOOD. Not just because she'd forced herself to do something unexpected, but because she'd been brave enough to come over and see Thaddeus. After telling him they couldn't go out, she'd been unable to stop thinking about him. That had to mean something.

Later, there might be guilt and recriminations, but today she was going to enjoy every moment and see where it all took her.

After he called his friends to say he was bringing a plus-one to dinner, they went down to her car, which took only three tries to find, then he drove it out of the parking garage and over to the valet parking in front of the Westin hotel.

"Why here?" she asked. "It's expensive."

He handed the keys to the valet and gave her the parking receipt. "It will be easier for you. Just give the guy a tip when you leave. The parking will be added to my account."

They collected the small overnight bag she'd brought with her and went into the hotel. "But you shouldn't pay for my parking."

"It's fine, Unity. I promise."

Once in the lobby, they went to a bank of elevators that required a special fob to activate.

"I'll get you a spare key and fob when we're upstairs," he told her. "You can take a skybridge over to the mall."

"You live in a hotel?"

"Above it. From the twenty-fourth floor to the top are condos."

They exited on the forty-fifth floor and walked to a double door. Thaddeus let them inside. Unity stepped into an elegant marble foyer and saw a dining room in front of her, along with floor-to-ceilings windows with a perfect view of Lake Washington and downtown Seattle.

"The kitchen is in here," he said, leading the way.

She trailed after him, spotting a half bath before finding herself in a huge gourmet kitchen. The cabinets were gleaming cherry, the miles of countertop were covered in the most beautiful patterned granite. The upscale appliances were brands she'd only ever read about in magazines.

"Butler's pantry," he said, pointing around the side of the kitchen. "Wine cellar. There's food in the refrigerator. The cleaning service keeps it stocked, so help yourself."

He showed her the living room, with windows on

two sides, the media room and a laundry room that was bigger than the master bedroom at her house.

They went down a different hall and he pushed open a door. "The guest room."

She went inside. The space was large, with a king-size bed, two nightstands and a TV mounted on the wall. In the corner was a chaise covered in a faux leopard print. She saw a closet with built-in drawers, enough hanging space for a boutique and a full-length mirror, before heading for the luxurious en suite bathroom with double sinks, a spa tub and a walk-in shower.

She felt like a country mouse seeing the big city for the first time. Knowing that Thaddeus was successful and seeing the proof of his wealth were two different things. Part of her felt unsettled and part of her wanted to bounce around on the bed. She went with a quiet, "Wow. Impressive."

"I hope you'll be comfortable here."

"I might not find my way back to the living room."

He looked at his watch. "It's nearly five. Let's plan to leave at five thirty."

"You're not going to show me the master?" she asked.

One eyebrow rose. "Best if I don't."

Because…why? Not that she would ask. She'd used up her allotment of bravery for the last two years and was running on sheer nerves. Yes, she knew she was doing the right thing, but it wasn't easy. Still, she was going to keep going because retreating was not a good plan.

Thaddeus left her, closing the door behind him. Unity quickly unpacked, then touched up her makeup. She used the rest of her time to study the fixtures. While her bathroom redo wouldn't be anywhere near this nice, she appreciated the inspiration.

At 5:28, she tried to get back to the general area of the front door. She only had to backtrack twice.

"How big is this place?" she asked when she finally found her way and saw Thaddeus waiting for her, a bottle of wine in one hand.

"Thirty-four hundred square feet."

"It's a condo. Aren't they supposed to be small?"

"Some are. Shall we?"

She nodded, thinking it was very possible he was much more successful than she'd internalized. Not that it mattered, it was just a little unexpected.

The idea that maybe she should have paid more attention to who and what Thaddeus was continued when the valet pulled up in a sleek, deep blue car. No, car was wrong. It was so beautiful, it was practically a sculpture.

She eyed the gorgeous lines and the grill in front. There was a stylized trident on the front of the car. A trident? Was that an upscale car brand?

"This is beautiful," she told Thaddeus as the valet opened the passenger door for her. "What is it?"

The valet, a young guy in the hotel uniform, stared at her wide-eyed.

"A Maserati GranTurismo," he and Thaddeus said together.

The valet flashed her a grin before closing the door. Unity had definitely heard of a Maserati before. To think she'd been excited to drive Ellen's Subaru.

She glanced at Thaddeus, taking in the handsome lines of his face. He was successful, he was incredibly good-looking and, hey, he had the body of a stripper.

"Why on earth do you want to go out with me?" she

asked before she could stop herself. Perhaps a question she should have considered before driving over and practically throwing herself at him.

When he glanced at her quizzically, she added, "You could have anyone. I'm not especially pretty, I'm not very girly, I don't have money and I'm an emotional basket case. I don't get the appeal."

"I like you."

Which was nice of him to say, but brought her back to the main question of why. What could she have done to get his attention?

"Is it a chemistry thing?"

"Partly. If nothing else, you're loyal."

"Some might say to a fault," she murmured, smiling at his statement. "Do your friends live in a normal house?"

"Define normal."

"Not a mansion."

"Ah. Yes, they live in a normal house. You'll like them. I've known Freddy since we were six. He and Lela married young and they have three kids. I'm the favorite uncle, which I like a lot. When I started buying buildings and needed a business manager, I hired Freddy and the family moved up here. Lela's a stay-at-home mom who has the organizational skills of a four-star general."

"They're family," she said.

He glanced at her and smiled before returning his attention to the road. "They are."

They sounded nice. Unity tried to ignore her growing nervousness and instead focused on how close she and Thaddeus were sitting. She wouldn't have to lean very far to her left to brush against him.

He'd changed from his suit into jeans and a long-sleeved shirt. His strong thighs were right there, she thought idly. It would be easy to just slide her hand over and rest it on his thigh. Then they would both be shocked, she thought, hiding her smile.

More quickly than she would have expected, they pulled into the driveway of a two-story house. She managed to climb out of the low car without flashing anything, then glanced back at the seat.

"Getting in is easy," she said. "You just kind of point your butt and fall back. But there is no way I could get out of this car in a pencil skirt."

"Do you own a pencil skirt?"

"Not at the moment."

"If you buy one, we'll take the Mercedes."

Problem solved, she thought humorously. Okay—note to self. Next life, try to be born rich.

Before they were halfway up the path, the front door opened and Freddy and Lela hurried out to greet them.

"I'm Lela," the pretty, very short brunette said, giving Unity a quick hug. "I'm so excited to meet you."

She hustled Unity into the house. Unity had a brief impression of a two-story foyer and a living room before she was shown into the open concept family room–kitchen.

"This is wildly exciting," Lela told her, leading the way to a massive sectional sofa. "I can't remember the last time Thaddeus brought a girl over." Her dark eyes were dancing with excitement. "I want to know everything about you, but if I get too intense, just tell me to back off. Freddy tells me I've gotten too good at interrogating the kids and it's spilling over to the rest of my life."

Unity had no idea what to say to any of that. She was spared from responding when Freddy and Thaddeus walked into the room.

"Hey," Thaddeus said, sounding stern. "You just ignore me? Is that where we are?"

Lela laughed and hugged him. "Sorry. I got carried away. You brought us a girl."

"She's a friend, not a sacrifice."

Freddy rolled his eyes at them, then held out his hand to Unity. "I'm Freddy. Obviously the crazy woman is my wife. She can be intense. Feel free to ignore any questions you don't want to answer."

She and Freddy were about the same height. He had dark hair and dark eyes, and there was an air of kindness about him. Unity liked him instantly.

"It's nice to meet you, too." She turned to Lela. "Both of you. Thank you for having me over to dinner."

"Anytime," Lela said, staring at Thaddeus pointedly. "I was thinking margaritas would help get the evening started. On the rocks or frozen?"

Unity wasn't much for drinking hard liquor. She and Ellen preferred ice cream and cookies on their girls' nights in. "Ah, on the rocks?"

"I'll have a beer," Thaddeus said easily, taking Unity's hand and pulling her down next to him on the sectional.

The U-shaped sofa had seating for maybe fifteen people. There was a square coffee table and a movie-theater-size TV on the wall.

"I sent the kids away," Lela said as she poured different liquids into a martini shaker. "It'll be quieter that way."

"Thaddeus said you have three children," Unity said.

Freddy handed Thaddeus a beer, then sat on the sofa. "Two girls and a boy. They're a handful, but Lela does great with them."

Lela brought over the margaritas, then joined her husband. She raised her glass. "Welcome, Unity."

Unity raised her glass, thinking dinner with his friends was a much bigger deal than she'd realized. Her mind returned to the question she'd asked in the car—why her? Only there wasn't time to consider it— not with Lela peppering her with questions.

"So you live in Willowbrook?" Lela asked.

"Yes. I grew up there. I have a small handyman business."

Lela raised her eyebrows and looked at Thaddeus. "An entrepreneur. You have that in common."

He leaned toward Unity. "She's not subtle. Just go with it."

"Hey, I heard that," Lela protested, then leaned against Freddy and sighed. "Don't they look good together?"

Fortunately for Unity, the cocktail hour of conversation quickly shifted to more general topics. Freddy and Thaddeus talked a little business, which Unity enjoyed. She didn't know much about what he did and liked hearing about different projects.

Thirty minutes into her visit, Lela invited her into the kitchen to "help with dinner."

Unity had a feeling that her presence was more about being grilled than offering assistance, but she didn't mind. Lela seemed enthused, not mean-spirited.

"I hope you like Mexican food," Lela said, sliding a 9-by-12 dish of enchiladas into the oven.

"I do. Very much."

"Good, it's a family recipe and I had them ready for tonight."

They sat at the large island.

"You didn't have to send your children away," Unity told her. "I would have loved to meet them."

"Next time." Lela picked up her drink. "Thaddeus mentioned you were a widow?"

Unity nodded. "My husband was in the army. He was killed in the line of duty."

"I'm so sorry."

"Thank you. I always knew it could happen, but I still didn't think it would, if that makes sense."

"Did you have any children?"

"No."

Lela glanced toward the family room. "I met Freddy when I was nineteen and married him when I was twenty. Six years later, we had three kids. As soon as the third was born, I told him to get snipped." She pressed a hand to her mouth, her eyes wide. "I shouldn't have said that. I blame the margarita."

Unity grinned. "I won't tell. Stuart and I got married at eighteen. He joined the army and I moved out to be with him as soon as he was done with basic training."

"You were a young bride, too."

"I was."

Lela leaned close. "Thaddeus was married before. She wasn't right for him. We never got along, which worried me, but I didn't say anything. I'm just the best friend's wife. But later, he found out she was being mean to his mother. What a bitch. I'm sure having your mother-in-law living right there isn't easy, but she had her own suite of rooms on the main floor and she was such a sweet woman. She loved Thaddeus."

Lela grinned. "When he was first starting out as a stripper, he would get paid in tips. After he moved his mom out to Las Vegas, she would take all the money he got and iron it for him." She made an X over her chest. "I'm not kidding. Every morning she would iron the bills so they were perfect. Plus, the heat would kill the germs." Her smile faded. "I miss her so much."

"She sounds like she was a loving mother."

"She was. I think she would have liked you. You're normal and normal is good. You would not believe some of the women he's gone out with." She sighed dramatically. "If they get to the point of meeting us, we know it's getting serious. Then it ends and they're all hysterical. A few of them have come crying to me. Like I'm going to take their side. Boo-hoo. I miss him. Boo-hoo, the sex was so good. Ha! How much of that was because of him and how much was because of the money?"

Lela covered her face with her hands. "Listen to me! I'm horrible. Stupid tequila." She dropped her hands to her lap. "Please don't judge me. I'm a really nice person."

Unity patted her shoulder. "You're protective. Friends should be protective. He's lucky to have you in his life."

"You're very kind. Thank you."

Thaddeus walked over. "What are we talking about?"

"You," Lela said with a grin. "I'm telling her stories."

He put his hand on Unity's back. "They're lies. All of them. Believe nothing."

"I have to believe some of it," Unity told him. "Lela was talking about your mom. She sounds wonderful."

For a second she worried she'd said the wrong thing.

Thaddeus's gaze darkened, but then he put his hand on her cheek and smiled.

"She would have liked you a lot," he told her.

UNITY ENJOYED THE rest of the evening. Dinner was great and the company was even better. The four of them talked well into the night before she and Thaddeus said their goodbyes.

"That was fun," she said on the drive back to his condo.

"There were way too many stories about me."

"Oh, I don't know. Now I have a much more well-rounded picture of you."

"It wasn't very flattering."

"It was charming."

She'd liked hearing about his childhood and the pranks he and Freddy had played. Knowing how modest his upbringing had been made his current success even more impressive.

Lela was funny and honest. Unity liked her. The conversations about her children had made her want to meet all three of them. They'd also been a stark reminder that there weren't any children in her life. While she knew how that had happened, the truth of it still shocked her.

She was thirty-four. She was supposed to be a mom by now. She'd always seen herself becoming a mother, yet here she was—childless. Worse, it was her own fault. She'd agreed to put off having kids. With the clarity of hindsight, she knew their plan had been foolish from the start.

They left the car with the valet and headed for the elevator. While they waited, Unity looked at Thaddeus.

"Thank you again for introducing me to your friends."

"They liked you."

"I hope so."

They stepped onto the elevator. Thaddeus used his fob, then pressed the button for the top floor. When he turned back to her, it seemed the most natural thing in the world to move close and put her hands on his shoulders. He responded by wrapping his arms around her and kissing her.

The feel of his mouth was exactly what she wanted. She parted instantly and he swept inside, brushing his tongue against hers. She immediately felt little zaps of excitement all through her body. Wanting stirred to life. Her breasts got heavy and her nipples tightened, just like they had after she'd watched him dance in that video.

The elevator doors opened, forcing them apart. Thaddeus took her hand as they walked to his front door. When they were inside, he cupped her face and kissed her again.

Unity tossed her small handbag to the floor and leaned against him. He was taller than she was used to, and strong. As their mouths claimed each other, she ran her hands up and down his back, liking the feel of him. Their tongues circled and teased, arousing her with every stroke.

This felt good, she thought, enjoying the dull ache low in her belly. Wanting him was proof she was still alive and somewhat functional.

They continued to kiss. He moved his hands to her waist, but no farther, while she continued her exploration of his arms, then moved to his chest. It was only when she brushed against his nipples and felt his breath catch that she realized they were playing two different games. She immediately stepped back.

"I'm sorry," she whispered, feeling awful.

"About what?"

She made a vague motion toward him. Her gaze dropped and she saw he was fully aroused. "I didn't mean to lead you on."

His mouth twisted. "No one has ever said that to me before. How are you leading me on?"

"With the kissing. I can't do more than that and you're…" She looked away. "You know."

He surprised her by smiling. "Hard? Unity, you're a beautiful woman I happen to like and we've been kissing for about fifteen minutes. What did you think would happen?"

"I wasn't thinking. I was enjoying myself."

"I was, too. I like kissing you and I like you touching me. I know we're not going to make love tonight. I don't expect that."

"You're not mad?"

He reached for her hands and pulled her against him. "I'm not mad. Now let's kiss for another ten minutes, then call it a night. You can sleep with the smug knowledge I'll be forced to take a cold shower."

She knew he was teasing her, but couldn't help saying, "I'm not being difficult on purpose."

"I know that. Unity, I do get it." He lowered his head. "Now shut up and kiss me."

So she did.

twenty

Ellen was feeling really good. She was a little sleep deprived, but that was okay. It was for a good cause. She finished putting on mascara, trying not to smudge her upper lid, which was difficult and her own fault. She couldn't stop smiling.

Life was good. Great, even. She loved the whole sex thing with Keith and she was even coming to terms with Cooper hanging out with his dad.

Okay, *coming to terms* was a little strong. She accepted it had happened, but she still didn't like it. But she would fake acceptance until he flew to LA. Then she would sob hysterically the whole time he was gone. Or at least for a few hours.

It was still about forty minutes until everyone met downstairs for breakfast. Ellen scanned her email and clicked on a link for a sale at Nordstrom. It took only a couple of minutes to find three dresses she really liked.

Even on sale they were pricey, though. Not Santa Barbara pricey but way more than she was used to paying.

Still carrying her tablet, she grabbed her key and let herself out of her room. She crossed the hall and went down two doors to Lissa's room, thinking she would ask her if the dresses were worth getting online or if they should go to the closest Nordstrom. A day trip to Seattle could be fun. Maybe Unity would like to come along, as well.

She was about to knock when someone from the housekeeping staff walked by.

"Did you want to go see your daughter?" the woman asked with a smile, then used her master key to open the door.

Ellen knew there was no reason to explain Lissa wasn't her daughter.

Ellen knocked once as she pushed the door open. "It's me. I have a fashion question." She walked inside, quietly closing the door behind her before she turned and nearly dropped her tablet.

Lissa was still in bed, but she wasn't alone. Luka was with her.

No, Ellen thought, blinking frantically, hoping she was having some kind of seizure and this was all an illusion. No, Luka wasn't *with* her. He was on top of her! And they were naked!

"Oh my God! You're having sex! Stop it! Stop it right now." Ellen glared at them as the truth slammed into her, making it hard to breathe.

Both teens stared at her wide-eyed.

"What are you doing here?" Lissa asked.

"I wanted to ask about some dresses on sale." Ellen pressed her free hand to her chest. "This is bad. This is so bad. How could you do this? You swore to your father you weren't sleeping with anyone. You lied to him." She turned slowly in a circle, trying to figure out what to do.

"So bad," she repeated. "Your dad is going to be pissed." She glared at Luka. "What were you thinking? How long has this been going on? He's going to kill you, Luka. You know that, right?"

Keith. Oh, no. He was going to find out and then what?

"I wasn't sleeping with anyone when I talked to my dad," Lissa said, pulling up the sheet. "It's no big deal."

"It's a huge deal and you know it." Ellen felt sick to her stomach. "I'm going to throw up."

"Ms. F, could you turn away, please?" Luka asked. "I want to get up."

"Oh, please. Do you think I care about your penis, you idiot? Your life span has been considerably shortened. That's what you should be worrying about."

"Okay."

Luka started to get up. Ellen immediately spun away, covering her eyes.

"I don't want to see you naked, you fool. What's wrong with you?"

"But you told me—"

"Don't try to make sense of this," Lissa told him. "She's gone over the edge."

"I'm not over the edge," Ellen muttered. "I'm close, but I'm not over."

"I'm dressed, Ms. F."

Ellen turned back to find Luka had pulled on jeans and a T-shirt. He looked more than a little chagrined.

"I love her," he said, looking both proud and scared.

"I have for a long time. I just got up the courage to tell her."

Which, under any other circumstances, would have been really sweet.

Ellen turned on Lissa. "So you thought it would be a good idea to have sex with him while on a road trip with your *father*?"

"I love him, too."

"Do you really think that has any relevance to this situation?" Ellen clutched her tablet to her chest. "I have to figure this out. We still have to visit the University of Oregon and then tonight and the drive home. If he finds out…"

She pointed at both of them. "We're all going to die and you're both to blame."

With that, she turned and stalked out of the room. But being away from the scene of the crime didn't help at all. She simply couldn't wrap her mind around what she'd seen.

Ellen managed to stumble back to her room where she stood by the bed, trying to figure out her next step. Keith was going to be furious and she couldn't blame him. She totally understood that, but what really got to her was the fact that she was going to have to tell him.

Just thinking about that made her stomach get all flippy and the need to throw up returned. She took several deep breaths to calm herself, which didn't work at all.

Someone knocked on her door. She pulled it open and glared at Lissa.

"How could you?"

Lissa stepped inside and waited for Ellen to close the door.

"It's not what you think."

"You're not having sex with Luka? Oh, please. I saw you and him. I'm going to have nightmares about it for weeks. I can't unsee it. So he tells you he loves you and you fall into bed with him?"

Lissa crossed her arms over her chest. "I didn't fall into bed with him. I've liked him for a while but I didn't think he liked me. He told me in San Diego and we've been hanging out ever since."

"You're not hanging out. You're having sex! Sex that I know about, so I'm going to have to say something. Imagine how well that's going to go."

Lissa touched Ellen's arm. "You can't tell him. Not while we're on the trip. He'll freak out and we're all trapped together. Please. He won't be able to handle it and he'll get mad at Luka." Her brown eyes pleaded. "As soon as we get back to Willowbrook, I'll tell him. I swear."

"I'm not sure your word is worth anything."

"I didn't lie before. I wasn't sleeping with anyone."

"No, but you wanted to."

Lissa groaned. "That's not against the rules. Haven't you ever wanted someone?"

Not a question Ellen was going to answer. She turned away and pressed a hand to her stomach. No way she would be eating breakfast this morning, or maybe ever.

"I don't like keeping secrets from your father," she said, knowing in her very upset gut that Lissa was right about not telling Keith while they were on the trip. He wouldn't take the news well and the trip would be ruined for everyone. "I don't like any of this."

"I'm not happy, either," Lissa grumbled.

Ellen put her hands on her hips. "Guess how much that matters right now."

"It matters to me."

Ellen raised her eyebrows and waited. Lissa sighed. "Sorry."

"Thank you." Ellen mentally worked through the logistics. "We'll be in Eugene later this morning, then we just have tonight before we head home. It's one night. We can get through that." She pointed to Lissa. "You will not have that boy in your bed tonight."

"You're really bossy."

"I am and you are going to promise me you will be sleeping alone."

"I promise."

Ellen walked to the door. "I still don't know how Keith isn't going to find out."

"You have to make sure that doesn't happen. He'll go ballistic. You know he will."

Ellen nodded and watched Lissa walk back to her room. When she was alone, she sent Keith a text saying she was running late and would be skipping breakfast. With any luck, he would think she'd overslept—a reasonable assumption considering the hours they'd been keeping.

She used the extra time to pack and fake her way into a calmer state of mind. If only she'd kept her fashion questions to herself, she thought glumly.

She saw Coop in the lobby and walked up to him. Her son turned and smiled. "Hey, Mom. I can't believe the trip's nearly over. It's been great."

She balled her hand into a fist and socked him in the arm as hard as she could, which, sadly, wasn't very hard. He yelped and jumped back.

"Why'd you do that?"

"Because you knew and you didn't say anything."

Coop stared at her blankly.

"That Luka is sleeping with Lissa. You room with him every night, so you knew he wasn't where he was supposed to be."

Her son flushed, then ducked his head—just the way Luka had. Did they practice looking all sorry and pathetic together?

"I couldn't say anything. It's a guy code."

"It's Coach's daughter and he is going to flail you alive. And guess what? I'm going to let him."

"Mom, Luka's my friend."

"I thought Coach was your friend, too. I thought he looked out for you and made sure you got a good interview at Stanford. I thought he did a lot of things and you repay him by not looking out for his daughter?"

Coop's discomfort seemed more genuine now. His expression turned guilty. "It's not like that. Luka really cares about her."

"Yeah, and Coach loves his daughter. What if she was your sister and one of your friends did this to you?"

"But she's not."

"Which isn't the point. How would you feel? You betrayed him, Cooper. When he finds out—"

Coop looked horrified. "You're going to tell him?" he asked, his voice cracking on the last word.

"Lissa is as soon as we get home. He knows you've been rooming with Luka, so it won't take him long to figure out you knew what was going on. I sure wouldn't want to be you when that happens."

"Mom, you have to do something."

"Like what?"

"I don't know. Protect me."

"I believe Coach going after you is part of the guy code."

With that, she walked toward the bus.

She knew she'd laid it on pretty thick. Keith wasn't going to hurt Coop—at least not physically. He might have a few things he wanted to say, but Coop deserved that. But if her son sweated his actions for a couple of days, she was fine with that. Let him worry. He'd earned it.

Now she just had to figure out how to act normally for the next thirty-six hours. Once they were home, it was all going to hit the fan and she would have to deal, but until then—

She stopped about twenty feet from the bus, then turned and quickly walked back toward the lobby. There was still one night left, she thought with a groan. One night where who knew what could happen.

She opened her tote and looked up the number for the hotel in Eugene. When she was connected with the front desk, she said as cheerfully as she could, "Hi, this is Ellen Fox. We have eight reservations for tonight. The high school group? I need to make a change."

It didn't take long to make sure her room had two beds and to cancel Lissa's reservation. When they arrived at the hotel, the teen would be forced to room with Ellen, thereby insuring there was no late night Luka visit. On the downside, Ellen wouldn't be sneaking into Keith's room either, which was a high price to pay, but worth it, considering the circumstances.

"Sometimes you have to take one for the team," she murmured as she hung up.

THADDEUS POURED HIMSELF a second cup of coffee. He'd been up early after a restless night spent wanting what he couldn't have. The shower hadn't helped at all. Knowing Unity was sleeping just a few feet away had kept him on edge until, at close to five, he'd decided to admit defeat and start his day.

He'd circled by the front door to see if her purse was still on the entry table where she'd put it the night before. He stared at the handbag, somewhat surprised she'd stayed. He'd half expected her to bolt in the night.

She was different this time, he thought as he put down the sports section of *The Seattle Times* and picked up *The Wall Street Journal*. More open, less sad. While he wanted to believe the change was real, he knew trusting her completely would be a mistake. Not that he was doing a very good job of keeping himself emotionally distant. Every minute he spent with Unity sucked him in deeper.

"Morning."

He looked up and saw her walking into the eating area off the kitchen. She had returned to her regular self—jeans, a T-shirt, no makeup and straight hair. While he'd enjoyed dressed-up Unity, this was the woman he knew and, well, liked.

"Good morning. Did you sleep?"

She smiled as she raised a shoulder. "I don't do well in strange surroundings. But the room is lovely and that shower is perfection. I'm thinking of doing some remodeling in the house and the bathroom gave me lots of ideas." She paused. "Coffee?"

He pointed to the second place setting at the table and the carafe. "Help yourself."

She sat down and took in the plate of fresh fruit,

the croissants and butter. "Very fancy. Do you do this every day?"

He folded the paper and set it on the chair next to him. "No. I can order room service from the hotel. This is from them. However, I am capable of scrambling you some eggs, if you'd like."

"This is plenty. Thank you."

She poured herself coffee, then took a croissant. After breaking it open, she looked at him.

"The kissing was nice."

Not the conversational opening he'd been expecting. "Yes, it was. I was worried you wouldn't be okay with it."

"I was. I haven't thought much about sex since Stuart died. It was nice to know that part of me hasn't atrophied from lack of use."

"You don't feel guilty?" A dumb ass question, but it was too late to unask it.

She shook her head. "There isn't any guilt. It's not like that. When I think about Stuart, I feel sad. I think maybe the not moving on is about staying connected to him. If I have a life, I leave him behind."

"He's not here to leave."

"I know. Which creates my dilemma. I think guilt would be easier to handle—that happens when you violate your own moral code. But for me, I've never been sure of what I'm allowed to do or not do. At the same time, I've assumed I'm the one making the rules. What if I'm not?" She picked up her coffee. "Do you want me to change the subject?"

"Not at all."

He didn't enjoy talking about Stuart but believed ignoring him didn't work, either. He was a part of Unity. Without Stuart, she would be a different person.

"It's like the kid thing," she continued. "Last night, when Lela was talking about her children, I had such an ache inside. I always wanted children."

"You had a plan. His mother dying changed the timeline."

She smiled. "You remember." She picked at her croissant. "It was a dumb plan. What were we thinking? That kids couldn't possibly be moved once they were in school? That's ridiculous. We shouldn't have waited. We shouldn't have taken the chance. I feel so stupid. I want kids. Sometimes I can practically feel what it's like to hold a baby in my arms."

She stared at him. "Oh, wait. I just remembered I'm not supposed to say that to the guy I'm dating. It's considered scary, right?"

He chuckled. "You wanting kids is so the least of it, Unity."

"I'm not pressuring you to be a father."

"I understand that."

"Good. It's just we put it off. We were always waiting for something. Having children, Stuart to retire so we could move back to Willowbrook. We lived by very clear rules, but why? We lived our lives waiting and now I'm wondering if I've just continued that habit. I feel like I'm waiting, too. But I don't know for what? Waiting to be sixty so I can move into Silver Pines? If I want kids, I should figure out a way to have them. If I want to be better, then I should be better. Somewhere along the way, I lost myself and I don't know that it started when Stuart was killed. I think it happened a long time ago." She sighed. "It's something I have to think about."

He didn't know what to say to that, nor could he assess how her words changed things, or even if they did. Yet he felt uneasy about most of what she'd said.

"I'm officially changing the subject," she said as she spread butter on her croissant. "What are you doing today?"

"Ironically, I'll be waiting, as well. In my case, it's for an inspection report on an apartment building I want to buy. If the report is favorable, then I'll go through with the purchase."

Her eyes widened. "That's really what you're going to do today?"

"Yes."

"Just like that?"

He smiled. "It's what I do."

"That kind of puts my tiny life in perspective."

"Your life isn't tiny."

"I'm not buying apartment buildings."

"You've never cared if I had money or not."

"That's true. I thought your car last night was called a Trident."

He laughed.

They talked for a few more minutes, then Unity said she wanted to get on the road. He rose and carried her small bag down to the valet.

While they waited for her car, she said, "Thank you for everything. I had a really good time."

"Me, too. You know how to get to the freeway from here?"

"I do." She pointed north. "I take a right at Northeast Eight, then get on 405 South. In a couple of miles, I merge onto I90 eastbound. Then it's a straight shot home."

The valet pulled up in Ellen's Subaru. Unity kissed Thaddeus once, and handed the valet ten dollars before getting in her car and driving away.

Thaddeus knew she had to get back to her business and her life. He didn't mind her leaving—that was inevitable. What he didn't like was the sense that somewhere along the way, he'd been left, as well.

SOMETHING WAS WRONG. Keith had felt it from the moment everyone had climbed on the bus, and throughout the drive to Eugene, the feeling had only increased.

He couldn't put his finger on what it was. Ellen had been quiet, but that was because she'd mostly been leaning against the window, dozing. The teens were also less talkative than normal. No doubt they were tired, too. It had been a long trip, but a good one. This was the last college and by late tomorrow afternoon, they would all be home.

He found his way to campus and parked. Ellen immediately opened her eyes and smiled at him. When their gazes locked, he felt the familiar jolt of desire that had been his constant companion since the trip had started. The difference was now he knew he could do something about it.

He undid his seat belt and angled toward her. "You're tired."

She immediately looked guilty. "I am and you must be even more tired." She glanced toward the back, where the kids were collecting their things for the day, and lowered her voice. "You have to handle all the driving. I shouldn't have kept you up so late."

He stretched. "It's for a good cause."

She nodded, then turned and dug in her purse. "I

have a text. I'll bet it's from Unity. Oh, the hotel." She looked at her phone. "Huh. That's, ah, weird."

"What happened?"

"There's a change in the reservation." She tucked her phone back in her bag. "They don't have enough rooms. It looks like I'm going to have to, ah, room with Lissa tonight. That's too bad. I'm disappointed."

The words sounded right, but there was something about her tone. "You okay?"

"I am. Just, you know. Sad."

The students walked to the front of the bus. He opened the door to let them out. When they were all outside, he got up.

"If you're with Lissa, then we're not going to be able to…" He glanced out the open door, then back at her.

"I know. I'm sorry." She brightened. "But you'll be able to sleep. That's good. It's a long drive home."

Something was off with her, but he had no idea what. She'd been herself when she'd left his bed, early that morning. What had changed?

"Ellen?"

She moved to the edge of her seat. "Keith, I'm fine. I swear. I'm not happy about the sleeping arrangements, but it's just one night."

"You're sure."

"I am." She leaned close and whispered, "I'll miss you. A lot."

He smiled. "I'll miss you, too."

"Hey, Coach," Andy called. "I have an appointment. You about ready?"

"Duty calls," Keith said.

"Tell me about it," Ellen muttered as she stepped off the bus.

twenty-one

UNITY STOOD IN the center of her living room with absolutely no idea what to do next. The evening with Thaddeus had been a kind of revelation. Not only had she been reminded what normal life was like—she'd enjoyed herself. She'd liked his friends and having dinner with them and the kissing and all of it. Even this morning, trying to explain her feelings, had been good if a little awkward. But Thaddeus had been kind and understanding, as always.

She'd spent the drive home trying to be clear about what she'd learned about herself and how she was feeling. She'd been forced to acknowledge that she hadn't once thought about Stuart. Not in the way she usually did. Even when she'd talked about him, he hadn't been a part of things. She could feel herself letting go, bit by bit. Part of her wanted to continue on the path and part of her wanted to retreat.

But the pain of where she'd been was too much, she thought sadly. Too exhausting, too depressing, too everything. She wanted to be happy again. She wanted to feel good about herself and what she was doing. Starting now.

She drove to the local sporting goods store and spent twenty minutes trying on swimsuits. Not the cute kind but the serious ones athletes wore. She bought two, along with a bathing cap and goggles, then headed for the swim club out by the baseball field.

It took ten minutes and a hefty charge on her credit card to join. She was given a quick tour and a lecture on pool safety before being shown to the women's locker room.

One o'clock in the middle of the week wasn't exactly prime time, so she was alone as she walked out to the Olympic-size pool. There were only two other swimmers doing laps. She paused to watch them for a second, all the while inhaling the familiar scent of chlorine. She walked to the far lane and stepped into the water. After spitting into her googles, she rubbed the lenses and slid them into place. She adjusted the straps for the right fit, then began to swim.

She was halfway across the pool when her sense memories ignited. Her body remembered the easy movements, the pace of her breathing. She was desperately out of shape, but still this all felt good.

She spotted the color change on the lane lines, warning her she was near the end of the pool. She eyed the wall before ducking down to start her underwater turn, only to miss the wall and accidentally inhale. She came up coughing loudly and hung on the edge until she could catch her breath.

"So attractive," she murmured before swimming out a few feet and trying it again.

The second time she was too close and couldn't push off, but the third, she executed a perfect turn and shot out into her lane, the push-off giving her momentum.

Victory, she thought proudly. Good for her. She continued to swim, enjoying the sense of freedom and the knowledge that a small piece of her had finally been found.

"WHAT DID YOU DO?"

Ellen did her best to look innocent as she stood in the lobby of the hotel in Eugene, Oregon, a pair of room keys in her hand. "Do? What a question. There was a mix-up and we're short a room. You don't mind if we share, do you?"

Lissa glared at her. "I'm not fooled. You did this on purpose. You want to make sure—" She paused to look around, as if wanting to confirm they were alone. "You want to make sure I don't sleep with Luka tonight."

"Sleeping is really the least of it," Ellen murmured. "It's one night. You'll live."

She wanted to add that Lissa wasn't the only one suffering, but that would lead to a conversation Ellen wasn't about to have with Keith's teenage daughter.

Lissa put her hands on her hips. "You're treating me like a child."

"Uh-huh. Newsflash. I have zero remorse."

Ellen expected her roommate for the night to explode or stalk off, but Lissa surprised her by linking arms with her and grinning.

"This will be fun. The desk clerk said there are microwaves in the room. Let's get some popcorn and then we can watch TV together. Maybe one of those dance reality shows. They're my favorite. To be honest, I'm kind of tired and could use an early night."

"Who knew you could be bought for the price of a bag of microwave popcorn," Ellen said as they headed for the elevator.

"It usually costs more, but I'm feeling guilty about what happened this morning. If you could have seen the look on your face." Lissa giggled. "You were not happy."

"No, I wasn't. And we still have to tell your father."

Not something she wanted to think about. So far she'd yet to figure out a way to have that particular conversation. No matter how many times she tried to come up with a great opening line, she couldn't find one that in any way distracted from the fact that Lissa was doing the wild thing with Luka.

"We don't have to tell him tonight," Lissa said cheerfully as Ellen let them into the room. "And look!" She waved a small bag of jelly beans. "I got them at the student bookstore. Only the good flavors."

"It will be a feast," Ellen teased.

They walked into the hotel room and stared at the two double beds separated by a nightstand.

Lissa sighed. "No offense, but I would much rather be with Luka."

And I would much rather be with your father, Ellen thought with a sigh.

"At least you don't have to worry about me leaving the toilet seat up," she said instead.

Lissa laughed. "You're right." The teen surprised her by hugging her tight. "Thanks for not telling my dad until we're home and thanks for worrying about me. It's kind of nice."

Ellen held her close. "I'm glad you think so." It would all hit the fan later, but for right now, this felt really good.

KEITH DROVE OFF the freeway off-ramp and headed for the high school. When they'd stopped for gas in North Bend, he'd told all the kids to text their parents to let them know the bus was about seventy minutes out of town.

The drive from Eugene had been quiet. Everyone was tired after their trip. Ellen had kept him company, sitting behind him on and off, talking about the different schools.

He'd appreciated the company as he kept his attention on the road. Like the teens, he was tired, although he would guess some of his reasons were different. Or at least one of them.

Ellen.

Things had not gone the way he'd expected, but he wasn't about to complain. They'd been friends for a long time and the fact that they were now sleeping together was a complication. Still, he wasn't sorry. However they were going to define their relationship, he wanted to keep seeing her in every way possible. Even needing a good night's sleep, he'd missed her last night. His hotel bed had been empty and cold without Ellen snuggling against him until dawn.

Maybe once Coop and Lissa were settled, they could get together. He wasn't sure how to go from their usual hanging out to the bedroom but he was sure they could figure something out. He smiled as he reminded himself she would be more than a little motivated. Since discovering the pleasures of a man-induced orgasm, Ellen had been eager to explore the concept and he doubted she'd been any happier about their forced estrangement.

At some point, they were going to have to talk about where they were in their relationship, as well. Going back to just friends was a possibility, but not one he liked the sound of. So were they going to date? Were they past dating and already involved?

He saw the high school up ahead and told himself he and Ellen would figure it out later.

"Wake up, everyone," he called loudly. "We're home."

Everyone started stirring. As Keith turned the bus into the high school, he saw several sets of parents waiting. He rolled into the parking lot to the sound of applause from the back of the bus.

He turned off the engine and opened the doors. "We made it," he said, standing and stretching. "Okay, check all around you to make sure you've got your stuff. If you leave it behind and I like it, I'm keeping it."

"Maybe I should stay on the bus," Ellen teased quietly, collecting her tote bag.

He grinned. "I'd like that very much." He dropped his voice to a whisper. "Were you bad today?"

Before she could answer, a couple of the moms walked onto the bus.

"You're back! Andy, darling, I missed you so much."

Andy hurried up front. "Mom, you could have waited."

His mother ignored that and hugged him. "You were gone for so long. You barely texted. My heart was broken."

"Oh, Mom."

They walked off together. Keith followed them and

opened the luggage storage compartments. Coop and Luka joined him and began setting out bags.

"Thanks for everything," Luka said, as he worked. "I gotta get back to see my mom. You know how she gets."

Keith handed him his duffel. Coop grabbed his.

"Yeah, thanks, Coach. This was great."

The two headed off together. Keith frowned. Wouldn't Coop go home with his mom? Unity would be picking her up any second. He shook off the thought and dealt with the other parents who showed up. It took only a few minutes for everyone to clear out.

"Unity's on her way," Ellen said, standing next to her luggage. "I know you're tired. You don't have to wait."

"I don't mind." He glanced at Lissa. "You can sit on the bus, if you want. I'll stay out here with Ellen."

Lissa glanced between them, sucked in a breath and said, "Dad, I slept with Luka on the trip."

Keith heard the words, but they didn't make sense. It was as if his daughter suddenly had started speaking Danish—not that he would recognize Danish, nor did he know why that language popped in his head. But whatever it was, it wasn't English. It couldn't be. If it was, that meant he could understand her and—

"Just like that," Ellen said, sounding more weary than shocked. "That was your plan? What happened to everything we talked about last night?"

Talked about? Last night? Last night when Ellen and Lissa had unexpectedly shared a room because the hotel had—

He spun to stare at Ellen. "You knew!"

She twisted her hands together. "It's not what you think. Okay, it's what you think but it's not…" She made a strangled noise in her throat. "Keith, I'm sorry."

"You knew!" He couldn't believe it. Ellen had known Luka and his daughter were—

"I can't even think it," he snapped, glaring at his daughter. "You lied."

"I didn't. I wasn't doing it the last time you asked."

"But you wanted to."

Lissa covered her face with her hands. "What is it with you thought police people? I refuse to be in trouble for thinking something. I just refuse."

He had no idea what to say to his daughter, so he returned his attention to Ellen. At least there he could give in to his rage.

"How could you not tell me?"

"I know. I'm sorry." She sounded desperate. "It was so awful. I went into Lissa's room in Medford. I wanted some fashion advice and they were there, in bed. I was so shocked. I told them to stop."

He narrowed his gaze. "You told them to stop? Wow. Great. Then I guess it's all okay."

"Keith, no. Please, I would never betray you. You know that. You know *me*. I wanted to tell you, but not on the trip. What would you have done?"

"Killed Luka." That was the obvious solution. He should have thought of it before.

"Da-ad!"

He turned to his daughter. "Your best defense might be staying quiet right now."

"Whatever." She flounced onto the bus.

Ellen watched her go. "I'm sorry."

"So you said."

She looked at him. "I mean it. Keith, I know this is shocking. I went through it myself. But there was no way to tell you while we were still on a bus. It would have been hideous for everyone."

"I trusted you."

"We were on the road. There was nowhere for Luka to hide." Her voice was pleading. "Keith, you have to see that."

"Do I?" His anger grew as a sense of betrayal fueled it. "We're supposed to be friends. There is nothing I care about in this life more than my daughter. You have Coop. I thought you'd get it. But you didn't. How can I ever trust you again?"

Tears filled Ellen's eyes. "Don't say that. Please. I wanted to tell you."

"Did you? Because it's hard to tell that from your actions."

She reached for him. He sidestepped her touch and watched her arm fall to her side.

"I want to explain."

"*Now* you want to talk." He shook his head. "I can't believe you did this, Ellen. It's unforgivable."

With that, he walked onto the bus, closed the door in her face and drove away. The last thing he saw was Ellen standing alone in the parking lot, tears streaming down her face, her and Coop's luggage piled at her feet.

ELLEN STOOD IN the hot parking lot, not sure how her life had gone from amazing to sucky in a single conversation, but it had. Desperate sobs clawed at her, making it hard to breathe. She'd screwed up—she got that—but the punishment didn't seem to fit the crime.

About five minutes after the bus had pulled out, literally leaving her in the dust, Unity drove up in Ellen's

Subaru. Her friend got out, took one look at her and held open her arms. Ellen ran to her.

"Everything went wrong," she said, crying harder, knowing she was a mess and not sure how to make it better.

"We can fix it," Unity told her, hanging on tight.

"You don't know that."

"I bought wine."

"Then I guess we'll be okay."

Ellen stood back and wiped her nose. They collected all the luggage and threw it in the back of her car, then Unity drove them to Ellen's place. Within a few minutes, the suitcases were unloaded. Ellen tossed Coop's into his room and set hers by her closet. By the time she got to the kitchen, she saw Unity had already piled the mail she'd collected on the counter and had set out food for dinner. There were four different deli sandwiches, a couple of salads, a pitcher of ice water and an open bottle of red wine. The table was set and there was a box of tissues in the center.

Ellen looked from the table to her friend and fought against yet more tears.

"I screwed up so bad," she admitted.

"I doubt that."

"Keith hates me."

Unity smiled. "I doubt that even more. You've been having the sex."

Ellen thought about how wonderful things had been, how she'd loved being with Keith, how he made everything fun and sexy and right and now he was mad at her.

Tears returned, as did Unity's warm hug.

"Come sit down and tell me everything. There's a

second bottle of wine right here and I don't have anywhere to be. Not until I go hunt down your kid."

Ellen nodded, then grabbed a couple of tissues and blew her nose. "He took off rather than face the reality of Keith finding out about Luka and Lissa. I'm sure he's with his friend now. There are going to be words and consequences for sure."

They sat at the kitchen table. Unity squeezed her hand, then poured them each a glass of wine. "All right. Start at the beginning. You were sitting on the bus, thinking Keith looked really hot and then what?"

Despite everything, Ellen managed a shaky smile. "It wasn't exactly like that. And you know most of it. But I'll start at the beginning."

Over the next half hour and a bottle of wine, Ellen explained about how things had gotten started with Keith and about Coop wanting to spend a couple of weeks with his dad and how she'd stumbled upon Lissa in bed with Luka.

"It all got really messed up then," she said with a sigh. "I couldn't tell him what had been happening."

Unity rolled her eyes. "Of course not. You were on a bus. You had to think about the other kids. Keith would have killed Luka."

"Or worse. I know I couldn't say anything, but now he's furious and I don't like how that feels."

"Because you care about him."

"Yes. He's my friend."

Unity raised her eyebrows.

Ellen shook her head. "It's not more than that, I swear. It can't be. We're friends."

"You said that already."

"Good friends."

"Who have a lot of sex."

"That part's really nice. He's so sweet to me. We've tried all kinds of things that I never thought of doing. When he touches me…" She reached for her glass of wine. "But what if he stays mad at me forever?"

"When has Keith ever done that?"

"He's never been mad before, so I don't know."

"He hasn't been mad at *you* before, but you've seen him mad at other people. He blows up and then he gets over it."

That was true, Ellen told herself. Keith didn't hold a grudge. She could only hope he didn't start holding one now.

"So that's my sad story," she said with a sigh. "Tell me what's been going on with you? And don't take that to mean I want a description about the latest remodel you're working on. Tell me about Thaddeus."

Unity surprised her by placing her arms on the table and resting her head on them. "I'm a mess."

"Possibly."

Her friend glared at her. "Hey, be supportive."

"I can't until I know what's going on. The last I heard you were pretending you weren't dating and he'd kissed you. That's kind of a lot. What's happened since?"

Unity straightened and finished her wine in a single gulp. "I spent the night with him."

Ellen felt the world shift as the space-time continuum tore, threatening all life as she knew it.

"You slept with Thaddeus and didn't tell me?" she asked with a shriek. "How could you not tell me? I thought we were friends." Shock battled with hurt and hurt won. "I told you about my sex."

Unity held up both hands. "I didn't sleep with him. I

spent the night at his condo, in the guest bedroom. But we did kiss. A lot."

Ellen's emotions died down. "Sexy kissing?"

Unity grinned. "Very sexy kissing."

"That's huge. So huge. Are you okay?"

"I honestly have no idea. I'm scared and upset and confused. I don't feel guilty, but I don't feel right, either. Thaddeus is great and I like his company but I always feel like I'm not sure about anything. Except he makes me feel safe and when we're not together I miss him, so it's complicated."

"Of course it would be. You've only ever been with Stuart and now you're dating some hunky guy." She paused. "He is hunky, right? Because you deserve that."

Unity pulled her phone out of her pocket and showed Ellen a picture. The man looking back at her was lean, with dark hair and eyes, and a penetrating stare. All of which were really interesting, but not as much as the fact that he was gorgeous.

She stared at her friend. "You never said he was that good-looking."

Unity's expression turned sheepish. "Yes, well, I didn't know how to work it into our conversation."

"I told you Keith and I did it doggy style and you couldn't cough up the fact that your boyfriend is prettier than Liam Hemsworth?"

"Oh, that's a really good point. Sorry." Unity glanced at the table, then back at Ellen. "Do you think it's possible that because I came to live with you and your folks after my parents were killed in that car accident that I started integrating their rules into my life, the way you integrated them into yours?"

"If you're trying to distract me from how incredibly good-looking the man in your life is, that's a really good way to do it."

Ellen got up and collected the second bottle of wine. They were obviously going to need it.

"Yes," she said after a few seconds. "I think you have a lot of rules that don't make sense. Your folks didn't have rules at all, so obviously they came from mine. Figuring that out is really insightful."

"I can't take credit," Unity admitted. "Dagmar's the one who thought it up."

"Do you know what the rules are? It's not always easy to define them, but if you can name them, you can decide if you want to follow them or not."

"That's what I've been thinking." Unity seemed to brace herself. "I lied about the challenge."

"What does that even mean?"

She writhed in her seat. "I was lying when I first brought it up. I hated that we were fighting and I wanted to show I cared, so I pretended I wanted to change, too. That way we were doing it together. Only I didn't want to change before. I thought my life was fine."

Ellen carried the open wine bottle to the table and took her seat. "Hardly shocking, my sweet."

"You knew?"

"No, but I'm not surprised. You like your life."

"Not so much lately."

Ellen filled each of their glasses. "Go on."

"I want to have a baby."

Ellen put down her wineglass and stared. "Okay, that's new. As in you want to get married and have a family or you want to have a baby on your own?"

"I think I want to have a baby with Thaddeus."

Ellen clutched the table to keep from falling out of the chair. "For real?"

"Maybe. I've been thinking about it."

"So you're in love with him?"

"I don't know. I like him. I want to be with him. But I don't think I love him."

"But you could?"

"I don't know."

Ellen was thrilled and stunned, pretty much equally. "I was gone like three weeks and the whole world changes. I'm going to need time to process this."

"Me, too." Unity managed a shaky smile. "There's other stuff I've been thinking about."

"I'm not sure how much more I can take, but go ahead. Shock me."

"I joined the swim club."

"Good for you." Ellen held up her glass. "I salute you. And?"

"I want to expand the business. I need to get real space and a couple of full-time people working for me. The guys I have do a lot of good work, but there are so many projects I have to turn down because I don't have enough help."

Ellen desperately wanted to ask if Unity was finally ready to move out of that mausoleum of a house she lived in, but sensed that would be taking things a little too far.

"For someone who didn't believe in the challenge, you've embraced the spirit of it."

"I know." Unity grabbed her hand. "You have, too. I'm kind of proud of us."

"I'm proud of us, too, all with the growing and changing." She held up her glass. "Girl power forever."

twenty-two

KEITH GAVE BOTH himself and his daughter twenty-four hours to recover from the trip. In his heart, he was hoping she would come to him and ask to talk, but when she didn't, he knew it was up to him. He was the parent— a fact he didn't like at this particular moment, but he couldn't ignore it or her.

He knocked on her half-open bedroom door.

"Come in."

He stepped inside and saw Lissa lying on her bed, headphones over her ears. She had a fashion magazine open beside her. When he turned the chair at her desk and sat down, she wrinkled her nose and took off her headphones.

"You're not here to talk to me about what I want for dinner, are you?"

"Nope."

"Sometimes you're so parental." She sat up and

shifted so she was sitting cross-legged, her expression one of long suffering. "I'm impressed you waited this long to yell at me."

He was going to tell her that he wasn't interested in yelling—that yelling didn't accomplish anything—only he couldn't seem to speak. It had been, what, only a few months ago that she'd been a chubby, happy toddler who loved her dad more than anyone in the world. He remembered how her face would light up whenever he walked into the room. She would stop whatever she was doing and rush to him. Becky had always been bitter about that, claiming she did all the work, so why was he the favorite.

There was no good answer to that, although he'd done his share, whenever he was home. He'd stayed up many a night when Lissa had been sick, and when he'd started coaching, he'd spent his summers with her. After the divorce, he'd been terrified of becoming a weekend father. He hadn't wanted that—he'd wanted to see her every day. Lissa was his daughter and he loved her. He always had.

All of which was easy. What was hard was realizing that his baby girl was nearly a full-grown woman and that he was going to lose her a lot sooner than he was ready.

"What?" she asked, rolling her eyes. "Why are you looking at me like that?"

Before he could answer the question, she stood and put her hands on her hips.

"Say it," she shrieked, her voice loud and intense. "Just say it. You want to get rid of me. You can't wait until I'm gone."

Lissa, like most teenagers, had moods, but until recently she'd never gone off on him like this. He felt as if he were staring at a stranger. Confusion held him immobile. He had no idea what to do and, in that second, was desperate to call Ellen and ask for help. Only this was his problem and he had to solve it.

"Just say it!" Lissa yelled again.

"I have no idea what you're talking about," he admitted. "Lissa, what's wrong?"

"You want me to leave. You don't want me here."

Suddenly talking about her and Luka seemed like a much easier path than this one.

"That's not true. Why would you say that? You're my daughter and I love you." He searched desperately for linkage to anything that had happened in the past few days. "Did you hear from your mom recently?"

"No."

There was something in her tone that made him circle back around the topic. "When did you last hear from her? Your birthday, right?"

She half turned away. "You mean did the great Becky deign to call her own daughter on her seventeenth birthday? What a silly question. She's far too busy for the likes of me."

The pieces all fell into place. "Lissa, I'm sorry. When I asked, you said she'd called."

"I lied."

He rose and pulled her close. "I wish you hadn't. Now I know why you've been acting so weird. You're feeling rejected."

"I'm not acting weird."

"You are a little."

He could call Becky later and tell her exactly what he thought of her. Okay, he wouldn't do that, but he would make it clear she had a responsibility when it came to Lissa. Blowing off her oldest daughter's birthday was unforgivable.

"I wish I could take the pain and handle it all myself," he said. "For what it's worth, I love you so much and I'm grateful to have you here."

She pushed away from him. "Don't lie to me."

"Lissa, you know I love you."

"For now. But what happens in a year? What happens if I stay past my expiration date? Are you going to throw me out, like spoiled milk?"

Was it him or was she talking crazy? "You're not making any sense. This is your home." There was something more, he thought grimly, but God help him, he had no idea what it was.

"And then I graduate and then we have the great college countdown. With any luck I'll go so far away, I'll never be able to come back. That's what you want. I'm surprised you're not looking at colleges in Australia. Then you'd never have to see me."

He got it then. Finally. He took in the hurt in her big eyes, her protective stance, the way she never wanted to discuss college, how she'd talked to Ellen about not having any idea about a major. He combined that with her mother's increasing distance and the real fear many teens had about leaving the relative safety of high school to step out into the unknown.

He reached for her again. She sidestepped him, but he had moves and it took only a second to capture her. Keeping a hold of her, he sat on her bed and pulled her onto his lap, just like he had when she'd been little.

"Stop it!" she demanded, struggling to get away.

"No." He held her firmly, forcing her head against his chest. "Lissa, you're the best thing I've ever made."

"That's disgusting. You ejaculated. Big whoop."

He knew she was trying to shock him into letting her go, but he continued to hang on tight.

"I love you so much. If you don't want to go away to college, that's fine with me. Stay here. Go to community college. Live in your bedroom forever. I don't want you gone, little girl. I know one day you'll want to get married and have kids, but we could make this house work. Build an annex or something. It would be fun."

Some of the tension left her body. This time when she pushed away, he let her go. She slid onto the bed and stared at him.

"You don't care if I don't go away to college?"

The wariness in her tone cut him to the heart. "Not if that isn't what you want. We always talked about it, so I assumed you were still interested. But if you've changed your mind, I'm down with that."

She winced. "Please don't say 'down with that.' We've talked about your attempts to fit in with teenagers. It's very sad." But she was smiling as she spoke.

"Do you want to stay here after you graduate from high school and go to community college?" he asked.

She sucked in a breath and then nodded.

"You're sure?"

Another nod. Her gaze met his. "I'm not ready for a four-year school. I don't know what I want to study and the idea of the quote, unquote, college experience scares me. I need time to figure things out."

"Can I use half your college fund to buy a real expensive sports car?"

"You're impossible."

"I know. But still, you're stuck with me." He studied her. "I love you and I'm totally fine with you going to community college. But you have to do something for me, too."

She crossed her arms over her chest. "I'm not going to like what it is, am I?"

"Probably not. I want you to see a counselor."

"What?" She scrambled off the bed. "Dad, I'm fine."

"You're not fine. You're dealing with a ton of crap and I should have seen that sooner. Just the stuff with your mom is probably enough to keep you in therapy for a couple of years, but let's agree that you see someone for the next three months. If it's helping, you can continue. If it's not, you can stop. But you have to put in the effort first."

He thought she would push back, but she surprised him by sighing heavily and then saying, "It's probably a good idea. I don't want to end up being a forty-year-old woman with mother issues."

"I wouldn't like that either."

She flung her arms around him. "You're a really good dad."

"Thank you. Now explain to me about how the hell you ended up sleeping with Luka. And when you're done with that, convince me not to kill him, because that's next on my agenda."

She flopped back on the bed. "Dramatic much? You're not going to kill anyone. You don't have the temperament."

"Want to bet? You're my daughter and he defiled you."

She sat up. "Dad, seriously? Defiled? It's not the fourteenth century."

"It's close enough and the word works. What happened?"

"Sometimes Mommy and Daddy share a special kiss and then a baby is—" She looked at him. "Not funny?"

"Am I laughing?"

She muttered something under her breath. "Fine. Luka and I have kind of been eyeing each other for a while. But when he wouldn't ask me out, I figured he wasn't really interested. On the bus trip, that changed."

"How?"

"You really want the details?"

"Every one of them." Knowing what had happened would help him decide how he was going to kill the kid.

"Fine. That first night, when Ellen wanted to go sing karaoke, Luka and I went for a walk. We started talking and he told me he liked me a lot." She paused, her mouth curving up into a secret smile. "We kissed and that was it. We were together."

Now he was sorry he'd asked for details. "You went from kissing to sex in less than two weeks?"

"Dad, we're teenagers with raging hormones and access to a hotel room. What did you think would happen?"

"Not that. You told me you weren't sleeping with anyone."

"I wasn't before the trip."

"You're grounded."

She tilted her head. "For what?"

"Having sex with Luka."

"There's no rule against sex."

Damn. She had him there. "You lied about it."

"I didn't. You never asked me if I was sleeping with him or anything. I haven't broken any rules."

Now he was sorry she was so smart. "You didn't tell me about Luka. Letting me know is implied in our relationship."

Her brows rose. "You didn't tell me you were sleeping with Ellen."

He came up off the bed. "How do you know that?"

Her smile turned smug. "I saw you sneaking out of her room at like five in the morning. You weren't fully dressed and I just knew."

He swore silently for about twenty seconds. "Are you mad?"

"Why would I be mad?"

"Are you threatened? Are you worried my relationship with Ellen displaces you?"

"No. Why? Oh, right. Because of Mom." She shook her head. "I like Ellen. She's great. I'm fine with you two being together." She shifted to her knees. "Dad, you can't be mad at her anymore. I'm the one who asked her not to say anything. She was really upset when she found us and wanted to tell you right away. It's my fault, not hers."

He was less sure about that, but this wasn't the time. He had bigger problems to deal with at home.

"I don't like that you're sleeping with Luka."

She studied him. "Is it the sex in general, or sex with him?"

"Sex with anyone."

She smiled. "So you like Luka."

"Not anymore." He sank onto the desk chair. "My head hurts."

"You should have had boys."

"The thought has crossed my mind." He met her gaze. "Tell me he's using a condom."

"Every time."

"And he's good to you?"

She flushed and dropped her gaze. "Dad, trust me. You don't want to have that talk with me."

True, but someone had to. "Pushing you beyond what you want to do is never okay. And when you're together, it shouldn't just be about him. You have, ah, crap." He sucked in a breath. "You're nearly grown and you have—"

He couldn't do it. He could not discuss sexual satisfaction with his daughter. If that made him a wimp, he was okay with that.

"He should make you happy," he hedged.

"Stop," she said, covering her face with her hands. "I beg you, stop. Yes, he takes care of me first, Dad. It's nice. I won't let him do anything I don't want him to do. He was a virgin, Dad. He told me."

As if. "Guys say anything to get in a girl's pants."

"So you've explained countless times." She flushed. "He didn't know what to do or where to put it or anything. So I'm pretty sure it was his first time, too. We figured it out together. He's a good guy. You should trust him."

"I do. With anything but you."

"Oh, Daddy. Can we please be done?"

He nodded, knowing he'd reached his limit. But that didn't mean the problem was solved. Make that problems. He still had to decide what to do about Luka and figure out how make sure Lissa knew what good sex was supposed to be like and deal with Ellen, although she was the most confusing of all and how had this all happened so damn fast?

ELLEN WATCHED COOPER stand at the barbecue, monitoring the chicken he'd put on the grill a few minutes ago. He was so much taller than he had been a couple of years ago, but the lankiness was the same. It would take him until his early twenties to put on all the muscle he wanted.

She knew that Keith was careful with the guys' training. When they wanted to overtrain, he reminded them that they were still growing and adding too much muscle would mean they wouldn't be as tall as they could be. It was enough to scare them into being sensible—something she appreciated.

She crossed to the outdoor table she'd already set. They were having a big green salad with their chicken. They'd both eaten plenty of junk food on the trip. She'd vowed they would have lots of vegetables and other healthy foods for the next few days to counteract the wildness. She'd already pureed the peaches she'd bought to freeze into a sorbet for dessert. So far Coop had only complained twice—a win in her book.

Life had returned to normal more quickly than she'd anticipated. Coop had done his laundry the day after they got home and had started his summer job. She was already working at the fruit stand in the afternoons. The only downside was she hadn't heard from Keith. He'd left her standing in a parking lot nearly forty-eight hours ago and hadn't been in touch with her since. She was going to give him until tomorrow, then she was going to find him and demand that he talk to her. She didn't like him being mad at her and she didn't think he was being fair.

More significant, she missed him. They'd spent so much time together on the trip and now she hadn't seen him in two days. She felt as if she were going through withdrawal. Not just from the sex, although she did miss that a lot, but also from him. She needed to see him and be with him to right her world. Every minute with him had been wonderful. Okay, not counting the last ten minutes—those had seriously sucked.

"I think these are done, Mom,"

She handed him the meat thermometer so he could check, then held out the serving platter when he nodded. The chicken pieces he'd just finished were piled on top of the previous ones. In most households that would have been enough for five meals. In hers, she was hoping to have leftovers for lunch. Her son could pack away more food than any five people she knew.

They took their seats at the table. Coop put three thighs and a breast on his plate while she served him salad in the side bowl.

"All your laundry done?" She asked. "You were using the washer all morning."

"I had some clothes from before." He gave her a sly smile. "You know, Mom. Some guys still have their moms doing their laundry."

"I've heard that. Would you like to go live with any of them?"

He shook his head as he sighed. "No. I want to stay with you, even if you won't do stuff like that for me." He pointed to the heaping platter of chicken. "You make me cook sometimes. It's unnatural."

"It's on a barbecue. I thought guys were into the whole fire thing." She made a low grunting noise. "Me like fire."

He chuckled as he tossed the thigh bones onto the

empty plate she'd left on the table. "I kind of like it, but the chicken's better with lots of sauce."

"We did a healthy marinade instead. Lucky you." She waited for his rueful grin before switching the subject to one that wouldn't make him as happy. "Talk to Coach yet?"

Coop put down the chicken breast he was demolishing. "Why would you ask that?"

So no, he hadn't. "How long are you going to hide from him?"

"A few more days. I don't want him to yell at me."

"Maybe if you'd tried to protect his daughter, you wouldn't be so worried."

"Mo-om, we've been over this. Luka's my friend. I wasn't going to rat him out. Plus, he really loves her. He'll take good care of her."

"If that's what you really believe, then you shouldn't be worried about talking to Coach."

Her giant son hunched in his chair. "I don't think he wants to hear that Luka's in love."

"You can't hide out forever."

"I can hide for a while more." He looked at her. "If he comes asking, don't tell him where I am."

"Oh, please. I'm not lying for you."

"Not telling him the information isn't the same as lying."

"Not telling him the information is what has you hiding from him in the first place."

"Mom, please. You don't know what it's like to have Coach mad at you. It's really, really bad."

Not information she wanted to have, because right now, Keith wasn't very happy with her, either.

"My advice is to go to him and tell him you're sorry.

Get it out of the way before the problem gets bigger. But it's your decision, so you'll have to live with the consequences."

Coop looked at her. "I'm hiding for as long as I can."

She sighed. "Some parents get to be proud of their kids."

"Some kids don't have Coach Kinne wanting to punch them out."

She patted his arm. "I'm sure he won't touch your handsome face."

"I'm more worried about my ass, I mean my butt."

"If it gets ugly between the two of you, I can always step in." Assuming she was still someone Keith listened to. Or cared about.

twenty-three

THADDEUS KNEW HE had it bad. The make-out session with Unity had changed everything for him. In those few minutes of mind-blowing kissing, he'd let down his guard and now he couldn't put it back up. Ironically, his guard was the only thing that would stay down—just thinking about Unity got him hard in about two seconds, a situation made all the more awkward when he was at work. Worse, he couldn't stop thinking about her. Their quick daily texts were a poor substitute to seeing her in person. Or even talking on the phone. But he refused to act like some lovesick kid. He was a man who knew how to handle himself and act with restraint.

All of which sounded great, but didn't explain why he was pacing in his living room when what he really wanted to do was call her and ask if he could drive over to see her.

"Note to self," he muttered. "Next time, find a woman who lives on my side of the mountains."

His phone buzzed. He lunged for it, nearly slamming his shin into the coffee table. Yup, he had it so bad.

Are you still at work?

He studied the text, grinning like a fool because it was her. God, he was an idiot. *No. I came home early.* "Because I couldn't stop thinking about you and getting a hard-on. I literally had to stay at my desk for an extra ten minutes before I could leave."

I thought maybe we could hang out.

He glanced at his watch. It was nearly four. By the time he got out of Bellevue and onto I90, it would be close to four thirty.

I could be there by six or six fifteen.

I'm glad you said that because I suddenly thought how awkward this would be if you had a date with someone else.

He read the text, but had no idea what she was talking about. Before he could ask, his doorbell rang.

He crossed to the foyer and opened the door to find Unity standing in the hallway. She had a covered casserole dish in one hand and a large tote bag slung over her shoulder.

"Surprise," she said softly, looking both happy and nervous. "Good idea or bad idea?"

She was here? He stared at her for a second before smiling and pulling her inside.

"Great idea, but I would have come over there."

"I had a free afternoon and I'd been thinking about you." She headed for the kitchen. "So this is lasagna. I made it myself. I'm hoping you have some kind of vegetable."

"We can order up."

She set the casserole in the refrigerator, then put her tote bag and purse on the counter. "Of course we can."

He raised a shoulder. "Hey, I have a lifestyle. I can't help it."

She laughed.

Unity looked good, he thought absently. She had on jeans and a short-sleeve sweater kind of thing that accentuated her body. Her hair was loose and he would guess she had on a little makeup. Without considering the consequences, he opened his arms.

For a single second, he realized she might not want to hug him. With Unity, he was never sure. But instead of stepping back, she surged toward him, wrapping her arms around his waist and leaning her head against his chest.

He held her tightly, liking the feel of her body against his. Not just for sex, but because hanging on like this felt good. Right, in a way.

"You smell good," she said, taking a sniff of his T-shirt.

"I worked out before I got home, so I showered. It's the fancy body wash."

She looked up at him. The corners of her mouth turned up. "I think maybe some of it is you."

"Could be. Want some wine?"

She nodded.

He kept his arm around her as he walked them over to the built-in wine cellar.

"Red or white?"

She hooked her thumb on his rear belt loop and leaned against him. "Would it be wrong to ask for champagne?"

"It's never wrong to do that. Do you have a favorite?"

She looked at him. "I believe I've explained my champagne inexperience to you before."

"Just checking."

He opened the wine cellar and pulled out a bottle of Dom Perignon, because he could. Yes, he was showing off, but so what? He was a sucker for the pretty woman next to him. The one who still had her hand on his back.

The touching was new. Or at least it was more than it had been in the past. Was it deliberate? Did he care? In a perfect world, she would slide her hand around to the front and rub her palm against his dick, but the world was far from perfect.

He collected champagne glasses and an ice bucket. After filling the latter about a quarter full of water, he added ice, then opened the bottle. He filled both their glasses then put the bottle into the ice bucket.

"Shall we?" he said, pointing toward the living room.

She took her glass. He grabbed his and the ice bucket before following her into the large room with the floor-to-ceiling windows that offered a killer view of the Seattle skyline, Lake Washington and the areas north and south of both.

They sat on the sofa, not next to each other, but close enough. She angled toward him.

"This is nice."

"It is."

She raised her glass. "Thank you for indulging me."

"Thank you for driving all this way."

"I wanted to see you."

That was heartening, he thought. But she'd burned him before, so he wasn't as trusting as he could have been.

"What are you thinking?" She asked. "You got very fierce for a second."

"I was wondering what you want from me."

He hadn't meant to say that, but refused to call the words back.

"Aside from champagne?" she asked, her voice teasing.

"Aside from that."

She sipped from her glass then set it on the coffee table. "The honest answer is I don't know exactly. I like you. I like being with you. I like thinking about you."

All good things, he told himself. "But?"

"Yes, but. This terrifies me." She waved between them. "You and me. Dating." She swallowed hard. "Sex."

"Are we going to have sex at some point?"

Her eyes dilated slightly. She reached for her champagne, then dropped her hand to her lap.

"I'd like to."

The whispered words had his dick stirring. He told himself and his wayward anatomy not to get any hopes up. Talk was cheap and Unity had issues.

"But," he said again.

"I don't know what the rules are. What I'm allowed to do."

"There aren't any rules except for the ones we make up."

She surprised him by nodding.

"That's what I've been thinking, too. That I'm following rules I don't even know exist. I'm trying to change that."

"What about Stuart? You don't want to lose him."

"He's already gone."

"Not for you."

Her eyes widened. "Is that what you think? That he's still with me?"

"Every day. He's a part of you."

"Do you think I'm ever going to get over him?" she asked.

"I don't know."

"Then why do you want to be with me? Thinking I'm still in love with him would be awful for you."

"It's not my favorite," he admitted.

He wasn't usually so honest in his conversations, but with her, he didn't hold back. He had no idea why—maybe it was like the chemistry. It simply was.

She leaned toward him. "I don't want to hurt you. I know that. I like you and I want us to be together."

"I want to believe you."

She nodded. "I'm sure my weird behavior doesn't help with that."

Not anything they needed to talk about. "What do you want from me?" he asked again. "Am I your transition guy? The one to get you over losing Stuart so you can move on with your life?"

Her eyes widened in obvious surprise. "I would never

do that to you," she said with enough sincerity that he believed her.

"Then what? Why are you here? Wouldn't it be easier to never see me again?"

He had no idea why he was pushing her like this. He supposed he wanted answers. Having her reject him and mean it would be painful, but then he could get going on recovering. Their current almost-relationship was punishing in its uncertainty. He was a man who liked to know what was going on.

"I like seeing you," she told him. "I like what I feel when I'm with you. Being around you shows me the possibilities. I'm tired of staying in one place. I want to heal."

"I want to believe you." He wanted a whole lot more, but knowing where he stood was a start. He wanted to take things to the next level or he wanted it done.

No, he didn't want it done, but thinking about her all the time, wanting her and knowing he couldn't have her was hellish.

UNITY COULD SEE the pain in Thaddeus's beautiful brown eyes. He was so strong and capable, yet looking at him this second made her ache for what she'd done to him. He had no idea what was happening between them, where this was going, and it was all her fault. She was a mess and she'd dragged him into her disaster of a life.

His questions were all fair ones. Of course he would want to know what was coming next from her. She thought about all she'd been through in the past couple of months. The fake-for-her challenge had turned into something real. She could feel herself getting better. The swimming was helping and she'd already looked at a couple of industrial parks where she could move her business.

But there was a bigger problem she had to deal with. It came down to a simple question: Did she stay where she was—living a half-life because Stuart was gone—or did she accept the pain of his passing, know she would love him forever and then admit that her heart had room for someone else? The choice was hers.

Only it wasn't a choice. She refused to stay stuck any longer. She was ready to start the next phase of her life. As for fear and the voices in her head, well, she was done with them, too.

She looked at Thaddeus who watched her cautiously. No doubt he was waiting for tears, or her to bolt, or something else awful. He was a good guy trying to give her the space she needed. She was lucky to have found him and she didn't want to lose him. Or them.

There were a lot of things she could say, but the man had no reason to believe her. Perhaps it was time to try something else. Something more direct.

She toed out of the flats she was wearing, then grabbed the hem of her shirt and pulled it over her head. Thaddeus's eyes widened in obvious surprise, but he didn't say anything, nor did he move. She sensed it was all up to her.

Terror gripped her, along with a feeling of dread, but under that, and growing strong, anticipation stirred. Her breathing quickened and an unfamiliar longing gripped her. She shifted so she could straddle him, her knees on either side of his thighs. Then she rested her hands on his broad shoulders, leaned close and kissed him.

The second her mouth touched his, he wrapped his arms around her and drew her close. She angled her head and parted her lips so he could deepen the kiss. Tongues stroked and teased and danced. She grabbed his hands and brought them to her breasts. Even through her bra, the feel of him touching her curves had her breathless.

She rocked against his erection, the friction arousing her to the point of incoherence. Wanting grew and with it came a sense of being alive. She was just about to suggest a more comfortable venue when he drew back.

Questions filled his eyes as he studied her. She didn't know what he would ask, but she had a general sense of the topic. She smiled and touched his face.

"I'm fine," she whispered. "I want you."

Need battled with wariness. She hated that she'd made him question what should be a natural next step and again decided showing was so much more clear than telling.

She stood and slipped out of her jeans, so she was wearing nothing more than bikini panties and her bra. "I have condoms in my bag," she said, holding out her hand. "I don't know how to be more clear."

He stood and smiled at her. "I'm beginning to think you're hinting at us making love."

"I am."

He kissed her, holding her tight and running his hands up and down her back before squeezing her butt. Nerve endings came to life, heating her body. The ever-present numbness faded and it was as if she could fully breathe for the first time in ages.

He stepped back and took her hand, then led her into the master. Once there, he undressed quickly. While he pulled back the covers and got a box of condoms out of the nightstand, she took in the honed lines of his body and his massive erection. Her insides quivered at the thought of him filling her.

They stretched out on the bed. He unfastened her bra and removed her panties. Any trepidation faded as he explored her first with his hands and then with his mouth. When he knelt between her thighs and kissed her intimately, her mind shut down as every nerve ending focused on the sweetness of his tongue against the very heart of her.

It took only a few strokes for her to get lost in a climax that left her calling out his name. Aftershocks lingered so long that when he pushed into her, she came again, an unexpected release that had her begging for him to go fast and deep, which pushed him over the edge in less than a minute.

She hung on to him, her legs wrapped around his hips, her body naked and satisfied, her senses happily muddled. She opened her eyes and found him watching her.

She smiled. "I'm not usually that quick," she said.

"I could say the same about myself." His tone was rueful. "I'd apologize except it's technically your fault."

She laughed. "Because I asked you to go hard and fast?"

"And you were coming. I find it difficult to resist the sensation of a woman climaxing around me."

"It is a first world problem."

He was still watching her, as if waiting for something. Then she got it.

"I'm not going to cry," she told him. "Or say I wish it hadn't happened or anything like that. I'm glad we did this. I want to do it again, as soon as you're ready."

All of which was true. Later, there would be tears

and confusion and maybe a little self-recrimination, but not now. Not when everything was so right.

"I brought my overnight stuff," she added. "I was hoping I could stay with you. Here. In your bed."

The last of the wariness faded. "You are always welcome in my bed."

"Even if I forgot to pack a nightgown?"

One eyebrow rose as he smiled. "Even then."

He bent down and kissed her. She wrapped her arms around him and knew that the first step had been taken.

ELLEN STARED AT the casserole dish on her counter. She and Unity had spent the morning cooking together. Unity had made lasagna, while Ellen had made her chicken parm recipe—the one that everybody loved, especially Keith. The oddness of them both cooking for a man was not lost on her, but while Unity was heading over to Seattle to see if she could seduce Thaddeus, Ellen was trying to get one to talk to her.

She still hadn't heard from Keith. This was the longest they'd ever gone without speaking. Even when he traveled with the team, he texted her. She knew he was mad, but come on. This was getting ridiculous.

She didn't like not communicating with him—it didn't feel right. They were always around each other.

After her shift at the fruit stand, she confirmed that Coop would be hanging out with his friends that evening. She changed into a thong and low-cut bra, then put on a cute summer dress and drove to Keith's house.

He answered on the first knock, but instead of looking happy to see her, he just glared at her.

"You can't still be mad," she said, pushing the casserole dish into his hands.

"That's up for debate."

She stepped past him into the house, glancing around to see if Lissa was nearby. When she saw the living room was empty, she turned back to Keith.

"I didn't know until Medford. I'm sure Lissa has confirmed that. I didn't want to keep it from you, but I had to. I arranged to room with Lissa so it wouldn't happen again on the trip. You know I'm telling the truth. You have to understand why I didn't say anything. It would have been awful for everyone."

He continued to give her that icy stare of his. She crossed her arms over her chest. "I would have kept it from you even if we hadn't been sleeping together. It was less than forty-eight hours. Come on, Keith."

He drew in a breath. "I'm not happy with you."

She waited silently.

"You probably couldn't have told me," he conceded. "I would have been forced to kill Luka and that would have created a lot of problems."

"You wouldn't have killed him."

"Okay, I wouldn't have, but I would have thought about it."

He led the way into the kitchen and set the casserole dish on the counter. They faced each other.

"I really am sorry," she said sincerely. "It was so horrifying. I totally panicked. And with us on the bus…"

"I get it."

"Then why have you been so mad at me? You haven't called or anything."

"I have had a lot to think about."

"Like?"

He pulled two beers out of the refrigerator, took the tops off both of them and handed her one. They walked into the family room and took their familiar seats on the large sectional sofa. Familiar but not exactly what she'd been hoping for, she thought ruefully. A few kisses and a suggestion they retire to the bedroom had been more in line of what she'd been thinking of, but maybe they should talk first.

"Lissa mostly," he said. "Lissa and Luka. She's growing up."

"She's seventeen. That's how old I was when I lost my virginity."

He winced. "Can we not phrase it that way?"

She hid a smile. "How old were you?"

"Fifteen."

"Wild man."

The corners of his mouth turned up. "She was sixteen, so older. It was nice."

"Fast?"

He grinned. "Very." The smile faded. "I just wanted to protect my daughter."

"You do. I know you had the condom talk and Luka isn't the type to take advantage."

"I know, but it's difficult. She's my little girl." He took a drink of his beer. "She doesn't want to go away to college. That's what all the acting out has been about. She wants to stay here and go to community college."

"Why would that be a problem?"

"She thought I was trying to get rid of her."

Ellen set down her beer and slid close to Keith. She put her arms around him. "I'm sorry. That must have been hard for you to hear. But you know that's on her, not on you. You've never done anything to make her think that." She felt a flicker of temper. "It's her stupid mother."

His arm came around her. "We shouldn't talk badly about her."

"You shouldn't, but I can call her the bitch she is. She never even phones her own daughter. It makes me so mad. I want to slap her."

He leaned back against the sofa, pulling her with him. She felt the tension ease in his body.

"Thanks for looking out for us."

"Always. We're friends and Lissa's a great kid who deserves better." She glanced at him. "It's actually your fault for picking that woman in the first place. Was it because of her boobs?"

He muttered something under his breath. "It wasn't her boobs. I fell in love with her."

"But the boobs helped." She sat up and smiled. "Speaking of which, I thought maybe we could take a look at mine, among other things."

She expected him to grin and drag her across him for a kiss, or stand up and push her toward the bedroom. But he did none of those things. In fact, he didn't smile at all.

"We have to talk."

She blinked. Talk? "About what?"

"Us."

She was still unclear. What about them? She shifted back and smoothed down her skirt. Obviously he had something on his mind. Better to let him get it out and then they could get on with the good stuff.

He straightened and angled toward her. "Ellen, we're home now. Things are going to be different than they were on the trip. We can't just have random sex whenever we want."

"Why not?"

"Because it doesn't work that way. We live in a small town. People will start to talk. We have to think about what we're doing. We also have to think about our friendship."

"What does that have to do with anything?"

"This could ruin our friendship, or don't you care?"

He wasn't making any sense. "Of course I care. You're incredibly important to me. May I point out that even though you were mad at me for no good reason, I made your favorite dinner and came over here to make up with you? I haven't liked us not talking. We always talk."

"Then you should respect what we have."

They were talking in circles. "What does that have to do with sex? I like us together like that and you do, too. So why do we have to stop?"

He glared at her. "Because this is real life. We have kids we have to worry about. And the town. We're both teachers. We can't be sneaking around, screwing in every empty closet we find."

"Why would it have to be in a closet? We already hung out all the time. No one talked about that. How would they know it was different now?"

"They would."

She genuinely had no idea what he was talking about. "Keith, are you saying you don't want to sleep with me anymore?"

"No, I'm saying we have to consider the consequences. There's more at stake than just a good time."

He seemed really mad and she had no idea of the cause. She stood and pulled up her skirt. "I wore a thong. Does that count for anything?" She wiggled her butt as she spoke, hoping to get him to smile.

He stood and took her hands. Excitement flickered in her belly.

"Can I be on top?" she asked. "And maybe we can—"

Only they weren't headed for the bedroom. He pulled her into the kitchen where he grabbed the casserole and pushed it into her hands, then opened the front door and eased her outside.

"Sex doesn't solve everything," he told her flatly before shutting the door in her face.

She stood on his front porch, her mouth hanging open.

What had just happened and why? She knew he was angry, but had no idea of the cause or what he meant by anything he'd said. Worse, she had a bad feeling that somehow her friendship with Keith had been permanently altered and not for the better.

She knocked, but he didn't answer. After a few minutes, she retreated to her car. Despite the heat, she shivered. Not only did she feel foolish and exposed, she was afraid. She couldn't say of what, but the knot of tension and worry sat like a rock in her belly and she had a bad feeling it wasn't going away anytime soon.

twenty-four

UNITY DROVE THE entire way home waiting to cry. She'd already planned she would get off at the closest exit and pull safely into a parking lot to have her breakdown, only it never happened. Not the tears, not the regret, not anything but happy aftershocks from a night spent with Thaddeus.

When she arrived back in Willowbrook, she drove past her own place and headed to Silver Pines where she parked in front of Dagmar's house. Her friend opened the door before Unity could knock and invited her in.

When they were seated on the sofa, coffee and a tray of cookies in front of them, Unity looked at her friend.

"I spent the night with Thaddeus."

Dagmar didn't look impressed. "You were there a couple of weeks ago, weren't you?"

"I spent the night in his bed."

Dagmar's eyebrows rose. "Ah, that's a different story.

Tell me—" She looked away and then back at Unity. "Oh, dear. I've found a boundary I can't cross." She laughed. "While I want to hear my dear boy is a wonderful lover, we are just too close." She smiled. "Just tell me everything worked out."

Unity grinned at her. "It did. You don't have to worry about him sullying the family name."

"Oh, good. Are you all right?"

A logical question. "I am. I'm good. Last night was incredible."

They'd made love several times and she'd slept in his arms. She had assumed it would be difficult for her to share a bed again, but she'd fallen asleep easily and had slept deeply until his roaming hands had awakened her in the most delicious way possible.

"I'm ready to let go," she said firmly.

Dagmar didn't look convinced. "Do you want to let go? Truly?"

"It's time. I've learned that I've spent my whole life waiting. Waiting to marry Stuart, waiting for our lives to start, waiting to have children. I've followed rules that made no sense because I thought I was supposed to." She swallowed. "I've wasted so much time I'll never get back. I want more. I want a man who loves me and babies. I want to be happy. I don't want to spend the next twenty years waiting to be old enough to move to Silver Pines so I can live out my life, waiting to die."

"Then start doing that," her friend told her. "Make a plan. Take the steps. You know the clichés. Some days it's easy and some days it isn't, but eventually you make progress." She took Unity's hand. "You're not going to forget him, my darling girl. Stuart will always be with you. Over time the memories become treasures rather than blows to the heart."

"I hope that's true. He was a good man, but he's not with me anymore." And while she didn't speak the obvious, she knew it down to her bones. Stuart would not be happy with how she'd been living her life. Or not living it.

Dagmar sighed. "You're going to break my boy's heart, aren't you?"

The question surprised Unity. "Why would you say that? Of course not. We're in a great place."

Sadness darkened Dagmar's eyes. "For now. But the reckoning is coming. Oh, dear. I should have seen that before. What was I thinking?"

Unity touched her arm. "I won't hurt him. I promise I won't."

"Don't promise that, silly child. The pain is inevitable. It's the afterward that will tell us the future."

THE WILLOWBROOK FRUIT stand had been located right off the freeway at mile marker 109 for as long as Ellen had been alive. What had started as a simple roadside stand had grown into a destination for travelers from June until early October.

The big barn had been converted into the actual market. In addition to local produce, they sold honey, baked goods, eggs and crafts. In the back was a petting zoo for the kids, a couple of friendly dogs, available for adoption from the local animal shelter, a picnic area and food stand that sold sandwiches, barbecued burgers and hot dogs, along with drinks and chips. There was a playground where kids could burn off some energy and very well-maintained bathrooms for all.

Ellen had started working summers at the fruit stand
when she was just fifteen. The hours were flexible and
the pay excellent—both of which she'd appreciated even
more, after she'd had Coop. Now that she was an adult,
she continued to work a few hours a week there in summer.

She'd just finished putting out several baskets of apricots when Coop wandered into the barn. He glanced
around, as if looking for someone, then smiled when
he saw her.

"Mom, I got the tickets!" he said as he crossed to her.

"I leave on Sunday," he said, practically bouncing
in place as he spoke. "I'm gone for two weeks." His
grin broadened. "And I'm flying first class. Can you
believe it?"

Each word knocked her around a little until she was
unable to focus on anything other than the Sunday part.

"You're leaving in four days?" she managed.

Coop looked concerned. "Why are you upset? We
talked about this."

They had talked about him going to visit his father
for a week and later in the summer. She pressed a hand
to her chest to try to catch her breath.

She wanted to throw herself at Coop and beg him
not to leave. She wanted to make him promise that no
matter what, he would come back. Because that was
her greatest fear—that Jeremy would be all perfect and
such a good time that Cooper would want to finish his
senior year at some upscale private school, and that he
would totally forget about his mother.

Coop was her baby, her little guy, her son. They'd
been on each other's team since he'd been born. They had
a good life and didn't need someone messing with that.

Only she knew Coop would see the situation differently. Of course he wanted to get to know his father, and she had to let that happen. She had to trust he would be okay.

"Mom?" Her son stared at her. "Mom, do you want me to stay home instead?"

Yes. Yes, a thousand times. Except she couldn't say that or even think it. This was her son and she wanted him to have the world—even if that world included his father. Just as important, if she put up a fuss about him visiting his father, she would undo all the work she'd done to convince him she would be fine when he went away to college.

"Stay?" She forced a laugh. "Oh, please. I want you to go. You'll have a great time. I just thought it was at the end of the month. I guess I got the dates wrong. Two weeks will give you more time to see the area and hang out with your half sisters."

He didn't look convinced. "I can tell my dad—"

She cut him off with a shake of her head. "The only thing you're going to tell him is to pick you up at the airport. You'll have a great time. Take lots of pictures and then when you get home, you can tell me everything."

The lies got easier as she spoke them.

"Get me the flight info, so I can be available to drive you to the airport," she said.

"Luka's going to take me."

An easy statement that hit her like an uppercut to the jaw. "That's nice," she managed. "Okay, I need to get back to work. When I get home, let's go through your clothes and figure out if we need to hit the outlet mall for anything."

Coop hugged her. "Thanks, Mom."

He released her and bounded out of the store, leaving her with a neat display of apricots and a shattered heart.

Telling herself everything was going to be all right didn't help at all. She unpacked a few cases of honey, then took her break. As she sat on a bench out by the picnic area, she told herself she was overreacting. She wasn't going to lose her son. So what if Jeremy was rich and in the movie business—she and Coop were tight.

Except he hadn't told her about Luka and Lissa and he'd kept the date of his departure from her until four days before he was leaving. Was he being a teenager or pulling back?

Uncertainty gripped her, making her stomach churn. She hurt all over and wanted to talk to a friend. But this wasn't Unity's area of expertise and while Ellen wanted to text Keith, she wasn't comfortable reaching out to him. They hadn't spoken in nearly a week—not since she'd gone to see him and they'd fought.

Not that she knew what they'd fought about. Keith was mad at her—that much she knew for sure. But she had no idea what about. How had things gotten so bad so fast? On the trip, they'd been happy and together and now... She just didn't know.

It was too much, she thought, feeling cold despite the near ninety-degree temperature. Fighting with Keith and having Coop go visit his dad. She didn't like any of it.

While she couldn't stop her son, she wondered if she could do anything about Keith. Only without knowing the problem, she didn't know how to fix it. Had the sex thing really changed everything so much? And if so, why? What was she missing? What wasn't he telling her? And even if they couldn't ever make love again—

a thought she found incredibly depressing—she didn't want to lose her friend. Not for anything. Because without Keith, nothing was going to be right.

LELA POINTED TO several patches of plants. Thaddeus dutifully dug them out, thinking they didn't look all that different from the ones that were left behind. Not that he knew the difference between a weed and a geranium.

"This is the easiest weeding I've ever done," she said, sitting next to him on the grass. "You should come help me in the garden more often."

"Don't you have a service that takes care of the yard?"

"Yes, but I like taking care of the flower beds. It's a beautiful day."

It was. Summer had arrived in Seattle, bringing warm temperatures and blue skies. Tourists flocked to the city, filling the museums and restaurants. Cruise ships on their way to Alaska could be seen at the port. As a rule, Thaddeus liked summer—just not today. Actually summer was fine. He was the problem, rather than the season.

"So, why are you sitting here in my garden at eleven in the morning on a Tuesday?" she asked, collapsing back on the grass and staring up at the sky.

The change in topic nearly gave him whiplash. Before he could stop himself, he said, "I'm in love with Unity."

He immediately wanted to call the words back. Lela's eyes widened as she stared at him.

"You're in love with her?"

He swore silently, but knew there was no distracting her from what he hadn't meant to admit out loud. "I don't want to be. As your daughter would say, it sucks to be me."

"Why? Unity's great. And being in love—" She reached for his hand and squeezed it. "The mighty have fallen."

"The mighty are about to get their asses kicked."

"Why would you say that?"

He stared at the grass. "She's not ready. She's still in love with her late husband. I don't know why she's been going out with me. Maybe to test the waters, maybe because she thought it would work out. Either way, I can see she's not ready to let go."

"You could be wrong about that. Even if she still has some things to work through, she could be in love with you, too."

"I doubt that."

He wanted to believe but he wasn't a fool. That night with Unity had meant everything to him, but he wasn't sure what it had meant to her. While she'd acted completely normal, he'd sensed there were emotions lurking under the surface.

He looked at Lela. "I want to marry her and have kids with her, but it's like she's under glass. I can see her, but I can't touch her. Not emotionally. I don't think she wants what I want."

Tears filled Lela's eyes. Her tenderhearted response warmed him. No matter what, he had good friends.

"What are you going to do?" she asked. "Tell her how you feel?"

"No. That would only make things more confusing for her. I don't want her acting out of guilt. I'm going to wait and see how it plays out." He hesitated, then admitted the truth. "It's not going to end well."

"You can't know that."

"I can and the hell of it is, I can't walk away from her." He managed a chuckle. "It's not fun to be the girl in the relationship."

"You're not the girl. You're a hunky guy and if she doesn't fall madly in love with you, then she's a fool and I'm sorry I ever thought I could like her."

"Thanks. I love you."

"I love you, too, Thaddeus. And thank you for trusting me with your secrets. I won't tell anyone."

"That only means you won't tell the kids, but you'll tell Freddy."

She laughed. "Very possibly." She pointed to the flower bed. "Let's finish this row, then you can go back to the office and take care of very important business."

KEITH'S BAD MOOD had persisted for days. He was grumpy, he couldn't sleep and he definitely wanted to take out his temper on someone, only he couldn't figure out who.

Since Lissa had come clean about her concerns, they were getting along. He still had a couple of weeks until football practice started, and he was ready for that. His truck was running fine, the house was in good shape, so why did he wake up every morning, wanting to rip the head off a bear?

Although he suspected the answer, he refused to acknowledge it. Nor would he call her or text her—mostly because if he came within ten feet of Ellen there was a better than even chance he wouldn't be able to refuse her and once he gave in, he wouldn't be able to resist her ever again.

God, he missed her. He missed everything about her.

Not just the sex, although he sure wanted that back in his life, but he missed being with her. The talking and laughing, the way she listened so intently and never judged. He missed her smile and having dinner with her. He wanted to sneak over and put gas in her car and maybe mow the lawn, although Coop took care of that.

He had it bad and he didn't know how to unhave it. It was eight in the morning, he'd been up since four and he had no idea what to do with himself or about Ellen or anything.

Maybe he should add on to the house—just to have something to do. Or tell Lissa they were going away for a couple of weeks. Something, anything, to break the pattern of wanting and not having.

The doorbell rang. He turned toward the sound, his heart suddenly racing. Finally. Ellen had come to him again. No doubt she would try to explain why he was wrong, all the while raising her skirt and flashing her perfect ass at him. He would give her about thirty seconds of talking, then he would kiss her until they were both senseless.

He needed her in his life and in his bed and even if this was totally messed up, he couldn't not have her anymore.

He pulled open the front door and deflated like a popped balloon. His temper returned and thankfully, he finally had somewhere to put it.

"You!" he growled.

Luka flinched. "Morning, Coach. I was hoping we could talk."

"Let me get my shotgun first."

Keith had to give the kid credit. Instead of turning

and running, he squared his shoulders, as if prepared to accept his fate.

"Do you want me to wait here or inside?"

Keith opened the door wider. "Get in here."

The teen stepped into the living room.

Keith motioned to the sofa. He didn't have to worry about Lissa interrupting him—she slept until at least nine and once she was out, nothing woke her.

Luka perched on the edge of a cushion. Keith remained standing. A dickish move to be sure, but he wanted the edge.

"Talk," he said sternly.

Luka swallowed. "I want to apologize for what happened on the bus trip."

"You mean the fact that you were having sex with my daughter? Is that what we're talking about?"

Luka went pale as he shook his head. "No, Coach. I won't apologize for that, but I'm sorry about what happened with Ms. Fox and how you found out. I should have handled the situation better."

"Or you could have not slept with my daughter."

"I love her."

The straightforward, honest declaration was an unexpected hit. Keith sank into a chair.

"You don't know what love is."

"I do and I love her. I have for a long time. Nearly two years. But Lissa is so beautiful and smart and perfect, I was afraid to say anything. What could she see in a guy like me, right?"

Keith thought of several scathing responses but decided to keep his mouth shut.

"On the bus trip we started hanging out. At first she was just helping me with my Spanish but then we were talking and I told her I liked her and she said she liked me and things went on from there."

Keith felt old by comparison. What was that line from *Men in Black*? Old and busted. That was him.

"She's my daughter," he said with a sigh.

"I know you're worried, Coach, but I'll take good care of her. You have my word. I always use a condom and I'd never force her and I'll always protect her. I'd die for her."

Dramatic, but possibly heartfelt.

"Just don't be a shit, okay? And don't just think about yourself." He muttered several swear words under his breath. "Don't hurt her, okay?"

"I swear."

Luka stood and held out his hand. Keith didn't want to take it, but given the fact that the kid had come to him and basically laid it all out there, what choice did he have?

They shook. Kcith sucked in a breath. "I still don't like this. No sneaking around. You'll respect curfew. And I never, ever want to walk in on you with my daughter. Is that clear?"

"Yes, Coach."

"I know you're going to keep doing it, but be careful and respectful."

"Yes, Coach."

"Now get out of here."

Luka nodded before bolting for the door. Keith changed into shorts and a T-shirt, then did a few stretches before heading out into the already warm morning. Maybe running for a few miles would clear his head.

He started at a slow jog. Old injuries woke up and

reminded him of their existence. That place in his left hip began to ache and his right ankle wasn't happy, but he ignored them all and increased the pace.

Luka had impressed him, he admitted as he began his second mile. The kid had a pair, coming to see him like that.

He smiled as he thought about telling Ellen what had happened. She would want to know all the details, then they would talk about what it all meant and she would have advice for him. Good advice.

He missed her, he thought, wiping sweat from his face. Missed them. They were so good together and being apart from her wasn't right.

But it was all her fault, he reminded himself. She was just so into the sex and nothing else mattered. Except the sex was new for her and he got that. After seventeen years, she deserved some time to play. Her interest in him, in them, that way, wasn't a dismissal of the rest of what they had.

Plus she was amazing in bed. Adventurous, fearless, totally up for anything he suggested. And when she came, it was magic.

Which made him wonder why he was so mad at her. If he believed she cared about him and he understood why the sex was so important to her and if he believed they were good together, then why were they fighting?

His left knee began screaming at him. It was always late to the party but when it got there, it made a lot of noise.

He ignored the pain and the sweat and the fact that he'd gone only three miles of the five he'd planned. He slowed to a stop as he turned the questions over in his mind. He shouldn't be mad at Ellen. She hadn't done anything wrong. So what was causing the low-grade dissatisfaction that he couldn't shake?

He started running again, only to stop a second time as the truth hit him like a three-hundred-pound linebacker. All the air rushed out of him and for a second, he thought maybe he was going to go down on the sidewalk.

The problem wasn't Ellen, he realized. The problem was him. He was totally and completely in love with her. Crazy in love. He didn't want to play—he wanted this to be real. Forever real, which should have been great except Ellen had never been in an adult relationship before. She was just starting to enjoy it all and there was no way she was going to be interested in settling on anything permanent before she'd had her time to explore the possibilities. Possibilities that might not include him.

twenty-five

UNITY BATTLED EXCITEMENT and nerves. Thaddeus was driving over to have dinner with her and stay the night. She'd cleaned the whole house, carefully planned a menu, had shopped for new lingerie and a sassy summer dress that she hoped was seductive and had brought a bottle of pricey-to-her wine. Perhaps most important, she'd sprung for a new mattress for the master bedroom. It had been delivered that morning. She'd carefully made it with the new linens she'd bought. She'd kept her things in the hall bathroom and would let Thaddeus use the small master bath.

At exactly five, Thaddeus knocked on the front door. She was smiling as she let him in.

"How was the drive?" she asked as he entered.

"Easy."

He carried a bakery box in one hand. After setting it on the living room coffee table, he turned to her.

She stepped into his embrace and raised her head to kiss him.

The feel of his arms and lips and just all of him was as delicious as she remembered. Anticipation sweetened the moment. This was good, she thought happily. Yes, it was difficult moving on, but it was also the right thing to do.

He stared into her eyes and stroked her face. "You doing okay?"

"Better than okay. I'm happy to see you."

Something flickered in his eyes. She couldn't tell what he was thinking, but hoped it wasn't anything bad.

"I'm happy to be seen," he said lightly.

She smiled and reached for his hand.

"We're having ribs for dinner. They've been marinating all day, so they should be delicious. We can eat inside or outside. It's still really hot outside, but the patio is in the shade."

He picked up the bakery box. "Eclairs. Dagmar said they're your favorite. These need to be refrigerated."

"I have a refrigerator. It's perfect."

They went into the kitchen. He glanced around, as if taking in everything.

"Is this your place or do you rent?"

"It's mine," she told him. "I know it needs major remodeling. I've been meaning to get to it, but I've been so busy with my other projects." She put the pink box into the refrigerator before facing him again. "I'm leasing office space."

Thaddeus's eyebrows rose. "You are?"

She nodded. "It's time. I turn away so much business. I'm signing the lease in a couple of days." She felt herself blushing, which was silly. "I've also started interviewing for a couple of full-time employees."

"That's big. Congratulations."

"Thank you. I'm terrified, of course. It's so much responsibility. They're depending on me for their paychecks. But I have a new accountant to help me with the paperwork."

"Forward progress," he said lightly.

"That's the plan." She fought the urge to cross her arms over her chest. "You've been so great to me. I know being around me isn't easy and I want you to know that I appreciate how wonderful you've been."

He tensed a little. "But?"

She moved close and put her hands on his chest. "No but. And I'm glad you're here."

His gaze searched hers. She grabbed his hands and put them at her waist, then leaned against him.

"I feel as if you're waiting for me to do something awful. I'm so sorry about that. I'm not going to change my mind about us. I'm really glad you're here, Thaddeus. I want this." She stared into his dark eyes. "I want you."

She felt him relax.

"I want this, too," he admitted. "You get to me more than I would like."

"That's kind of nice to hear."

"For you," he said ruefully.

"I hope you know none of this has been a game."

He brushed his mouth against hers. "I know. You're doing the best you can."

"Thank you for understanding." She stepped back. "Okay, I bought the beer you like along with some very fancy Scotch. Which would you prefer?"

"I'm not sure I can resist fancy Scotch."

She got out the bottle and a glass for him, then mixed herself a vodka and tonic.

"Let's go outside," she said. "If it's too hot for drinks, then we'll move back inside."

She led the way through the small dining room, down two steps into the family room.

"This used to be part of the patio," she told him. "It was closed in about twenty-five years ago." She looked around at the big room with the sagging sofas and old recliners. "There is a sense of going back in time here, so brace yourself."

Instead of responding, Thaddeus crossed to a table in the far corner of the room. A table that was so familiar, she didn't even notice it anymore. A table covered with framed photographs of Stuart and his family and her wedding to Stuart.

Thaddeus studied them for nearly a minute before picking up a picture of Stuart right after he'd finished basic training. He looked impossibly young in his uniform—but also proud and happy. There was another picture of her clinging to his arm as they both smiled at the camera.

Thaddeus looked at the wedding photos, lingering on one of just her.

"You were a beautiful bride," he said quietly.

Her stomach twisted as she watched him. She knew this was really bad, even though she couldn't articulate why. They were just pictures. Thaddeus knew she'd been married before, so there weren't any surprises. But the sense of dread only grew.

Finally he looked at her. "You said this is your house." A statement, not a question.

She nodded. "Stuart's mom died a few years back, leaving it to him."

"And he left it to you."

She nodded again.

He walked back to the kitchen and put down his drink. After looking at the living room, he stepped into the hallway.

She followed him, even though she knew what he would see. The wall of photographs marking the passage of Stuart's life.

Thaddeus studied each one before glancing around at the doors leading off the hallway. Only one was closed. He reached for the handle.

Her protest died unspoken. She didn't want him going in there, didn't want him to see, but knew there was no point in trying to stop him. The damage had been done. Seeing Stuart's room would only confirm what he'd already guessed.

Thaddeus walked into the bedroom she used. She stayed where she was, able to know what he was seeing from her own memories. The posters on the wall, the trophies in the bookcase. In the closet he would find her clothes commingled with Stuart's. She slept in his bed, wore his T-shirts as pajamas and left her hairbrush on a dresser next to an old signed baseball he'd always treasured.

Tears filled her eyes. She let them fall, the trail branding her. She'd been so sure, she thought sadly. She'd convinced herself that she'd moved on, that she'd healed, but she hadn't. Not really. The things she'd done were just a facade. The truth was there for Thaddeus to see. He wouldn't even have to look very hard.

Shame tightened her chest and made her feel sick.

She'd been a fool. Worse—she'd been cruel, and without even trying.

When he stepped back into the hall, there was no accusation in his gaze. No anger. Just a bone-crushing sadness that nearly made her gasp from the pain of it.

"I've suspected for a while," he said quietly. "That you're not available. I told Lela it was like you were under glass and I couldn't touch you emotionally, but it's more than that, isn't it? You're still with him."

She wanted to say that wasn't true. That she'd bought a new bed for them, that this wasn't Stuart's house, it was hers, only she couldn't. Not in the face of all he'd seen.

"I'm sorry," she whispered.

"That's why it wouldn't work," he continued, as if she hadn't spoken. "It was never just the two of us. There were always three people. That's why I couldn't reach you. I should have figured that out."

"Thaddeus," she began, then pressed her lips together, not sure what to say.

He moved toward her. After brushing away her tears, he lightly kissed her.

"You said you weren't ready," he told her. "I should have believed you. I'm sorry."

More tears fell. "Don't say that. Please don't say that. It's not what you think."

"I wish that were true, but it's not. You don't want to move on. You've said it again and again and no one has listened." Despite the pain in his eyes, one corner of his mouth turned up. "I'm listening now, Unity. I get it."

More tears fell. "I don't want to lose you," she whispered. "Please, give me another chance."

"I want to, more than you can possibly know, but

there's no point. You're still married to him. I'm willing to share you with your past but I won't share you in the present." He jerked his head back toward the bedroom. "Your heart belongs to that guy. I never had a chance."

"Don't go," she said, her voice shaking.

"I don't belong here."

She threw herself at him. He could have sidestepped her, but instead he pulled her close and held her so tightly, she couldn't breathe. But she didn't mind—she wanted to feel his arms around her, wanted to be surrounded by his strength. He was such a good man, she thought fiercely. A once in a lifetime kind of man. And she'd lost him.

He stepped back.

"You didn't do anything wrong," he told her. "Don't think otherwise. You're doing the best you can. Be true to yourself, Unity. No matter what. I will always—" He looked past her for a second, then returned his gaze to hers. "I'm glad I got the chance to meet you. Stuart was a very lucky man."

With that he moved past her and walked out of the house. Seconds later she heard his car start up and then he was gone.

The tears returned, this time with more intensity. Cries turned into sobs and she sank onto the floor, pulling her knees close to her chest as she gave in to the sadness. She'd lost again and this time she had no one to blame but herself. It wasn't fate or bad luck or anything but her being unwilling to let go of the past. She had exactly what she'd said she always wanted—an empty house and the memories of Stuart.

As she curled up on the floor and let the pain wash

over her, for the first time in three years, a little voice whispered in her ear, asking if that was really going to be enough.

ELLEN SAT ACROSS from Unity, watching her friend carefully.

"I'm okay," Unity told her, her voice raspy from the crying.

"Don't take this wrong, but you don't look okay."

Unity's face was pale, her eyes were red. Ellen didn't know how long she'd been crying before she'd called and asked Ellen to come over. She'd managed to recount what had happened with Thaddeus, ending with him leaving.

"From what you said, he wasn't mad at you," Ellen said.

Unity grabbed more tissues. "He wasn't. He was very kind about all of it, but I know I hurt him." She covered her face with her hands. "Why didn't I put away the pictures? I don't see them anymore. They're just a part of the landscape. But to him—it must have been a slap in the face."

She looked at Ellen as more tears filled her eyes. "He said there were three of us in the relationship."

"He's not wrong about that. You've never wanted to let Stuart go."

"Doesn't that make you worry about my mental health?"

An interesting question, Ellen thought, not sure how honest to be. "I always figured you'd move on when you were ready. You've made a lot of progress already with the business."

"I bought a new bed," Unity said in a whisper. "For Thaddeus and me. I thought he'd spend the night."

"That's good."

"Is it? This is like a ghost house. A ghost lives here and I invited Thaddeus over. What was I thinking?"

"Are you upset about Thaddeus or Stuart?"

"Thaddeus. I was so stupid."

"You weren't stupid. You like him. You wanted to keep seeing him. That's not stupid."

"Tell that to him."

Ellen moved next to her on the sofa. "Stop beating up my friend. I love her and you can't be mean to her."

"That's kind of twisted."

"Maybe, but it's true."

Unity looked at her. "Am I broken?"

"Yes."

"It is fixable?"

"That's entirely up to you."

ELLEN WAS PROUD of herself for getting through the entire evening with Unity without once mentioning her own heartache. There were times when friendship was a two-way street and times when it went only one way. Unity had needed her and she'd been there.

But the next morning, she woke up feeling sick to her stomach. After starting coffee, she logged onto her email account and saw that once again, there wasn't anything from Cooper. Since arriving in Los Angeles six days before, he'd texted exactly once to say he'd arrived and that had been it. He'd posted on social media, so she could follow everything he was doing. There were great pictures of a gorgeous house with a massive swimming pool. Jeremy's daughters were the cutest ever. It was all so perfect and she was over a thousand miles away, stuck in a tiny town, sorting fruit, while her son was having the time of his life and probably planning his future away from her.

She kept herself busy doing chores she usually avoided, like washing the baseboards and polishing the silver tea service her grandmother had left her. She spent the afternoon at the fruit stand, letting the general business there distract her, but when she returned to her empty house, hopelessness descended, nearly smothering her.

She hated how quiet everything was. She hated that no one left dishes in the sink, or drank all the milk without telling her or left sports equipment in the living room. She didn't want peaceful and tidy, she wanted loud and messy. She wanted Cooper back. Now!

But that wasn't possible and she still had another week to go. A week she wasn't sure she could survive without slipping into some form of madness. She pulled out her phone and stared at it. Her fingers twitched as she considered texting him.

"That's a bad idea," she said aloud, then unlocked the screen and started typing. She couldn't bother Unity right now—her friend was in too much pain. That left only one person.

I don't care that you're mad at me for some reason. I don't care that we're not speaking. Cooper's gone and I'm freaked out and if you were ever my friend, you'll come over right now and tell me everything is going to be all right.

For nearly a minute after she sent the message, her screen didn't change. Then three dots appeared.

I'll be right there.

She felt a whisper of relief and hope that Keith would help her feel better, then tossed her phone on the sofa and walked outside to sit on the front porch.

In less time than she would have thought, a pickup truck pulled into her driveway and Keith got out. She studied him, taking in the broad shoulders, the familiar face, the easy stride that ate up the distance between them. He didn't hesitate, instead walking directly toward her. When he was right in front of her, he held open his arms.

She launched herself at him. He grabbed her and held her tight. He was warm and safe and strong and after nearly a week of suffering, she could finally tell herself everything might be okay.

"I hate this," she said. "I want to call him and tell him to come home."

"You can't do that," Keith said, his lips inches from her ear. "You know his generation can't handle phone calls. You'd have to do it in a text."

That made her smile, which should have helped, but instead she started crying. Keith made soothing noises as he guided her into the house and got her to the sofa. They sat down and she buried her face in his shoulder, not exactly sure what she was crying about. Yes, the whole Coop thing was awful, but somehow this breakdown felt bigger. As if she was releasing all kinds of stress and tension she hadn't known she was carrying.

When she was done, or at least able to stop sobbing, she drew back. "I need tissues."

"You are a mess, aren't you?"

He went into the hall bathroom and returned with a box of tissues, then settled next to her, his expression concerned. Ellen mopped her face and blew her nose.

"He's not going to come back," she said flatly. "Being with his dad is going to be so fun that he won't want to come home. I'm waiting for him to tell me he wants to finish out his senior year in LA." She tossed the tissues on the coffee table and sniffed. "Jeremy can introduce him to all kinds of interesting people. Movie stars and stuff. He can probably get him cast in a sitcom. I can't compete with that. I'm just his boring mom." More tears filled her eyes. "I can't believe I've lost him."

Keith's gaze was steady. "You about done?"

"I have more but I can pause."

"You haven't lost him. Yes, he's having a good time, but give it a few more days. He'll be ready to come home." He touched her shoulder. "You're his family. His life is here. Once the shine wears off, he'll see Jeremy for what he is—a guy who didn't bother for seventeen years."

"I want to believe you but he didn't even ask me to drive him to the airport."

"He's a teenage boy. It's much cooler to go with a friend."

"I know that in my head, but my heart is sad."

"Trust him. Trust yourself. You raised a good kid. He loves you. He'll do the right thing."

"But it hurts."

"I know."

He shifted and put his arm around her. She snuggled close, liking the feel of him next to her.

"Why are you mad at me?" she asked.

"I'm not."

"You are. You won't talk to me and we haven't hung out even once since we've been back." She scooted over so she could look at him. "Tell me what I did wrong."

He looked away, then back at her. "There's no easy answer to that."

She took his hand in hers. "Keith, we're friends. That can't be lost. It can't. We enjoyed ourselves while we were gone. There has to be a way to make that work now that we're home."

"It's not that easy."

"Why not?" A horrifying thought occurred to her. "Have you lost interest in me sexually?"

"Of course not."

"Then why aren't we together?"

He pulled his hand free and shifted back so there were a couple of feet between them. The chilling effect was instant, making her chest hurt and tears burn. She blinked them away, determined to listen before reacting. She needed to know what was wrong so she could fix it. She needed Keith. Him pouting was one thing, but if it was more than that, she had to know.

"What do you want from me?" he asked.

The question surprised her. "I want what we had on the trip. Our great friendship and lots of sex." She pressed her lips together. "I shouldn't have said that. You'll get mad."

His eyebrows rose. "Why would you say that?"

"Because every time I mention sex you get mad. Because you're avoiding me and I don't know why. I get you were upset about the Luka thing, but you know why I did it and you should be over it. You're not trying to have sex with me and when I tried, you threw me out."

"I wasn't mad." He sighed. "Answer me this. After the sex, then what?"

Why couldn't he speak English? "We cuddle?"

He smiled briefly. "No, I mean, we're friends and having sex. Then what?"

And there it was—she understood each of the words, but didn't know what he wanted from her. "Why do I have to want something more?"

She expected a quick comeback, but instead Keith's expression turned stricken, as if she'd stabbed him right in the heart.

"What?" she asked quickly. "Tell me what's wrong? Why am I losing you?"

"You're not." He drew in a breath. "I understand you've never had a real adult relationship. I'm trying to give you space to grow into what's happening, but it's difficult."

She opened her mouth, then closed it. His words bounced around in her brain. She'd never had an adult relationship before? Oh, God! She'd never had a boyfriend or a date or anything other people took for granted. She was emotionally stunted and he didn't want to deal with that.

"Am I doing everything wrong?" She did her best not to sound too pathetic as she asked the question.

"You're not doing anything wrong. We're in different places."

"What does that even mean?"

"You want to play around. It makes sense—I'm not judging. After we're done, you'll want to find someone else to sleep with, and someone after that. You need to experience all the things you should have gone through when you were in your early twenties." His expression turned regretful. "I can't do that, Ellen. I won't. I've done the casual sex thing too many times and now I want more."

She couldn't take it all in. "You won't sleep with me because you think I want to go sleep with a bunch of other people? Where did that even come from?"

"You deserve the chance to live the life you were denied. I get that, but I can't be a part of it."

"A part of what? I'm not interested in anyone else."

She stood and paced to the window. Her mind was swirling. She'd never dated. That was embarrassing but also true. She'd never had a boyfriend or anything remotely normal and now Keith was mad at her because she didn't have the right skill set and in some weird way, he wanted her to go out and have experiences with other men?

She looked at him. "So if I'd had a bunch of relationships before, you'd sleep with me now?"

"It's not just about the sex."

"But you would."

"Maybe."

One of them was crazy and she was starting to think it wasn't her. "What aren't you telling me?"

He stood and glared at her. She had no idea where the anger was coming from, but it was plenty real.

"You want to know? Fine. I'm in love with you. I probably have been for a while, but I didn't realize it. Now I know and while I respect the fact that we're in different places emotionally I will not be some boy toy you use and toss aside when you're ready to move on to a real relationship." He shook his head. "Let me be clear. I get the irony of the situation. After years of women begging me to love them back, here I am, in the exact same position. I want it all, Ellen. You and me in a committed relationship. I won't settle for anything else, which puts us in a bind, because I don't think you want that with me."

In love? With her? Keith?

Her legs started to give out so she sank into a chair and stared at him. There were no words, no thoughts, just total and complete shock.

"That's what I thought," he said, sounding more resigned than angry.

Before she could stop him, he'd headed for the front door and was gone.

twenty-six

UNITY STOOD IN the master bedroom, staring at the made bed—the one that had never been used. She thought about her plans for the remodel and how she'd been so excited to pick out tiles and fixtures and do the work herself. Only now she couldn't summon the energy to do any of that. Once again she was going through the motions of living when in truth she was—

"What?" she asked aloud. "Dead inside? Or am I just scared?"

Scared of living and scared of moving forward and scared of being alone. Because as long as she lived as if Stuart was still with her, she wasn't alone. Not really. She could pretend that her grief was so large, it left no room for things like trying again or growing or failing.

She'd managed to rent office space and hire a couple of guys, but that wasn't enough. She spent her days feeling slightly sick to her stomach. She was avoiding her friends, she was missing Thaddeus more than she'd thought possible. She was a mess and there was an uncomfortable sameness to all the feelings swirling through her.

"I'm tired of myself," she whispered, then said it again, more loudly. "I am tired of myself. Of all of this. I can't do it anymore. I can't be sad. I can't be alone and afraid and stuck and all those things. I can't. I won't. I won't."

She turned and headed for the front door, grabbing her car keys along the way. Forty minutes later, she was back home. She carried in a dozen moving boxes and began taking family photos off the wall.

She wrapped them carefully, placing them standing up in the box. Picture by picture, she emptied the hallway wall. She didn't linger, didn't pause to trace the lines of Stuart's face, she kept moving until they were all packed. Then she stared at the empty space and waited for her heart to break.

Only it didn't. It stayed right there in her chest, beating steadily, reminding her that she was alive and healthy and still relatively young. So what was next?

By three that afternoon, all the pictures in the house were packed. By six, she'd taken down the posters in Stuart's bedroom, had packed up his trophies and started a donation pile in the living room. By seven, she was tired and sad, but functional. She went into the kitchen, poured herself a shot of tequila and downed it in a single gulp, then she reached for her cell phone.

One of her sources of income was local real estate agents who hired her to do a quick spruce on a house ready to go to market. She knew who she liked and who she thought was fair. After scrolling through her contact list, she pushed a button.

"Felicity, it's Unity. I would like to talk to you about a listing for a house here in Willowbrook."

"Great. Let me grab a pen so I can take some notes. Who are the owners?"

"I am. It's my house and I want to put it on the market."

"I'M FAINTING. This is me fainting."

Ellen threw herself back on the sofa and closed her eyes. Unity's wan chuckle drew her upright.

"You're really that shocked?" Unity asked.

Ellen stared at her. "That you're selling Stuart's house? Yes, I'm shocked. Or stunned. We can go with that."

When Ellen had called her friend to ask if they could get together and talk, she'd never expected Unity to be the one with the unexpected announcement. But she had been. Before Ellen could even bring up Keith, Unity had said she was listing the house. As in selling it. Just like that.

"What will you do?" she asked. "Where will you go?" She pressed a hand to her chest. "You're not moving out of town, are you? I don't think I could take that."

"I'm not moving away, but I am moving out of the house. I've already rented a condo. One of those horrible new ones by the north end of town. It's nothing I want, but I only have a six-month lease. I need to consider my options."

"That sounds so adult and rational. Are you really okay?"

Unity raised a shoulder. "I'm trying to be."

Ellen searched her face. There were smudges from a lack of sleep, but otherwise, her friend looked good. Determined and a little sad, but very much herself.

"You're moving on," she said softly.

"I have to," Unity admitted. "I'm getting annoying, even to myself. I can only imagine what everyone else has been thinking."

Ellen smiled at her. "That we love you."

"Thank you for being so patient. I didn't realize how incredibly determined I was to stay in one place. I was going through the motions. It was like my grief was a badge of honor."

"You're not the first person to do that. What about Thaddeus?"

At the question, Unity's mouth drooped and her shoulders rounded.

"I don't know."

"But you still like him, don't you? I thought he was a great guy."

Unity nodded slowly. "He is and he's been really good to me. I miss him so much."

Ellen waited a second, then said, "But?"

"But I'm not going back to him until I'm sure. I put him through a lot and he waited a lot longer than I deserved before walking away. I'm going to get my act together before I go see him."

"You know there's a risk in that."

"He could move on to someone else." Unity looked at Ellen. "I think about that all the time and it terrifies me. But I can't go back and then be unsure."

"Are you unsure?"

Unity smiled. "Less and less each day." The smile

faded. "I think I might have fallen in love with him. At least a little."

"Seriously?" Ellen slid forward on the sofa and hugged her. "That's huge. I haven't even met him, so we have to take care of that right away. In love?"

"I don't know. I miss him and I think about him all the time. He's a good guy, but so different from Stuart. Can I love them both?"

"Of course. You'll always love Stuart. If he hadn't died, you would still be together and you wouldn't have given Thaddeus a moment's thought. But he's not with you and there's this wonderful man who is so good to you."

"That's what I tell myself." Unity smiled at her. "Okay, enough about me. Speaking of potential boyfriends, what's going on with Keith?"

Ellen planned to say something funny but shocked herself, and possibly Unity, by bursting into tears.

"I'm a mess and so is my life."

Unity handed her tissues. "Tell me everything."

Ellen explained about making Keith come over to talk about Cooper being gone and how that had morphed into a conversation about their relationship and that he'd basically told her he was in love with her, all the while ending things.

"He thinks I'm emotionally stunted and can't be with him," she finished, then blew her nose.

Unity rubbed her arm. "He said he's worried you need to have more life experiences before settling down."

"Maybe. I don't know why he had to get all touchy-feely about things. What we had was great. All of it."

"And now he wants more." Unity's voice was gentle. "He's in love with you, Ellen. Of course he wants to know you feel the same way."

Her stomach knotted. "I like him a lot."

Unity looked at her expectantly.

"What?" Ellen demanded. "I have to say it back? Why can't we just have fun? Why does there have to be a commitment?" When did everyone get so traditional? She didn't want anything to change with Keith. She wanted to go back to how it had been on trip.

Unity studied her. "Keith figured out there was a problem, but he's assuming the wrong thing."

"What does that mean?"

"You're not interested in sleeping with a bunch of guys, you're scared to fall in love. You never have and I wonder now how much of that really was a lack of opportunity and how much of it was about you believing that love comes at a price."

Ellen didn't like the sound of that. "I have no idea what you're talking about," she said primly.

"You know exactly what I'm saying. Your parents put a price on love and affection. We used to talk about it. You vowed to be different with Cooper and you were. You love him no matter what. But giving your heart to a man is a lot harder than loving your child. What if you tell him you love him and then he puts a bunch of conditions on you?"

She wanted to say Unity was wrong, but in her gut, she knew her friend was telling the truth.

"I'm scared," she whispered. "Or more accurately, terrified."

There had been so many rules, growing up. After she'd gotten pregnant with Coop, things had only gotten worse. Yes, her parents had supported her and yes,

she'd screwed up, but they'd never once said they would
be there for her, no matter what. She'd spent the next
six years waiting to be tossed out on her butt for not
doing everything exactly how they wanted. Once she'd
graduated from college and gotten a job, they'd basically left town. As if their work was done and now they
could move on with their lives.

After they moved away, she rarely spoke to her parents. There were bimonthly phone calls and a visit every
five or six years, but that was it. They weren't interested
in her or their grandson.

Loving Unity was different. Her friend had always
been there for her, and loving Coop was easy. The second she'd held him, she'd known she would do anything
for him. She had friends and a good life, but she'd also
avoided anything like romantic love. Unity was right—
it wasn't an experience problem, it was *her* problem.

"I can't give my heart," she said.

"Really? Because loving Keith would be so awful?"

"What if he—" She paused, not sure what the what-
if would be. Keith had always been there for her. The
man took care of her car and helped with Cooper and
kissed her until she melted. Still, to risk everything
seemed impossible.

"He's right. I've never had an adult relationship. I
don't know what I'm doing. We should go back to being
friends."

Unity made a clucking sound. "Chick, chick, chicken."

Ellen glared at her. "You think you're in a position
to be giving me advice?"

"Someone has to. You've pretty much been in love
with him from the moment you met him. You hid it behind friendship, but it was there. That's why everything

was so easy on the trip. You're good together. This is your chance, Ellen. He's a hunky, sexy guy who's in love with you. Not handing over your heart is about as dumb as spending three years of your life hiding from the chance of healing and finding happiness."

"Why are we so scared?"

"Because we've both been hurt. It's hard not to flinch."

"I want to be brave," Ellen said. "Maybe."

Unity hugged her. "We could be brave together. Just join hands and take a leap of faith. Oh, I know. We'll add being brave to our lists."

Ellen laughed. "Great idea. You first."

KEITH GRITTED HIS TEETH, then knocked on his daughter's half-open bedroom door. Lissa looked up from the book she was reading.

"Hey, Dad." She sat up on her bed. "What's up?"

He set two books next to her, careful not to look at her or the titles. "I got these for you. I don't want to talk about them. Just read them and if you have any questions, you'll have to ask someone else. I'm sorry, but that's the truth."

She read the titles, then looked at him, her eyes huge. "Dad, these are books about sex."

He retreated to the door and stared over her head. "If you're going to do that with Luka, I want to make sure you're doing it right. He should be, ah, taking care of you and he's just a kid, without a lot of experience." He dropped his gaze to her face. "Lissa, I love you more than anything, but I can't explain that stuff to you. I don't have it in me."

Honestly, he would rather be shot. "But that doesn't mean you don't need the information."

Now it was her turn to look away. "You don't have to worry about that."

"It's my job to worry about everything where you're concerned."

She studied both books, then returned her attention to him. "I've had an orgasm, Dad."

He took a step back and tried not to wince. "Could we not talk about that?"

"I'm just saying we're figuring it out together. Guys are so easy. It's not really fair. You barely touch them and they—" She waved her hand. "You know. But it's harder for girls."

Where was that bolt of lightning when he needed it? "That's why I bought you the books. So you could read about different things." He waved his hand. "It's all in there."

Lissa scrambled to her feet, raced toward him and wrapped her arms around his waist. "You're the best dad ever."

"This is not my favorite part."

"I know, but you did it anyway." She looked up at him. "Thank you."

She was so beautiful, he thought, brushing the hair out of her face. "I love you, little girl."

"I love you, too. Now what's going on with Ellen? You can't still be mad at her about the trip."

"I'm not."

"Then why are you grumpy?"

"She's a difficult woman."

Lissa stepped back. "That's not the reason. You should marry her."

392   SUSAN MALLERY

Keith sagged against the doorframe. "Yeah, well, I don't see that happening. I broke things off with her."

"What?" she yelped. "Why? You're crazy about her."

"It's complicated."

Lissa's expression softened. "Dad, she's totally into you. We can all see it. Maybe she's just scared."

He wanted it to be that easy. That she just had to overcome a few fears, but he knew it was more than that. Ellen wanted to play. She'd just come into her own and now she was ready to experiment with a lot of different men. His head understood but his heart wanted to claim her as his own. He didn't want to share Ellen and he couldn't play when his feelings were so real.

"It's not going to work out," he said at last.

Lissa hugged him again. "She'll come around. You'll see."

He had his doubts. He'd laid it on the line for Ellen and she'd not only let him walk away, he hadn't heard from her in days. As signs went, that was a damned clear one.

SERENA WAS A beautiful redhead with more curves than should be legal and a warm, nurturing personality that should have been exactly what Thaddeus was looking for. She was in her early thirties and a partner in a local cupcake company. They'd met two weeks ago at a charity luncheon and this was their second date.

"Two years in, he said he'd changed his mind about having kids," Serena said in answer to Thaddeus's question about what had ended her first marriage. "I was blindsided by the information. We'd always talked about having a family. Kids are a priority for me. We tried counseling, but he was firm in his decision and that was the end of things."

"I'm sorry," he said, thinking the fact that she wanted children was a plus.

"Me, too. I felt betrayed in a way, if that makes sense."

"It does. He changed the rules."

She smiled. "We're probably getting a little too serious for the second date. Let's change the subject. The Seahawks are looking good for the season."

"You're a fan?"

"I am." She ducked her head, then looked at him from under her lashes. "I have season tickets and I go to every home game. One of the goals of my business is to make enough money so that I can afford a suite there. I'd love to have friends and family with me for the games. What a great experience for everyone. Like the perfect party."

"You're a football fan, then."

"I'm a Seahawks fan. There's a difference." She had a zest for life he liked. She smiled easily, had a great sense of humor and seemed ready to be in a relationship. In a word—perfect.

It was as if the Universe had closed a door and opened the proverbial window. He should be dancing for joy, or at least humming with excitement. Instead he found himself thinking about Unity and wondering what she was doing right now. Did he ever cross her mind?

He'd been unable to let her go. At night, when he was alone, he imagined her with him. Sometimes he dreamed about her. She was—

"Thaddeus?"

He looked at Serena. "Yes?"

She smiled. "You got a little lost there for a second."

"Sorry. I was just…"

He looked around the restaurant. It was nice enough and the dinner was good. Later, he could drive Serena home and kiss her, maybe more. She was everything he should be looking for and there was not a single part of him that wanted to take this to the next level.

"I was in a relationship recently," he said abruptly. "It was serious and as much as I like you and think you're beautiful and smart and sexy, I can't do this right now. You probably won't get the irony of what I'm about to say, but I'm not ready to be with someone else."

Disappointment tugged at her mouth. "I'm sorry to hear that."

"I am, too."

"We should go," she said, looking for the server.

"Don't you want to finish your dinner?"

Tears glistened in her eyes. "There isn't any point, is there?"

Guilt kicked him in the gut, followed by a wave of regret. Not just for screwing up things with Serena but for the fact that he was in an impossible situation. He wanted a woman he couldn't have and he didn't want the one that wanted him.

twenty-seven

THREE DAYS OF not sleeping made for a difficult morning. She was a mess in every way possible. She missed Cooper and worried constantly that she hadn't heard from him. He was still posting on social media, which made things both better and worse. While she knew he was having a great time, she also knew he was having a great time. As in why would you come back to some ridiculously tiny little town when you could drive around Santa Monica in a convertible and meet girls on the beach?

But as much as she needed her son to come home, she had to admit that the majority of her pain came from her confusion about Keith. Or rather her confusion about how she felt about him and if it was safe to give her heart and if she didn't give her heart, how could she survive without him because the not seeing him was starting to crush her soul.

Was Unity right? Had she been in love with Keith from the very beginning? She supposed it was possible, but there was no way to really know. They were great friends. They got along well and she'd honest to God never thought about wanting more. Which made sense, what with never dating or anything like that, she hadn't actually known what she'd been missing. And if she, for the moment, agreed all that was true, then she could see how she wouldn't have any trouble suppressing sexual interest, what with not understanding what it was. Over time, they'd become close friends who were a part of each other's lives.

Was that love? Honestly, she had no experience with the matter. Not romantically. She knew she liked being around Keith. She enjoyed his company and looked forward to seeing him. She liked their rituals, the conversation, the way they took care of each other. She'd been the one to look after him when he'd had shoulder surgery a couple of years ago and they always spent Christmas together. Once they'd started making love, well, that had been fifteen kinds of magic. The things he did to her body were incredible. She loved the heat and the feelings and the play and the laughter. She liked how he never made her feel foolish for asking dumb questions.

Was that love? How was she supposed to know?

She thought about what he'd said—how he'd worried that she would want to be with a bunch of other men. Yes, he was her only real lover, but she was okay with that. Even if the physical act might be better with someone else—a fact she couldn't begin to imagine—why bother? An orgasm was just like a sneeze if Keith wasn't there to share it. She wasn't interested in a bodily function, she wanted to feel him with her, listen to his breathing, his own groans of pleasure. She wanted to talk to him about what they'd done and then cuddle next to him while they watched a game or talked about their kids. Keith would be there if she got the flu and help her with Cooper and tell her if she had something stuck in her teeth. She liked being there for him, as well. Taking him shopping for Lissa and helping him buy a sofa and making double batches of whatever she was cooking for dinner to share with him.

She dropped the dust cloth onto the coffee table as she tried to figure out what she was feeling and what she wanted. No conditions—that was for sure. Not sternness and rules. Only Keith was never like that. He was always—

Her doorbell rang. She opened it and saw Lissa standing on the porch.

"Hi," she said, stepping back to let the teen inside.

"Can we talk?" Lissa asked.

"Sure." Ellen motioned to the sofa. "What's going on?"

Lissa perched on the edge of a cushion, twisting her hands together. "It's about my dad."

Ellen sat suddenly as all the strength left her legs. "Is he okay?"

"Oh, nothing happened. That wasn't what I meant." Lissa looked at her and swallowed. "Is it because of me? Is that why you don't want to be with him? That I won't go away to college? Because if I'm the problem, I can go somewhere so you can get together."

Ellen heard the words but couldn't process them at first. When the meaning finally sank in, she reached for the teen and held her tight.

"Is that what you think? I'm so sorry. Of course it's

not you. Lissa, I love you. I hope you know that. You're great and I'm so proud of you for knowing what you want and don't want. That's huge. Some people go their whole lives without ever figuring that out." She drew back a little and smiled. "I would really like to have you in my life more. You're fun and smart and easy to be around. Plus, I need you for fashion advice."

Lissa relaxed a little. "Then why don't you want to be with my dad? I thought you were in love with him. Was I wrong?"

"It's complicated."

"How? Is it because of all the other women who are constantly throwing themselves at him? You know he doesn't care about them. Dad's really loyal. He was faithful to my mom the whole time." She wrinkled her nose. "I heard them fighting about that once. She was mad he hadn't cheated because it would have given her a reason to leave sooner. Which didn't make sense to me because not cheating is a good thing."

Lissa paused. "You didn't answer my question. Was I wrong when I thought you loved him?"

"I…" Ellen had no idea how to answer that, mostly because she wasn't sure how she felt about anything. Who defined love? If she admitted she loved Keith, then she was the one defining the emotion for herself. Did it work that way?

"I don't know what he expects from me," she said with a sigh.

"Why don't you ask him?"

Duh. She could do that. Keith was always straightforward with her. There were no secret rules that if she broke, she would have to pay a price.

"He's not my parents," she whispered. "He's not like them."

Lissa's expression turned wary. "What does that have to do with anything?"

Ellen stood and laughed. "I will tell you another time. But right now I have to breathe in the fact that your father is a very good man who would never try to use his feelings to manipulate me or punish me or anything else." She pressed her hands to her chest. "Your dad said he loved me. I can't believe I didn't say anything back. I can't believe I let him walk away thinking, well, I don't know what, but something bad."

She turned to Lissa. "Where is he?"

Lissa grinned. "He's at home. I'm going to go hang out with Luka for a while and I won't be back until after dinner. Just so you know."

Ellen smiled at her. "Use a condom."

"You, too."

Ellen ran to get her handbag, then hurried to her car. It took what felt like ages to drive the couple of miles between their homes. She parked next to his truck, then raced up to the front door. Thankfully it was open as it always was. She hurried inside to his study where he sat staring at his computer.

"I'm in love with you," she announced.

He looked up, obviously startled.

"Don't say anything," she continued. "Let me get this out. I'm in love with you. I think I have been from when we first met, but I didn't know what love was and I didn't date so it never occurred to me to be more than friends or that I would want to be more than friends."

She took a step toward him. "I didn't react before, when you said you loved me, because I was scared. It's not that I want to be with other guys or that you're my test boyfriend. I was holding back because I was afraid of the rules. That you would treat me like my parents did. I liked what we had because it was so easy and comfortable and amazing and great, but now I realize it's not because we were playing, but because I'm in love with you."

She paused to catch her breath. "It's not just the sex, although I really like that. It's you and me and how we are together. I want to be here for you. A real partner. I want this to be everything you want it to be. A committed relationship." She realized she'd been talking a long time and he hadn't said a word. "Unless you've changed your mind or something."

He continued to study her for several seconds before standing up, circling the desk, taking her face in his hands and kissing her. Really kissing her. With lips and tongue and passion and promise.

She wrapped her arms around him, leaning against him, feeling the love wash over her. When he drew back, he said, "I haven't changed my mind."

"I'm glad."

"I love you."

"I love you, too."

"I'm not changing my mind."

"Me, either. I really don't want anyone else, Keith. Just you. And Lissa, but you know, as a daughter. And I don't have a lot of experience with relationships, so I'll be learning as I go. If you're okay with that."

"I am."

She put her hands on his chest. "So, we're in a committed relationship?"

"We are."

"Can we have sex now?"

"Yes. Sex is very much part of the bargain."

She looked into his handsome face. "I've missed that but I've missed you more. We're really good together."

"I'm glad you think so. Will you marry me?"

"I—" Her mouth dropped open as tears burned in her eyes. "You want to marry me?"

"More than anything."

"No one's ever wanted to marry me before." Tears fell. "Why am I crying? This is happy. Yes, of course I'll marry you." She kissed him, unable to stop crying. "What's wrong with me?"

"You're having a moment. I kind of like it."

"I'm being ridiculous."

"It's sweet, but if it's okay with you, I'm going to assume that us being engaged means these are happy tears and I can ignore them."

She nodded, still sniffing and wiping her face.

"Good."

He took her hand and led her back to his bedroom. When they got there, he closed and locked the door, then pulled off his T-shirt. The sight of his bare chest and that big bed was just enough of a distraction to stop her tears. A different kind of happy swept through her as wanting burst to life in all her girl parts.

This, she thought stepping into his embrace. This was how it was going to be for the rest of their lives. And she couldn't wait to get started on loving every second of it.

DAGMAR HAD ON a caftan in a paisley print. The swirling shades of purple matched the streaks in her hair.

Bangles jangled on her wrist and bell-shaped earrings hung from her ears.

Unity studied the other woman, admiring her style, her strength and her ability to accept what life had to offer. She wasn't there yet, but she was getting closer.

"You've been in hiding, little one," Dagmar said without judgment. "I've missed you."

"I've missed you, too. I'm sorry to have disappeared but I needed time to think and plan."

Dagmar poured them each tea, then offered a plate of scones. There was a bowl of clotted cream and several types of jam on the tray in front of them.

"You know I rented office space," she said.

"Yes, Howard does love to gossip. I also know you've hired two men to work for you and from what I hear, they are both very nice-looking. The ladies of Silver Pines will be so pleased."

Unity grinned. "I hired them for their skills, not their looks."

"Two birds and all that. What else?"

"I'm selling the house."

Dagmar's eyebrows rose. "That is a surprise. Are you sure?"

"It's not a comfortable decision, but it's the right one for me. It's time. I can't live with his ghost anymore."

"How does that feel?"

"Hard. Uncomfortable. Necessary. I've moved into a little condo I'm renting for a few months. It came furnished, so in a way it's like living in a hotel, but I think I need that for now. I've packed away all the important things like pictures and a few things that belonged to Stuart. Everything else I either sold or donated."

"I'm very proud of you," Dagmar said with a smile.

"It was time." Unity sipped her tea. "I'm seeing a therapist. A good one. She's helping me through the grief and I'm learning about all the ways I didn't handle it well the first time around. It's work and it's painful, but I'm getting stronger and more grounded. I'm still swimming."

"Excellent."

Dagmar talked about what had been happening in Silver Pines. There were several new residents and a few moves into assisted living. Unity listened politely, trying to work up the courage to ask about Thaddeus.

She still thought about him, missed him, wanted him, but she knew she wasn't ready. She'd put him through so much—she was determined not to see him again until she could offer herself as someone ready to be in a healthy, adult relationship. Assuming he was still interested.

"I admire you for not asking," Dagmar said unexpectedly. "It would have been my first question."

Unity didn't pretend to misunderstand. "I'm not sure I have the right to know and I'm scared the news will be bad."

"What defines bad news?"

"That he's in love with someone else."

"Was he ever in love with you?"

"I don't know. I doubt it." But she hoped. Or if not love, then maybe enough interest so that he would give her another chance.

"Thaddeus and I have made a pact to never discuss his love life again," Dagmar told her. "And I have promised to never get involved with it. I'm sorry to tell you, Unity, he's cut me off and I don't know a thing."

Not exactly what she wanted to hear, then reminded herself it would all be fine. She had a plan.

"What's your time frame?" Dagmar asked. "To go see him?"

"When the house closes. Once that part of my past is behind me, I'll be ready."

"Are you sure?"

"No, but I'm done waiting to live my life."

Dagmar squeezed her hand. "Good for you, child. Good for you."

ELLEN WAITED OUTSIDE of security at SeaTac Airport. Cooper had surprised her by texting her to ask if she would pick him up at the airport. She'd immediately agreed, eager to see him.

She watched as passengers filed out, on their way to baggage claim. According to the app on her phone, his flight had reached the gate a few minutes ago. He should be—

She waved when she spotted him. Coop saw her and grinned, then broke into a run. When he reached her, he grabbed her around the waist and swung her around.

"Mom! You're here. I'm so glad to be back. Two weeks was too long. How's everything? Did you miss me? Can we have meatloaf for dinner?"

She laughed and hung on to him, then stepped back. "You're taller."

He grinned. "It was two weeks. I can't be taller."

"You look taller. Yes on the meatloaf. I've already bought everything for it. I knew you'd want that tonight." Because it was his favorite after-a-trip food. She had no idea why, but there it was.

They walked to the escalator that would take them down to baggage claim. "You had a good time?"

"I did. Dad's house is amazing and his wife is nice enough. The girls are annoying. They wanted to hang out with me all the time and they're not into anything interesting. Dad took me to the studio and that was fun and I met a few movie stars, which was cool."

He paused to check the board telling him where to get his bag, then put his arm around her. "But it wasn't as much fun as the bus trip. I missed everybody and my room and stuff."

"I'm glad you had a good time," she said diplomatically, secretly cheering that Jeremy hadn't won him over. Not her finest hour, but she could live with that. "When are you going to go see your dad again?"

"I don't know. He said something about winter break, but it's my senior year and I'll have a lot going on." He looked at her. "I know he wants to get to know me but I keep thinking I've been around for seventeen years. He should have tried before."

"I don't disagree with that, but he's still your dad. It might be nice to have him in your life."

"Maybe. We'll see." He spotted his bag and walked over to collect it. "So what's been going on while I was gone?"

She led the way to the parking garage. "Funny you should ask." She held up her left hand.

Cooper stared at it and the diamond ring on her left hand, then looked at her. "What?"

She waggled her fingers. "The ring?"

"It's nice. Is it new?"

"You're such a guy. I'm engaged. Coach and I are getting married."

Coop came to stop, dropped his bag then pulled her close. "For real? You mean it? You're marrying Coach?"

The intensity of his voice surprised her. "I am. Are you okay with that?"

"Okay?" He drew back and wiped away tears. "Mom, it's the best. I've been hoping for a long time that you and Coach would get together, but it seemed like you only wanted to be friends. Lissa and I talked about how to get you two together, but we couldn't come up with a plan that wasn't totally dumb. This is great. When's the wedding? Are we moving? Our house is too small, but if we move in with Coach, you shouldn't sell it. You should keep it and rent it out, for income and stuff."

He picked up his bag. "You know, if you marry Coach, that's going to increase your income for Stanford. Is that a problem? Want me to ask Dad for tuition? I'd probably have to go see him for a week or something to get it, but I'd do that."

There was so much love welling up inside of her, she thought she might float away. "You are the best son ever," she whispered. "I love you."

"I love you, too, Mom. But about college…"

"It's going to be fine. Keith and I have talked about it. We're going to get a house together that is comfortable for all of us. Lissa has already been looking online and she can't wait for you to get back so you two can talk about it. You're right, I will be keeping our house for income property. That will help pay for Stanford, and Keith is paying the rest of it."

Because he wanted to and as he'd pointed out, he'd made good money in the NFL and he wanted to spend it on something that mattered. If she hadn't already totally been in love with him, that statement would have pushed her over the edge.

"Don't worry about money or me or anything but enjoying your senior year and keeping up your grades so you can go to Stanford, Coop. That's what matters to me."

He nodded, then fell into step with her. "Is there going to be a wedding soon? You know all the guys will want to come, so you'll have to order a lot of food. And can we wear tuxes because I look good in a tux. And, Mom, you totally have to wear a dress and everything because you'll be a beautiful bride and I know Lissa wants to be a bridesmaid. And I can stay with Luka when you go on your honeymoon. Lissa should probably stay somewhere else, because they're like together and I don't want to be responsible for her because if I messed up Coach would be mad."

He stopped again and stared at her. "Mom, Coach is going to be my stepdad." He grinned. "The guys are going to be so jealous. And for the new house, Lissa and I can't share a bathroom. She will hog it all the time because you know how girls are."

"How long have the two of you been talking about Coach and me getting together?"

"I don't know. A couple of years. She swore there was something going on, but I didn't think you were interested in him at all. I mean you never dated and stuff. I was worried about you."

She thought about the conversation she'd overheard nearly two months ago. "That was very sweet of you, but not necessary. I'm going to be just fine."

"I know. You'll have Coach. I'm happy. This is a great day."

She linked arms with him and thought about the promise that was their future. "It really is, Coop. Come on. Let's go home."

UNITY SIGNED EVERYWHERE the escrow officer indicated. It took only a few minutes to finish with all the paperwork.

"That's it," the pretty, dark-haired woman said with a smile. "The buyers have already signed, so we should fund later today and close tomorrow. As we discussed, the proceeds will be wired to your bank and be available the day after."

Unity nodded. Her throat was tight and she felt a little disoriented, but otherwise, she was holding it all together. Beside her, Ellen squeezed her arm.

"It's a wonderful home," Felicity, her real estate agent, said as they all stood. "The buyers are very excited."

"I wish I'd remodeled that master bath for them," Unity said, pulling the key out of her jeans pocket and handing it over.

"They appreciate the lower price on the house and the chance to make it how they want it," the agent told her.

They all shook hands then she and Ellen walked out into the bright fall morning. The days were noticeably shorter and the leaves were changing. Time marched on, Unity thought.

"You okay?" Ellen asked.

"I think so. It's weird that the house is sold." She smiled at her friend. "For the six hundredth time, you didn't have to take time off work to be here with me."

"Oh, I think I did. It was two hours. No big deal. How are you feeling?"

"Scared. Happy. Hopeful." She laughed. "So normal considering the circumstances."

"When are you driving over to Seattle?"

"Now."

Ellen hugged her. "You're a wonderful person and he would be a fool to not fall at your feet and instantly propose."

"At this point I would be happy if he just wanted to go out with me."

"He will."

Unity was less sure, but knew there was only one way to find out.

"Just be back by Thanksgiving," Ellen teased. "You're my maid of honor and I need you at the wedding. Plus you're staying with Lissa and Cooper while we're on our honeymoon."

"That's three weeks away. I'll be back long before that."

"You never know. Things could take a turn for the I-don't-want-to-get-out-of-bed."

If only, Unity thought.

She opened the door to the small four-wheel-drive SUV she'd recently purchased. "I'll let you know what happens. Say hi to your handsome fiancé."

"You know I will. I love you and I can drive over if you need me to be there."

"Thanks. I do know that. Love you, too."

Ellen waved and got in her Subaru. Unity followed her out of the parking lot before turning toward I90 and going west.

There had already been snow in the mountains but

the highway was bare and dry. Unity sang along with the radio in an effort to distract herself from her nerves. She practiced her calm breathing and told herself whatever happened, she could be proud of how far she'd come. Even without Thaddeus in her life, she had healed and if he didn't want her, eventually she would find someone who did. Because she was ready to be in a relationship with a good man. He was her first choice but if it didn't work out, she wasn't going to lose herself. Not again.

She made good time into Bellevue and drove into the parking garage. Minutes later, she was in an elevator, being whisked up to one of the top floors. She went into the office and gave her name to the receptionist.

"I don't have an appointment, but if he has a few moments, I would really like to speak with him."

The woman nodded, then picked up the phone. She gave Unity's name and the message. In the seconds before there was an answer, Unity felt her heart pound. She was both cold and hot and a little shaky but determined.

The receptionist put down the phone and smiled. "He's free right now. Do you know your way back?"

Unity nodded and started toward his office. She wasn't sure her legs were going to continue to support her, but she kept moving and then she was walking into the big open space with the killer view. But all she cared about was the man standing beside his desk.

He looked good. Tall and fit and handsome enough to make her go weak all over. His gaze was steady and she had no idea what he was thinking, but for now it was enough to simply see him and be in the same room with him.

"This is unexpected," he told her. "How are you?"

"Good. I need to tell you something, if that's all right."

His neutral expression turned wary, but he nodded.

She sucked in a breath. "I've missed you. A lot. But I knew I needed time to figure out my life. And I guess me. I've been seeing a therapist—a good one this time. I've sold the house and expanded my business and I'm still swimming."

She told herself that wasn't the important part and that she should get to it.

"I shouldn't have gone out with you before. I wasn't ready and I acted badly. I took so much from you and gave nothing in return. When I think about how I acted, I'm embarrassed and ashamed. I apologize. I didn't know how bad things were until it was too late."

He continued to study her, not saying a word or hinting at what he was thinking.

"I've grown. I will always love Stuart, but he's gone and I'm not willing to wait to die anymore. I want to live my life. I want to get married and have a family. I want to be happy and I want to make someone else happy. I want to be a wife and a mother and be really good at both jobs. I want to offer my heart to a wonderful man who will love me in return."

Her chest tightened, making it hard to breathe. She was terrified, but she told herself she was strong. Strong enough to do the right thing. "I was hoping that man might be you, Thaddeus." She waved her hand. "I don't mean I'm proposing or anything. That would be really scary. I mean maybe, if you're still willing, we could go out again and see how it goes. And before you tell me what you think about that, I want you to know that

I'm in love with you. And, well, I'm hoping you still like me enough to give me another chance."

She paused, wondering if she should say she would understand if he didn't want to, but wasn't sure if that was too much or if she'd said it wrong or—

"What did you have in mind?" he asked.

Hope filled her chest, but she told herself not to read too much into the question. "I need a date to a wedding in three weeks. Between now and then I thought we might get some dinner or something. If you'd be interested."

He didn't respond in any way. His dark gaze searched her face, no doubt trying to figure out if she meant it this time or if she was going to go cray-cray on him again.

"About the being in love with me part," he said. "You're sure?"

She nodded. "Yes. I'm in love with you, Thaddeus."

Putting it out there laid her bare. She felt vulnerable and scared and yet stronger than she ever had.

He crossed to her in three long strides, then pulled her close and kissed her. The second his mouth touched her, the fear left. She was back where she belonged and she knew everything was going to be all right.

They clung to each other, holding on as if they were never letting go.

"I can't believe you're here," he told her. "I thought I'd never see you again."

"I'm sorry for what happened and how I acted."

He looked at her and smiled. "I know you weren't doing it on purpose."

"That doesn't mean I didn't torture you."

"It was worth it." He kissed her again. "You're worth it."

The band around her heart eased. "I want to be with

you, Thaddeus. I mean that. Totally and completely. I love you."

"I love you, too. Believe me, I tried to get over you and I couldn't. I guess you're stuck."

"Lucky me." She smiled. "So you'll be my plus-one at the wedding?"

"I will. Want to stay and go out to dinner?"

She nodded and leaned against him. "So what does your afternoon look like?"

"I might be able to clear my calendar. When do you have to go back to Willowbrook?"

She looked at him. "I told the guys I was hoping to be gone through the weekend."

One eyebrow rose. "It's Tuesday."

"Well, I said I was hoping. If that's too long I can—"

He cut her off with a kiss. "Stay through the weekend. Stay forever." He frowned. "Dammit, your business is there. I'm going to have to move to that little town, aren't I? Dagmar will be thrilled."

He released her and walked to his phone. After pressing a button he said, "I'm going need you to clear my calendar for the rest of the week. Freddy can handle anything urgent."

With that, he grabbed his suit jacket and took her hand in his. "Ready?"

"Absolutely."

They walked out together. Unity had no idea what was going to happen next but… Okay, she knew what was going to happen next, but the after that part was less clear. Regardless, she knew that she and Thaddeus would be together and for her, that was all that mattered.

As they waited for the elevator, she pulled out her phone and sent a quick text to Ellen.

It went well. See you on Monday. Then she put her cell back in her bag and stepped into the next chapter of what had turned out to be a very happy life.

epilogue

Six years later...

"FORTY LOOKS GOOD on us," Unity said, her arm linked with Ellen's as they studied their reflections in the sliding glass door.

Ellen laughed. "It does and that makes me happy."

The April weather was perfect in Maui—warm and clear with a light breeze. The rental property where they were spending their vacation had cost the earth, but it had been worth it. Not only so she and Unity could celebrate their birthdays together, but so both families could spend a wonderful week hanging out.

Unity and Thaddeus were in the main house with all the kids and Dagmar. Ellen and Keith were in the smaller bungalow, and enjoying every moment of what felt like a second honeymoon.

Cooper had gotten time off from work—he'd graduated with a degree in chemical engineering the previous year and was working with a biofuel company down in Houston. Lissa was wrapping up the final year of college and would be graduating with her nursing degree. After community college, she'd transferred to the University of Washington, so had moved to Seattle, but she came home at least a couple of times a month.

"Mommy, Mommy, I want to go in the pool." Four-year-old Alana ran toward Unity and held out her arms to be picked up. "Daddy said to ask you if that was okay."

Alana, already a beauty, dimpled as she spoke. "I knew you'd say yes."

Unity swept up her daughter and held her close. "Did you?"

"Uh-huh. I'll wear my water wings and everything."

Unity laughed. "Then it must be all right."

Thaddeus walked toward them, two-year-old Jason resting on one hip. "This one wants to go swimming, as well. You up for a little water sport?"

"My children are turning into fish," Unity said with a smile. She looked at Ellen. "Sorry. Our girl time is going to have to wait."

"I'm thinking we should let the girl time go until we're back home," she teased.

"Do you mind?"

"Of course not." Ellen touched Alana's cheek. "How about if I join you in the pool?"

"That would be the best!"

"I think so, too."

They walked toward the large backyard with the huge pool and hot tub and a view of the ocean.

Dagmar lay in the shade, Lissa in the chaise next to her. Coop and Keith were playing water basketball, but put the ball away when they saw the younger kids. Coop scooped Alana up in his arms.

"How's my best girl?"

Alana dimpled. "I'm coming into the water. Mommy said."

"Are you? That's great. Let's go find your water wings."

Her big, strong son handled the little girl expertly. He surprised everyone with his skill with both kids. One day, when he stopped playing the field and got serious about someone, he was going to make a great husband and father.

Keith pushed himself onto the edge of the pool, then stood. "You going to join us?" he asked her.

"Sure. I just need to put on my suit."

He grabbed a towel from the stack by the chairs and fell into step. "Need any help?" he asked, his voice low and teasing.

She laughed. "I think I might."

Interest brightened his dark eyes. He moved close, put his hand on the small of her back and guided her toward their bungalow. Ellen glanced over her shoulder and saw Unity's knowing smile. Ellen grinned in return. Just the previous afternoon, she and Keith had watched the little ones for a couple of hours while Unity and Thaddeus had shared some "adult time."

This, she thought happily as they stepped into the bungalow. This life, this love, was something of a miracle and she was both grateful and happy for all that she had. Her friends, her family and, most important, the man who loved her for who she was.

Keith closed the door behind them, then pulled her close. She went into his embrace and knew this was exactly where she belonged...for always.

* * * * *

THE FRIENDSHIP LIST

SUSAN MALLERY

Reader's Guide

HQN™

Questions for Discussion

Note:
These questions contain spoilers, so it's recommended that you finish the book before reading the questions.

1. Every satisfying novel shows character growth. In what ways were Ellen and Unity different at the end of the book than they were at the beginning? What happened in the story to convince each woman that she had to make a change in her life? How did the challenge lists change them? Which character changed the most?

2. Why do you think the neighborhood of Silver Pines appealed to Unity so much? What did it represent to her?

3. Which woman did you like more? Why?

4. Early in the book, Ellen and Unity had a falling-out. What caused the rift? How did they heal their friendship? How did they stay connected with each other even when Ellen was out of town?

5. Susan Mallery is renowned for her in-depth characterization, and a big part of that is giving readers a clear picture of the characters' lives before the story even started. Discuss what you know about each of these characters from prior to page 1: Ellen, Unity, Keith, Thaddeus. How did their lives prior to this point affect their actions in the story? (Shout-out to Thaddeus's late mom for ironing his tips!)

6. If you had to choose, which guy would you marry, Keith or Thaddeus? Why? If marriage is off the table and we're just talking about a hookup, would your answer change?

7. What did you think of Ellen's reaction when she walked in on Lissa and Luka in the hotel room? Did she do the right thing? Why or why not? What would you have done?

8. Did you guess what was bothering Lissa before she blurted it out to her dad? Looking back through the story, discuss the ways that you could tell that Lissa was hiding something. Should Keith have realized sooner? Why or why not?

9. What surprised you in the story? Which scenes made you laugh? What moments are sticking with you?

10. Name something you would put on your own personal challenge list. Would that help you grow in some way and, if so, how? What has held you back from doing it already?

Recipes

Baked Zucchini

Author's Note:
If you prepare this first and put it in the oven after you've made the sauce but before you start assembling the chicken cutlets, both dishes will be done at the same time.

Ingredients:
4 whole zucchini, sliced into 1/4-inch thick rounds
2 Tbsp olive oil
Garlic salt & pepper to taste

Directions:
Preheat oven to 400 degrees. Toss the zucchini pieces with olive oil. Layer them in concentric circles in a pie plate or tart pan. Salt and pepper each layer. Bake for about 30 minutes.

Ellen's Chicken Parm

Sauce:
1 small onion, diced
2 Tbsp olive oil
2 cloves of garlic, minced
1 28-oz can of crushed tomatoes or tomato puree
1 tomato, diced
1 Tbsp basil
1 tsp oregano
1/2 tsp thyme
1/4 tsp cayenne powder
1 bay leaf

Chicken:
3 boneless, skinless chicken breasts
1/2 cup flour
1 tsp garlic salt
1/2 cup flour
1 tsp garlic salt
1/2 tsp ground black pepper
2 eggs

1 cup bread crumbs, plain or Italian seasoned
1 Tbsp olive oil for brushing the pan
Oil for frying

Topping:
1 cup shredded mozzarella
1/4 cup shredded parmesan

If desired, serve over cooked spaghetti noodles.

For the sauce:

Heat 2 Tbsp olive oil over medium heat. When glistening, add the onions and sauté until translucent. Add the garlic and cook until fragrant, about 30 seconds longer. Stir in the remaining sauce ingredients. Cook to a simmer, stirring regularly, then lower heat and continue to simmer while assembling the chicken.

For the chicken:

Brush a 13x9-inch pan with 1 Tbsp of olive oil and set aside. Heat oven to 400 degrees. Place three dishes side by side next to the stovetop. In the first, mix flour with garlic salt and pepper. In the second, whisk the two eggs. In the third, place the bread crumbs. Heat 1/4 inch of oil in a heavy-bottomed pan over medium-low heat.

Slice each breast in half to make six cutlets. Pound each cutlet to about 1/4-inch thick. Dredge in flour, then egg wash, then bread crumbs. Sauté until both sides are brown, about four minutes per side. Add oil as needed.

Assembly:

Place chicken cutlets in 13x9-inch pan. Pour sauce over chicken. Top with shredded cheese. Put into the oven and bake until cheese is melted, about ten minutes. Turn oven to broil and move dish closer to the heat. Broil until cheese is browned, checking every minute or so to make sure it doesn't burn.